ASH & RUIN

ESSAERISTS WAR
BOOK ONE

NICHOLAS TAYLOR

Ash & Ruin

Essaerists War Book One

Text copyright © 2025 by Nicholas Taylor

ISBN-13: 978-1-938387-19-7

www.NicholasTaylor.co

This book is dedicated to my wife, Stacia. You have been listening to me talk about this series for years. You've listened patiently as I prattled on about research, world-building, and magic systems, and you've endured all the times I vacillated back and forth on what to do with the story and characters. I couldn't have asked for a better partner in life. Thank you for all your support, and I love you.

PRONUNCIATION GUIDE

Characters

Mariokos (mar-ee-O-kos) | Xavieno (za-VEE-e-no)
Fioralba (fee-o-RAL-ba) | Caelwen (KAYL-wen)
Valfric (VALF-rik) | Wulfgren (WULF-gren)
Treftune (TREF-toon) | Biankara (bee-an-KA-ra)
Aelric (AYL-rik) | Ilara (I-LAR-a)
Ilfthandor (ILF-than-dor) | Nefeli (ne-FE-lee)
Thraindel (THRANE-del) | Durnara (DUR-na-ra)
Gaelrik (GAYL-rik) | Garethor (GAR-eh-thor)
Kernvald (KERN-vald) | Durgard (DUR-gard)
Yrthorn (YR-thorn) | Aresio (a-RE-see-o)
Theoliano (thee-o-LEE-a-no) | Alessandros (a-les-SAN-dros)
Damianello (da-mee-a-NEL-lo) | Helioz (HE-lee-oz)
Erastos (e-RAS-tos) | Luciakos (lu-see-A-kos)
Geraldox (ger-AL-dox) | Isaios (i-SY-os)
Pandros (PAN-dros) | Feliciano (fe-li-CHEE-a-no)

Countries

Gwenthari (GWEN-thar-ee) | Lysandrian (ly-SAN-dree-an)
Ulfgarath (ULF-ga-rath) | Wulfharboria (WULF-har-bor-ee-a)
Valfarans (VAL-fa-rans) | Eirfrosti (EYE-er-fros-tee)
Rothmornian (ROTH-morn-ee-an)

Places / Things / Misc

Essaerist (es-SAY-rist) | Essaeris (es-SAY-ris)
Essaerite (es-SAY-rite) | Essaerithon (es-SAY-ri-thon)
Valfglidea (VALF-glee-dee-ah) | Wolxaran (Wulks-ah-ran)
Holtstag (HOLT-stahg) | Treowholt (TREE-oh-holt)
Duskell (DUSK-ell) | Holtkern (HOLT-kern)
Dionisiana (dee-o-nee-SEE-a-na) | Dionisio (dee-o-NEE-sio)
Hroldenfell (HROL-den-fell) | Bryndraught (BRIN-drawkt)

PROLOGUE

Valfric kept low, staying behind a thin tree. The feeling of the rough bark under his hand grounded him in the here and now. As he took a deep breath in he felt his lungs fill with the scent of grass, dirt, trees, and people around him. He kept his breathing calm and slow. He didn't need to. The Lysandrians that were coming couldn't see or hear him, but he kept his breathing and movements slow anyway. Being a warrior was about control and knowing when to act.

Valfric's gaze swept out into the narrow valley before him. In the middle of that valley was a gravel road, where a small caravan could be seen in the distance, kicking up a cloud of dust that curled and wafted above the carts, people, and animals. He took another breath in, his eyes scanning the valley. The caravan wasn't a concern at the moment, but everything he couldn't see, everything he wasn't aware of—that was the real concern, wasn't it?

The day was warm for this time of year, though he knew in the evening they would start to feel the slight bite and chill of winter's approach. He was thankful for the weather. The grasses beyond the trees he hid in hadn't started to brown or die off yet with fall. The blades were still high and able to help keep him from sight. Granted, once they were on the horses, there was no being hidden, but that was for later.

He closed his eyes and reached out with his mind and power to one of his Essaerites in the area. It was in the form of a large wolf. The animal kept low to the ground. Valfric altered its fur, thickening and lengthening it, making it like that of the grass, and the fur took on a matted green color. With its appearance and how low it kept to the ground, it would be invisible to anyone looking out over the field. The wolf's gaze shifted about, taking in everything around it. Useful as the eyes were, he was more interested in its nose.

As Valfric inhaled through the wolf's sensitive nose, he caught the sweet whiff of wildflowers and grass, mingled with the scent of dust and the animals that were pulling the caravan forward. The wolf looked up, seeing down the road in the direction that the group was traveling. The wind was not in Valfric's favor, but that couldn't be helped. He shifted to another wolf, this one behind the assortment of carts and wagons. Again, he sniffed, catching the breeze, not trying to smell the caravan, but to smell anything that might be behind it. Perhaps legionnaires or something else that could give his team away or cause problems. The Essaerite breathed in deeply, but Valfric didn't sense anything. He pulled himself back into his body.

As he pulled back into himself, he glanced over at the people next to him. His raiding party was small, and that's how he preferred it. There might be ballads sung and stories spun of large war parties, but in Valfric's experience, you just wanted a handful of people. Small teams were quick and effective. You could get in, get out, take what you needed or wanted, then kill everything else. It also meant you learned and knew the people you fought and killed with better than you ever could in a large group. This group had been with him for a while, save for the one newcomer.

He glanced over at Yrthorn, the newest member of their group. He was barely eighteen, with shaggy hair and several days' worth of stubble littering his chin. Yrthorn, like all of their group, had the signature blonde hair and blue eyes that all Ulfgarath and Valfarans shared. The young man's tall, lean form was pressed against the ground as he peered around a tree, watching the Lysandrians in the valley.

"Are you sure you're ready for this?" Valfric asked softly.

It was no small thing raiding for the first time.

Yrthorn looked over at him, his expression showing a slight bit of concern at the question. His eyes moved to the ground as he thought. "I'm ready," he said softly, and then with more confidence, "I'm ready."

"Be sure you are. Today Ulfgara watches you from her hall in the immortal lands," Valfric said, referring to the goddess of war.

Yrthorn considered Valfric's words. "Will she give me aid?" he asked, his voice colored with hints of concern.

Valfric shook his head. "No. Today is your first raid. You must prove yourself to her if you want to garner her favor. She wants to know your worth before she guides your blade and spear," Valfric said.

It was true. Today, Yrthorn would have to prove himself not just to Valfric and his party, but to the gods as well. They would be watching so they could judge his worth. No one truly knew how they would perform the first time they saw blood, death, and battle. Some faltered, unworthy of Ulfgara's favor, but others—even ones you wouldn't expect—could rise to the challenge.

"I ask again, Yrthorn. Are you ready to prove yourself to us and the gods?" Valfric asked.

As he held the young man's gaze, he saw Yrthorn's expression settle into resolve. He gave a quick nod. "I am."

Valfric heard a soft chuckle from Thraindel next to him. "Yes, I'm sure you're ready, Yrthorn. You'll do well." He said with an excited smile.

Thraindel lived for raiding and battle. He had been in Valfric's raiding party for some time. He was a little younger than Valfric, only in his middle twenties. He had long, shaggy hair that he kept slicked back down to the nape of his neck. He was muscular but still had a lively build about him. His eyes shifted from Valfric and Yrthorn out to the field, as he scratched at his short, scruffy beard.

Thraindel was not always the most forward-thinking of Valfric's group, but he was an excellent warrior, and he kept everyone in a good mood. Valfric could almost feel the pent-up energy coming from Thraindel and Yrthorn as they waited for Valfric to give the order to attack.

On Valfric's other side was Ilara. She too had been with Valfric for some time, and he trusted her more than most. She was younger than he was, but not by a lot. Her icy blue eyes looked out around her, watching the caravan. Her long curly hair was held back behind her head with a leather cord.

Ilara was one of the most unique women he'd ever met. She was stunningly beautiful and a skilled fighter who killed with ease. He had never seen anything quite like her. In one moment, she could look at him in a way that made his mind shut off with lust, and then in the next moment, she would say something crude or uncouth or tell a joke that could make the most hardened warrior blush.

On Ilara's other side was Aelric. He was everything that was feared in a warrior. The man towered over all; his neck as thick as his head. He was bald, with a short, bristly beard, and his face wore a permanent scowl. He wasn't as good a fighter as Valfric, but sometimes, even Valfric was scared of him. He was brutal in battle and fought more like a force of the gods than a man.

Their horses were behind them, hidden by some branches that they had leaned against trees. Behind those horses were the pack horses they brought with them to carry whatever they looted. Leading the pack horses was one of Valfric's other Essaerites. He didn't like creating beasts of burden. They were a waste in so many ways, and he wasn't good at them, but it would be useful today.

"What do you see?" Aelric asked.

Valfric put his focus back on the caravan. "I don't see anything behind them. Or I should say, I can't smell anything behind them. Closer to the settlement, it is hard to tell," he said.

Aelric grunted. "We need to be quick," he said.

Valfric agreed. They would need to move quickly. They were close to a Lysandrian settlement, and there was a risk that there could be a Lysandrian Essaerist in the area. There wouldn't be enough time for them to send out any help for the caravan, but if Valfric's party dawdled, they could be captured or followed.

"We'll need to wait for them to get a little closer," Valfric said. "I have something that will check out the caravan."

He closed his eyes again and moved to another Essaerite, this one in the form of a puppy. He had found these to be useful. To the Lysandrians, this territory was on the edge of the frontier—or what they called the frontier and what Valfric and his people called home. But it wasn't so far into Gwenthari territory that the Lysandrians suspected everything around them.

The puppy ambled its way along the road up toward the caravan. There were tricks to doing this right. One was to make sure that the dog didn't look wild. It needed to look like something a Lysandrian would expect to see. Two, it needed to look like it was in good condition, perhaps as if it had just run away from home and was lost. It made people trusting.

The Essaerite was too far away from Valfric to make many alterations to it, but he didn't need to. It had its hidden abilities. The little dog wandered up to the caravan, not scared in the least. As it approached, one of the mules that was pulling a cart snorted at it, and the puppy gave it a little bit of a berth. A little girl came tottering out with curly dark hair and dark brown eyes. She squealed when she saw the puppy and ran up to it, picking it up.

"What is your name?" the little girl asked.

Valfric let the Essaerite lean into the nature he'd given it. It licked the girl's face, and she giggled in delight. She carried it along, and as she did, Valfric saw through its eyes, marking everything in the caravan.

He spoke to his people. "It's small—only a few men and women in the group. I don't see any soldiers," he said.

The girl was still laughing at the puppy and bringing it up to a young woman. "Nefeli, look what I found."

The puppy looked over at the woman that the little girl was speaking to. She was in her late teens or early twenties, with olive skin, green eyes, and long, dark brown hair. She was attractive, and Valfric could make out the subtle curves of her body.

"That's very cute. I wonder if it has an owner," the woman said.

Valfric pulled his attention away from the puppy.

"They're nearly here. I don't see anything out there. What do you think they're carrying?" Thraindel asked.

Valfric shrugged. "It looks like basic goods—maybe some spices, food, and personal belongings."

He nodded. "Do they have any decent slaves?"

Valfric connected to the puppy again, looking around. "No, they don't have any slaves with them," he said, disappointed.

"How about any that might become good slaves?" Thraindel corrected.

Valfric smirked. "I think there might be one or two down there you might like," he said, "but we need to be quick. We can't fuck around."

Thraindel huffed and nodded. "Right, right, we're close to the settlement," he said.

"And it's the boy's first raid," Ilara said.

Yrthorn blushed and smiled.

"You excited?" she asked.

Yrthorn nodded.

"Alright, let's mount up," Valfric said.

He stood and walked over to his horse. He hoisted himself into the saddle, as did the rest of his group. They moved closer to the treeline.

"I'll distract the caravan with the puppy," Valfric said. "Then the wolves I have out in the grass will move in on the lead and rear cart. I don't see any horses, so they're not going to be able to get away. Most of them are on foot. Come in quickly and work fast. We are not here to play. We can play later," he said, eyeing Thraindel.

The caravan was so close now, and it was time to move. He gripped his saddle and connected into the puppy that was being carried around by the little girl. It looked sweet and playful, just like any puppy. But its teeth were like knives. It would make quick work of the girl. In a way, he was thankful for how this was about to play out. He never liked having to deal with kids. There was something distasteful about it.

With a flick of his mind, the puppy's jaws latched onto the girl's throat. She let out a gurgling scream, and Valfric could feel the Essaerite's mouth fill with blood as its teeth dug deep into her soft flesh. It began to jerk its head around, ripping and tearing her neck open. Next to her, the woman that the child had been talking to screamed and grabbed at the puppy. The entire caravan turned to look and see what was going on. As they did, he sent the command to the wolves that were out in the fields.

He'd created two of them for today—one at the front and one at the back. The wolf at the front darted out of the grass, jumping at the lead mule, latching onto it and attacking. The animal bayed and screamed. At the same time, the one from the back attacked the rear cart. There was pandemonium.

Valfric pulled back into himself. "Go! Go! Go!" he shouted to his people.

He spurred his horse, and they began to run out of the trees toward the Lysandrians. He saw the little girl drop as she bled out, and the puppy was ripped free from her. They tried to throw it into the field, still unaware of what was going on. It darted back and latched onto the calf of one of the men, who went down, howling in pain.

Others were starting to realize that something was wrong as the mules went down. They grabbed spears and swords that they had hidden in the carts, but Valfric could see they were old and rusty. These were not weapons that were used. The people using them were not warriors—they were what warriors killed. Valfric was closing the distance with the caravan quickly.

He drew his sword and raised his shield. He let out a bellowing war cry that ripped through his throat and soul. Those around him did the same, all feeling the same exhilaration of what was to come. As he reached the front of the caravan, he reached out with his sword, hitting a man in the chest with it.

He felt the handle jerk in his hand as the blade made contact with bone and tissue. It bit deep into the man's chest with a crunch, and gouts of blood spouted out around the blade, coating its surface. The man let out a gurgled scream of pain, his eyes widening in horror. Valfric let go of the sword as his horse reared onto its hind legs and knocked the man over, driving its front hooves into his ruined chest. As the horse came down, Valfric turned and swung with his shield, hitting a woman who was trying to move out of the way. The shield caught her face, sending her to the ground.

He dismounted his horse and pulled the bloody blade from the man. All around him were the sounds of screaming, dying, and fighting. He grabbed a spear that was lying next to the slain man. The woman he'd hit in the face was back up and running for the field. He reached back and threw the spear, hitting her in the lower back. She dropped to the ground, screaming as the spear dug into her. She flopped around and made a pathetic attempt to crawl away. Valfric laughed and directed one of his wolves to her. It latched onto the back of her thigh, causing her to howl in pain. She tried to bat the wolf away, and it grabbed onto her forearm and thrashed its head back and forth.

He spun, looking for anyone. He saw an old woman scuttling underneath a cart. She kicked at him as he pulled her out by her ankles. He drew a dagger from his belt and jammed it into her back. Feeling the blade pass through ribs and organs, she gurgled and moaned as he twisted it. As the blood gushed from the wound, it coated his hands in warmth. He wiped his hands off on the woman's tunic and stood back up, sheathing the dagger.

It was already over.

His team was moving about, checking for unaccounted-for survivors. Valfric came around the cart to see the body of the little girl lying on the ground, her blood pooling in the dirt, turning it into mud.

Aelric was reaching down to the woman who had been with the girl. Nefeli was her name, if Valfric remembered correctly. Aelric grabbed her hair, pulling her up bodily, making her scream. "Ah, looks like we had one that lived," he said.

Nefeli muttered and sobbed, begging.

Thraindel came up laughing. "It does look like we have a good one. What should we do here?" he said. Then he glanced over to Yrthorn. "It is the kid's first raid!" he said.

Aelric grinned. "This is true. There should be a reward for that. What do you think, boy?" he said.

Yrthorn's eyes were wild, his face covered in spatters of blood. He had done well—or at least Valfric was pretty sure he had. Yrthorn was alive, and he didn't have any cuts on him, and the blood on him wasn't his own. That was a good sign for a first raid. Valfric grinned, and he grinned back at him.

"I suppose that's true. He does deserve a reward for that," Valfric said.

Thraindel laughed. "That he does!"

Aelric pushed the woman toward Yrthorn. "First raid, first thrust. How does that sound?"

Nefeli screamed in horror.

"Don't waste time," Valfric barked. "You can play with your toy later."

"Oh, don't be like that," Ilara said, chiding. "This is a special occasion for Yrthorn."

Valfric sighed; it was true, and it was something he had to recognize, even if they didn't have the time for it. "Fine. But the rest of you, take what we can."

He turned as the small procession of the pack horses came into view, being led by his Essaerite.

It roughly resembled a horse in shape, but it was smaller. Its back was as wide as that of the other horses, but its body was hollow and missing organs. The legs were thin and long, and the whole thing looked to have been made of clay come to life. Despite its appearance, it was strong and didn't need water or food. He reached out with his mind, telling the wolves in the area to start looking for danger. They started running down the road toward the settlement and back up the way the caravan had come.

He turned his attention to one of the carts in front of him, climbing up on it, cutting a rope, and opening up a bag, looking through what he could find. He could hear what sounded like laughing and screaming coming from just down the train.

"Make it quick," he reminded, and then he turned back to the bag that he was looking at. He pulled out spices, some papers, and a few small trinkets and baubles. Next to him, Ilara was on a cart of her own, looking through it.

"Finding anything good?" she asked.

"No, nothing all that valuable yet. The spices might fetch a little bit of a price," he said.

She grunted.

"How about you?" he asked.

She fished out something and held it up. "Looks like actual gold."

He smiled. "We may have gotten something useful out of this trip, after all."

He started packing everything he could onto the horses, and a few minutes later, the rest of the party joined him. He walked up to the Lysandrian woman. She was wearing the remains of a pale blue dress that had wrapped around her body. Her eyes were red, and her face was streaked with tears and covered in dirt. He reached out his hand while tapping into his Essaeris. A simple slave collar materialized in his hands, and she gaped at it, trembling in fear.

"We wouldn't want you running off now. Slaves are valuable, and we don't want to lose anything valuable now, do we?" he said.

He hooked the collar around her neck. "Alright, let's move," he said to his party.

He tugged the woman along by her collar and got up on his horse. He pulled her up in front of him. She whimpered and sobbed. "Don't think about doing anything stupid," he growled into her ear. "Things can get much, much worse."

He spun his horse around and started heading back toward the woods.

———

Valfric pulled back into himself. "No pursuit," he said.

The camp was in a small clearing surrounded by trees that stretched high above them, casting the area in cool shadows. Valfric was sitting on a stump he'd created at the edge of a small fire. A pot sat in the coals, bubbling and gurgling with stew. Next to him, Ilara was wrapped in a gray woolen skirt as she sewed closed a rip in her pants.

Valfric glanced over, inspecting the repair.

"You're a shit seamstress," he commented.

She glanced up at him. "Fuck off," she laughed, then sighed, looking at the repair before setting the pants on her lap. "I am shit at this," she admitted.

Aelric was sitting opposite Valfric, finishing his dinner. "So, nothing?" he asked.

Valfric shook his head. "Nothing. A fire tonight is still a bad idea."

Aelric grunted his agreement. They could hear Thraindel and Yrthorn finishing up in Yrthorn's tent. The Lysandrian woman had stopped making sounds a while ago. Thraindel came out, followed by Yrthorn. Valfric heard Ilara chuckle.

"Having fun, boys?" she asked.

Thraindel wiped sweat from his brow and ran a hand through his hair. "Got to teach the boy how it's done, don't I?" he said with a laugh, socking Yrthorn's arm. "And he's doing well so far."

Yrthorn beamed at the praise, and Ilara snorted. "I didn't know you knew where it belonged, Thraindel. I assumed Yrthorn was teaching you."

Yrthorn and Valfric laughed, and Thraindel shook his head. "Ah, now, Ilara, you know I know where it goes, but I still respect the banter."

She smirked and nodded.

"We should give the bitch to Yrthorn," Thraindel announced as he and Yrthorn took a seat by the fire.

Valfric looked up from the flames. "He's too young for a slave," he said, then corrected himself, "A fresh slave."

Thraindel sat back. "What's a fresh slave? A slave is a slave, Valfric, and he earned her. You may not have seen him, but I did. He did well today."

"He did do well today," Ilara confirmed seriously.

"Valfric is right. He's too young for a fresh one," Aelric said, glaring at Thraindel. "And there is a difference. She was a free woman until today, and she hasn't been broken or trained."

Thraindel scoffed. "What do you mean she isn't broken? She is, and if she's not, she will be by the end of the night! And what training does she need?"

Valfric shook his head. "It's not the same thing. She's never been a slave. She'll need to be taught her place, and Yrthorn will as well, for that matter."

"I can do it," Yrthorn said with the confidence that can only come after a successful raid.

Valfric knew that feeling all too well—the feeling that you are the master of the world and that everyone and everything should bow to you. "You aren't ready. Take one of the settlement slaves when we get home."

"Come on!" Ilara said. "He has to learn sometime. Unless you think he's going to fall in love with some Lysandiran bitch, why not give her to him?"

Valfric resisted the urge to huff. He looked up at Yrthorn, seeing excitement in his eyes. Valfric could hold his ground and say no, but he could see that it would crush Yrthorn's spirit. He sighed. "Fine. She's yours. We will make her a proper collar when we get home. Until then, she'll wear the one I created."

Aelric huffed softly and glanced at Valfric. They shared a look, and Aelric nodded softly in understanding. Thraindel was clapping Yrthorn on the shoulder. "What a day, huh?"

Yrthorn grinned.

Valfric took a scoop of stew out of the pot and ladled it into a bowl. He blew on it, letting the steaming liquid cool before he took a bite. The air was getting chilly, and he glanced at the sky, watching clouds begin to turn shades of orange and pink.

Softly glowing veins wound up the trunks and branches of some of the trees around them and began to pulse with dim light—mostly purples and blues, but there were other colors as well, sometimes around the rims of leaves. Some of the night flowers also began to give off soft, glowing hues. He caught a glimpse of a few other lights bob in the darkening forest and heard the sounds of night animals as they woke. The trees nearest them didn't pulse with light, and they wouldn't with any kind of fire nearby.

"It's getting dark. Eat so we can put out the fire," Aelric said.

Thraindel grabbed a bowl, as did Yrthorn.

Valfric finished his stew and held the bowl over the pot. He released the Essaeris he'd used to create the bowl, and it vanished. The bits of food that had been clinging to the sides fell into the pot. He stood. "It's going to get cold tonight," he mused, stretching as he ambled over to his tent while the others began to talk and banter with each other.

The sounds from outside were muffled as he entered his tent. He pulled off his shirt and tossed it aside. On the ground was a pile of furs and blankets, most of them created using Essaeris. He flopped down on the pile. The flap opened, and Ilara stepped inside. Valfric's eyebrow shot up. "Need something?"

She smirked at him as she closed the flap. "Yes, as a matter of fact, I do. Everyone has gotten to celebrate our successful raid today but me," she said, kneeling next to him. She placed her hands on either side of his head, her expression serious. "I did well today too, and I want to celebrate."

He fought a grin. "And you're here why?"

She straddled him. "I'm here for you to do your manly duty, of course," she said coolly.

It took every ounce of his will not to pull her to him. "My duty?" he said with a laugh.

Her eyes tightened in the most piercing and seductive way. She nodded. "Your duty."

"Why not one of the others?" he asked, running his hands up her thighs under her tunic.

Her lips twitched into a crooked smile. "They are spending themselves on Yrthorn's new toy."

Valfric felt himself getting hard as she looked down at him.

"Aelric isn't," he said.

She bit her lip. "I know, but we have to ride tomorrow, and Aelric is a monster," she said softly. "I can't ride comfortably after a night with him. I need something more... comfortable," she said in a teasing voice.

He laughed deeply, and she smiled. She leaned over and kissed him. "Besides, even if they weren't busy, Yrthorn would blow if I so much as touched him, and Thraindel thinks much too highly of himself." She kissed him again. Her eyes smoldered. "And you, Essaerists, have that control skill going for you."

Control was something he felt himself losing. "We're going to come back around to that 'comfortable' comment," he said.

She kissed him, her lips warm and insistent on his in a way no other woman could be. His hands slid to her ass and squeezed. She sighed and flicked her tongue in his mouth. She leaned back and pulled her tunic off. Valfric's gaze roamed up her belly to her round breasts. He gripped her ass with one hand as the other moved to palm one of her breasts. Soft flesh filled his hand, and he ran a finger across her nipple, making it harden. He sat up a bit and pulled her closer, taking the nipple into his mouth.

She moaned softly as he sucked on it. He nipped it gently, making her gasp, and he looked up at her. "Your tits are one of my favorite things," he said and kissed her.

She molded to him, kissing back deeply. She broke the kiss and smirked. "I thought my cunt was your favorite thing about me."

He smiled and kissed down her neck. "I said your tits were one of my favorite things." He kissed her neck. "But speaking of my favorite thing..."

Her laugh sent energy pulsing through his spine. *Gwendara, help me,* he thought. She pushed him onto his back and looked into his eyes. "My celebration, remember?" she said as her hands reached down to his pants, pushing them down. "I plan on getting my fill. Understand? You do whatever you need to do to keep control," she said wickedly, and then got to work.

When he finally exploded inside her, he felt like the weight of the world had been lifted from him. He panted, pulling out of her and rolling onto his back. They were covered in sweat. They lay there catching their breath, his heart still pounding in his chest.

"Now that was celebrating," Ilara panted as she rolled onto her side.

He laughed and pulled her close. She kissed his neck, then smacked his chest. "What was that for?" he demanded.

She glared. "Dammit, Valfric, now I will be sore when we ride tomorrow."
Valfric laughed hard.

PART ONE

CHAPTER I

Mariokos's eyes fluttered open. Warm light seeped into him as a breeze drifted in from the window, running across his back. In his arms, Biankara slept soundly, her body soft and warm against his. A little too warm, if he was being honest. There had been a slight chill the night before, and he had thrown on an extra blanket when they had gone to bed. Now, the bed felt almost too hot and stuffy. He moved, and Biankara stirred. Biankara was twenty, just like Mariokos. Her long, dark brown hair was wavy and splayed out on the bed. Her dark green eyes were sleepy as they looked at him.

"Sorry, I didn't mean to wake you," he said.

She yawned and stretched in his arms.

"It's fine," she said as she rolled onto her back. "It's hot in here," she added with another yawn.

He chuckled softly. "It is." Mariokos reached out and pulled off one of the blankets, instantly feeling a small amount of heat leave the bed. "Better?"

She yawned and stretched again. "Yes, much."

He rolled onto his back, and she rolled onto her side, her head moving to his chest. Biankara's gentle breath caressed his skin, and his hand went to her back, absently running up and down her soft skin. She sighed and closed her eyes. He glanced at the window and was hit with the light streaming in. He squinted slightly as it dazzled his eyes, driving any remnants of sleep from him. As his eyes adjusted, he looked out, seeing a blue sky with only a handful of clouds.

"It looks nice today," he commented.

Her eyes opened, and she glanced out the window. Her fingers ran slowly across his chest and abdomen. "It does look nice out. Would you like breakfast?" Her fingers glided over his chest and arms. Her voice took on a softer tone. "Or should we stay in bed a little bit longer?"

He thought for a moment. "I guess we could have breakfast. That sounds good."

He felt her hand stop moving, and she tensed for just a moment.

"Okay, breakfast," she said, slightly off.

Fuck, that was the wrong answer, he thought to himself. Of course, it was the wrong answer. How could it have been anything but the wrong one? Mariokos was a lot of things, but being good with women was not one of them. Before he had a chance to correct himself, she was rolling out of his arms and out of the bed. She stood and put on a pale blue, loose dress. It looked similar to a tunic but was longer, sleeveless, and made of flowing silk.

He sighed and rose, getting dressed and pulling on a tunic. It wasn't that he didn't like the idea of staying in bed with Biankara in the morning; it just hadn't been the first thing that had crossed his mind, and he couldn't quite pin down why.

Biankara was talented, smart, well-connected, and all the other things that anyone could want in a woman—not to mention she was one of the only single Essaerist women in the entire Dionisiana province—but for some reason, nothing seemed to click for him with her. *This was only the third night you've spent over here,* he reminded himself. Though, shouldn't that have made him more eager to take her up on her offer? How many men turned down sex from a naked woman in their arms? Not many.

After they got dressed, they walked out onto a patio. They had stayed the night at one of Biankara's family estates. It was a place that Mariokos could never have imagined when he was younger, but now he had been to many places like it.

The round patio was paved with white stone. Above them, a pergola was held up by intricately carved pillars. Vines with blue, red, and yellow flowers wove their way around the slatted roof of the structure. Mixed in among the vines were pieces of glass in every hue that dappled the area with colored light. The patio was at the edge of a large garden where he could see several slaves, they were working on tending to the flowers and various plants. They were all dressed nicely and well-kept.

Biankara sat at a small table, and he sat across from her. The garden gave the area a soft, sweet smell, and Mariokos found it relaxing to look at all the flowers.

"What plans do you have for the day?" she asked, with just a hint of tartness to her voice.

You fucked up, he thought to himself. This was a pretty common thought for him when it came to Biankara. He needed to try harder. He needed to learn how to court, and he decided he would talk to Xavieno about it later today.

"I just have training, and then we have the feast tonight," he said, hoping this line of conversation would brighten her mood.

She perked up a little at that. "The Harvest Feast should be fun," she said. "And what are you and Xavieno going to be doing during training today?"

She knew Xavieno, of course. They were all Essaerists and had trained together from a young age. They'd started as a group of young people from diverse backgrounds and lives, and they were like family.

"Nothing too amazing. Probably some combat Essaerites knowing Xavieno," he said with a smile.

Biankara smirked. "Yes, we all know how much Xavieno likes being a warrior and being a good fighter and legionnaire who protects us from the many foes of the empire," she said mockingly.

Mariokos laughed. This was one of the few things the two of them seemed to have in common, and that came naturally for them. Mariokos was a good fighter, and he was good at using his Essaeris when it came to combat. But where he truly excelled was in all the other things. When it came to creating Essaerites to build or to farm or to do any other tasks, that was where his strengths lay. And it had always been that way.

It wasn't exciting or sexy or any of the things that songs were written about or that people swooned over, but they were the things that helped keep society moving, in his opinion. Frankly, it was for Biankara as well. She may have liked the high life and enjoyed having expensive belongings and having people do things for her, but she understood the power of work and the power of money.

A woman came to the table, setting down a tray of food. Mariokos looked up, noticing the slave's collar around her neck. The metal was woven with copper wire and blue glass. She nodded slightly at him as she set out plates and arranged the food.

"Would you like anything to drink this morning?" the woman asked respectfully.

Biankara considered for a moment. "Wine."

The slave looked over at Mariokos. "Just some juice, thank you," he said.

The woman bowed slightly and walked off. On the tray was an assortment of fruits, breads, cheeses, and cured meats. He picked out a couple of pieces of flat-bread and some cheese, spreading it on the bread. He picked up a Dolcianos. The skin of the fruit was almost black and smooth under his touch. He took a bite. The inside of the fruit was a vibrant green, filling his mouth with sweet juice as he chewed.

"How about you? What are you up to today?" he asked.

Biankara nibbled on a Dolcianos of her own.

"Just this and that around here, and then getting ready for the feast this evening," she replied.

The slave returned and poured them both their drinks. He reached out and took a bowl of Berrianos jam that still had some of the dark berries whole or slightly crushed in it. He slathered it onto some bread before taking a bite. It tasted wonderful; it had the perfect balance of sweetness and bitterness. He reached out with his power, feeling the jam, getting a sense for it. His Essaeris pulsed. He created a little blob of the jam on another piece of bread. He took a taste of it, thought, and then took a taste of the real jam. Biankara looked over at him.

"Success?" she asked.

He handed her a piece of bread. She took a bite and nodded in approval. "It's almost perfect," she said.

"Thank you," he said with a smile. "Would you like to feel it?"

She shook her head.

He didn't push the subject. One of the lessons they had learned early on was how to sense and recreate things with their abilities. One's power could feel a creation of a willing Essaerist and could recreate it, but it was a skill that had to be developed. It was much easier to create something that had already been made by another. It was as if one person's Essaeris could talk to another person's. But you could do it with anything, even if it wasn't something made of Essaeris. One of the more practical applications of this technique was with food. You couldn't digest it. You could eat it, but you needed to release it before it was digested.

This was easy enough to do. For Mariokos, he always had food items constrained to disappear after they had been in a warm, wet environment for a while—like, say, a mouth or stomach—or as soon as they hit acid. Usually, he had both in effect. The upside of this ability was that you could turn bland food into something much more palatable, or you could flavor water to taste like wine or juice or so many other things.

He could see where for Biankara it wasn't a skill that she thought she really needed. She'd always had whatever she wanted and always would. But for him, part of being an Essaerist meant being a legionnaire for a few years, and legion-naires' diets, while hearty, didn't exactly come with the best-tasting food.

He was happy that he had been able to mimic the jam.

Biankara's family always seemed to find the best-tasting foods, and both Xavieno and his wife Fioralba would be happy with the find. He finished his breakfast and noticed the sun getting higher in the sky.

"I need to get going," he said.

Biankara nodded. "I figured. Will you be by to collect me this evening?"

He smiled. "Yes, I will." He got up and kissed her cheek. "I hope you have a wonderful day."

She smiled. "You too."

Mariokos made his way to the training grounds for the legion. There was a special section for Essaerists, though there weren't many in the area right now, which gave Xavieno and Mariokos mostly the run of the place. He saw Xavieno standing next to an Essaerite that towered over him. Mariokos walked up to the man and patted his shoulder.

"Good morning, how is it coming along?" Mariokos asked.

Xavieno turned to him, giving him a wide smile. Xavieno was taller than Mariokos, with shaggy hair that came down to his chin. He wore a broad smile, and his brown eyes were lit with excitement.

"Good. So how was it last night?" Xavieno asked.

Mariokos resisted the urge to roll his eyes. "It was fine, I guess. It just feels off," he said, and before Xavieno could say anything else, Mariokos reached down into his Essaeris and created a small blob of jam. "But I did get this."

Xavieno raised an eyebrow, poked the jam, and tasted it. His eyes lit up. "Ooh, that's a good one. And don't try to change the subject," he said.

Mariokos released the jam, and it vanished. "I thought you'd like it. And why are you so concerned with how my evening went? Biankara and I have spent the night together before. And aren't we a little old to be talking about sexual conquests?"

Xavieno waved his hand. "I'm not interested in if you had sex with her or not. I was just hoping that things were going better with her, is all." He smirked. "And we both know that sexual conquests aren't something that exactly describes you."

Mariokos chuckled. "Whatever." He thought for a moment. "That still doesn't explain why you want this to work out for me." Mariokos eyed his friend. Xavieno seemed to cave just a bit.

Xavieno sighed. "Fine, it's selfish. But Fioralba agrees with me."

"What's selfish?" Mariokos asked.

"Look, you're like a brother to us, and we want you to be happy."

"But?" Mariokos prodded.

Xavieno shrugged. "But it might be nice to be at a feast or having dinner with another couple that seems like they're... you know? A couple." He went on. "Haven't you ever had that one friend in a group that makes it awkward for everyone else?"

"So you're saying I'm awkward?" Mariokos said, trying not to sound irritated.

Xavieno snorted. "On your own? Erosino no! And Biankara isn't either. But since you two started courting..."

Mariokos sighed, feeling disheartened. "See? Something's off with it. But it's not like either of us has a lot of choices."

"She does. She may not like all of them, but there are a few other single Essaerists in the province. They're a bit older, but that's not uncommon for Aristolios," Xavieno said.

It was true. In some of the lower social classes, large gaps in age were rarer, but for those in the Aristolios class, it wasn't uncommon for a man to prove himself before settling down. Mariokos always had to remind himself that while he was an Aristolios, it wasn't by lineage but because he was an Essaerist. All Essaerists were automatically Aristolios. Biankara was born an Aristolios, and it was the only life she'd ever known.

Mariokos looked over at Xavieno's Essaerite, which was standing next to them. All Essaerists were born with the same potential, but that didn't mean they were equal. At the beginning of his journey of becoming an Essaerist, Mariokos hadn't been able to do much more than create the occasional twig or rock. That had changed with years of training. The same went for Xavieno, Fioralba, and Biankara.

As they'd grown, their creations had become more powerful and complicated. They could create more of them, and they could do it faster and with less power. What stood before Mariokos now was one of Xavieno's masterpieces. Mariokos looked at the thing. It was a four-armed statue shaped like a man, but it was tall, almost towering over him. Its skin was white scales that were hard to the touch, like they were made of stone or metal. Mariokos glanced over at his friend. He had watched the slow progression of the Essaerite before him for a few years, but he was always curious about Xavieno's thinking, and the scales were new.

"Scales?" Mariokos asked.

"I think it's better than armor," Xavieno said. "Plate might be stronger, but this distributes impact better, and swords and spears struggle to penetrate it. I still gave it shields," he added.

Mariokos continued taking in the statue. Its legs were like those of a dog, minus the hair. They were covered in the same scales as the rest of its body. The legs looked powerful.

"So you decided to go with animal legs?" Mariokos commented.

Xavieno nodded. "I did. They give it a lot more agility and speed. The only problem is the feet," he said, looking down at them.

Mariokos looked at them. "What's wrong with them? It seems to work fine for wolves and other animals."

"The weight," Xavieno said. "These Essaerites weigh more than your average legionnaire with a full kit by a decent amount. I'm worried about it in mud, but I can make the feet wider if I need to," he mused.

Xavieno started walking around the Essaerite with Mariokos. It was exquisite and terrifying in many ways, but that was also the point of it, and there was an elegance to the design. Xavieno was good at that: balancing the aesthetic with functionality. It was something that Mariokos rarely thought to do. Xavieno didn't have to think about it; his Essaerites always resembled forms of art. Each and every one was a statement.

The statue had a large square shield, just like the legionnaires had, though it was bigger. Mariokos could see little ribbons that ran along its arms and back. He looked over at Xavieno.

"Compressed Essaerites?" he asked.

Xavieno nodded. All Essaerites took Essaeris, but you could store some of it in mini Essaerites that had simple forms. They'd have predetermined forms when they were activated, but they took less power to maintain than fully realized ones did. Mariokos could see them all over the statue. Xavieno's statue would be able to activate and deactivate the mini Essaerites at will, giving it more options and flexibility.

Mariokos had these as well. They were handy. You could only create so much at any given time, and then you had to wait for your Essaeris to rebuild itself. He had learned over the years to keep a certain amount always on hand and to be able to build it up faster than he had when he was younger. Still, having objects that could quickly turn into something else was useful.

For example, Mariokos had three large beads that were on his belt. When activated, they turned into replacement legionnaires that were the same size as a man, complete with armor, a shield, a helmet, and a spear and sword. They were as good of fighters as Mariokos, but were most effective when working as a group. All Essaerists in the Legion were expected to be able to create ten replacement legionnaires if given enough time. It was a pretty easy task to hit once you'd been doing it for a while, but they weren't the only things they used. In fact, they were a rarity.

What Xavieno had in front of him was more common for what you would see an Essaerist create for combat. Most had creations that represented the pinnacle of their abilities. Xavieno had chosen to create something that he could make multiple versions of. For Mariokos, he'd taken a different direction and gone down the path of creating a single large Essaerite called an Essaerithon.

"Have you hit your creation goal?" Mariokos asked.

Xavieno nodded. "Yes, now that I have the design finalized, I can create five of them, but I think with a little bit more time and focus, I should be able to get up to six."

Mariokos nodded in appreciation. "They'll be effective. How many can you create right away?"

Xavieno thought. "Two, maybe three," he said, "but two seems more likely." He said, almost disappointed.

Mariokos snorted. "That's pretty good for how advanced these are." He continued to walk around it. He looked up at the eyes, which were glossy black spheres. "The black eyes are unsettling," he said with appreciation.

Xavieno grinned. "Aren't they? Look at this," he said, and the Essaerite smiled, its teeth also glossy black.

Mariokos felt a chill run down his spine, and he chuckled in approval. "These will terrify any enemy."

"Our own people too," Xavieno said. Mariokos raised an eyebrow, and Xavieno explained, "The difference is our people will know these things are fighting with them and not against them. I think it might be a morale boost."

Mariokos smiled. "You're good at seeing all the angles, Xavieno. You always have been. How much can you alter them in combat?"

Xavieno grimaced. "I can't really. When I create them, I can make tweaks— like if I need bigger feet or if they're going to be in mud or sand—but not too much else. At least not for a while. Maybe in time, they'll take me less focus and effort to create, but I'm not very confident about that."

Mariokos wasn't surprised. This was the limitation of powerful and advanced Essaerites, especially for a group of them like what Xavieno created. Mariokos' Essaerithon was large but more rudimentary, with part of its design being around alterations in the field.

"It's impressive," Mariokos said.

Xavieno grinned. "Thanks, I know it's not as amazing or wonderful as what your Essaerithon and the smaller versions of it do. They dig, right?" he said teasingly.

Mariokos punched him in the arm. "Yes, they dig, but they can also cut down trees and do all sorts of construction," he said. "And don't give me that look like you're bored. In our time in the legion, have we spent more time digging or fighting?" he asked.

Xavieno held up his hands in surrender. "That's fair. You know when we were growing up and they said the legions were half warrior, half builder, I didn't quite believe them, but now? Well, now I'm kind of wondering if it's full-time builder, part-time warrior," he said.

Mariokos chuckled. "So more digging then," he smirked. "But if we ever get deployed, though, I suspect it'll be almost even. So, are you going to the feast tonight?" he asked.

Xavieno nodded. "We are. Are you and Biankara going?"

Mariokos sighed. "We are. She's excited about it."

"And I take it you're not?" Xavieno asked.

Mariokos shrugged. "It'll be fine. It'll be good food, good company, drinks, music, dancing, and all of those things."

"Yes, it will be, and with a beautiful woman, right? Biankara is attractive," Xavieno said.

Mariokos chuckled. "Yes, she's attractive. And she's smart, and she's talented, and she's connected, and everything about her is wonderful."

"Until?" Xavieno asked with a knowing smile.

Mariokos sighed. "Until she opens her mouth—but not all the time," he said in defense of Biankara.

Xavieno laughed. "Yeah, she has that effect. She always has. But what are you going to do? The best Essaerist female in the area is taken," he said.

Mariokos smiled. "I suppose I won't fight you on that one," he said fondly.

Mariokos, Xavieno, and Xavieno's wife, Fioralba, along with Biankara, had all learned and trained together as they grew up. It was something that happened with all Essaerists, and with Essaerists being rare, there weren't that many of them, so you got to know the ones that were in your area.

Xavieno and Fioralba had always been inseparable, and it hadn't been a surprise when they had gotten married. Mariokos was happy for them. Essaerists only married other Essaerists in Lysandrian society, so that meant he could marry Biankara or stay single and maybe someday marry someone else. The same went for her. She could marry Mariokos, or she could maybe find an older gentleman who was an Essaerist who had lost his wife or had never gotten married. There weren't many options. It wasn't that he didn't like her. He did. It just didn't feel right.

His relationship with Biankara was taking up more and more of his mind, and he wanted a break. "Why don't we train?" he said.

Xavieno gave him a knowing smile and nodded. "Alright, sounds good. Let's train. Start with basics?"

Mariokos smirked. "What else is there?"

Xavieno laughed, and they wandered over to a shaded corner of the training yard. Essaerites were fun to make, but they weren't what made an Essaerist. It was the little things that did it. Mariokos created a cushion, and he knelt on it. Xavieno did likewise. Mariokos closed his eyes and focused on his breathing. He felt inside of himself, feeling his power. He opened his eyes and reached out with his power. A spear appeared in front of him on the ground. As it appeared, he felt his Essaeris fade a bit. He dismissed the spear, and it vanished. He could feel his Essaeris slowly replenishing itself. He created the spear again and repeated the process, with each repetition, he went faster and faster while trying to use as little energy as possible.

They moved on to other items, changing the objects rapidly. The idea was to make it so they could create simple objects almost as fast as they thought about them. There was a time when these exercises would wear them both out for the rest of the day, but now it almost made him feel energized. When they were done, they got up and started creating legionnaires. Mariokos felt his mind move into one of them. As he shifted into it, he could see, hear, and feel everything from it, almost like it was his own body.

It had been disorienting the first few times he'd been in an Essaerite like the one he was controlling now. It was also odd being able to see yourself but from something else's perspective. The legionnaire felt human to him, except that Mariokos didn't feel pain or heat in the same way. He could make it so he could feel pain or heat just like if it were like a person, but that wasn't useful.

Instead, he felt damage and how severe the damage was. The same went for heat. He'd know if it were to be burned or be in danger of it, but he wouldn't feel it, per se. The skin was tougher than that of a man, being closer to the toughness of leather. He walked around as the Essaerite and flexed its hands and muscles. After a moment, he lost himself to it.

Xavieno was controlling one of his own. It was the best way to practice fighting. There were no real rules, and you didn't get tired out. Mariokos drew a short sword, as did Xavieno. They started working through some basics that got more and more advanced. Once it turned into a real fight, Xavieno was going to dominate Mariokos. He knew this and was fine with it. Xavieno was a skilled fighter; it was his passion in life. Mariokos did not have the mind for fighting. Not like Xavieno did.

He saw himself and Xavieno sitting on cushions with their eyes closed.

"Maybe let's not hit ourselves today," Mariokos said through his Essaerite.

The one Xavieno controlled lacked some of the character and features of a human face, but Mariokos could still make out a sheepish expression. "Good call. I still have a sore spot on my head."

The day before, they'd gotten carried away, and the Essaerites had ended up toppling onto Mariokos and Xavieno. Thankfully they were spared any shame as no one had seen it, but today Mariokos wanted to avoid that happening again.

They squared off, each creating shields and spears. They began to circle each other. Mariokos gripped his spear tightly, waiting for Xavieno to strike. After a moment, Xavieno thrust forward, and Mariokos moved his shield, deflecting the spear. He thrust out himself, and in a smooth movement, Xavieno caught the strike with his own shield and used Mariokos's movement to redirect the spear away. Xavieno slammed into Mariokos, knocking him off balance.

As he righted himself, his Essaerite registered a spear piercing his thigh. From there, the rest of the fight went downhill.

CHAPTER 2

Xavieno entered his chambers and turned, closing the heavy wooden door with a soft thunk. The failing light of the sun shone through the high slit window. Against the wall to his left was a bed, and across from it sat a brazier. The walls were a soft gray stone, and the worn wood floor had a rug covering much of it.

Sitting in a chair, looking at herself in a polished bronze mirror, was his wife, Fioralba. She turned and smiled as he entered the room. He smiled back, enjoying how his heart still did little skips sometimes when she looked at him. Fioralba's light olive skin brought out the deep richness of her green eyes. Dark brown hair flowed down her shoulders and partway down her back. Xavieno was of the belief that Bellisara, the goddess of beauty, had taken the time to personally create Fioralba's face in her own image—something he told Fioralba often.

He took a few steps across the room, closing the distance to her, as she stood. He leaned over and pressed his lips to hers.

"Good evening, Bellisara," he said.

Fioralba wrapped her arms around his neck and laughed softly. "Good evening, my love. I hope the day never comes when you stop pursuing me."

He held her closely, loving the feel of her soft form against him. He ran his fingers through her long hair, feeling the silky strands slip through his fingers. "I don't see a day when I stop," he smiled and kissed her lightly. "How was your day? And are you looking forward to tonight?"

"It was good, and I'm not looking forward to tonight. How was your day?" she said, her voice tinged with resignation.

He gave her a small squeeze before stepping back. "Tonight might be better," he said. "My day was good," he said as he pulled off his tunic.

He reached inside himself, pulling on his Essaeris. A large brass basin winked into existence before him. With a flex of power, a tall, spindly Essaerite appeared. In one hand, it held a pitcher of steaming water, and in the other, a brush.

Xavieno stepped into the basin and created some soap. The Essaerite poured the hot water over him, the pitcher never running out. He began to scrub himself. Rough bristles scraped off the dust and dirt of the training yard.

"Mariokos learned a new jam today," he said as he lathered up. He had the soap and water constrained to the space above the basin so as droplets of water and soap flung off him they vanished. The Essaerite with the pitcher poured more water on him.

Fioralba sat down, and an Essaerite of her own started weaving her hair into an intricate braid. She glanced at Xavieno through the mirror. "Did he now? One of Biankara's, I assume?"

"It is; you'll like it," he said, as warm water and soap washed away the grime of the day.

"Did you learn it?" she asked.

He looked sheepish. "Mariokos can—"

"I know what he can do," Fioralba said, giving him a playful glare. "But what if you ever want it, and Mariokos and I aren't around?"

As he stepped out of the basin, the water vanished from his feet and body. The Essaerite took the basin and tossed it along with its contents out the window. Xavieno released everything he'd created, and they vanished lest someone outside get hit with a basin full of water.

He walked up to his wife. "Now, don't be like that. One of you will always be around to take care of me. Speaking of taking care of—" he began.

She laughed and placed her hand on his belly, keeping him away. "Clothes," she said with a smirk. "If we are late to another one of these things, we'll hear about it."

He grinned. "But what if I want to be late? And you look so stunning in that dress... Besides, who will we hear it from?"

She looked up at him with a seductive, playful glint in her eye. "If you'd come in before I started my hair, I would have been open to being late," she glanced down his body and back up to his eyes. He grinned. "But," she said, "I don't want to mess up my hair. And we'll hear it from your other wife."

"Other wife?" he asked.

His Essaeris rushed out of him, creating deep red fabric that wrapped around his body. He preferred tunics, but wraps were the expected garments of feasts and formal gatherings. The fabric was soft and felt good against his skin. All in all, they weren't bad to wear unless it was summer. But tonight should have just enough coolness to it to keep the wrap from feeling hot or oppressive.

He created a mirror and inspected himself. He ran his fingers through his hair a few times and noted the stubble on his chin. He debated shaving, but he liked the way it looked.

"Mariokos," she said.

Xavieno barked a laugh. "He's not my wife, and he won't care if we're late."

"No, he won't, but Biankara will, and she'll complain to him about it, and then we'll have to hear about it from both of them," she said.

He peered over at her. "She won't care."

Fioralba stood and inspected his outfit. "Tangelo is hosting this feast, and all of command will be there along with every other important person in the area. We're Aristolios, and Biankara will view tonight like a battle."

He sighed, feeling resigned. "She will, won't she?"

Fioralba nodded, so he relented and let her finish getting ready.

By the time her hair was done, the sun had set outside. Xavieno sat on the edge of the bed. Along the slitted windows at the top of the room, little vines from outside curled in through the opening. Little buds began to slowly pop open. The nocturnal flowers resembled orchids in their shape. These ones were white with violet running around the petals. The flowers slowly began to glow. The center of each flower was a deeper shade of violet than the edges of the petals. Xavieno always enjoyed watching them bloom in the evenings. There was something soothing and relaxing about it.

The night air had a pleasant coolness to it as Xavieno and Fioralba walked to the feast. Luminescent flowers all over the city were opening, casting their gentle light on walls and people. Some were vines that crawled up the sides of buildings, casting their light against the gray or white stone of the structures, coloring the buildings in kaleidoscopes of various hues. Others were on trees, and little bugs and moths could be seen flying and darting around them.

A few of the trees had colored bands running up their bark that glowed and pulsed lightly. He saw a moth split into three versions of itself, with each version visiting a different bloom. Essaeris in nature was so practical and elemental in Xavieno's mind. He sought elemental grace in his Essaerites but rarely practicality. That was the territory of Mariokos.

Xavieno held his wife's hand, feeling her slight fingers intermingled with his. "Tonight's going to be fun," he said reassuringly.

She looked over at him. "I know. I'm sure it will be."

These events were far worse for her than for him, but he felt for his wife, and her stress translated into his. He felt it edging its way up his spine with each step they took. He breathed out slowly and calmed himself.

It'll be fine. People will move on, he thought. And they would move on at some point. The question was when and what it would take to make them move on. While he was all too happy for him and Fioralba not to be the center of conversation or pity, he didn't want somebody else to have to deal with something that would cause that same attention. And it was pity that they faced. Not some scandal. Not hatred. Just pity. And it wasn't that the pity was unjustified or even unwelcome. More it was that each nice comment or understanding look brought up the cause of it.

He knew for Fioralba that it also came with a sense of defeat and shame. She saw herself as failing in some way, but miscarriages happened all the time. It would have been worse for the child to have been born just to pass. But it was different for an Essaerist woman. It was harder for them to bring a baby to term, and the whole pregnancy was complicated by their Essaeris fluctuating and going out of control.

Essaeris was just like a part of one's body, and he was sure that months of that part of you fighting you was embarrassing and frustrating, but at least tempered by the prospect of joy just beyond the horizon. It was unfair to have that joy ripped away from anyone. But that was the will of the gods.

As they neared the plaza where the feast was being held, he could make out decorations along the walls of the building. Out front, he saw a group of men and guards who were checking to make sure that anybody trying to go into the feast was allowed. Standing next to them were six people.

"I told you she would look at tonight as battle," his wife said.

Xavieno grimaced a little bit. Yes, it appeared Biankara was looking at tonight as a battle. Not the type you fought in, mind you, but the political type. She was standing with Mariokos, who was wearing a wrap similar to Xavieno's, in a rich brown. Next to him, Biankara wore a stunning dress of expensive silks and exotic fabrics. The outfit was adorned with a handful of jewels and gold and silver chains. Unlike Mariokos, Xavieno, and Fioralba, Biankara's outfit was not Essaeris. In her family's opinion, wealth was something to be seen. It denoted power, and she'd always railed against creating clothing with her powers despite the prodding of their instructors.

For Essaerists, creating clothing had little to do with status; it was discipline and practice. It was about keeping yourself at a point where your powers were able to easily handle all of your needs, save for food and water. Self-reliance was the mark of the Lysandrian Essaerist. For Biankara, she'd only created clothes in training, looking at the task as something beneath her.

Behind Mariokos and Biankara were four slaves. Two males and two females. All appeared to be in their early twenties, and their collars had bits of blue glass on them. The collars were immaculate, as were their clothes. All wore tunics of creamy white and leather sandals that looked new. Xavieno suspected that they came from a line that Biankara's family had owned for generations.

Fioralba sighed as they approached the group. Before she could speak, Biankara said, "Don't sigh at me. You are all Aristolios, not some common Citizanos. You need attendants. Mariokos already lost this battle tonight for the three of you."

Xavieno scoffed. "Mariokos is not my champion... She is," he said, nodding to his wife.

Biankara laughed. "So should we skip me winning again for the evening? Though I do enjoy the practice... Well..." she shrugged. "I suppose on second thought it's not my place to try and tell you what to do. You are a powerful man and warrior who can make his own decisions." Her expression became apologetic. "It was presumptuous of me. I'll send your attendant home," she said and pointed at one of the male slaves.

The slave had a soft appearance that still held the foundations of masculinity, and his eyes and lips were perfect. Xavieno felt himself waver a bit. "I suppose if you already have someone here, it would be rude of me to refuse."

Biankara's lip quirked up in a smile. "Oh, it's fine, Xavieno. I know you are anything but rude. It was my fault, and it's not bothering me, really," she said politely.

Next to him, Fioralba smirked playfully. "See, my love? We got what we wanted. Thank you for respecting our choice, Biankara."

He turned to his wife. "You're agreeing?"

Fioralba looked confused. "Yes, we won. Or I should say I won because I am your champion after all. And I know you don't want an attendant. Especially one with eyes like that," she said emphatically. "Honestly, Biankara, how could you even think this is something my husband would like? But it does seem like a waste of time to have him leave. Perhaps he can be my attendant, and my husband could have..."

Xavieno caught Mariokos attempting to hide his amusement by inspecting a pebble at his feet.

Xavieno cut Fioralba off. "I'll take the male," he huffed, his eyes darting between his wife and Biankara. "You two enjoy this too much," he glanced at Mariokos. "And you?"

Mariokos shrugged and chuckled. "Biankara already told you I lost before we got here. I was just enjoying the show."

Xavieno rolled his eyes and began to walk.

"And I am a powerful man and warrior—and man," he grumbled at Biankara.

"Mmmhmm, I noticed," she said with a laugh.

He had to admit Biankara knew him well.

Their attendants followed them as they walked. As they walked through the entrance, they were met with the rich smells of the feast. He inhaled the rich aroma of meats cooking, and his stomach instantly growled.

The feast was the harvest celebration for Corianthus, the god of harvests, and while Xavieno's leanings were more towards Bellamara, the goddess of war, he always enjoyed the harvest feast.

All around the courtyard were tables where people stood eating and drinking. In the center was a massive stone altar at the feet of a statue of Corianthus. The statue towered above them. Corianthus had a crown of wheat and barley, his muscular arms were adorned with tattoos depicting the seasons, and his tunic was made of leaves and vines. Light from fires danced across the marble of the statue, almost seeming to make it come to life.

The altar was covered in dark brown fabric—the color most associated with Corianthus—and the reason for Mariokos' brown wrap. The altar was piled with all manner of vegetables and fruits from the harvest as a sacrifice. Braziers stood at the sides of the altar with sweet-smelling smoke rising and curling in the air. They approached it and offered a small prayer of thanks.

Xavieno could see why Mariokos resonated so much with the god. Where Xavieno saw the joy of battle and the honor and majesty of it, for Mariokos, it was the small things. It was watching a harvest come in, watching a plant grow, watching something be built. It may not have been what drove Xavieno, but he could respect it.

They stepped back from the altar after giving their thanks. Xavieno took in all the feastgoers. Senator Tangelo had invited much of the legion's leadership and some of the more known members of the city as well.

Of the three free classes in Lysandrian society, two of them were represented. Aristolios were the highest class of society, with Citizano being the middle class. Most of the Aristolios had attendants following them. Notably absent were the lowest members of society, the Subaltero. The class was composed of those who had once been criminals, freed slaves, or were just unfortunate enough to have been born at the bottom. That was Xavieno's heritage. Of course, that changed when he became an Essaerist. Now, he was at the top, and his family had moved up to the class of Citizano.

Slaves with red glass in their collars moved with trays of food, setting them on the tables and collecting used dishes. They worked quickly and effectively, being as inconspicuous as possible.

Xavieno turned to his group of friends. "Well, shall we find something to eat and a place to stand?" he said.

Biankara was smiling politely and looking around, her eyes gauging everyone. "Yes, I think we should start with drinks," she said.

Biankara waved at the attendants to get drinks and then guided Xavieno, Mariokos, and Fioralba to a table that was large enough for four people to stand around. Biankara positioned herself so that she could see into groups of people around them. As they walked, Xavieno caught a few people glancing their way—not at Biankara or at him, but at Fioralba. He felt a pang in his gut for her, and he could see her shrink back into herself just a little bit.

Biankara fixed both Xavieno and Fioralba with a warm but stern stare. "The two of you are going to start smiling and laughing, and you are going to appear to have a good time this evening," she said.

"Biankara, it's just—" Fioralba started and was cut off.

"No, it's about perceptions. Look," she said earnestly, "I understand that you don't want to be the center of attention, and I understand you don't want pity. I don't want that for either of you. I am upset about what happened to you, but these people don't need to be thinking about it. So tonight, you're going to show them that you've moved on, whether you have or haven't." She took on the tone of an instructor. "So this evening, you are going to laugh, you are going to drink, you are going to make it appear as if this is one of the best Harvest Feasts you've ever been to, and there's nothing else that's on your mind."

Xavieno was about to speak when Mariokos interjected. "She's right. As soon as people stop thinking about it, then you don't have to worry about the attention anymore. And as soon as it looks like you're no longer thinking about it, they won't either."

Next to Xavieno, Fioralba tensed and sighed. "I am over it. I am fine. We are. We really are." She said like she was trying to convince herself.

Xavieno knew that's exactly what she was trying to do. Convince herself. He was in the same spot, and he decided that Biankara and Mariokos were right. He didn't think about it all the time anymore, and only really did when he saw others look at them or heard a hushed comment.

Biankara smiled tightly. "Okay, then prove it. Prove it to these people and prove it to yourself," she said.

Xavieno nodded slightly. "You're right. It's only difficult when people remind us," he said. "Or at least, that's usually when it's difficult," he said, gathering himself. "If we don't give them a reason to remind us, then maybe they won't. We can do this," he said to his wife.

She nodded. "We can do this. And it's not like we're the first couple to have something like this happen," she said.

Biankara spoke. "No, far from it. And that's why everyone is looking at you this way. Everyone knows what it's like or knows that they could have to experience something like it at some point, and they know it's more likely for us Essaerists," she said kindly. "Not everything is easy for us. And sometimes people like being reminded of that—even if they don't know that they like it."

Their attendants returned with wine. Xavieno took a glass and drank, tasting the sweet liquor as it filled his mouth and rolled down his throat. He took another sip.

"You're right. Tonight, we will eat, we will drink, and we will forget," he said.

Biankara nodded, satisfied. "That you will. All while playing the perfect picture of Aristolios," she said with a smile.

Mariokos chuckled.

Xavieno barked a quick laugh. "Yeah, fine, that too."

———

FIORALBA GROANED SOFTLY IN CONTENTMENT AS HER ATTENDANT WORKED ON A KNOT IN her shoulder. She was sitting with Biankara in one of the parlors off to the side of the main courtyard where the feast was being held. She lounged back in a soft chair as the slave worked on her shoulders.

Xavieno was off enjoying his attendant somewhere, and Biankara sat in a chair next to her with her own attendant massaging her feet. Fioralba's mind swam and buzzed slightly with the wine from the evening, and her belly was almost painfully full.

The slave's ministrations were pleasant, but her pressure was just a bit off, as was the placement of the woman's hands. Well, and the rhythm of her movements. It wasn't her fault; she just couldn't feel what Fioralba was feeling.

"Are you sure I can't use an Essaerite to do this?" Fioralba said to Biankara. She looked up at the attendant. "Not that you're not amazing at what you're doing, but an Essaerist's own Essaerites can't be beaten," she said. The attendant didn't give any indication other than a small nod but kept working.

In fairness to the slave, this wasn't the first time Fioralba had made this argument. The first time she'd said something, the woman had stopped, which resulted in Biankara telling her that, other than requests for where and how she was to massage Fioralba, she wasn't to listen to Fioralba.

Fioralba looked over at Biankara, who just shook her head. "You can do that later. Besides, doesn't this feel wonderful?" she said.

"Yes, it does, but not as good as an Essaerite does. It's nothing against a human; it's just my creations know exactly what I want because, oh yeah, they're a literal part of me," Fioralba said flatly.

She understood the value of creating clothing that looked expensive and learning how to act like a member of the upper crust. What she didn't understand was the use of slaves by Essaerists at events like these. It was just a show of wealth, which in the case of Fioralba and her husband, they didn't have.

Biankara rolled her eyes. "This is just fine. Besides, I didn't see your husband complaining."

Fioralba chuckled. "No, I'm sure he's enjoying himself just fine." She smirked. "You really took the wind out of his sails with that one."

Biankara smirked as well. "I may know a thing or two."

"Speaking of the men in our lives," Fioralba said, "where's Mariokos? I somehow doubt he's enjoying his attendant the same way Xavieno is."

Biankara shrugged. "I'm not entirely sure, to be honest with you. He had been speaking to some people before, you and I went to go sit down and relax. I suspect he's discussing farming or roads or something of that nature with them," she said with a warm smile.

"Is he doing a good job of politicking this evening?" Fioralba asked.

Biankara laughed heartily. "No. No, of course not. That is nothing that Mariokos is ever going to be good at, I dare say." She said.

"But he's a good man," Fioralba said.

Biankara's expression softened. "Yes, he is. He's a very good man. And one of the only eligible Essaerists in the area," she pointed out. Biankara sighed and looked at her friend. "Don't give me that look. I know he feels the same way."

Fioralba tried to keep her expression even. "He likes you."

"I know he does. And I like him. We've been friends for years. We've known each other for a long time," she said, looking up at the ceiling and thinking for a moment. "And it's a good partnership for what it's worth."

Fioralba looked at her. "But?"

"But it's not the best partnership," Biankara said. "It may be the only one that I have available to me, and Mariokos has so much going for him, but he also has to spend time in the Legion. And when he comes back... well, what is he going to do?" she said.

"I'm sure Mariokos will keep himself very busy and be very productive," Fioralba said.

"Yes, but with what?" Biankara shook her head. "Look, I know all of you tolerate my views and my politicking and everything of that nature, but you have to remember that for me, this has been my whole life. This is my family's legacy, and I'm an Essaerist," she said.

Fioralba tried to look at it from Biankara's point of view. It was true. She was different from all of their friends. Yes, Essaerists were born just as often in the higher classes of society as they were in the lower. It's just that there was so much less of the upper class for it to happen with. So when it did, they were something of an oddity and special.

It also wasn't uncommon for Essaerists who were born into Aristolios families to marry someone else in the same situation. It just was good business for the families. Marriage for political or financial gain was common for Aristolios. But Essaerists only married other Essaerists, which greatly limited who they'd end up with. Had they been closer to the capital, it would have been a different story.

"You can find a way to make it work," Fioralba said. "And while Mariokos may not have the political connections that you'd like, he's very talented and is an extremely good Essaerist, and he understands how the world works and functions," she said.

Biankara nodded. "Yes, I know. That's crossed my mind. Frankly, it has my family's too. My father sees a great deal of potential in Mariokos," she admitted.

"So what's the problem then?" Fioralba asked.

Biankara motioned for her attendant to move from her feet over to one of her hands. She sighed softly as the man began to massage her hand and wrist.

"It's just not what I expected growing up. I always assumed I would end up with a man like my father," she said matter-of-factly. "I know it sounds childish to be bothered that life isn't going how I planned it would when I was a little girl, but it's what it is. Also, I always expected to be marrying somebody who was... I don't know, established."

Fioralba could empathize with that. It was also common amongst the higher members of society to have an age gap between males and females. It made sense. The men would establish themselves, build their empires, and put their focus on that when they were younger, and then they would look for a wife. They'd start a family and raise the next members of their mini-empires. Mariokos was the same age as Biankara, which, while common for Fioralba, Xavieno, and Mariokos' families, wasn't for Biankara.

"So, what are you going to do?" Fioralba asked.

Biankara sat back. "Continue doing what I am now. Mariokos is a good man, and we are good friends. And while that connection or love may not quite be there, why would you need love for marriage?"

Fioralba didn't have a response for that. Again, their upbringings had been so different. For Fioralba, marrying Xavieno had been about love and them being together forever. But for Biankara, a spouse was a partner, and you had to find a way to make it work. Of course, for Biankara, as soon as she became an Essaerist, that had changed. The pool of people was much smaller, and now she was forced to try to pick what was available or wait and hope for a marriage of political gain and value. It was a risk.

Xavieno came walking into the parlor. His wrap was slightly askew, and he had a broad smile on his face. His expression was relaxed.

Fioralba smiled, happy to see him looking relaxed. "Did you enjoy yourself?"

His attendant came walking in behind him, his hair ruffled. Her husband grinned.

"I did. How are you?" he asked.

She smiled softly. "I'm enjoying myself," she said. And she was. It was relaxing, and they'd had a good evening.

She was happy that Xavieno had gone and blown off some steam that evening. It was something that he needed to do. She looked over at Biankara. "Thank you for tonight."

Biankara smiled. "You are welcome. Just always remember I know everything, so just trust me and don't argue."

Xavieno snorted a laugh. "Like you would ever let us forget anything like that," he said playfully.

Biankara grinned.

Fioralba smiled and drained the last of her wine, setting it on a table next to her. "Well, is it sufficiently late that we can go home?"

Biankara smirked. "Oh, it's been sufficiently late for that for some time," she said. "It's not my fault your husband has been dilly-dallying with his attendant for so long."

Fioralba snickered. "Yes, he does that," she said with a smile and stood. She took Xavieno's hand. "Well, shall we, my love?"

He gave her hand a small squeeze and looked over at Biankara. "Thank you again for the evening. See you soon," he said, and they walked out of the parlor.

CHAPTER 3

Caelwen bent over and inspected a mushroom at her feet. The mushroom was growing on a stump near the edge of a small pool on the forest floor. She glanced at the water, and her reflection looked back at her. In it, gone were the last vestiges of her teens. Instead, a young woman with vibrant blue eyes and a face framed with fiery red hair peered back at her. Her gaze moved back to the mushroom.

She reached down, holding it with one hand and cutting it free from the stump with the other. She stood, placing the mushroom in a bag. The morning air was cool and thick with mist and moisture. It clung to the plants and trees in the form of dew that, in the coming weeks, would turn into frost.

Her boots were slick with moisture, as were her cloak and the hem of her tunic. The forest was dim, with the sky covered in gray clouds. It was pleasant. Caelwen enjoyed this time of year. Around her, the trees soared, their canopies connecting and weaving amongst each other, their bark covered in moss, and their roots tangling on the ground. She stepped over to another log and inspected some more mushrooms.

In the trees, she heard chattering, and she looked up and smiled. A little flying squirrel, called a Valfglidea, jumped from the trees and stretched out its tiny arms. It glided down towards her, landing on her shoulder. She barely felt its weight.

Its long, bushy fur was a shade of green that turned to blue as it landed on her. Its cheeks were full, and its big black eyes looked at her. Valfglidea were intelligent, mischievous, and thieving. They also had the lifespan of several humans and were unreasonably cute.

This particular one was named Treftune. Caelwen smiled as the little critter moved to a bag that she had slung across her back. It emptied its mouth into the bag, and she heard the sound of Holtkern nuts clattering inside.

Treftune came up and nuzzled her cheek. "We're not supposed to be looking for Holtkern nuts right now," she reminded him. "Remember? Duskells, we're looking for Duskells." She said, referring to the nut of the Duskwood tree.

He chirped again and wound his way around her neck, almost making a type of scarf. His fur was soft and warm against her skin. She scratched him behind his ears as she continued to walk, searching for more mushrooms or anything else that might be edible or of value. She heard some rustling in the trees, and a Valfglidea flew down and landed on her shoulder. It looked up at her expectantly. She held open a different bag, and the creature poked its head in and dumped out some triangular nuts.

"Now that's what we're looking for," she said.

The nuts were coated in saliva that vanished as soon as the little being jumped off, away from her. One of the nicest parts about Valfglidea was that they were Essaerists and could create multiple versions of themselves. Treftune could make about five versions of himself, all of which were busily foraging for nuts. *Hopefully, most of them are looking for Duskells,* she thought. Valfglidea were clever and could change their fur, ears, and teeth. They had exceptional senses of smell and hearing, and their sight wasn't too bad either.

To outsiders, Valfglidea seemed a rarity and almost magical, but anyone who knew anything about them knew that they were everywhere. They were just exceptionally cautious, and it was rare for them to bond with a human. Caelwen was thankful for Treftune; he was a wonderful companion and had been her mother's before he'd been hers.

More versions of Treftune showed up and emptied their mouths into bags. Thankfully, unlike their creator, the Essaerites seemed to do a good job of finding Duskells to collect. She felt a nudging against her mind from one of her own Essaerites, a weasel-looking creature that she had created.

She had several of them in the area. They had a strong sense of smell and were busy rooting about looking for truffles. One had found one. She hiked up the side of the hill, weaving through trees, vines, and branches until she found the Essaerite. As she got there, it wandered off in search of another truffle. Caelwen dug at the base of a tree until she found the truffle and pulled it out. Treftune chirped at her, and she sighed, handing over a small chunk of the truffle to him, which he gobbled down eagerly.

Valfglidea were horrible at digging, and she knew how much he loved the mushrooms. She placed the rest of the truffle in an Essaeris bag that she sealed off lest her fuzzy companion got it in his mind to steal. Treftune came to the bag and pawed at it, chirping in annoyance. She smiled.

"Those are not for you. You had your reward," she commented. Treftune chirped in response and climbed up her body, winding around her neck.

Caelwen stood and closed her eyes, breathing in deeply, feeling the scent of the forest saturate her lungs and mind. She breathed out, relaxing. She continued wandering around, hunting for mushrooms, and was about to head back home when she felt another one of her Essaerites. This one was a particular type of trap. It had caught something. Hopefully, it had caught what it was supposed to. She made her way to it and found it in a small bowl between several trees.

The Essaerite was a collection of vines that were wrapped around a struggling wild hog. The creature thrashed a little and squealed in frustration and irritation. The vines tightened around it, keeping it in place but not harming it. She smiled. This was what the trap was supposed to be trying to capture. The hogs were not the easiest prey to catch, but they tasted good and were destructive.

They were the bane of farmers everywhere, as they would root out crops and break fences. But they were a nightmare to hunt, trap, or catch. For Caelwen, they weren't so bad. She'd set out a trap and maybe some bait, and she'd catch a few of them.

She liked the meat but was tired of it, though they fetched a decent amount of coin, and it made the farmers in the area happy. She reached out with her powers and altered the Essaerite. It wrapped itself tighter around the hog, and then six of the vines turned into short legs. The hog squealed as it was lifted. She directed it to go back to her home and drop the hog off in the pen. She'd sell it in the next few days.

Caelwen secured the bags to her back and began picking her way down the mountain and through the dense forest. She couldn't see her breath as her breathing picked up, but the day was cool, and she liked it. Her home was along the edge of the settlement, and it started to take shape as she neared the edge of the trees.

The cottage was modest, with an enclosure for a few animals outside. She saw the hog that she'd caught along with two others in the pen. They rooted around in the mud along the fence, trying to get out, and otherwise seemed displeased about their new home. That was fair. The cottage was dug partway into the ground, its thick thatched roof sloped steeply. A ribbon of smoke curled up from the chimney as she walked up to the front door.

Caelwen took two steps down into the cottage and was met with the warmth of her home and the smell of dinner cooking. Along the far wall was a fireplace with a few embers burning, their scant light casting the inside of the cottage in a warm, flickering glow. In those embers was a pot with the evening stew simmering and bubbling inside it.

She shrugged off her cloak and hung it on a hook by the door. Near the wall to her right was a rough wooden table with two benches. A couple of jugs of Bryndraught sat atop it. She moved the jugs out of the way and set her bags on the table.

She walked up to the fireplace, grabbing a few pieces of wood and tossing them onto the coals to start burning. To her left, one wall of the one-room cottage was overshadowed by shelves that had various beads of glass filled with different herbs and tinctures, along with jars of other items that she had made or created.

On the table was an Essaerite working on Duskells. While the task of producing Duskwood oil was straightforward, the Essaerite was one of Caelwen's more complicated-looking ones. It looked like a chunk of wood that had several small vines with fingers reaching out of it. Some of the vines were reaching into a basket with Duskells in it. They'd pick up a nut and plop it into a metal cracker that would crack the nut and dump the meat into a small mill. Once milled, it was put in a press that pushed out the oil into a small ceramic cup. There were four crackers, two mills, and one press, all working in perfect harmony. But complicated though it appeared, most of Caelwen's other Essaerites were more complex and harder to make.

The process was normally very tedious, time-consuming work for most humans, but for Caelwen or any Essaerist, it was relatively easy to do. Duskwood oil burned for a long time without any smoke and was bright. It fetched a high price on the market and was one of the more profitable things that she sold. The only real catch to it was that the Duskwood tree didn't fruit until it was ten years old, and even then, only every five or six years after that, with each tree producing a small quantity of Duskells. While the trees were common enough in the forest, the nuts were rare and hard to find.

Caelwen grabbed one of the bags from the table and created a bucket of warm water to rinse the Holtkerns she'd collected. The warm water would help all the dirt and grime from the forest come off them. After that, she walked outside, making her way between her cottage and the pen. The hogs squealed in disdain, but she paid them no attention. Next to her home, she found another bucket full of water and Holtkerns, though the water in this bucket wasn't Essaeris.

The Treowholt trees that produced Holtkerns were all over. In the fall, the nuts littered the ground all over the settlement, but finding ones that would make it through the winter and didn't have cracks or bugs in them was a different story. That was where Treftune did a great job. With their keen noses, Valfglidea were able to find the best nuts, and with a little prepping from Caelwen and some Essaeris, the Holtkerns would make it well into next year.

The ones in the bucket she held now had been soaking for a day or so and had been ones that she had found around town. Many were broken or had obvious defects. The mixture smelled horrible, and she saw a few drowned worms floating on the surface, but the hogs would love it. She dumped the bucket out into the pen, and the hogs went over and began chomping away.

As she watched the hogs, she noticed a figure coming up to her house. She peered closer, seeing a man in a ratty tunic with a collar around his neck. His hair was long and greasy, as was his beard. Eilfgar, one of the settlement's slaves. He came trotting up to her.

As he neared, she was hit with the stench of him. It made her want to take a step back, but she resisted the urge.

"Caelwen, there is a caravan coming on the main road," he said.

"What kind of caravan?" she asked, her interest piqued.

"Carts of goods, it looks like. I think they're merchants looking to trade," he said.

"How many carts?" she asked.

He held up five fingers.

She nodded. "Does my uncle know?"

His head bobbed. "Yes, he does. He's who told me to tell you. He said they might be staying a bit."

"I'll come by in a bit," she said.

As he walked away, she released the trap Essaerites she had in the forest along with the weasels that had been truffle hunting. She had plenty of Essaeris left in her, but she wanted all she could have. The power welled up in her, and she created two small owls. They flew off in different directions. She normally had them out at night. They weren't for hunting, mind you, but to watch for trouble. Her settlement was small and looked like a great target if a group had a mind for it.

She let the feeling well up in her again, and this time when it came out, she felt the pull much harder. There was a swirl of soft colors that resolved into the form of a puma. Its fur was charcoal black, and its eyes shone with cunning and intelligence. Pumas came to the area from time to time, but their fur was a golden brown, not black. In Caelwen's experience, when someone saw a two-hundred-pound cat, it was best if they could tell it wasn't natural. The Essaerite's color would ensure that anyone who saw it would suspect Essaeris and be less likely to shit themselves. But it would also put them on notice with the message being clear: behave yourself or face the consequences.

She went back inside the house. "We're going to have company soon," she said to Treftune and made her way over to a stone bench that was in the corner. She released the top of the bench with her Essaeris, the stone vanishing and revealing the contents inside.

There were several jugs filled with Duskwood oil, along with some pouches full of coins. She pulled out some of the coins and inspected the Duskwood oil inventory that she had, sucking on her bottom lip. *This would be the best time to sell,* she thought to herself.

It wasn't like she was the only one who sold the oil or the only one who made it. There were plenty of people in the settlement who foraged for their own Duskells and made their own oil. However, it was the time of year when people were starting to think about what they needed for the winter, and they would be hoarding it, or wanting to buy some. Now would be the time it would fetch the greatest price.

She looked over the jugs, trying to add up their value in her mind. Of course, she didn't need any oil for herself. She could always just create some or create a light if she needed to. The oil was a means to an end for her. There were things she needed to buy throughout the year, and oil helped her with that. She thought, *Hmm, I want to see what they have before I bring this up,* she thought to herself. If the caravan was loaded with oil, they wouldn't give her a decent price, but in her experience, it was rare for a caravan to have a lot of the oil this time of year.

"Come on, Treftune, let's see who came to town," she said as she walked towards the door. The little Valfglidea uncoiled himself from his spot by the fire and ran over, crawling up her leg and back to settle on her shoulders.

She wound her way along a narrow road that moved through the settlement. She passed by a few small farms and cottages. It appeared that nobody was out on their farms but were checking on the newcomers.

As she came towards the center of the settlement, she could see more activity. Here there were a few buildings for meeting or drinking. And in the center of it all, there was a small courtyard where five carts were, with everybody in the settlement talking to the newcomers. Caelwen waited, taking her time, knowing that there was always the rush of people that came first; she could wait.

As people cleared away, she slowly meandered up to the carts, inspecting the various items they had. There was nothing she needed. She wanted to sell. That said, she would go for an odd spice or something of that nature. As she looked around, a man with blonde hair and blue eyes looked down at her.

"What are you looking for?" he asked.

She eyed a few of their wares and shrugged. "Not looking to buy, but maybe looking to sell," she said, glancing up at him.

He had a firm jawline and a scar running up the side of his face. He grinned. "And what could you be looking to sell?" he asked.

"Duskwood oil," she said. "I have a few jugs of it."

The man looked thoughtful. "Really? What are you doing with a few jugs of Duskwood oil that you're looking to get rid of? Most people are stocking up."

She smiled sweetly. "That's why I'm looking to sell."

He seemed thoughtful. "You're going to have to prove you have it before I make an offer," he said.

She shrugged. "Fair enough. Come by and take a look? Unless you'd like me to lug them down here."

He leaped off the cart and towered over her. He smiled. "Show the way."

She did so, turning and starting to walk towards her home. She caught a few hushed comments from some of his party along with a snicker. He was soon striding alongside her.

"Are you married?" he asked.

She glanced up at him and shook her head. "No, I'm not."

She noticed him eyeing her appraisingly as they walked. He was attractive and seemed to be confident. She'd give him that. They moved away from the settlement proper, and as they did, he eyed her more.

"You live on the edge of the settlement? With your family?" he asked.

She smirked. "I live alone."

Caelwen understood the confusion. She was young and didn't look like a fighter. She was one, but it wasn't her center. She figured that he either assumed she was stupid and a nice target or that he was walking into something he shouldn't be. As they neared her cottage, she could see him tense. *Going with the latter, huh?* she thought.

"Relax, I'm an Essaerist," she said casually. "I'm not going to rob you."

He eyed her, and she made a cube of wood pop into existence. His eyes widened for a moment. "Huh, I guess that's why you have the oil to sell," he commented, his voice sounding a little shaken. "I've always wanted to bed an Essaerist," he said in an attempt to regain some semblance of confidence.

She snorted a laugh. "I wouldn't count on it tonight."

She resisted the urge to smile. She didn't dislike the idea of sleeping with this man. In fact, after a moment's thought, she was planning on doing it. Her settlement was small, and she wanted a pre-winter distraction. But with how he'd looked at her and the comment he'd made, along with all of the hushed things his friends had said to him, it told her that he wanted her more than she wanted him. *Good,* she thought. Horny people tended to make poor business decisions. She wasn't immune to it either; she just wasn't at a disadvantage this time.

As they neared her home, she saw him tense again as he spotted the Essaerite Puma lying in front.

"Don't worry, it won't do anything to you," she said.

"Why is it here?" he asked.

She shrugged. "There's a caravan of newcomers in town. One can't be too safe," she commented.

He breathed out a little.

"Really, you're fine. Essaerites aren't like normal animals. It just looks like a puma, but it's not actually one," she explained. And then she added more brightly, "it's far more deadly. Normal animals have organs and all that, that weigh them down. That cat is all muscle, teeth, and claws." She smiled warmly at him and walked to her door, enjoying the look of shock and horror on his face. *That should keep you in line,* she thought to herself.

She walked in with him behind her. As he walked through the door, he glanced out at the paddock with the hogs in it.

"They don't mind that thing?" he asked, curious.

She shook her head. "They don't know about it. They can't see it, and Essaerites don't have a scent unless we give them one. So the hogs can't smell it, see it, and it doesn't make any sound."

He nodded. "But if they did see it?" he asked.

She laughed. "If they saw it, there'd be problems."

He breathed in. "It smells good in here," he said. "Well, despite the smell of Duskwood oil." He said as he walked over to the table, "You weren't joking when you said you had some to sell." He said, looking at her Essaerite that was busy pressing some oil into a cup.

"I have two jugs. I'll sell them for twenty each," she said confidently.

He looked back at her and smiled tightly. "Ten," he said.

She eyed him. "Twenty, and I'll include dinner," she hedged.

He looked over at the pot by the fire as it bubbled. "What's for dinner?" he asked.

"Stew, and some bread that's about to go on," she said. As she said this, a stump in the room changed, growing legs and arms. He stepped back for a moment, his breath catching. She snickered. The Essaerite went and found a bowl of dough; it began to knead the dough and placed it on a flat rock next to the fire. "Dinner will be done soon."

He ran his hand through his hair. "That's not fair," he said.

She smiled up at him. "Twenty?"

He laughed. "Maybe fifteen. It'll depend on how good the stew is," he said.

She chuckled. "Oh, I see."

She turned to the table and started to clear away the oils and nuts from earlier in the day. She felt two very large hands on her hips, she looked back at him and raised an eyebrow. His expression was confident, if not a little cocky, and she felt her heart flutter a bit.

"Maybe if you sweeten the deal, I'll go for twenty," he said, his lips close to her ear.

The feel of his breath on her made a spike of energy slither down her spine.

She turned around slowly, doing her best not to let her eagerness show. She gazed up at him, noticing all the details in his blue eyes. Her gaze moved to the line of his jaw. She made a point of moving her eyes down and up him before she spoke.

"Hmm, maybe it should be the other way around," she said breathily, her eyes moving up and down him again. "Maybe if you do a good job, I'll be willing to sell to you for ten."

She leaned back against the table, her palms against its rough surface. She held his gaze and bit her lip. She watched his expression crack, and his hands went to her waist.

His head gave the smallest of shakes. "Fuck," he said, his voice rough. "You're going to win this, aren't you?"

Her hands moved down the fabric of his tunic to his belt. She nodded softly. "Yes, I am. You're going to pay twenty."

She unfastened his belt. "This is how it's going to work. Your caravan will be here for a day or two. So tonight, I'll let you have your fun. But by morning, you'll pay me what I want for the oil and then pretty much do whatever I'd like you to do."

His eyes narrowed for a moment, and then he laughed. "Yeah, I'm not even going to argue with that," he grinned, and it made her heart kick.

He leaned forward, his lips catching hers. She kissed him back, her arms going around his neck. His tongue slipped into her mouth, and she gave a soft sigh. She was looking forward to her pre-winter distraction.

———

WHEN THEY'D HAD THEIR FILL, THEY GOT DRESSED.

Caelwen smirked. "So how was having an Essaerist for the first time?"

He grinned. "I could get used to it." He ran his hand through his hair and gave her an almost longing look. "And before you say anything, I'll pay you twenty."

She chuckled and walked over to check the progress of the stew and bread. The stump Essaerite began getting bowls and spoons and placing them on the table. It went and grabbed the pot and ladled some stew into the bowls. She watched as the man observed the Essaerite with wide eyes.

"I take it you haven't been around a lot of these?"

He shook his head. "No, never actually. I guess I shouldn't say that; there was one that came through our settlement once, but otherwise, no," he said, looking a little dumbfounded.

She smiled. "We're rare," she said as she sat down. She tore off a chunk of bread, dipped it in the stew, and took a bite. He sat across from her and did the same, watching the Essaerite. His eyes moved around the inside of her cottage, seeming to notice it for the first time.

"I didn't notice any fields. I did see the pen. I take it you're not a farmer," he said.

She nodded. "Nope, not a farmer."

"So are you a healer or something like that?" he asked, noticing some of the bottles on the wall.

"Something like that," she said. "But mostly, I forage and scout around and fight if needed."

He took a bite of stew and sighed. "This is good. Did the—" he said, searching for the word.

"Essaerite," she supplied.

"Right, the Essaerite," he nodded. "Did that make this?"

She shook her head. "It stirred throughout the day, but I did most of the cooking for it this morning. Essaerites can cook and can do it well, but I needed something to do," she said with a shrug.

He chuckled. "I guess I could see that with these. They're probably a whole lot more useful than slaves," he commented.

"They certainly are," she said. "Well, at least when you get more advanced. When I was younger, I couldn't even create a stick," she said.

"And you're a warrior too?" he asked, not sounding surprised.

It was common for Gwenthari Essaerists to be warriors. In fact, that was the norm. Caelwen was a little special in that she didn't put all her focus on fighting and instead spent time working on more practical creations like the stump and Duskwood oil Essaerite. Though she was good at fighting as well.

"Aren't we all warriors?" she said dryly.

He took another bite. "I suppose so. It's the way of life. The strong win, don't they?"

She nodded. "So we've been told." She looked at the scar on his face. "Is that how you got that scar? Was it a great battle?"

He grimaced and looked down. "I want to say that it was, and the men in my caravan will give me no end of shit for admitting this, but it wasn't in battle that I got this scar," he said.

She cocked an eyebrow. "Do tell."

He sighed. "I tripped and fell."

She looked at him for a moment and then started laughing. "That sounds like something a woman would say when her husband beats her. Was that how it played out? Did someone beat you? Was it a woman?" she asked.

He glared at her playfully. "No. I did trip," he said.

She laughed and placed her hand on his. "Don't worry, I'll protect you," she said.

He shook his head and laughed. "I knew I shouldn't have told you."

She laughed softly, and he said, "I tripped. It was in a forge, so yeah."

She gritted her teeth. "Ooh, that does not sound enjoyable."

He shook his head. "It really wasn't."

They ate the rest of their meal silently. As they were scraping the last of their bowls, she said, "It's getting late."

He nodded. "I guess I should be off."

She smirked coyly. "That would be rude, wouldn't it, to send a guest home at night?" she said.

He grinned. "Looking to sweeten that pot a little bit more?"

She smiled. "Maybe you're the one who needs to earn his breakfast," she said, standing up.

He grinned deeper. "I think I can do that. My name is Faelric, by the way."

"I'm Caelwen," she said and took his hand, giving him a tug. "Now show me how good of a breakfast you're expecting."

CHAPTER 4

Caelwen woke with a yawn. Faelric's large arm was draped around her, and they were buried under a collection of furs and blankets. She yawned again and stretched, feeling him shift next to her. The sound of a fire crackling in the fireplace soothed her, and she resisted the urge to close her eyes. Instead, she shifted in Faelric's arms, rolling over and seeing him look around her cottage.

She turned her head to see what he was looking at. He was watching her stump Essaerite, which was gathering some dishes and putting them on the table in preparation for breakfast. It skuttled about on four short legs resembling those of insects, but made of wood. Its arms were a bit longer and ended in long-fingered hands. It carried items on top of its flat head; stumps were useful that way; there was always a place to set things. Caelwen glanced back over at Faelric, noting a slight tenseness in his eyes. She raised an eyebrow.

His eyes darted to hers for a moment. "I don't like it."

"You don't like what? The Essaerite?" she asked.

He nodded slightly. "There's just something off about it. I don't see how you can trust it," he said, looking at her.

"You don't see how I can trust the thing that's a part of me and that's making our breakfast and putting some logs in the fire this morning so that the cottage is warm?" she said.

He looked back at the stump. "A slave could do the same thing," he commented, "and that you can trust."

She snorted. "Wait. You would trust another human who has been forced to work for you, forced to be your property, who has been abused by you and at their core hates you, over an Essaerite that has no emotions, no thoughts or feelings, and just does what I want?"

He looked down at her. "My argument doesn't sound as good when you put it that way."

She laughed. "It really doesn't, but I guess I understand. It's not like the Essaerite looks like a person or anything like that."

"Can they?" he asked.

She nodded. "They can look like anything you want and be anything. It just depends on how skilled you are. I couldn't make one that looks just like a person. I've seen other Essaerists who use Essaerites that are more human-looking, but they never fully look like a person. I'm sure there are Essaerists who can do it, I just haven't seen one. But the almost human-looking ones seem to bother people."

"So you made a stump that moves around like a giant bug with vines that turn into hands, and that's not supposed to bother anyone?" he asked flatly.

He had her there.

"Do you want breakfast or not?" she asked, changing the subject.

After they ate, Caelwen fetched the two jugs of Duskwood oil and gave them to him.

"I can get you payment when we walk by the caravan," he said, looking at the jugs.

"That sounds good. Do you have any other trades planned for the day?" she asked.

He nodded. "A couple of people talked to us yesterday. How about you?" he asked.

"I have three hogs in the pen out there. I think I can sell two of them today," she said.

"And what are you going to do with the third?" he asked.

She shrugged. "I may sell it, but I'm thinking I might salt it or smoke it for the winter," she said.

"Are you pretty good at catching those things?" he asked.

She smiled. "I'm the best," she said.

Caelwen grabbed her cloak and they walked outside. They were met with thick fog and mist that enveloped the landscape, accompanied by a light drizzle of rain. She breathed it in, feeling it fill her lungs. Next to her, Faelric glanced down at the Essaerite puma, which hadn't moved since she had created it the night before.

She smirked. "If you don't like that or the stump, you'll definitely not like this."

She felt her Essaeris build within her, and she reached out her hand, pointing to the ground and releasing her energy. There was a shimmer as vines came into existence, forming into four legs carrying a cage made of vines, twigs, and leaves. She created another one, making Faelric gasp, and they scuttled over the side of the paddock. He watched as the hogs inside panicked and started running around. From one of the Essaerites, a vine snapped out, grabbing one of the hog's legs and pulling it towards it.

It pulled the squealing animal closer, wrapping more vines around it and hauling it into the cage. It stood up on its four legs and scuttled over the paddock wall next to Caelwen. She watched Faelric's expression, a mix of horror, excitement, and fascination, as the other Essaerite did the same with one of the other hogs. It, too, joined them. She looked up at him.

"Did you like it?" she asked.

He glared at her slightly. "I'm not going to say that I didn't, but I'm not going to say that I won't have nightmares from that either." He breathed out. "Those things are powerful," he said after a pause.

She shrugged. "They're rudimentary. They're basically just vines and branches that I've created. There are far more advanced ones out there, but for these hogs, they're pretty useful. If I just tried to bring them along with a rope..."

He laughed. "Now that would be entertaining. You may be powerful with your Essaerites, but I would love to see a girl your size try to control two wild hogs with just a rope."

She laughed. "Oh, I'm sure it would be entertaining. As it is, the hogs don't get hurt this way, and they'll calm down in a bit. Plus, I don't have to be dragged through the mud," she said with a smile.

"And I get some nightmares," he said dryly.

"And that too."

They began walking towards the center of the settlement. Behind them, there was the occasional squeal or grumble from one of the hogs. She noticed Faelric made a concerted effort not to glance behind him. As they approached the caravan, she could see a couple of the people who had been with him the day before. They eyed the Essaerites, then their companion, and finally Caelwen, each giving a little smirk. She glanced over, noticing that Faelric had a smile on his face, and she shook her head. When they reached the caravan, he handed over the money for the jugs, and she went on her way.

She left the caravan with her two hogs and made her way toward one of the farms. She had a couple in mind, but the first one she was going to stop at was Grenulf's. She hummed to herself as she walked, enjoying her morning. She'd had a good evening, made a sale, and was hopefully about to make two more. And if the gods were smiling on her, she'd have another good evening.

Grenulf's home was a little larger than Caelwen's cottage, and it had a small barn. She saw a paddock where there were some sheep and goats next to his fields, which had been cleared from the harvest. As she approached, she could see Grenulf standing outside. She waved at him. From around the corner, another figure came out, and her smile faded.

"Fuck, seriously." She groaned to herself.

In the distance, she could see a thin man with a long white beard and white hair. He was her uncle, and she sighed. "Such a cunt," she muttered to herself. She walked up to the farm, approaching the two men. Grenulf smiled amiably at her and almost appeared a little relieved that she was there. Her uncle gave her a fake smile.

"Good morning, Grenulf," she said to him. She glanced over at her uncle, Ilfthandor. "Uncle," she said flatly.

"Good morning, Caelwen," her uncle said. "What do you have here?"

She looked back. "They're called hogs," she said sarcastically. "They're a type of animal that lives in the forest and likes to get into fields. Have you heard of them before?"

Her uncle scowled at her, and she noticed Grenulf trying not to snicker.

"Don't be petulant," Ilfthandor said.

"Don't ask stupid questions," she shot back.

Caelwen was the only one in the settlement who would dare speak to her uncle that way. Well, her or her brother, but he was off with a mercenary group at the moment. Caelwen's uncle had taken over after Caelwen's mother had passed away. Her father used to lead the settlement, but he died long ago in a botched raid set up by her uncle. Then, her mother had taken over, and when her mother had passed, Caelwen and her brother had been too young to take charge.

Her uncle was disliked, but he was the richest man in the settlement and was slightly feared. Caelwen did not share that fear. She turned her attention to Grenulf.

"Can I interest you in a hog?" she said.

Grenulf looked over at the hog. "Yes," he said awkwardly.

She raised an eyebrow. "What's wrong? You said you wanted one yesterday," she said.

Her uncle cut in. "Yes, and I think he still does. He was going to provide one for a feast this evening," he said, smiling broadly.

Caelwen sighed, understanding. "You want Grenulf to provide a hog that he's about to buy from me for a feast tonight? So are you buying the hog from him?" she asked.

Her uncle frowned a little. "No, everyone provides for feasts. You know that, Caelwen. We have guests," he said.

She snorted. "I'm sure. And what are you providing, uncle? Oh, wait, never mind. You're providing all of the arrangements," she said.

Grenulf looked like he didn't want to be part of the conversation, and her uncle glared at her. Before he could speak, Caelwen said, "I'll provide the hog for this evening if Grenulf will cook it. How does that sound?" she said. "That's very generous, don't you think?"

Grenulf seemed to perk up at that.

Her uncle grumbled. "Yes, very generous."

"Good then." She smiled broadly and glanced over at Grenulf. "I have an extra hog if you're still looking to buy one."

His expression softened, and he nodded. "Yes, if you're still willing to sell, I am," he said.

"Ilfthandor, we'll see you this evening," Caelwen said.

He gave her a glare and went on his way. As soon as he was out of earshot, she said, "Cunt." She looked over at Grenulf. "I'm sorry for volunteering you to cook tonight," she said.

He shook his head. "No, thank you, Caelwen. I thought I was going to have to buy this hog and then cook it and then find something else to try to store away for the winter," he said.

She patted his arm. "Well, good. I'm glad it worked out this way."

He looked at her. "But will you be alright?" he asked.

She smiled. "I'll be fine. I've got lots of Holtkern, and I have another hog as well. I can keep it, or I can probably catch another one of the little fuckers if I decide to sell it," she said, looking at the hogs.

She directed her Essaerites over to his pens and released the hogs, which instantly scrambled around inside the pen, free and agitated.

"Let me know if you need anything," she said to Grenulf.

———

CAELWEN CAUGHT THE SCENT OF A BONFIRE AND A HOG ON A SPIT WELL BEFORE SHE SAW the feast. The buildings in the center of the settlement glowed with light and people sang and danced around the fire. Its flames roared and shot high above the gathering. Many of the people had tankards of Bryndraught that they were drinking from, and someone had busted out a keg of mead.

She was looking forward to the evening. She could smell the mead and Bryndraught on Faelric's breath as he greeted her. She laughed as he scooped her up in a hug and spun her around.

"How's the mead?" she asked.

He set her down. "Wonderful, and I can't wait for that hog to be done," he said, pointing at a hog that was slowly turning on a spit.

One of the men from his caravan came over and started talking to Faelric, while Caelwen looked around at the gathered people. She spotted her uncle sitting off to the side near the fire but not so close that it was too hot. He was sitting with some men from the caravan, speaking to them. He looked over at her, and she sauntered over.

"Good evening, uncle," she said, sounding pleasant.

She didn't like him. She thought he was an ass, and a fuck, and stupid, and also an ass and a fuck, but he was also her uncle, and they were around outsiders, which meant that Caelwen was going to play nice and be a good niece. It also meant that he wasn't going to be his normal crusty self with her either.

He smiled warmly. "Caelwen, my dear, how are you?" he asked, standing up.

She hugged him, and he hugged her back. "I'm good. Thank you for throwing this feast tonight," she said warmly.

"Of course, my dear. Sit down and join us," he said.

This was the game they played; adversaries sometimes during the day or around the settlement, but always on the same side and team when there were others around.

"Are you discussing business, or are you enjoying this wonderful feast you've put together, uncle?" she asked.

He smiled. "Both, my dear, both. I am discussing some sales right now with one of these good men."

She smiled. "Very well, but promise me you'll enjoy yourself tonight," she said sweetly.

This, too, was part of the act. Caelwen, while known and respected in her settlement, was an unknown to outsiders, and to them, she was a pretty, unmarried girl who didn't have the look of a warrior. She was underestimated. She was the niece of a settlement's leader, just a spoiled brat—probably seen as ignorant and stupid. She liked it that way. That's how she wanted to be viewed.

Eventually, outsiders would figure out that she was an Essaerist, something these men already knew. Not that she thought there was a threat here, but still, it was always good to play.

She got some meat and bread, along with some Bryndraught. She went back and sat next to her uncle, eating, drinking, laughing, and appearing to watch those around her while instead, she listened intently to her uncle's conversation. He was making a deal.

Her uncle was by far the wealthiest man in town. He had the most property, the most slaves, the most belongings—he had the most of everything. He also had deals set up that were completely in his favor with most people who lived there. From the sound of the deal he was making now, it appeared that he was being taken and not the other way around, something she very much doubted was the case.

He was speaking to one of the men about the price of some sheep. Part of her was tempted to stop him or ask questions, but she didn't because this was part of the game. The sheep were too expensive, and he'd be overpaying significantly. Something she knew he wouldn't do.

It made her feel uneasy. *What are you up to, uncle?* she thought. She didn't like his scheming, and she didn't like his dishonesty. It had been detrimental for their settlement and, in her opinion, it had been bad for their relationships with other settlements in the area. He had become cocky over the last few years. There were some men in the settlement who were good fighters, her brother being one of them. But those men were gone now. They would be back soon, but they had been hired to fight in some war in the south. When they came back, they would have spoils and riches, but there may not be as many of them. It was foolish for her uncle to count on that now, but he was also counting on Caelwen.

Essaerists were nothing to mess with. Though Caelwen didn't see herself as advanced, her presence gave other settlements pause, and they were right to be wary. The puma she had patrolling the outskirts of the settlement could easily kill several men, and she always had something wandering or flying around. Most times, it wasn't for raiding parties, but for wolves, foxes, or other animals that would come into the settlement to steal. But it meant that it was hard to get the drop on her people, and also meant that if you came in with a small group, you would have to deal with something like the puma and everything else she could create.

People were respectful of Essaerists; they had to be. They were powerful. But Essaerists were rare, and being rare meant that they were misunderstood. Her uncle was one of those people who misunderstood them, even though his niece was one. He, like so many, worked under the assumption that Essaerists could create beings so powerful that they could defeat almost any force, and that just wasn't the case. There were limits to what they could do, and Caelwen knew she was very limited.

There were many Essaerists who were far more capable than she. There just weren't any in the area. So she listened to the conversation, trying to figure out her uncle's angle and what he was doing to either screw the people in the caravan or those in the settlement. Most likely, it was a scheme that would screw everybody, and the only person who would come out on top would be her uncle. She took another drink of Bryndraught.

As the evening continued, her uncle moved away from business and joined in the merriment of the feast, as did the men of the caravan. All of them were drunk now, as were most of the people in the settlement. She checked on her Essaerites before deciding to join in on the festivities. It didn't matter how drunk she got or if she blacked out until tomorrow evening. The puma would still do its job. It would wander around, looking for trouble. She also had a few owls flying over the settlement. They would find anything that was amiss, and if they did, the puma would act.

This was the peace and comfort her settlement had. They knew they could lose themselves in the evening and not have anybody get the jump on them. So she grabbed another tankard of Bryndraught and downed it. Then she started in on the mead. She found Faelric, who was extremely drunk and wobbling around, singing some off-tune song that she couldn't quite understand.

"Caelwen," he said as she approached, his voice slurred.

She smiled.

He scooped her up in a hug. "Dance with me," he said.

She laughed and heard some people start playing music. They began to dance, or at least they tried. Caelwen was sure at the moment that it looked good, but she suspected that anyone who wasn't drinking would think other-wise. She downed her mead and spun around with Faelric, who was far too big for his own good, especially with the alcohol. They crashed to the ground a few times, laughing and joining in the song and dance, until finally, the alcohol won out, and Caelwen went to sleep.

———

SHE FELT LIKE SHE'D BEEN HIT IN THE HEAD WITH A WARHAMMER. THAT WAS THE ONLY explanation for how she felt. Caelwen groaned, her head throbbing as if it was going to rip open and explode. There was an oppressive weight on top of her, and she was lying on something hard. She shifted, took a breath in, and then coughed.

Next to her, there was a grumble. It was Faelric. His eyes cracked open, blood-shot and red. She looked at him.

"Wh-what? What happened last night?" she asked.

He groaned and rolled onto his back. "Mead. Mead is what happened." he said softly.

She rolled, feeling pain in her shoulders and hips, and more pain in her head. Where was she? She looked around. She was lying on wood. She shifted and found that she was in the center of her settlement, lying on one of the carts from the caravan. She wasn't alone. There were other people lying around, but most, it seemed, had made it home that evening.

There were a few crackles and pops from the coals left from the bonfire from the night before, but mostly it was just people slowly coming to and staggering around. Her jaw hurt from sleeping on the wood. She looked over at Faelric.

"Did we have a good night?" she asked.

She thought. She was pretty sure they had. She remembered flashes of it—there was bad dancing and singing, and... there was something. Her uncle had made a questionable deal. That was still in her mind, but she couldn't remember much after that.

Faelric sat up and looked thoughtful. "I think we did." He looked down at his clothes and moved them around, "but I don't think we had a great night; we're both still dressed."

She laughed and then instantly stopped, grabbing her head. "Oh, no."

He did likewise. "No laughing," he said.

"No laughing," she echoed, groaning.

She stood and jumped off the cart. As her feet hit the ground, she wobbled a little, her leg asleep from the night before. Faelric jumped down as well; his landing was not as graceful as hers. Other people in his caravan were getting up. She tilted her head, hearing her neck pop.

"When are you guys leaving today?" she asked.

She heard a voice from behind her, from the caravan leader. "In less than an hour," he said, all smiles. He looked at Faelric. "I told you not to drink that much last night," he said cheerfully.

He started yelling at some of the other people in his caravan—not angrily, mind you, just to yell. There were a few grumbles as some of the settlement people woke up and heard the yelling. They slunk off to their homes. Faelric winced.

"You're gonna have a good day," she said.

He looked over at her. "That was uncalled for."

She smiled. The caravan leader barked another command, and Faelric began shuffling around. He looked back at her.

"Well, Caelwen, it was... it was enjoyable," he said.

She smiled and hugged him. "If you come back through town, I'd be happy to sell you more Duskwood oil," she said.

He smiled. "Sweeten the pot, and I might buy it from you again," he said with a smirk.

"I think I can manage that," she said.

She kissed his cheek and began to walk home. She would like to say that as she walked, she was graceful or proud, or that he watched and thought to himself, 'there's the one that got away.' But she heard him begin to work, and he was in no state to think, and her walk resembled more of a stupor than a walk. Her leg was stiff. She really didn't know what she had done to it the night before, but it loosened up a bit as she moved through the settlement back towards her cottage.

She entered her home and found a hot breakfast waiting for her: boiled oats and some flatbread. She tried to move to her bed, but she heard chirping and looked up to see Treftune on the table. He looked at the food and then at her, and then chirped.

"I don't want to eat," she said. He chirped again, a little bit more insistent this time. She sighed. "Fine."

She sat down and scooped some of the food into her mouth. Her jaw hurt, but she chewed and swallowed, and then took another bite, feeling a little better, and then another. The stump Essaerite gave her a glass of water, and she downed it eagerly, feeling her body and mind start to come back to her. She yawned and looked over at Treftune. "Treftune, I think today is going to be a day spent inside," she said. The little Valfglidea chirped happily and jumped up on her shoulder, wrapping around her neck and warming her. She smiled softly and scratched behind his ears. "I'm glad you approve," she said as she took a bite of her bread.

CHAPTER 5

Caelwen yawned, waking up from a nap. She stretched, noting how much better her body felt. Her headache was all but gone as well. Curled up next to her was Treftune. He was on his back; his fur was currently a soft brown, and his little chest rose and fell slowly as he slept. His leg twitched a bit, and she smiled as she gently stroked his belly. He grumbled a little and snuggled in closer to her.

She laid her head back and thought for a moment. *I wonder what time it is,* she mused. She reached out to the puma in front of the cottage and had it look up. The sky was the same as it had been when she'd come in, telling her she'd only been asleep for an hour or two at most. But in that time, the ground had gotten wet, and she suspected that it had rained a little.

She sat up, disturbing Treftune, who grumbled. As she moved, her head throbbed slightly, and she felt a twinge of irritation with herself about her choices at the feast. She got out of bed and looked down at Treftune. "Do you want to go with me to feed the hog?" she asked.

One of his little black eyes opened and peered at her for the briefest of moments. Then he grumbled again and curled back up, putting his tail over his eyes. *So that's a no,* she thought. Her leg was stiff as she walked to the door. *Fucking mead.*

After she fed the hog, she went back into her home. She had the stump put some water on to boil and walked to her wall to pluck one of the glass cubes off of it. Inside, she could see dried herbs and leaves. The glass was Essaeris, but the herbs weren't.

When the water came to a boil, she poured it into a mug and dropped in the glass cube. She released the glass, allowing the herbs and leaves to float around in the water, tinting it with color and flavor. She swirled it around and sat, waiting for the tea to steep. As she did, she grabbed some of the Holtkerns that she had gathered the day before and finished washing them off.

She scooped some of the nuts out of the bucket and put them on a plate. The shells were dark from soaking, and she looked at them, focusing on the Essaeris water. She slowly began to release the water. As she did, the shells lightened as they dried. She'd learned the hard way that if she released the water too quickly, the nuts could crack. She repeated the process until all of the nuts in the bucket were dry.

She felt her power within her, and let it well up and spill out in the form of oil, which she poured into the bucket. She stirred the nuts around and then altered the oil, letting it get thicker as it clung more to the nuts. After a few stirs, she dumped them out onto the table. As they left the bucket, the oil changed and hardened around each of the nuts. They clinked and rolled around.

She picked each one up, altering its exterior, making it smooth and hard, encasing the nuts in a glassy rock. It took very little effort for her to do, and the upshot was that nothing could get into them. She could store them outside in a barrel throughout the winter, and they'd be fine; nothing could get in, no moisture, no bugs, no rodents—nothing would even smell them.

Caelwen took a sip of her tea, feeling the hot liquid course down her throat into her belly. She took a few more sips and relaxed, feeling her headache fade even more.

She glanced over at Treftune. "What should we do with the rest of our day?" she asked him. "Perhaps another nap? I'm thinking another nap," she said, gulping down more tea.

She felt a nudge from the puma outside and she turned her attention to it. "Cunt," she muttered as she saw her uncle walking toward her cottage. She wasn't in the mood for whatever shit he had planned.

She walked out of her home to meet him outside. He eyed her as he closed the distance to her cottage. Caelwen stood with her arms crossed. He walked with a slight limp—a souvenir from when he'd gotten her father killed years ago. She didn't know everything about the botched raid other than Ilfthandor had failed in some task, and it had resulted in a catastrophic failure of the raid.

He wore a dark tunic under a cloak made of wolf skin. In his hand was a walking stick that was intricately carved, and she could see the outline of a sword hanging from his hip under the cloak. *I wonder if he even remembers how to swing it anymore?* she thought to herself.

"Good afternoon," Ilfthandor said as he neared Caelwen.

Maybe he wasn't here to be a prick. She felt a few raindrops hit her, and she sighed, deciding to keep things civil. "Good afternoon. Would you like to come in?"

"That would be nice," he said.

She turned and opened the door. He followed her in, and she had the stump start boiling more water. Ilfthandor looked around as he sat at the table.

"I wish you'd consider moving closer to the center of the settlement," he said.

She grabbed him a mug. "Why is that?" she asked. "Don't tell me you're worried about me out here on the edge of the settlement."

He didn't bother lying. "Of course I'm not worried about you," he said. "You're an Essaerist. I doubt there's anyone in the settlement whose safety I need to be less concerned with than yours."

The stump poured the water, and she placed some tea in each mug. She knew why he wanted her in the middle of the settlement. He wanted to control her if he could, and she strengthened his position. She was both a risk and an asset to him.

She was in line to take over should her uncle and then older brother die. Eventually, the former would happen, or he'd become too old to lead. Having Caelwen on his side could help him avoid that. She was also an asset because she was special, and marrying her off could be used to solidify a large treaty or agreement. Though she wasn't sure he'd ever play that hand. If she got married off, she wouldn't be in the settlement anymore, and that could weaken him.

"So how did your trades go?" she asked, changing the topic.

He nodded. "That's actually what I wanted to talk to you about."

Her eyebrows went up. "How so?"

He took a sip of his tea, trying to look concerned. "Some of the residents reported that they had a few items go missing last night, and that the men in the caravan weren't...honest in their dealings."

She sat back in her chair. "I didn't have any issues. And if people make bad deals, that's on them, isn't it?"

He held up his hand. "Yes, of course, it is. But the theft? We can't have that," he said, shaking his head.

You son of a bitch, she thought. She'd thought his deal the night before seemed off. She waited, looking at him expectantly. She knew where this was going, but she wanted to make him say it.

"Some of us feel that something needs to be done. It's unfortunate, but it is also the way of the world. The way of the strong," he said.

She rolled her eyes. "Raiding a caravan after making a bad-faith agreement isn't the way of the strong. It's the way of the shitty and dishonest."

He flared up. "How dare you!" he said, his face tinting red.

There was a time in her life when this man's anger frightened her and made her cower, but those days had long since ended. She'd also learned to read him. His anger was real but not directed at her accusation. Rather, it was aimed at her unwillingness to bend to his whims.

"It's true," she said evenly.

"You need to stand with your settlement, Caelwen," he said, talking down to her.

Now it was her turn to get angry. "I need to? No, uncle, you need to! I stand with them every day while you cheat people and come up with stupid plans like the one you're coming up with now!"

They were both on their feet now, and she saw his hand move back. His eyes were narrowed in rage, but his hand stayed still. Caelwen didn't budge and held her ground. If he wanted to hit her, so be it. She'd had worse from him, and she knew he wouldn't. Likewise she wasn't going to hit him. He was the leader of the settlement, and she couldn't just hurt him; there would be consequences.

She could challenge him if she liked and let the people decide. He was too old for her to challenge in combat, but the settlement could overthrow him. But that wasn't why he stayed his hand.

They both knew what the people would decide. Ilfthandor would stay in power. What stayed his hand was that deep down he knew that with a flick of her mind, he'd be dead, and no matter the consequences for her, there was no bringing someone back to life.

He took a few breaths to calm himself. "The caravan is stopped for the night. The road is mud. Unless you want to be branded a traitor and coward, you will join the group tonight that is attacking them."

Her teeth clenched. "I don't care what you brand me," she said in challenge.

He sneered. "Tell me. There are people who have grievances that will be there tonight. Do they live without you? But you could kill the caravan all on your own, couldn't you?"

She felt her face heat up. "Then don't send them."

His sneer deepened. "You didn't answer my questions."

"No, they won't live," she said, and added, "and I might be able to take them all on my own, but it's not a guarantee. There were twelve of them. And they had horses."

"Then scatter them," he said.

She barked a laugh. "Scatter them? Do you really think there wouldn't be anyone that got away? And what? So they can go home and tell their people what happened?" She shook her head. "Do you ever think past next week?"

He seemed to calm. "Then make sure they don't live. This is the world, Caelwen. You'll help, or the blood of those you know will be on your hands."

He turned and stalked out of her home. "Meet at the edge of the settlement tonight." He shut the door.

———

As Valfric cleared the forest, he took in the settlement before him. He stretched in his saddle.

"It's good to be home," he said to the group.

Next to him, Ilara gave her agreement, as did Aelric and Yrthorn. Thraindel made a comment from the back of the group, and Valfric looked back at the slave girl, who didn't say anything. She kept her eyes down, focused on her saddle as the horses trudged along.

Their settlement wasn't large, but it wasn't small by any stretch either, and there were many good fighters in it. But Valfric and his team were the best. They followed the main road into the settlement, passing by cottages. People waved at them and said their greetings as they passed. He saw farms with animals moving around, and he spotted the occasional slave working in a field or a stable. The settlement had many slaves, and Valfric's team was responsible for a lot of them.

As they got closer to the center of town, he felt himself relax more. It was always good to be home. In the center of town were a series of buildings that were for gatherings, a few inns, and businesses. They rode to the main meeting hall. He got off his horse and walked up to the heavy wooden door of the meeting hall and opened it. "We're back," he announced as he walked in. The room was mostly empty, save for a woman who sat in a chair at the far end. She looked over at him.

"Valfric," Durnara said with a toothy smile.

The woman had long blonde-gray hair and blue eyes. She was thin and had probably once been stunning. Now age had taken its toll, as had the stress of leadership. She stood and moved over to Valfric and his friends. She looked at each in turn.

"How was the raid?"

"It was good," Aelric said. He looked over at Yrthorn. "For the boy's first raid, he did well."

Durnara looked at him and nodded in approval. "We need more young warriors."

"We always do," Ilara commented, "and we always will have them."

Durnara glanced over at the other woman and then back to Valfric. "So it was a good raid, then?"

Valfric nodded. "Yes. Yrthorn did well. We got a slave that we gave to him, and we found a few other items—some of them useful, some not. It was a small Lysandrian party that we found, but we were able to make it pretty deep into their territory."

She nodded. "That's good. I'm glad to hear it. It sounds like food, rest, and drink are in order. After you're settled, Valfric, come and see me," she commented, giving him a look.

He nodded, understanding the look. There was something she was worried about. He looked over at Yrthorn. "Alright, let's get you all set up, now that you're a man and a warrior and all."

His team clapped Yrthorn on the shoulder and congratulated him.

Valfric turned and called to Yrthorn. "Come on, boy," he said.

They walked out of the main hall, and his gaze shot over to the Lysandrian woman. "Come on," he barked at her.

She flinched but walked alongside them. Her eyes darted around the settlement in fear, and Yrthorn looked over at her and smirked. "You've already had the worst of it. Don't worry, honey," he said with a chuckle.

Valfric glanced at Yrthorn and thought to himself again that the boy was not ready for a new slave, but there was nothing to be done about it now. They walked past various shops and made it to a smith. They found the smith outside his forge banging away at some metal. As they came around the corner, he looked up.

"Valfric, good to see you," he said, walking over to Valfric for a quick embrace. "How was your raid?"

"It was good. So good, in fact, the boy here needs something from you," he said.

The smith looked over at Yrthorn. "And what do you need?" he asked, glancing over at the Lysandrian woman.

"I need a collar," Yrthorn said.

The smith smiled. "Your first slave—congratulations! How did you win her?" he asked.

"I killed her companions," he said.

Valfric saw the woman look down, her eyes welling for a moment.

"Good for you," the smith said. "Get over here." He barked at the woman.

She moved forward, and the smith looked at her neck, wrapping a cord around it to measure the length. "I have one that will work already. We lost one the other day," he said to Valfric.

"That's too bad. What happened?" he asked.

"A horse saw a snake, spooked, and trampled them," the smith said with a huff. "Too bad too; they were skilled."

He walked over to a drawer, pulled out a leather and metal collar, and brought it over to Yrthorn. He hefted it in his hand, and the woman looked horrified. Valfric released the Essaeris collar, and Yrthorn wrapped the new one around her neck.

"There, look at you now! You're proper," he said and slapped her ass. She gasped slightly. The smith laughed.

Valfric turned to him. "Thank you. Drinks later?" he said to the smith.

"Of course, and you're paying, right? I mean with the raid and all..."

Valfric laughed. "Fine. I'm paying."

They began to walk off. "Do you have an idea of where you're going to keep her?" Valfric asked Yrthorn.

"Probably just on my property. Where else would I keep her?"

"The settlement has an area for some of them, but your property is good enough. Remember, that's not an Essaeris collar on her now, so you'll need to make sure she doesn't run off, especially if you want to keep her on your property," he said.

Yrthorn eyed her. "She wouldn't dare. She knows better. Don't you?"

Her head bobbed. "Y-yes, master. I know," she said, her voice tinted with fear.

Valfric made a mental note to talk to Yrthorn more when the woman wasn't around. She may have been broken, but she wasn't obedient yet. She was trying, and she was certainly scared of Yrthorn, Valfric, and all of their people. But that was when they were in the woods, on the trail, and after she had just watched all of her family be butchered. Over time, that could change, and if Yrthorn didn't know what he was doing and didn't instill the correct behaviors, it could go badly for him.

Valfric tried to push this from his mind as they walked. That was a problem for another day. He needed to know what was on Durnara's mind.

"I need to talk to Durnara. I'll talk with you later," he said to Yrthorn and patted his shoulder.

Yrthorn nodded happily and pulled the woman along. "It's time for you to see your new home, Nefeli. You might even come to enjoy it," he said to her as they walked.

He found Durnara alone in the central meeting house. She watched him enter, a look of concern on her face.

"Do you think Yrthorn is ready for the responsibility of a new slave?" she asked.

Valfric shook his head. "No, I don't, but it's done."

She nodded. "It's done." She sighed and sat in her chair, staring out at the center of the meeting hall for a moment, lost in thought. "You know, there was a time when I wanted this so badly."

"What? Controlling the settlement? You say that like you still don't want it."

She looked up at him, a tight smile on her lips. "I do still want it, but sometimes," she said, shaking her head. "Sometimes I think I'm a fool for wanting it."

He nodded. "We're all fools in some way. What has you concerned?" he asked, getting to the point.

"Not so much concerned," she said, "but curious and maybe a little worried about Wulfharboria raids coming from the north."

This got his attention. "Were we attacked while we were gone?"

She shook her head. "No, we were not, but there are rumors. Wulfharboria has been pushing deeper and deeper. So have groups from Valfarans," she said.

Valfric sighed. "That's not new. Our people are weak—not our settlement, but our people."

She nodded. "We have become weak. You're right. You and yours are an excellent example of what we should be and what we've lost. Still, we have to deal with these threats, or we might have to."

"Why have Wulfharboria groups been pushing in over the last few years?" he asked.

She shook her head. "Rumor has it that to the northeast, conditions haven't been as good. They've had farmland failing. It doesn't help with the plagues that have ravaged our people over the last generation. It's made us easy pickings, and we've become weak," she said harshly.

This he agreed with. Valfric's people were supposed to be warriors. They were supposed to be raiders and rulers, the terror of all around them. But that had changed in the last generation. He scoffed.

"The others forget what we once were. We were the ones that made Lysandrian children tremble in fear at the stories their parents told. We made the

Valfarans question their own safety—and the same with Wulfharboria. And now look at them?" he said.

She nodded. "Yes, the Valfarans have been coming and picking but the Wulfharboria has been the biggest problem. And you're right about Lysandrian; it is most certainly a concern. It's been ten years since they stopped trading with anyone in Ulfgarath," she said.

"Well, I guess it's a good thing we've stepped up the way we trade, then," Valfric said with a grin.

She smiled. "Yes, it is. These are far better deals you're getting by just killing and taking what we need," she said with a smile. "And it reminds them of why they shouldn't fuck with us."

That had been much of the reason Valfric and his team had been moving more and more into Lysandrian settlements. It had nothing to do with the spices they took, or the slaves they occasionally captured, or even some of the better goods. It was to remind the Lysandrians not to fuck with his people.

"Does that mean you want me to go raiding down there again?" he asked.

Durnara shook her head. "No, not right now. I don't think we need to worry about Lysandrian for the moment. But some of the Wulfharboria settlements could use a bit of a reminder."

He nodded. "Very well. What did you have in mind?"

"Many of the Wulfharboria had settlements that had mercenaries goto war down south. That war is over, and they should be coming back to their settlements laden with spoils," she said with a smile.

He grinned. "Well, that doesn't seem right. Wulfharboria doesn't need gold and jewels or anything else."

She nodded. "They don't. And the rest of our people need to see what's out there," she said sternly. "They need to see what happens when you are a strong people. When you are a settlement that commands respect." She said with flint in her voice.

He nodded, feeling energy build within him. Yes. He would raid and take and steal and kill. And stories would spread. And as they spread, so too would the memory of what his people had once been.

"Kill them all or leave them alive?" he asked.

She looked at him. "Most need to live. They need to know they were beaten. They need to tell their fellow settlement mates. They need to tell the rest of the Wulfharboria what's waiting for them. Why they should go back north or why they should just push south."

He nodded. "We'll leave in a few days."

"Good," she said.

"Is there anything else?" he asked.

She shook her head. "No, nothing else of note. I'm glad the boy did well," she said softly.

"I am too. He'll continue to grow, and he'll continue to get stronger."

"That he will," she said. "Bring his new toy on your raid. If he's going to be training her and breaking her in, he needs to be the one doing it."

Valfric nodded. This was how it should be. "Agreed. I'll make sure she comes with us. It shouldn't be a problem, and we can always use the help on the road," he said.

He left the meeting hall and went back to his home. He unsaddled the horse and put it in the paddock by the house, then opened his door, carrying in his bags. He breathed in the stale air of a cottage that hadn't been lived in for a few weeks. He looked over in the corner, seeing his bed, and smiled.

As he set his things down, he heard a door creak behind him and turned to see Ilara standing there.

"So, when are we leaving again?" she asked.

He turned back to what he was doing and smiled. "What makes you think we're leaving?"

She walked inside, stepping down onto the dirt floor. "Because Durnara talked to you alone."

"The Wulfharboria has been moving in on other parts of the territory," he said. "She thinks they need reminding of who we are."

Ilara sat in a creaky chair and set her feet up on his table. "Oh, I see. We're out teaching a lesson. And who are we teaching a lesson to?" she asked.

"They should have groups of warriors returning from the war down south," he said.

Ilara nodded. "I like it. They'll be full of spoils. I assume it's not just going to be our little band going, though."

He shook his head. "I don't think so. We're going to need more than the five of us. It'll be good for the other people in the settlement to remember who they are and what they are."

"Yes. Yes, it will be good for them," she said.

"And we're going to leave most of them alive," he commented.

"So that way they can go back and remind everybody what they're facing," she smiled. "Durnara always was a crafty one, wasn't she?"

"You say that like she's not around anymore," he said.

Ilara shrugged. "She is around for now, but she's getting older," she said.

He knew where this conversation was going. "But she's not dead yet," he said. "And I'm not taking power by killing my predecessor."

Ilara didn't give any reaction other than to say, "I know, and I think that's smart. I'm just saying you need to be crafty like she is."

"And why is that?" he asked.

"Because someday when you're in charge, you're going to need it," she said.

He sighed. "Yeah, the crafty ones do seem to do better, don't they?"

"So when do we move out?" Ilara asked.

"In a few days," he said. "I'll let the others know and give them a chance to sleep in their own beds for a couple of nights, and then we'll be off."

CHAPTER 6

The sun had long since set by the time Caelwen made it to the edge of the forest. The cool night air was thick with fog and mist, making the grass slick and the ground muddy. The only real benefit of the moisture was that it dampened sounds.

Caelwen sighed as she saw two figures standing at the edge of the woods. "Just the two of you?"

The two men started, both turning to look at her. One was the settlement's smith, Durgard. He was wearing a helmet and had a shield, a spear, and a sword at his belt. Next to him was Kernvald, one of the farmers in the settlement.

"When Ilfthandor told me that there were people in the settlement who'd had issues with the caravan, I thought there would be more than two," she said.

Durgard shifted a bit. "I didn't have any problems with them, but Ilfthandor told me that we were going to take out the caravan tonight." He shrugged. "He said it was important."

"I see," she chose not to comment on the 'important' part of his statement.

"I'm glad to see you, Caelwen," he said.

Kernvald shifted from foot to foot. He was average in every way possible. He wasn't a bad man or a good one. Caelwen didn't have negative views of either of the men with her.

Caelwen looked at Kernvald. "And were you taken by the caravan?"

He sighed. "I made some bad deals, maybe, but they took advantage."

Caelwen nodded. "So the three of us are supposed to kill, what, twelve or thirteen of them?"

"Well, that should be easy for you, shouldn't it?" Durgard said. "You're an Essaerist."

Of course, this had been her uncle's plan all along: to have Caelwen do it all.

To kill the caravan, to deal with anything that went wrong, and to have the blood on her hands. She sighed. "Cunt," she muttered under her breath. "I didn't have any problems with them, but here we are, and no, I won't be able to kill all of them. They have horses, and I know some of them are strong men."

"So what are we going to do?" Kernvald asked.

Caelwen shrugged. "Our best? We're going to have to be smart about it, though. And the two of you are going to have to pull your own weight. I'm not going to be able to do all this, nor am I willing to," she said sternly. They both nodded, seeming uncomfortable. *Good,* she thought to herself. They should be uncomfortable.

Kernvald shuffled a bit more, his eyes darting to the treeline. "Should we say a prayer to the gods?"

"Who? Ulfgara only blesses warriors and the brave. We aren't warriors, and we're attacking at night while they sleep, so we're not brave either."

"Thrain then?" he asked.

She snorted. "Did Thrain give you wisdom when you made a bad deal?" She shook her head. "Let's hope that Durnhelm would rather have the men in the caravan tonight and none of us. Otherwise, we're on our own."

She closed her eyes, reaching deep inside herself, feeling power welling up, bubbling toward the surface. She held it in and breathed out. It surged and flowed out of her, creating an Essaerite that roughly resembled a panther, but not exactly. The creature was large, around four hundred pounds or so, and had a similar body plan to a cat, with four legs, a jaw, a mouth, a tail, and fur. But it wasn't a cat. Its jaw was deeper and larger, giving it the ability to wrap halfway around a man's chest.

Its hide, while covered in black fur, was thick and leathery, making it difficult to stab or cut through. Its paws were similar to those of a cat's but with more dexterity and longer fingers. It couldn't work with tools or build something, but it could roughly grab onto things if need be. Likewise, the claws were unique. Each toe had two claws, both metal, stacked on top of each other. The first set of claws was long and razor-sharp, able to slice through anything—be it metal, wood, flesh, or bone. On top of those was another set of claws that were wider and almost dagger-like. When the Essaerite extended its claws, they looked to be one, but in reality, what happened was the first set of claws would dig into something and then retract, leaving the second set—not to slash through the prey or victim—but to grip onto it, so that the Essaerite could use its powerful muscles to rip it apart.

This creature didn't need to breathe, drink, or eat. It could make noise. That was something she found to be useful, but its teeth were longer than those of an average panther of this size and were metal, as was the entire interior of the mouth. There was nothing inside the mouth that could be cut or damaged.

As it came into existence, the men shifted. Caelwen felt down inside herself, sensing more Essaeris sitting beneath the surface. It rippled in her, and a second cat appeared.

The two men looked at the animals, and Caelwen smirked, always enjoying seeing people's reactions. The Essaerite's shoulders came up to her lower ribs, making them much larger than any cat that lived in the area. The eyes were special, able to see in the deepest dark and track movement. The noses were keen, and the ears were as well. She could make the eyes glow if she wanted to, though that wasn't something she planned on using tonight.

Next, she focused on herself. Presently, she was wearing a tunic and pants, along with a pair of boots. That wouldn't do. She closed her eyes, breathing in, feeling the Essaeris deep within her. This would require more. "Give me a minute," she said to the two men. They stood stock still, quiet, letting her do what she needed to.

She took a deep breath, feeling her power build. As she breathed out, she held the energy in place, and she took another breath, and then another, she felt Essaeris build up inside of her, trying to claw its way out. She focused her mind's eye on what she wanted to create. The power didn't come out in a rush as it had with the cats. Instead, it slowly trickled its way out of her, wrapping around her body. Not in the form of energy, but in the form of vines and branches. More of them began to come into existence, crisscrossing around her body, growing and snaking around her, covering her.

She heard creaks and groans as the vines turned into thick branches. She lifted her foot, and they zipped underneath, creating a type of boot that was more like a tree stump, its roots clinging to the ground. She lifted the other foot, and the next one formed. She opened her eyes, feeling herself moving up just a bit as the legs extended. She brought her arms to her chest, and the vines reached out off her shoulders, creating arms.

She looked down at her tree-like body, seeing thick arms. The tree suit began to create wrists and long fingers made of wood. Along the forearms, she created blades that were similar to axe heads. Unlike the rest of the suit, the blades were not made of wood but metal. Inside other parts of her forearm, there were other blades that could shoot out should they be needed. Along her back, two vines grew, thick as a man's arm. At the end of them were four digits, but just inside the vines were long metal spikes.

Before, the men had each been a foot or so taller than her. Now, she was about a foot and a half taller than both of them. She felt the Essaerite snake its way around her face and head, creating a helmet. This was the part she had enjoyed creating. She knew there was something to showmanship and striking fear into your opponents.

The helmet resembled the skull of a deer, with long antlers coming out of it. The sockets had deep, round, black eyes with no whites. These too she could make glow, but again rarely found the need. She could see through the eyes, and she closed her own, looking out through the Essaeris' ones. It took her a moment to orient herself, but all of a sudden, she was the Essaerite—not herself, not Caelwen, standing inside this monstrosity. She was the monstrosity.

Its arms and legs were thicker than any man's thighs. She was tall, intimidating, and menacing. In the suit, she was stronger than any human ever could be. She looked down at Durgard and Kernvald.

"Are you two ready?" she asked.

The men's heads bobbed and wobbled a bit. She smiled. *Good,* she thought to herself. There were some benefits to things like this. She almost never used this Essaerite, but she knew there were Essaerists out there with far more powerful and better ones than this. But it was still intimidating to a normal person—terrifying in so many ways. For her people, it was also a point of pride. After all, this monster was on their side, but it also made a point. It reminded the people of what Caelwen was and what she was capable of.

Part of her wished that her uncle had been there as well so that he could be reminded of what she was, but that was for another time. She reached out to an owl that she had in the area and found the caravan not far from them. "If we take the woods, we can be there in less than an hour," she said. The caravan had had to wind around on the road, which had taken them some time. With the rain and mud, it had slowed them. They'd finally stopped in a clearing.

As Caelwen watched through the owl, she felt a pit form in her gut. She only knew one of the men in the caravan, and he'd been a good one. He'd been kind and honest with her and didn't deserve what was coming. She tried to push it from her mind.

"They're spread out," she said.

"They are?" Durgard asked, surprised.

"Yes, they have no reason to be concerned." The owl swooped over the area. "It also looks like one of their carts got stuck in the mud. I suspect they wanted to avoid the same fate happening to the others," she commented.

"Okay, what do we need to do then?" Kernvald asked.

"You two are going to take the lone cart. I'll deal with the rest." She sighed. "Alright, let's do this," she said as she began to walk.

The Essaerite she was in was surprisingly quiet, the roots of her feet able to sneak around and barely touch the forest floor, keeping it from creating sound. She changed the bark to a deep bluish-green, making her large form vanish in the shadows. The two cat Essaerites were likewise quiet and dark, slinking their way through the forest. She could hear Durgard and Kernvald moving as quietly as they could, but there were limits. There was no moon out this evening, and even though some of the trees glowed faintly, one could never see all the roots on the forest floor, forcing them to pick their way with care.

For Caelwen, it was a different story. All around her, she could see perfectly. The eyes of the Essaerite were able to make out all of the scenery around her. It was a deep blue that was accented by the colors of the various glowing trees, flowers, plants, and bugs, along with the occasional animal that would move on the forest floor or in the trees above. It was beautiful in so many ways, and something she enjoyed. There was a serenity to it, and the forest was silent. She lost herself in it as they walked.

As they came to the edge of the trees, she could make out the caravan ahead of them. She felt that same pit in her gut as she had before. "Sorry," she said under her breath. She looked around, inspecting the caravan. The horses would be problematic, but she suspected her uncle Ilfthandor wanted some of them. "Cunt," she muttered under her breath.

The cart that had gotten stuck in the mud was a ways back from them. It looked like there were a couple of men around it—maybe three or four at the very most. She looked over at Durgard and Kernvald. "I'm going to attack the main carts first. Give me a minute before you move in on the other cart. With any luck, they'll focus on me, and you'll only have a couple of men to deal with."

Durgard and Kernvald nodded.

She slinked off away from them, as did her cats. They moved low, keeping behind trees and brush. For Caelwen, it was much easier to move because she looked like a tree. Whenever the men weren't looking in her direction, she would move quickly, not making a sound, circling around until she was getting closer to the unsuspecting people.

She slowed, coming almost to a stop at the edge of the trees. On either side of her, the cats did the same. They hunched down, their bellies touching the cold, wet ground. Caelwen looked at the caravan. Everyone was still awake, which was something she'd have preferred wasn't the case.

She could sense what the cats were thinking and planning. All her Essaerites could work together and through her. It had felt eerie the first time she'd felt it. The cats hunted much like their flesh-and-blood counterparts, but with the benefit of being one mind and not being worried about injury or death.

She'd have them attack first. It was cowardly in a way. The Essaerites didn't have feelings or emotions. They didn't care if they killed or maimed. Caelwen did. She didn't mind killing when it was necessary, but this wasn't necessary. This was Ilfthandor making bad-faith agreements and turning his niece and the settlement's people into robbers and murderers.

In so many ways, this was the way of the world: kill and take what you want, but Caelwen didn't care for it. It was a waste. She moved her focus to her cats. They'd moved from the cover of the trees and were slinking their way closer to the caravan. No one saw them. Nor would they until it was far too late.

She readied herself. As soon as the cats attacked, she'd need to spring into motion. The faster this all went down, the better for all involved. One of the cats was crouched, its powerful back legs ready to jump.

There was a yell from the cart stuck in the mud, followed by another.

"Shit, shit, shit," she hissed.

Kernvald and Durgard hadn't waited for her to attack first. On the carts before her, men stirred, grabbing weapons. There were more shouts. She sent a thought to the cats, telling them to attack. They did so, leaping at the nearest men to them.

One launched itself, crashing into the back of a large man. Its front paws gripped the man's arm and shoulder. He let out a scream of shock and pain that turned into a gurgle as the Essaerite's jaws clamped down at the base of his neck.

The animal's sharp claws retreated, leaving only the ones that gripped. They sunk deeper into bone and muscle. There was a popping, ripping sound as the Essaerite pulled with its jaw and paws. The man's gurgled scream was cut off as his neck began to separate from his shoulder.

Blood poured from the man like a bucket being kicked over. Bone and fat were exposed as the Essaerite continued pulling, ribs separating from the man's spine, and the shoulder blade shining in the dim light. The cat finished separating the shoulder and arm before dropping the corpse to move on to the next. Brutal as it had been, it was over almost as soon as it had started.

There was another cry as the other Essaerite worked on another man. Other men were running for horses and scattering. The attack had started far too soon. She stood and made the Essaerite she was in roar. It was a blend of several animals, giving it an unnatural sound that was both high and keening and low and rumbling at the same time. Despite it coming from her, Caelwen felt a zing up her spine at the sound, and her hairs stood on end.

Men turned to the sound, and she made the eyes blaze a vivid green. Little rivulets of green light pulsed up her helmet and antlers. They ran down her arms and body, making the whole Essaerite pulse with lines of light and color.

The lights and roar did what they were meant to. The men stared in shock and terror as she ran at them. In the moments of pause, her cats did their deadly work, dispatching more of the people in blood and brutality. Caelwen was there now, her mind cleared of her second thoughts and hesitations.

One of the vines on her back lashed out with the dagger end, spearing a man in the chest. She swiped at another who had the sense to grab a shield. As her arm moved, the roots on her feet dug into the ground, holding her in place as her long arm made contact with the shield. It splintered as the blade on her forearm hit, and then it made contact with the man, cutting through cloth and bone. Air left him in a whoosh as he was knocked ten feet from her. He hit the ground and rolled lifeless.

She spun as a man came at her with a sword raised high. His face was full of fear, but she gave him credit for bravery. A long blade came out of her wrist from her left arm, and she stabbed him before he could get close enough to swing at her, for all the good it would have done him.

Caelwen was in no danger tonight. Her Essaerite was thick and strong, and she very much doubted anyone would be able to pierce it. She looked around as the sounds of battle faded. Torn bodies littered the ground around Caelwen and her cats.

"Caelwen!" She heard a voice yell.

It was Kernvald's. She moved away from her killing ground, crossing the distance to the other cart quickly. She could hear Kernvald's frantic voice yelling out.

"What is it?" she asked when she got there.

As soon as she arrived, she saw what it was. Laying on the ground, groaning and holding his gut, was Durgard. She could see red soaking his tunic.

She released her helmet, and the body of the Essaerite opened up. She stepped out of the being, and her foot hit the muddy ground, making a squelching noise as she approached Durgard. She knelt down.

Durgard writhed in pain, groaning and clenching his gut. She tried to move his hands.

"Durgard, let me look. Let me look!" She felt a frantic worry creeping up her spine, filling her.

She pulled away his hands and saw blood. She moved the tunic, seeing a deep slice along the side of his abdomen. She pressed hard on it.

"Keep pressure on it," she said to Kernvald. "It doesn't look like he had anything vital hit; otherwise, he'd be dead," she said. But she wasn't sure. There was no telling what the blade had actually cut.

She looked around, seeing corpses on the ground.

"We're missing someone," she said.

"One of them got away," Kernvald said.

And she knew who it was. She'd seen the faces of every man she or her Essaerites had killed. Faelric wasn't among the dead. Part of her felt relief, but mostly she felt concerned.

Kernvald was covered in blood, but it wasn't his own, from what she could gather. He had a broken nose and a split lip.

"Shit," she muttered under her breath. "On foot, or horseback?"

"Horseback. You can run it down though, can't you?" he asked.

"No," she said. "Shit. Shit. Shit!"

She connected to her owl and had it swoop around looking. It didn't take long to find the figure of a horse running down the road away from the settlement.

"Shit," she said again.

As the owl approached, she recognized the man sitting on the saddle, confirming her earlier assumption that it was Faelric.

"What do you mean you can't catch it?" Kernvald said. "Those cats are..."

She cut him off. "Those cats are large and meant to rip things apart, not to run them down," she said. "There were what, three that you two had to deal with?" she spat. "This is so stupid," she said under her breath. "There's nothing we can do about that now. We need to get Durgard back to the settlement," she said as she stood up.

Kernvald looked around at the carts of the caravan. "What about all the..."

She reached out, her fist connecting with Kernvald's cheek, sending him sprawling.

"What about, what? Your spoils?" she growled. "They'll be here. There's nothing here to take them, and I will keep one of my Essaerites around to keep your precious spoils safe," she said venomously. "Gather the horses before they run off. I need to get Durgard back to town."

She got back in her suit and held out her arms, creating a plank.

"Get him on here," she said to Kernvald.

Kernvald got himself under the other man and groaned as he hoisted him up and placed him on the plank.

She began to move to the edge of the forest.

"You're not going to take the road," he asked.

"No, it'll take too long. It'll be faster this way," she said, trying to control her panic.

She began to move as quickly as the Essaerite could. She crashed through the underbrush, doing her best to keep Durgard from being hit by any branches. Without having to move at the speed she had before to keep quiet, she was able to cover the ground to the settlement fairly quickly.

When she broke the treeline, she made a straight path for her home. She needed to get there, needed to see if she could keep Durgard alive. He was mumbling, and his face was turning a deadly pale.

She jogged quickly across the settlement, making it to her home. With a flick of Essaeris, a few vines came into existence, and she set the plank that had Durgard on it atop them. They scuttled inside her door, and she stepped out of her Essaerite, moving in behind them. They hoisted Durgard onto the table. He didn't seem to be moving anymore.

"Shit, shit, shit!" she said.

She held her ear next to his mouth, hearing him breathe softly.

"Good," she said.

She pulled up his tunic, ripping it, and saw where the cut was. She focused on her Essaeris. She didn't have a lot left, but she had enough. She created a bandage that she wrapped around him and pressed into place, trying to stop the bleeding. Then she rummaged through her cupboards, looking for what she needed.

She found the catgut she was looking for and went back over to Durgard. She removed the bandage, seeing it already soaked with blood. She created a bottle of acid that she poured over the wound. It was a mild acid, that helped to keep wounds from going bad. He moaned but didn't move much. She worked quickly, stitching the cut, hoping it wasn't too late.

As she finished up, her Uncle Ilfthandor came spilling into the room.

"What happened?" he asked.

She looked up from Durgard, glaring at him. Caelwen felt anger seethe inside her.

"There were three of us for twelve of them, you idiot. What do you think happened?" she snarled.

"Girl, don't you..." he began.

"Not now, Ilfthandor," she said in a deadly cold voice.

He looked at her like he wanted to say something but then noticed who was on the table.

"Is that Durgard?" he said.

"Yes. It's Durgard," she said.

"Is he going to make it?" Ilfthandor asked.

She looked up at her uncle. "I'm not sure. I don't think anything important was cut, but that doesn't mean it won't go bad or that he won't be bleeding on the inside," she said.

She could see it in his eyes. She could see the mistake that he knew he had made now. If they'd lost Kernvald, that would be sad. Losing anybody in the settlement would be. But Kernvald was just a farmer. Durgard? Durgard was the only smith they had. Losing him would be a loss.

"Do what you can," Ilfthandor said.

"What do you think I'm doing?" she snapped. "Get out of here!"

He hesitated as he turned to her. "Caelwen?"

She looked up at him. "Don't worry. You didn't lose anything," she said. "Now get out!"

CHAPTER 7

Caelwen stared at the two jugs of Duskwood oil sitting atop her table. They stood like beacons, accusing her and judging her for her failures. She glared at them, *fuck you jugs,* she thought.

In the days following the raid on the caravan, she'd gotten over her guilt for attacking them. After all, it was the way of the world, and even though she didn't like it, the one person she liked in the caravan had gotten away. Of course, that was also part of the problem and one of the accusations being thrown at her by the jugs.

Faelric had gotten away. Caelwen wouldn't have been able to pursue him had she wanted to, and in the days following the raid, no one had seen him. That wasn't surprising; he'd been on horseback and was heading away from the settlement. She didn't know where he hailed from, but she doubted it was one of the nearby settlements. By now, he'd be clear of the area, and she'd be hard-pressed to find him.

The question now remained: was Faelric being alive going to be a problem for the settlement, or not? She wasn't sure. Caravans being raided and robbed were common enough. That's why there'd been so many men with the group—to help dissuade people from doing what Caelwen's people had done.

Treftune jumped from one of the high rafters of the ceiling and glided down, landing on her shoulder. She looked over at him.

"What do you think, Treftune? What do you think's going to happen?" she asked.

He glanced between her and the jugs, his eyes keen and intelligent, in a way that she always found astounding for an animal. He chirped and rubbed his face against hers. She smiled and scratched behind his ears.

"Yeah, I don't know either," she said.

Her mind reached out to some of the birds of prey she had circling the area. The chances of reprisal were low, especially because it was difficult to sneak up on their settlement, but also because Caelwen was pretty sure that Faelric's caravan hadn't been part of a larger one. Or at least he hadn't said anything about it.

There was something enjoyable about being in the birds as they flew. She hadn't made them in a way that they could feel anything, per se. They could tell if they were falling or if they were struggling to fly, but otherwise, they weren't the same as real animals. Still, there was something to the sight of being above the trees and land, seeing the rivers wind through the area, and the occasional animal out in a field. It relaxed her.

"Alright, Treftune, let's get going for the day," she said to the little creature.

She went outside and checked on some barrels that were full of Holtkerns. The lids were still in place, indicating that nothing had tried to get into them—not that she suspected that there would be. Every one of the nuts inside the barrels was encased in glass-like Essaeris that would make them impossible to smell. But diligence demanded that she take a look and make sure.

She'd ended up selling the hog, so the pen was empty, which was kind of nice. She always hated the smell of the animals and hearing them squeal and rummage around. She would need to catch something soon if she wanted to have any meat for the winter. Well, if she wanted to have any meat for the winter that she didn't have to pay for.

Caelwen felt restless energy building inside her. She needed a distraction to take her mind off the potential problems Faelric might or might not cause. She glanced over at a pile of logs that needed to be split. *That'll do,* she thought.

She walked up to the pile and grabbed a few pieces. She set them on the ground next to a log and reached inside herself to her Essaeris, letting it well up and flow out of her in the form of an axe. She set one of the logs on the stump and gripped the axe tightly. She lifted it above her head and brought it down. There was a satisfying thunk and crack as the log split in two.

She could have an Essaerite do this, but there was something about the work that she enjoyed, and she didn't have much else to do, so splitting wood was a good outlet for her nerves. She felt her skin warm as she brought the axe down again and again. With each swing, her mind cleared a little bit more. As her mind cleared, she reached down and felt her Essaeris swirling inside of her. She grabbed another log, put it on the stump, and swung down again, splitting it. The action kept her body in motion and occupied, letting her mind sink down into her Essaeris—to play with it, to massage it, and feel it play back with her.

Caelwen had loved it when she had first come into her power. She felt insane that first time, of course, feeling Essaeris, but that feeling of insanity had gone away, and she had seen what a true joy it was. Now the energy was a constant comfort for her, something that she looked forward to and that was as much a companion for her as Treftune was.

Her serenity was broken as she heard someone call her name. She shifted her gaze away from the logs and scanned the road that ran in front of her house. In the distance, she saw someone jogging in her direction. It was a young woman in her early teens. She wore a tunic of pale blue that hugged her thin features. Her hair was a long, wavy red, and she was breathing hard as she jogged up to the house.

Caelwen knew her. "Ulfiel," she said, walking to the road. "Is everything okay?"

Ulfiel made it to her and stopped. "It's my father," she panted.

"What's wrong with Durgard?" Caelwen asked.

She hadn't been sure if Durgard was going to make it the night of the raid. He'd lost so much blood and had gotten pale as a corpse, but by morning he was moving around and seemed to be doing better. The next day he was even better still.

Ulfiel's face was etched with concern and worry. "He hasn't been feeling good. He stumbled today, and he's been having a hard time getting up. I think there's something really wrong with him."

This had been a risk. Caelwen wasn't sure what had gotten into the wound when he'd been stabbed, and there hadn't been much that she could do to help him. All she could do was hope that everything went well. "Take me to him."

They made their way as quickly as they could to Durgard's house. The forge where he worked stood a little ways away from the house. It was one of the few stone buildings in the settlement.

Ulfiel led Caelwen up to the house and inside. It was similar to Caelwen's, though a little larger. She was met with the smell of a fire in the fireplace, and she saw Rothia, Ulfiel's mother, standing over a bed. Rothia resembled her daughter, though an older, more defined version. Caelwen was sure that at some point in time, Ulfiel would be no different. In the bed lay Durgard.

Rothia's expression was concerned.

"What happened?" Caelwen asked as she walked into the room, approaching Durgard.

"He said he was going to go out into the forge," Rothia started. She shook her head. "I told him he shouldn't yet. He didn't make it far when he fell over and grabbed his side."

Caelwen studied Durgard, who was in bed, his face scrunched up in pain. She saw a sheen of sweat on his forehead. "Durgard, did something tear?" she asked him.

He shook his head. "No, I don't think so," he said through gritted teeth.

She pulled up his tunic, not caring if she was exposing the man to his family or not. She heard a small gasp from Ulfiel, but Rothia didn't react. Caelwen peered down at the wound she had stitched shut the other night.

"Shit," she muttered under her breath.

Shit was right. The wound was red and swollen, and she could see some pus leaking out along the stitches. She reached down and felt around it; the skin was hot to the touch. He winced a little. "What is it?" he asked.

"There must have been something that got in the cut when you were stabbed," Caelwen said, concerned.

She'd cleaned the outside of the wound and had poured acid on it, but she didn't have a way to clean inside it. Either there was something that had been on the blade that went through his abdomen, or something had been nicked inside of his body. She thought the former more likely. She felt around his swollen side, feeling the heat, and then she felt his forehead. He was burning up.

"What are we going to do?" Rothia asked.

Caelwen thought for a moment. "What we can." She needed supplies. She thought about having her stump Essaerite bring them, but it was slow. She turned to Ulfiel and said, "Go back to my cottage. I want you to fetch some things for me. I have an Essaerite that looks like a stump; it will be waiting for you with what I need."

Ulfiel's head bobbed. "Yes, ma'am," she said and ran for the door.

Once Ulfiel was back with the supplies, Caelwen got to work creating a poultice that she wrapped around Durgard's belly, covering his wound with herbs she had ground up. He sighed softly at the coolness. She began working on making some tea and tinctures to give him. As she worked, Ulfiel and Rothia stood by him, wringing their hands.

I can only wonder what this is like for them, she thought to herself. But then she realized she did know exactly what it was like for them. She'd been in the same position when her mother was dying. Caelwen felt a pang for the two women and focused on preparing a tea with medicines in it that she thought might give him the best chance at survival. *Guide me, Caelith,* she thought to the goddess. But she wasn't sure Caelith would aid her. After all, Durgard was hurt when he tried to kill people, and while Ulfgara might appreciate that, Caelwen suspected the goddess of nature, growth, and life wouldn't.

"Here, drink this," she said.

She held the back of Durgard's head and brought the cup to his lips. He took a sip and coughed, "Gods, Caelwen, that is disgusting!" He coughed again, "Are you trying to poison me?"

She snorted, "Baby. And I'm not poisoning you, but whatever is making you sick. Now drink."

He drank more of the tea, and then she made him force down a few tinctures that made him cough and gag a bit, which, in her experience, meant that they were probably exactly what he needed. He seemed to calm down and then fell asleep, his chest rising and falling slowly.

There was a knock at the door, and Caelwen turned to see her uncle standing in the doorway, a concerned look on his face. She noted that it wasn't the normal look of concern that he wore—the fake one. This was real. He was concerned about Durgard. Ulfiel stayed next to her father and Rothia as Caelwen joined Ilfthandor outside.

He held her gaze. "So, tell me?"

Caelwen shot a glance over at Rothia and then back to her uncle. She shook her head. "It's not good," she admitted. "The wound is festering, and I think there's something inside," she said.

"Will the poultice you put on help?" Rothia asked.

Caelwen shrugged a little uncertain. "I think so, but I don't know for sure. If there was something inside the wound, it's going to be up to his body. All I can do is try to give him an edge," she admitted.

Rothia wrung her hands, and her eyes filled with tears. Ilfthandor went to pat the woman's shoulder, and she shied away a little. Caelwen touched Rothia's arm.

"Give me a moment with my uncle," she said.

Rothia nodded and went back into the house. Caelwen met Ilfthandor's gaze.

"We cannot lose Durgard. Some people in the settlement are more important than others," he said in a hushed tone.

She hated words like that, but they weren't untrue. The reality was that many people in the settlement could be replaced. The smith, not so much—especially not when they had enemies, enemies they had thanks to her uncle.

"I'm well aware," she said softly, "but there's not much that I'm going to be able to do."

His gaze was thoughtful. "Is there anything that we need that could help?"

"Maybe, but I wouldn't know what it is. And if we're being honest, I'm one of the best healers in the area," she said.

She didn't mean this to sound boastful. It was just a fact. Her grandmother had been a healer and was one of the best in the area. She had trained Caelwen's mother, who had trained her. Caelwen had continued to learn afterward. Being an Essaerist had given her the time and abilities to hone her craft, but she had limits.

Oddly, Caelwen's limits and abilities as a healer were something her uncle never seemed to question. He might criticize how she had fought or question a deal she had made, but he knew nothing of healing. He only knew its importance, and she could see stress in his eyes.

"I shouldn't have asked you to raid that caravan," he admitted.

"No, you shouldn't have," she said, though her voice didn't hold the harsh coldness that it usually did when she was agitated with him. It would do no good in this situation. What was done was done.

"I'm surprised you're not more angry with me," he said.

She shrugged. "I was."

"And now?" he asked.

She shrugged again. "What's done is done, and it's the way of the world. Just because I didn't like it and I thought it was shitty doesn't mean that it doesn't happen all the time. If we'd had a few more people, maybe it'd have been different, or if they had waited to attack until I'd started mine, but who knows?"

"There are so many things that could have gone differently. Or maybe, with all those in place—if we had more people, or if they had waited for the right time—maybe instead of being in bed hurt right now, Durgard would already be dead. We just don't know what the gods have planned for us," she said.

He gave a small, tight smile. "You're a lot like your mother. She was wise, too," he said, then sighed. "Let me know if anything changes."

Caelwen nodded. "I will, but there's not going to be much more that changes tonight. I'll go home in a few hours and check on him tomorrow or the next day. But now, it's up to Durgard."

———

VALFRIC'S HORSE SLOWLY MOVED BENEATH HIM. THEY WERE ALMOST OUT OF THE settlement now, and he took one last look around, making sure they didn't have any stragglers. With him was his normal team, but in addition, there were another twenty men. Some of them had brought their wives, daughters, or sons to learn and help. There was also a handful of slaves with them, along with pack horses. It was a bigger group than Valfric liked being a part of when it came to raiding, but he understood they needed a lot of people because they didn't know the size of the caravans they'd be hitting. They also wanted to ensure that they won each of those fights and needed people to carry away the goods.

Next to him, Aelric rode, looking ahead. "Are you looking forward to going raiding?" Valfric asked his friend.

Aelric glanced back at the group of people and sighed, "I suppose there's a joy to it," he said halfheartedly.

Valfric chuckled. "But the large group?" he said knowingly.

Aelric nodded. "More people to watch after. The boy and you are more than enough already."

Valfric laughed. "Good to know. I'm glad to know you feel like you have to watch over me," he said and reached out to slap his friend's shoulder.

Aelric gave him a grunt and a quick nod. "Of course I do. You would die every time if not. I just let you think that you're a good warrior."

Valfric shook his head. He looked back again, seeing Yrthorn riding a few horses behind them. Behind him on his saddle was his slave, Nefeli. She appeared to be settling in all right. She still cast her gaze around at everyone with fear, which was something that was good for a slave—especially a new one—but she wasn't as broken as she had been before. Yrthorn appeared content as he rode.

He chose not to make a comment to Aelric. They both were of the same mind, and there was no use speaking about it. As they entered the forest, Valfric sent out a couple of Essaerites to scout ahead of them, looking for any potential danger. Most of these were in the form of wolves that stayed out ahead of the horses. All of the horses in the settlement knew not to be afraid of Valfric's wolves. They appeared slightly different from their flesh-and-blood counterparts, and they didn't have a scent. Having the horses accustomed to the wolves was useful, as he didn't like the idea of keeping the wolves away from their group.

He relaxed in his saddle and rotated his perception around from one wolf to another, making sure that everyone was making it through the forest okay and were not spreading themselves out. He noticed Aelric looking at him.

"What?" Valfric asked.

"Are you using your Essaerites to mother-hen everybody in the group?" Aelric asked.

"And if I am?" Valfric asked.

Aelric shrugged. "It's just too bad you weren't born a woman. You would have made such a wonderful mother."

From behind them, they heard a snort, and Valfric turned around to see Ilara chortling.

"What? It's true," she said. "You have such wonderful maternal instincts. Really, I feel like less of a woman being around you," she said in mock seriousness.

"Fuck all of you," Valfric said.

He heard Aelric and Ilara both chuckle.

"Don't be like that, sweetheart," Aelric said.

"Yes, Valfric," Ilara crooned. "Don't be like that. You're so sweet, so kind," she said.

Aelric turned back at her. "Does he have a nice tight twat, too?" he asked her.

She guffawed and then composed herself. "The tightest," she said seriously.

Valfric shook his head and chuckled. "Again. Fuck you all," he said and spurred the horse a little faster.

CHAPTER 8

Mariokos stepped onto the top of a small hill and looked down on the training field. He saw various groups of men working and training. At its core, the legions could be broken into four main groups when it came to battle. First, there were the skirmishers. These men, or in Mariokos's experience, boys, were new. The skirmishers had never been members of the Legion before. These individuals had no training and oftentimes came from families with no means. This was where most men started when they joined. Legionnaires were required to buy and maintain their own armor, weapons, and equipment. They could purchase gear from the state or merchants, so long as it fell within the specifications the legions set forth for the type of unit they were in.

For those in the skirmish lines, they didn't have any of that property, which meant they had the most basic equipment available. Skirmishers were paid less than the other Legionnaires, and they tended to pull more undesirable duties. But if they did well in this group, then they moved up to the first line.

The first line was what most people in the Empire associated with the Legions. These men had far more training and experience, though they were still relatively new and young. The first line had better pay, better equipment, and far more discipline to go along with it. Then, you had the second line. This was comprised of men who had been in even longer and had more experience. If you were from an Aristolios family, this was where you might start your journey if you joined the Legion. Then, you had the third line. The third line was composed of veterans who had been fighting for many years or for those who were exceptionally skilled or if you were an Essaerist like Mariokos.

Not that he wasn't skilled enough to make it into the third line on his own, but the reality was that skilled though he may have been, he would probably have been in the second line if he had joined without having been an Essaerist first. Not that Mariokos would have joined if he hadn't been an Essaerist. He very much doubted he would have found himself in the Legions, but he understood why many did it. It was the easiest way to move up in society.

One could be the lowest member of society, and at minimum, if they served their time in a Legion, they'd become a Citizano. If you did well in the Legions and were renowned, you could even make your way up to Aristolios. The pay increased with each rank in the Legion you moved to, along with the type of work you did. This was also in part because the longer you were in the Legion, the more skilled you became.

When Mariokos had joked about being half builder and half warrior, it hadn't been a falsehood. The more advanced ranks of the second and third lines were almost like artisans when it came to their craft and were faster and better builders than those in the lower ranks. As a result, they tended to be assigned more desirable tasks.

In this, the legions built the empire and moved it forward. Not only did they protect the empire from danger, but all the roads, aqueducts, and many of the major buildings were constructed by the legions. When they weren't fighting or doing construction, they trained. Boredom was not something that legionnaires knew much about.

Mariokos looked at the field, searching for the man he was supposed to be working with that day. His name was Theoliano, and he was a major. Mariokos liked Theoliano. He had been in the Legion for years and was a no-nonsense kind of man when it came to combat; he knew exactly what war was and what it was about. He made no apologies for what they did and how they worked, but he was fair, and he did a good job of running any groups he oversaw.

Mariokos walked up to Theoliano, seeing him inspecting a group of troops in front of him. He had short, bristly brown hair and a scar running down the side of his face from his temple to his firm jawline. Like most men in the legion, his build was lean and muscular, and he held himself with confidence.

"Good afternoon, sir," Mariokos said.

Theoliano looked over at him and nodded. "Good afternoon, Mariokos." He looked back out at the groups of men.

"What is the plan for the day?" Mariokos asked.

It wasn't uncommon for an Essaerist to help train other legionnaires. Essaerists could provide something that you just couldn't have with real troops, meaning you had something that men could actually kill and hurt. It gave them the chance to get a feel for it before actual combat.

Theoliano pointed at a small group of men. Mariokos shifted his attention to them. They looked young, but they were members of the first line. He could see that most of their equipment was new, if not on the cheaper side, and they didn't quite hold themselves with the discipline and experience that you'd expect of other members of the first.

"New?" Mariokos asked.

Theoliano nodded. "Yes, they're just learning the basics of formations and how to work as a unit." He said, "I want you to create normal men today that are going to come at them as if they were a horde of barbarians to test their lines."

"Anything in particular other than that? Is there something you want me to push?" he asked.

Theoliano looked thoughtful for a moment. "I just want to see how they're doing right now, but I suspect we're going to need to work on them keeping together as a solid unit. Most of these guys have been on the skirmish line for a couple of years. They're used to just running around and doing whatever they need to on the battlefield."

This was one of the harder transitions for those coming from the skirmish line. The skirmishers at the beginning of a battle would run in front of the Legion and throw javelins and darts at the enemy and otherwise try to keep the enemy from forming a solid line. Then, they'd run behind the main lines and continue to throw javelins and darts, along with shooting arrows at the enemy. Should someone be hurt, those in the skirmish line would pull them away from the line of battle and take them to a healer if they could.

If things were going poorly and a squad or line needed cover as they were pulling out, the skirmish lines would come in and try to do what they could. If there were any breaks in the line, the skirmish line was there to hold it until other legions could come in. It was a dangerous job. The men typically had round shields and short swords, in addition to the javelins and spears issued by the Legion. It had a high mortality rate, but if you were someone who was a brawler or who enjoyed fighting on their own, it could work for you. It also gave you the opportunity to move up, and it came with food and a place to stay.

Mariokos was thankful he never had to experience it; it was a meat grinder. His Essaerites would join in the group of skirmishers, oftentimes throwing javelins with more precision than the skirmishers ever could, but he himself had never had to be part of the line. When men moved into the first rank from the skirmish lines, they tended to struggle, moving from a spot where they ran around and essentially did whatever they wanted when fighting the enemy to having to work as a cohesive unit. If they could master it, they could survive and do well.

Mariokos reached inside himself, feeling his power grow. He pulled on it and began creating Essaerites that resembled men. They didn't look exactly like people; their skin was gray, almost like stone, and their eyes were plain. They had no hair or clothes, nor any definition to their bodies other than smooth forms. He could create ones that were almost passable for humans, or at least passable for a legionnaire on the battlefield, but that took too much Essaeris for training purposes.

The other thing that the Essaerites had was that they carried all of Mariokos's combat training, experience, and expertise. This made them highly skilled on the battlefield and during training. Part of why Mariokos was a good fighter was that every male Essaerist served in the legions; once they came into their power, they were trained in combat. He had years of experience over other

Legionnaires his age, but the training had also focused on having him master every aspect of battle so he could create Essaerites for any role.

Theoliano looked at the Essaerites. "These will work," he said.

"Do you want me to hamstring them?" Mariokos asked.

Theoliano pinched his chin for a moment, thinking. "I don't think any of these men have ever fought an Essaerist before," he commented. "Keep them at their full abilities," he said. "At some point, there's a chance that these men will end up having to fight Essaerites that look just like enemy soldiers. They need to know what they're going against. They need to know to fear something that looks different."

"Alright, kick their asses, I understand," he said with a smirk.

Theoliano grinned quickly. "It's the best way to learn, isn't it?" he said and slapped Mariokos's shoulder.

Theoliano barked an order, and the group of soldiers formed into a shield wall. Theoliano explained that they were to hold their ground and hold the wall. This wasn't a test to see who the greatest of them was or if they could take out Mariokos's Essaerites.

The men had real weapons and equipment, though for this first exercise, their weapons were off to the side. Mariokos' Essaerites swords, battle axes, and spears looked real but weren't. The men in the squad could get roughed up today, and Mariokos fully planned on roughing them up. But none of them would break any bones or get stabbed or cut. The men would feel what it was like to have their weapons sink into flesh and bone, but they wouldn't risk their lives today.

While Theoliano talked to the men, Mariokos made a few tweaks to the Essaerites, giving them variations in appearance. Some were tall or short. Others were thin.

At a word from Theoliano, Mariokos turned his attention back to the shield wall. The men looked ahead, their eyes fixed on the Essaerites. He noticed a few of them looking worried and concerned. *Good,* he thought, *be wary of Essaeris.* His barbarians began to move forward, slowly approaching the shield line.

Mariokos knew that the men would do fine at the beginning. They'd all hold the line because they were clear-headed, and none of them had been laid out flat by one of his barbarians. Holding a line wasn't hard when your head was in the fight. Mariokos would need to try and get their heads out of it.

His group of barbarians raised their weapons and ran forward in a blur of speed. They made contact with the line. Swords and axes hit shields as others tried to stab through gaps in the wall. The men held their ground and kept the wall. Some of his barbarians slammed themselves into the shields, and he saw one man's foot slip. Another barbarian took advantage of the slight gap in the wall to thrust his spear into the opening. Another soldier dodged away from it, catching an axe blow to his shield. The barbarians disengaged, and the men reformed the line.

Mariokos watched the men's expressions shift now. The initial nerves were gone, and they had some confidence. Mariokos's barbarians came forward again and again and slammed into the shield wall. The men pushed back and tried to knock the Essaerites over. Mariokos could see the men's confidence grow.

He smirked; it was time to push them. He focused on the man who had slipped, seeing his expression turn to anger. An Essaerite moved forward as if it were going to hit him with a sword and then ducked down, swinging its blade under the shield. The man's feet moved quickly as he tried to avoid the strike. The Essaerite launched itself up, slamming into the man's shield, knocking him back and making him fall.

To their credit, the other men quickly formed up, re-establishing the wall, but the man who'd been knocked down was up and yelling in rage. He'd dropped his shield and was reaching out toward the Essaerite, his face red.

"Halt!" Theoliano yelled.

Mariokos's barbarians stopped moving, and the men looked at Theoliano.

"You are not here to fight! You are here to learn how to hold a line. That's why none of you have swords or spears yet," Theoliano said in a commanding tone. "Later today, you will have weapons, and you will have your chance at cutting one of these things. But not yet. Right now, you need to learn. Keep your heads on, or you will die."

Mariokos stood back and listened as Theoliano lectured the group of men. He'd been there once himself. Everyone had at some point. As Theoliano spoke, Mariokos turned his attention to sensing and feeling his Essaeris. He stoked it a bit, trying to help it build. Right now, the soldiers were the ones pushing themselves, but that would change throughout the day as Mariokos had to repair Essaerites. The soldiers wouldn't be the only ones tired at the end of the day, and Mariokos wanted to ensure his reserves were at top level before the day became taxing.

"Alright, again," Theoliano called.

———

Mariokos groaned softly as he stepped into the hot water in the bathhouse. He took another step in, the water coming up to his knees, and then another step, up to his waist, and another step. With a few more, the warm water came up just below his nipples, and he sighed in contentment.

High above him, light filtered in from slitted windows, lighting clouds of steam and making the water shimmer. The room was cavernous, with stone pillars surrounding the large bath, which could hold dozens of people, along with servers and a handful of musicians who played quietly in the corner. The air was thick with moisture that filled his lungs with each breath.

Next to him, Xavieno also groaned as he entered the water. Mariokos loved the bathhouses. Honestly, what wasn't there to like? The water was warm and felt amazing. There was usually good company and conversation to be had, along with wine and food along the edges. He breathed in deeply, inhaling the scent of incense and herbs, feeling it relax him more.

"Long day?" Xavieno asked.

Mariokos smiled. "It wasn't too bad. Just training with Theoliano," he said as they ambled deeper into the bath.

They nodded at other men who were standing, having conversations with one another.

"How about you?" Mariokos said.

Xavieno shrugged. "It was fine. Nothing all that exciting. Just some training with the rest of the Legion. Basic formation work."

They trained with the rest of the third line often. Even though it wasn't common for an Essaerist to actually be in the lines themselves during combat, it was good for them to know how to do it, and there were times when it was necessary, especially if they were using Essaerites that resembled legionnaires. For Xavieno, he tended to do it a lot more, as he liked to be in the action if there was a fight.

Though they hadn't seen many of those during their time in the Legion. It wasn't that the Empire didn't have legions that were out actively engaged in combat; just not theirs. He suspected at some point, that would change.

They walked to a nice open part of the bath and leaned against the wall. Mariokos felt the warm stone under his arm as he leaned against it.

"So, are you seeing Biankara tonight?" Xavieno asked conversationally.

Mariokos thought for a moment. "Yeah, I'm going to go over later and see her. Her father's in town, so we're going to have dinner."

Xavieno chuckled. "Have fun with that."

Mariokos laughed. "Oh, I'm sure I will. How about you? Have anything exciting going on this evening?"

Xavieno winked at him. "Wouldn't you like to know? The goings-on of a married couple are none of your concern," he said with a smirk.

Mariokos rolled his eyes. "So nothing, I take it?"

Xavieno stretched his arms over his head luxuriously. "Yep, nothing at all. I'm telling you, you gotta get married," he said, "it's great."

―――――

CAELWEN WAS EXHAUSTED. SHE YAWNED AND FOUGHT TO KEEP HER EYES OPEN. SHE wasn't sure how many hours of sleep she'd gotten over the last few days, but it hadn't been many.

Shortly after Durgard had fallen ill from his injury, a pair of Wolxaran had moved into the area. The creatures were rare and one of the few predators that could use Essaeris. Like her Valfglidea Treftune, the Wolxaran could create other versions of themselves. They were slightly smaller than wolves and resembled foxes with long bushy tails. They could change the color of their fur and could alter their teeth as well. They had exceptional senses and, like a Valfglidea, lived for multiple human lifespans. They were incredibly intelligent creatures and were associated with the gods. On occasion, they would bond with a human, but it was rare for this to happen. Normally, they bonded with one another, creating a mating pair.

Caelwen had dealt with them over the years, but only sparingly, and she had never dealt with a pair before. It was extremely rare for a pair to go after a settlement or to go anywhere where humans were in general. They tended to be very skittish creatures that avoided people. That was fine with her.

The ones she had encountered in the past had all been juveniles looking for easy pickings with the settlement's livestock. It hadn't been difficult to get them to go away. Caelwen's pumas did a fantastic job. But the ones she was facing now were far from juveniles. The juveniles could create two or three versions of themselves, and with Caelwen's pumas, it was relatively easy to keep them at bay. But with the adults, they could create closer to five or six versions of themselves. And with two of them, it was overwhelming her abilities.

Between her exhaustion and the constant strain on her Essaeris, she could only create and maintain four pumas, and they were nowhere near as formidable as the ones she had used when they'd attacked the caravan. These ones were all under two hundred and fifty pounds. Two of them together could easily handle a juvenile. But the adults were proving difficult.

It was known that Wolxaran never attacked with their own bodies. They always sent in their Essaerites to do it. This allowed them to take on far more challenging prey, and other predators generally avoided them. Thus far, with this pair, she had counted ten Essaerites. Far more than her four pumas could handle.

But she did have an advantage. The settlement had moved as much of its livestock as it could into more centralized locations, giving her a smaller area to protect. She still had to watch for homes to make sure that people didn't get attacked, but at least the livestock was less of an issue.

She also had a couple of owls in the area circling around that could find and track the Wolxaran's Essaerites, but it was pushing her hard. They were nocturnal and almost only attacked at night. During the day, they slept.

For Caelwen, her days were consumed by taking care of Durgard, whose condition was worsening. She yawned again and bounced around from owl to owl. Normally, she didn't have to stay awake to guard the settlement from predators. If she had a puma or two in the area, it would be more than sufficient, but as it was, the Wolxaran were too smart and too adept. Caelwen had to be awake, had to watch, had to check everything.

The first night hadn't been too bad. The Wolxaran had come, and her pumas had been able to easily scare them off. She had hoped it would end there, but the next night they came again, and this time they hit a different part of the settlement. Again, she rebuffed them. Now they were back. She could feel it. Her owls had caught a few glimpses of them darting in and out of the trees all around the settlement, and this was going to be one of the biggest problems. She didn't know where all of them were and what area they would target, so she had to spread her pumas thin.

In the center of the settlement, people were arguing with her uncle. They were angry that the Wolxaran were attacking their livestock. Their anger wasn't directed at Caelwen. They were grateful for her. They were furious that the Wolxaran were there to begin with. For them to go after a settlement like this was bad luck.

They'd angered the gods. Or at least that's what some of the people were saying. They had a lot going for them. There were the Wolxaran, the town smith being ill, and possibly going to die. All of it could be traced back to her uncle and his decisions. Part of her wished she could be in the settlement meeting right now, arguing with him about it. But as it was, she was more engaged in this activity. Her uncle would worm his way out of whatever trouble he'd gotten himself into; that she had no doubt of.

She sighed, her eyes drooping. One of her pumas thought it caught sight of something. She snapped her attention to it and focused on the Essaerite. It was on the outskirts of town, on the opposite side of her. It was peering into the dark woods. Some of the trees pulsed with faint light, but many of the other night plants had withered for the season. It gave the animals plenty of darkness to move and hide in.

"Come on, where are you?" Caelwen said to herself.

Another puma thought it saw something, and she shifted her attention to that. It was also peering into the forest. The Essaerite wanted to move into the forest to hunt, but she pulled it back. As she pulled into her own body, she heard a howl from outside. It sent an involuntary shiver through her body. There was no way to stop it. When Wolxaran howled, people trembled. Then there were more and more howls. She heard them from all of her Essaerites.

It was like a chorus all around the settlement. She got up and checked her door to make sure that it was locked tight and that nothing could get in. She didn't like the idea of something entering her home while she was connected with one of her Essaerites. From the rafters, she saw Treftune tremble a little and hide, his fur changing to a dark brown that matched the wood of the rafters.

One of her pumas saw something, and she connected into it. Coming from the forest, she saw three of the Wolxaran darting for it. "Shit," she said to herself. With a thought, she sent another puma heading to assist the first, but it stopped as it saw Wolxaran coming for it as well.

"Shit, shit, shit," she muttered.

She ordered her pumas to start falling back, back towards the livestock and the center of town. But the Wolxaran were closing quickly. "Shit!" she exclaimed.

The first puma wasn't going to make it anywhere near town. It wheeled and launched itself at the first of the Wolxaran. They were exact copies of the animal that created them. This gave them disadvantages. They had normal teeth, fur, flesh, and claws. This was not a problem that Caelwen's pumas had. Like the cats she had created for attacking the caravan, they had metal mouths, teeth, and claws. One puma was more than a match for two of the Wolxaran Essaerites, and it could possibly hold its own against three.

It didn't make any sound as it attacked. There was no scaring these animals away or freaking them out like she had been able to do with humans. The puma latched onto the neck of one of the Wolxaran and bit down hard, thrashing. As it did so, it registered a bite on its hindquarters. It let go of the Wolxaran and spun, swinging its paw out and raking its claws down the side of one of the others. The animals backed away, surrounding the puma. It spun around, snapping at one of the Wolxaran that came in towards its hindquarters, trying to bite it.

Caelwen felt her Essaeris growing inside of her. She was going to need to assist one of them. In the corner of her mind, she registered that the other puma was also being engaged now as well. "Shit," she said.

There were four going after that one. With a thought, she sent one of the pumas that was heading back towards the center of town to help the one that had four. In the moment of thinking about it, the three attacked the first puma. She connected in as teeth and claw met. There were growls from the Wolxaran, and the puma lashed out, gripping onto one of them, ripping it in half. She felt a surge of pride as the Essaerite did its work, and then her heart instantly sank as two of the Wolxaran were able to gain a purchase on it. "No," she groaned.

The other puma was now being joined by the second one. They were driving off the Wolxaran quickly, and she focused all her attention on the first puma, which was down to two of them. It swiped with its claws, catching the jaw of one of the Wolxaran and ripping it open.

She smiled. She was going to win. And then it all went wrong. Three more of the Wolxaran came out of the woods and joined the one that was left. She felt her heart drop as the animals synchronized their attack, hitting her puma from all sides. It rolled and moved, trying to keep anything vital from being bitten or clamped onto. But one of the Wolxaran managed to seize the base of the puma's spine. There was a crack, and she felt the puma go down.

Her Essaerite started to lose quickly, and it didn't take more than a few seconds before it was over. She could pump more Essaeris into it, try to heal it, try to recover, but it was too late, and she knew that. She still had three more pumas left, and she brought them in towards the center of the town. Her heart hammered. This was going to be a long night. She reached down, feeling her Essaeris, and felt a well of fear and disappointment. She didn't have enough. She couldn't create another puma.

"We'll just have to hold out for the night," she said to herself. "We'll just have to hold out."

CHAPTER 9

Caelwen's exhaustion pressed down on her like a wet blanket thrown on a dying fire. She, like the fire, sputtered and struggled to keep going but couldn't make it. It was too much.

The Wolxaran had finally departed the area, or at least she hoped that they had. The night before, in the early hours, when they had been howling and otherwise trying to breach her defenses, they finally had a break. Up to that point, Caelwen had lost puma after puma, to the point where she could barely keep anything moving at all.

She'd been worried that she was going to have to move down to smaller animals or try to create something like the stump she used in her home that did her housework to defend the settlement, but as the Wolxaran howled, one of the stolen horses from the caravan panicked and was able to jump the fence.

She'd watched through one of her owls as the animal bolted away from the settlement and saw the Wolxaran approach it. She wouldn't have been able to stop it.

She watched as the horse was taken down, and she held her pumas in place. She could have shooed the Wolxaran away, maybe, but for what? So she could guard over a dead horse, and allow the Wolxaran other Essaerites to come to the settlement?

She'd watched as the other Essaerites belonging to the Wolxaran came into view, and at some point, the two actual Wolxaran themselves. There were twelve in total that she had seen. She wasn't sure which was real, but they made relatively quick work of the horse. She saw their bellies extend and distend as they gorged themselves, and then they slunk off into the forest.

Essaerites didn't need to eat or drink, and their stomachs didn't digest anything, but they could be used for storage. And that's exactly what the

Wolxaran Essaerites' bellies did. Their Essaerites would store the meat and anything else they caught in their bellies. And when the Wolxaran were hungry, they would release the Essaerites and eat the contents of the stomach, just as fresh as if they had just been killed.

This was the way of the Wolxaran, and it was effective. The Wolxaran would retreat to some den secluded in the mountains to wait out the winter. Their Essaerites would hunt for them and bring back food. The horse would be an excellent start, helping them build up their fat reserves so they could have a relaxing winter in their den. It ensured survival, and she respected it.

Normally, she would have found it amusing that it was one of her uncle's horses that was killed, but as it was, she didn't have the energy for amusement. She didn't have the energy for anything. Durgard's condition had steadily worsened with each passing day.

His infection had depleted her entire winter stockpile of herbs. During the day, she couldn't forage; she was too exhausted, and she didn't have enough power left to create anything that could venture into the woods to look for herbs. No one else in the settlement knew what they were looking for, and it was too dangerous to go out in the woods with the Wolxaran in the area. That had meant that Durgard's condition had declined day after day, without Caelwen being able to do anything about it.

The once muscular man was now a shadow of his former self. Even if he were to survive, he wouldn't be swinging a hammer or working in a forge for months to come, and even then, it would take him years to regain his strength. Not that he was going to make it. Caelwen knew that, and deep down inside, Rothia did too. But Durgard's daughter, Ulfiel, seemed to still be holding out hope that her father would live. Caelwen felt for her. She felt for both of them. This was a horrible thing to witness—watching a loved one dwindle away to nothing and knowing there was nothing you could do about it. No way to stop it.

Durgard's skin had taken on a gray pallor and was clammy to the touch. There were blotches of red covering his body as the infection spread. He hadn't woken in a few days, and Caelwen hoped he wouldn't again. She could only imagine the suffering that would result from it. His wound had festered, leaking pus and smelling rancid. She tried changing the bandages and doing what she could, but she knew it was just for show at this point. There was no stopping what was coming. The settlement was already feeling the loss.

Durgard had constantly built and crafted for the people of the settlement. Be it items for farming equipment, weapons, or repairs, he always had something to do. His forge was full of projects that were left undone. The winter was going to be hard. There was no doubt about that. And for Caelwen, she needed to find a way to try to resupply her herbs if she could. The few cold snaps that had already happened had probably killed most of them off, which meant it was going to be a harder winter if folks got sick.

The room was dim, with the fire barely burning in the hearth. In the corner, on a pile of straw, Ulfiel was curled up, sleeping fitfully. Next to Caelwen was Rothia. She was holding her husband's hand, looking down at his face.

"Is there anything you can do?" Rothia asked softly.

Caelwen shook her head. "Be here."

Rothia slowly closed her eyes and nodded. "I understand. Thank you."

Caelwen reached out and placed her hand atop the other woman's, giving it a squeeze. What else could she do? There was no way of saving the man, and there was no way of really comforting Rothia, but she couldn't leave her alone either.

"You should go get some sleep. There's nothing more you can do," Rothia said.

Caelwen gave Rothia's hand another squeeze. "I'm staying right here with you," she said softly.

Rothia looked at her and smiled faintly. "Thank you, Caelwen. You're like your mother, you know that?"

Caelwen returned the smile, but it didn't feel genuine to her. After all, she wasn't feeling anything right now. She was just in a haze. "Thank you."

Rothia looked back to her husband. "She was like you in that she cared about the people of this settlement. She cared fiercely about us, and she did everything she could. I don't know how many beds she sat next to as people passed away. You're like her in that regard," she said, "and you're tough like she was too." Rothia shook her head. "I don't know where the women in your family get it. I've never seen people as tough and practical as you are," she said with a soft smile.

Caelwen smirked a bit. "I've heard that we're practical, among other things."

Rothia chuckled softly, "among other things, I'm sure." She got serious. "But she cared about us. Your brother does too. I wish it were him or you that were in charge of this settlement," she said with a sigh. "None of this would have happened."

Caelwen felt a pang of guilt in her gut about this—not that she could unseat her uncle from power, but that it was even a thing at all. That it was a member of her family that caused so much of this.

"I'm sorry, Rothia," Caelwen said.

"Not your fault. At some point, you or your brother will take over," Rothia said with a smile. "And the settlement will support you when that time comes," she said, then shrugged. "I think," she added, unsure. "Your uncle does have some loyal followers."

It was true; her uncle had made the right people well-off, and it kept him from having any real opposition. But this last incident with the caravan might have gone too far. They were going into winter, and losing a smith. The chances of merchants coming into town were going to be rare if word spread of what had happened. And they'd had the Wolxaran, so even the gods were mad at them.

Caelwen thought that when her brother came back, there was a chance, albeit a small one, that he could challenge Ilfthandor. And maybe they could have a decent leader. But that was if her brother came back. She didn't know when those men would return or if they would at all, let alone what mood or mindset they'd be in when they arrived.

Durgard made a little gurgling sound, and his mouth twitched a bit before he went back to sleep. Caelwen looked down at him, seeing his skin take on even more of a pallor than before. She knew this look. She saw tears streaming down Rothia's cheeks.

"It's happening, isn't it?" Rothia asked.

Caelwen felt tears in her own eyes. "Yes," she whispered. "Ulfiel?" she asked.

Rothia's head bobbed. "Yes. Yes. Get her."

Caelwen got up and walked over to Ulfiel. She gently shook her shoulder, waking the girl. Ulfiel looked up at her.

"What is it?" she asked.

Caelwen's voice was thick. "Ulfiel, it's time to say goodbye."

The girl was instantly awake, her face scrunching up and turning red. "No," she moaned. "No, not yet," she said. Ulfiel scrambled to her feet and rushed to the bed. She leaned over her father. "No, Papa. No, not yet. No, please," she sobbed. Her tears fell onto her father's chest.

Caelwen stood back, not wanting to intrude on this moment for the two people in front of her. Rothia and Ulfiel hunched over Durgard, and she could hear them sobbing, could hear their sorrow.

She watched Durgard's chest rise and fall slowly and softly, getting shallower and shallower until, eventually, it didn't rise again. She felt her heart sink, a part of her feeling like she had failed. She had failed to protect Durgard in the first place. She had failed to change her uncle's mind. She had failed to keep Durgard's infection from raging through his body.

If she had managed to find a way to drive the Wolxaran off sooner, she could have kept forging, but she knew that wouldn't have been enough. Her mind and her heart were at odds. Her mind knew that as soon as that blade had pierced his skin, it was over. It had just been a question of time. It wouldn't have mattered if she had driven the Wolxaran out or if she had killed everybody in that caravan three times over again. The only way to have kept Durgard alive would have been to keep him away from the caravan to begin with.

———

VALFRIC WATCHED AS A GROUP OF PEOPLE SET UP A CAMP IN A SMALL VALLEY. THE GROUP was smaller than the one he had with him, but he was wary of them. There were a handful of women and children, but what caught his attention the most was a wizened old man riding a dark horse with the group. He wore furs and appeared to be older than time itself, with a beard that reached down to his waist and long hair with the top of his head balding.

"Caelbercht says we can take them," Yrthorn said as he sat next to Valfric.

Aelric grunted. "Caelbercht's a fucking idiot."

Valfric agreed. Caelbercht was indeed an idiot. He hadn't been on many raids before, but now that they had been out for a little while and had a few successful raids, Caelbercht and some of the others had decided they were experts and warriors to boot.

"Caelbercht is an idiot," Valfric said. "You see that man down there? The old one?" Valfric said to Yrthorn, trying to make this a teaching opportunity.

"What about him?" Yrthorn replied.

Yrthorn's tone had changed as well. He'd gone from being the unsure youngest member of the crew to being a little on the cocky side. He'd also been spending his evenings with Caelbercht and the others, drinking themselves into a stupor with wine and Bryndraught they took from their victims. When he wasn't drinking, he was tormenting Nefeli. Valfric had grown tired of being kept up at night with her screams and pleas for mercy. As it turned out, Yrthorn was a sadistic drunk.

Valfric shot a glance at the boy. "He's an Essaerist," Valfric said, "and an old one."

Yrthorn smirked at Valfric. "Oh, you can't handle an old man?"

Valfric fought the urge to growl. "In hand-to-hand combat, yes, I'd expect even you to be able to take an old man," Valfric said with venom in his voice, "but it wouldn't be hand-to-hand combat. It would be with Essaeris, and with that, he has years of experience on me. You see those bighorn sheep wandering around their camp?" he said, pointing.

Yrthorn looked down at the four bighorn sheep that were wandering around. He snickered. "You're scared of sheep? Come on, Val. Your wolves can take them out."

Valfric gritted his teeth. "Do you think they're actually sheep, or are you that stupid?" he asked. "Do my wolves seem like normal wolves to you, Yrthorn?"

He saw uncertainty cross the boy's face. "Well, I guess, no, I guess not."

Valfric smiled, but it wasn't a kind smile. "See? Maybe you don't know everything." He looked back down at the camp. "Those sheep will not be sheep."

"But there's just four of them. There's more of us," Yrthorn said.

"Yes, there is more of us than there are of them, but we don't know how many Essaerites he has or how good he is with them. We know that he's good enough that he doesn't mind having women and children along with him, people that he seems familiar with. And the men who are with them don't seem overly concerned," Valfric said. "Yet they have carts full of riches that they just got from being mercenaries down south."

Ilara added to the thread. "Yrthorn, these are not going to be easy men to take. They've been battle-hardened and fighting for a long time. And to Valfric's point, we don't know what other Essaerites he can make."

"Or if those are even all the Essaerites he has right now," Aelric said. "For all we know, there might be others in the area and some watching us as we speak," he commented.

Yrthorn was looking more and more unsure of himself. He huffed, "Whatever," he said, moving away.

Aelric, Valfric, and Ilara exchanged glances.

"Caelbercht's starting to get under my skin," Aelric said.

"Mine too," Valfric commented.

Valfric didn't like it. The group they were watching was a threat but not to their settlement. They had traveled far from home and were near the Lysandrian and Rothmornian borders, raiding groups moving up from the south. The pickings had been good, with the groups thinking they were safe being close to the borders. It had made his people overconfident in their abilities, and they were also used to being the only side with an Essaerist.

Later that evening, Valfric sat with Ilara, Aelric, and Thraindel around the campfire. They were on the edge of the camp, looking in, seeing all those from their settlement who were busily getting drunk, yelling, and being rowdy. *This is what you wanted,* he reminded himself. He wanted them to remember what it was like to raid, rape, and ravage. He wanted them to remember their heritage, and this was part of it.

The one that was going to be a problem, though, was Caelbercht. Caelbercht was a large man and a competent enough warrior, but he had a lot of bravado that he hadn't really earned. He was busy getting drunk, laughing, and talking with Yrthorn while they tormented Nefeli.

Valfric had no problem enjoying one's slaves. He didn't even have issues with torturing people, but he didn't think it was wise for Yrthorn to be doing this. There was a difference between torturing someone for fun when you planned to kill them, and another when it was cruelty just for the sake of fun with something that was supposed to be a servant. Slaves were tools and wealth, not some bobble to be gained and lost.

Presently, Nefeli was naked and screaming, begging them to stop. Yrthorn was watching, laughing, as Caelbercht and some of the other men held her down and pressed hot coals from the fire to her back. Her body was covered in bruises, burns, and scars in various stages of healing. The once beautiful woman was on her way to becoming grotesque and disfigured.

"It's stupid," Ilara said next to him.

"Yes, it is," Valfric said, "but there's nothing we can do. She's his property."

Ilara looked at him. "I'm sorry."

"Sorry for what? I didn't know you knew how to say that word," he commented dryly.

She chuckled and hit his arm. "I'm sorry for not backing you with Yrthorn. You're right; he's too young. He doesn't understand."

"No, he doesn't," Aelric said, watching.

Aelric was probably the most violent, brutal person Valfric had ever met. But he was also cunning and smart, able to see down the road. And what Yrthorn was engaged in wasn't going to end well. It ended in one of two ways. One, the slave would fight back, which could end poorly for him. Yrthorn had been allowing her to sleep in his tent or forcing her to do so, which was fine. But in Valfric's experience, you wanted someone you could trust beside you, not someone who was just afraid of you.

The other possibility was that Nefeli would die. There was nothing wrong with killing people, and nothing wrong with killing a slave, but it was a waste, in Valfric's opinion. Nefeli was young and able-bodied. There was so much she could do. There were so many ways she could make Yrthorn's life easier. She also would have fetched a high price before he and Caelbercht had ruined her, but Yrthorn had chosen the path of entertainment.

Yrthorn came stumbling over to them, obviously drunk. He sat next to Thraindel, who glanced at him.

"Having a good time?" Thraindel asked.

Yrthorn grinned. "I am. I'd be having more fun if we'd attacked that group today, but there's always tomorrow," he said, smiling.

"We're not attacking that group tomorrow," Valfric said, looking at the fire.

"Caelbercht thinks we can do it. I agree with him. He thinks you're just being weak," Yrthorn said.

Valfric's head snapped to Yrthorn. "What did you say to me?"

Yrthorn held up his hands. "I didn't say I agree with him about you being weak. I just said what he said."

"You need to do a better job of picking your friends, boy," Aelric said. "Caelbercht is not one of them. Look at him over there right now. What is he doing?"

Yrthorn looked over and chuckled. "He's enjoying Nefeli," he said with a cocky grin.

Aelric smacked the boy upside the head. "Would you do that with a horse?"

Yrthorn looked taken aback. "What do you mean, would I do that with a horse?"

"Answer the question," Aelric said. "Would you do that with a horse?"

Yrthorn was silent for a moment. "Nefeli's not a horse."

"That's not the point," Valfric growled.

Yrthorn instantly fired up, the alcohol giving him more bravado. "She's a slave, and I can do what I want with her," he said evenly.

It was Ilara who spoke this time. "You're right, Yrthorn. You can. She's yours to do whatever you want to. Just like it would be if she were a horse. And you're right. She's not a horse. She's much smarter, more capable, and far more valuable," she said acidly. She pointed at Caelbercht. "And you're letting those men destroy your property. Do you think she'll be any good after this trip? Do you think you're going to be able to do anything with her if she even survives?"

Yrthorn shook his head and stood up. "Caelbercht was right. You four just carry on with the rumors of your success and your power and your prowess." He paused, and Aelric gave him a hard look.

"Choose your words wisely, Yrthorn. Friend or not, drunk or not, you can still get laid out on your ass," Aelric said icily.

Yrthorn looked like he wanted to say something, and Valfric looked up from the fire. "Go to bed, Yrthorn. And take Nefeli with you. I don't want to hear her screams all night long."

Yrthorn looked like he was about to say something, and Valfric stood up, looking him in the eyes. "Are you ready to do this? Are you really ready to challenge me?" he asked, his voice cold.

Yrthorn's eyes quivered. He shook his head softly. "No. No, I'm not. I'm sorry, Valfric. I'm sorry." He backed away. He called to Nefeli and scuttled off to his tent.

Thraindel spoke, "You're going to need to do something about Caelbercht."

Valfric sat back down and looked at the fire, sighing. "I know I am."

CHAPTER 10

Valfric stirred, his eyes opening to see the ceiling of his tent. The air had a cool bite to it, and he sat up, yawning as he did. His mind reached out to his wolves; he had four of them. Two were in the camp, with one lying next to his tent. The other two were close to camp and to the west.

He didn't think the other Essaerists in the area knew about Valfric and his little band, nor did he believe that if he did, the other Essaerist had any reason to harass them. But he still wanted the wolves on the side of the camp nearest the other group. Just because he didn't think something would happen didn't mean that it wouldn't. He pulled off the furs he'd been sleeping under and crawled out of the tent into the soft morning light. The sky was covered in a dome of gray clouds. A few of them hung over the peaks of distant mountains.

Around him, the camp was in a state of disarray that could only be the result of drink and carelessness. Smoke rose from the dwindled remains of several campfires, with men lying around the embers' dying warmth. But most people were in tents. Piles of loot lay about the camp haphazardly.

It drove Valfric crazy. His team always left everything on carts or stacked neatly for quick loading should problems arise. It was a pain in the ass, but raiding was as much about needs and wealth as it was about the thrill and joy of it all. *But this is what you wanted,* he reminded himself. He'd wanted the people to enjoy themselves and to know what their ancestors had. Part of that was letting them get a taste for it. Later, they could learn restraint and organization.

He stood and walked over to Ilara's tent. He stuck his head in, seeing her eyes open. He resisted the urge to smile. Ilara wasn't someone you could sneak up on.

"How'd you sleep?" he said.

She yawned. "I slept well last night. They drank themselves into a stupor faster than most nights, so it was quiet."

She got up and joined Valfric outside her tent. Thraindel and Aelric were likewise getting up. Thraindel's head swiveled, inspecting the camp, and she smirked.

"Look at them all, just lying there begging to get their throats slit," he said warmly.

Aelric glanced at Thraindel. "Don't tempt me. Where is the boy?"

"Probably still passed out," Ilara said with a hint of irritation, "the little shit fits right in with this group." She nodded at some sleeping men on the ground.

Aelric grunted. "He needs to come down a peg or two before he does something regrettable."

Valfric grabbed some wood and tossed it onto some coals. The coals popped and crackled as they began to heat up the wood. Valfric knelt and blew on them, making flames start to lick up the sides of the fresh wood.

He kept tending to the budding flames until a small fire burned. He felt its warmth reach out, warming his face and hands. Ilara handed him some flatbread that he placed near the flames to warm up. He created four stools and took a seat on one.

"Do we have anything else to eat, or did these fucks eat it all?" he called over to Thraindel, who was looking in one of the carts for food.

Thraindel huffed. "They ate through all the meats and cheeses," he said, coming back empty-handed.

Valfric handed him a warmed piece of bread.

"There might be some in the other carts or in some tents," Thraindel said.

"Sure there will be," Ilara commented. "So we get to hunt today unless Valfric's Essaerites want to do that for us?"

He glanced over at her, seeing her smiling hopefully. He shook his head and chuckled. He thought it was time for the group to start learning how life was on the road.

"I can probably get us something," he gestured to the others from their settlement, "but not enough for all of them. These fucks are going to need to learn that it's not all getting drunk and eating until your gut hurts."

Aelric took a bite of bread and nodded. "Agreed. And I can think of who needs to learn that lesson the most," he said, standing up.

They all smirked and watched as Aelric strode over to Yrthorn's tent. Aelric ducked inside, and Valfric waited, wondering how rude of an awakening Yrthorn was about to get.

"What the fuck!" Aelric bellowed.

His tone had all of them on their feet and rushing over. Valfric looked in the tent, seeing Aelric leaning over Yrthorn. The blood drained from Valfric's face.

Yrthorn was lying on his back, the skin on his face a light gray. He was covered in blood. Aelric was on top of him, trying to wake him.

"Shit," Valfric said, pushing into the tent. "Yrthorn!"

His furs were soaked in drying blood that stuck and coated Valfric's hands as he reached out for the boy. Yrthorn's skin was cold as ice, and Valfric felt his heart drop.

"What is it?" Ilara asked with Thraindel.

Valfric felt his heart sink. "He's dead," he said softly. "Someone's killed him."

Rage built inside Valfric as he saw Yrthorn's bloodied form. He gritted his teeth. "Where's the girl?" he asked, to no one in particular.

Thraindel swore softly. "I don't know. Let me see," he said, stalking off.

Valfric looked over to Aelric, seeing his veins bulge and his skin redden with anger; the big man's whole form shook with the force of it. They backed out of the tent and stood. People were starting to stir, hearing the sounds of commotion.

Aelric growled. "Where is that Lysandrian bitch?"

Valfric's mind reached out to his Essaerites. He had the two in camp come over and start searching for the girl. They picked up her scent in a moment and began wandering around the camp looking for her. Valfric joined them, looking around, kicking people, and waking them up.

"Get up," he ordered. As he did so, he noticed that a group was missing. "What the fuck?" He grumbled to himself. He glared at a man who appeared to have been up for a while.

"Where the fuck is Caelbercht?" he demanded.

The man looked up at him, a flash of fear in his eyes. "I-I don't know. They left this morning. Something about doing a little hunting?"

Valfric gritted his teeth. "Did they have a woman with them?"

The man shook his head. "No, they didn't."

His wolves had finished pacing around the camp and were now searching the outside. One of them picked up a scent moving to the south. It started slowly tracing the trail.

"Damn it," Valfric muttered to himself.

He called over to Aelric. "Aelric! They caught her scent."

Aelric, Thraindel, and Ilara walked up to him. He could see the anger and pain on all of their faces. Yrthorn had been a prick lately, but he was still one of them. He was a brother in arms, and Nefeli had taken that from him. That would be something she would gravely regret.

"Good. I'll grab my horse," Aelric said. "I'm going to enjoy running her down."

"We might have other problems," Valfric said. "Caelbercht went out this morning with some friends, hunting. And don't worry, the wolves will grab her and bring her back," he said. "They'll keep her alive," he added with venom in his voice.

"Good. I hope they do," Aelric said, his teeth clenched.

"I want to find Caelbercht, too," Valfric said. "He should have been on watch this morning, and instead, they wandered off hunting or doing whatever the fuck stupid things they're up to. They should have been here to see her leaving. Even those idiots would have noticed someone covered in blood walking out of the camp."

With another flick of his mind, he sent other wolves to search for Caelbercht and his company. The time for being nice with the people from his settlement was over. Someone was dead, and while they probably couldn't have stopped it, Valfric was at his wits' end with them.

His mind went into the wolves that were looking for Nefeli. They were moving deeper into the woods. This only made Valfric angrier. She'd been gone for hours. How long had Yrthorn been dead? But her scent was getting stronger, and she wouldn't be able to outrun the wolves.

He turned his attention to Ilara. "We might need to go bring her back. She's out pretty far."

But then one of his other wolves caught his attention.

"Hold up," he said to her as she started to walk to her horse. He went into the other wolf's mind. It, too, was smelling blood, but it was to the west of them. He had it breathe in deeper.

"What is it?" Aelric asked.

"Something's wrong." Valfric felt his gut turn. "Wake everybody up, now!"

The others didn't question him. Instead, they started yelling for their compatriots to get up and get ready for whatever Valfric thought was coming. The scent of blood grew stronger the closer the wolf got to camp.

And then the wolf saw it. Valfric felt his heart drop.

"Fuck," he groaned.

"What is it?" Thraindel asked, looking at him.

"I found Caelbercht," Valfric said, his eyes looking through that of the wolves. Caelbercht was almost back to camp, but he wasn't going to make it there. The man was covered in blood, his clothes and armor hanging from him, his flesh also hanging in meaty strips. He fell to the ground, and the wolf came up to him, inspecting the soon-to-be-dead man.

The wolf paced around Caelbercht, coming up to his face. Caelbercht turned to it, his face covered in blood and gore. His breath was shallow. He looked at the wolf, recognizing it as one of Valfric's. Then he wheezed, "Coming."

Valfric pulled from the wolf. "Shit," he said and yelled to the people around him, "Get ready. We have Essaerites coming!"

Ilara's head snapped to him. "What?" she asked, concerned.

"I just found Caelbercht in the woods. He's torn up. It doesn't look like something that men did," he said, anger filling him. *I told them not to fuck with the other Essaerist,* he thought to himself. And now they were going to have to deal with the fallout from it.

He called back the two wolves that had been looking for Caelbercht's group, and his mind reached out to the ones that had been looking for Nefeli. They were almost to her. They could see her in the distance, running through the woods. The wolves were running fast after her. She had to know she was being pursued. He felt indecision and anger roiling in him as he saw them close in on her.

"This will just have to do," he said softly. They wouldn't get to enjoy taking Nefeli apart and making her pay for what she did. She would just have to go for as clean and quick of a death as the wolves could give her.

As the wolves closed the distance, though, he heard something: a strange guttural call. He pulled himself back into his body and looked around, scanning for anything as the people around him rushed about looking for weapons. He found the source of the sound. On a rock that jutted high out from some trees, he saw a figure. It looked like a bighorn sheep. As he looked closer, he could see that the hooves looked sharper than a normal sheep. It looked down at the camp, and its eyes seemed more intelligent than any animal he'd ever seen.

Then he heard the sound again, that same guttural noise. The bighorn sheep opened its mouth, except it wasn't a normal mouth; it exstended down, taking up much of its neck. As its jaws opened, he could make out rows of sharp, vicious teeth. It bellowed a sound deep and guttural, and he felt ice in his chest. As the head moved, he saw the slight amount of light from the cloudy day glint off of the teeth. They were silvery and metallic, and he felt his heart sink further.

His mind reached out to the Essaerites chasing Nefeli. They were mere seconds away, but seconds weren't something they had. He cursed himself and the world and everything that had been going on, and with a tug of his mind, he pulled the wolves back. He was going to need them. He was going to need all of them.

The camp was chaos as people scrambled to grab weapons and prepare for whatever was coming. Valfric's mind reached out, checking to see where his wolves were. They were making their way back. The two that had been searching the area nearest them were already back in the camp. His eyes roamed around, trying to find the other Essaerists, Essaerites.

Amidst the shouts of people, he heard something crashing through the underbrush. His eyes turned, and two rams came running out of the forest. The first one slammed into a man, sending him sprawling. As it hit, it turned, stopping quickly, rounding on another person, its mouth and neck opening up, clamping down on a man who screamed. Blood sprayed as the ram twisted and jerked its head quickly, ripping through flesh, throwing the man to the ground.

In the forest, a figure approached. Still high in the trees, Valfric made out the form of a wizened old man. He was tall, standing much taller than a horse, taking long strides. He wore a robe of deepest black. In his hand was a staff formed of gnarled wood, with gemstones on the top. Valfric locked eyes with the man, seeing him grin. His teeth were black. Atop his head, he wore a helmet with ram's horns curling about it. Valfric felt his heart hammer. He had never gone against another Essaerist before, but he would have to now.

Valfric held his gaze and reached out, creating a shield and spear. He saw the other man's eyes narrow just a little bit as recognition that he was fighting another Essaerist crossed his face. This gave Valfric a little confidence and a little happiness. *That's right; you're not the only one here.* He grinned. If today was the day that he died, at least it would be facing a worthy adversary. Ulfgara would welcome him into her halls for that.

In front of him, one of the mountain sheep was staring him down, its head held low, ready to charge. Valfric was in his own world. Nothing else mattered; around him was pandemonium as people tried to form up, tried to defend themselves. He registered three other sheep in the camp sowing destruction.

But none of that mattered. All that mattered was Valfric and the one he was squaring off with. He held his shield in front of him and pointed his spear toward the animal. He had no doubts in his mind that this thing could and would kill him, but he just needed to hold it for a while. He noted two of the sheep disengaging, heading back toward their creator. He grinned. This seemed to confirm what he thought. This man didn't know that there was another Essaerist here, and he wasn't prepared. That would be Valfrics people's only saving grace.

The sheep began to move forward, running at him.

As it came close, Valfric dropped his shield and stuck the butt of the spear into the ground, altering it, making it extend out and thicken, not ending with a point but changing it to a thick round shield. The ram crashed into it, and he felt the vibration of the impact jolt his hands. The shaft of the spear shattered. The ram rolled, hitting the ground, and as it began to get up, Valfric's wolves were there and were instantly on it.

The sheep spun, throwing the wolves off. Valfric pulled them back lest the sheep be able to fully engage. He wasn't going to lie to himself. These Essaerites were far more advanced than what he had, and he couldn't go toe-to-toe with them. The sheep backed away from the wolves that darted around, nipping at it.

People from the settlement were starting to form up now, making a wall of shields. He saw Aelric at the fore, shouting orders. Valfric joined the wall. His heart felt like it was going to rip out of his chest, and he felt the thrill of fear and excitement course through him.

His other two wolves were back, wrapping around the people of the settlement to flank the Essaerist. The two sheep before them turned and ran back to the Essaerist. *Good, we have him pinned down, but not for long.* They needed out.

"Get the fucking carts loaded now!" Valfric bellowed.

In the trees, the other Essaerist was surrounded by his sheep and Valfric's wolves. They didn't have time. Valfric was working under the assumption that the old man had more sheep and that they would be there soon.

The shield wall broke as frazzled people rushed to grab what they could. He threw a few things over his pack horse and saddled up himself. He panted, his blood roaring in his ears.

"Quickly, quickly," Aelric was bellowing at the others.

They didn't have time. *If there were two or three more, they couldn't handle it,* he thought to himself.

The old man peered down at him and gave him a toothy, knowing grin and a nod of his head. Valfric felt a slight sense of relief. The nod was so much more than just a nod. It spoke of someone giving credit to a younger, less capable opponent but also said, "I'm giving you another day to live, boy, if you take the opportunity."

And Valfric fully intended to take the opportunity. He got on his horse and spurred on.

"Move, move, move," he yelled to everyone. People were scrambling onto their horses and beginning to move, pulling carts and dragging slaves along. They'd be leaving over half the loot they had gathered over the last while, but they were leaving with most of their lives, and that was something.

Valfric, Aelric, Thraindel, and Ilara stayed to the back of the group as they moved, and Valfric pulled his wolves in close. He fused more Essaeris into them, healing their wounds and making them stronger. As they began to move and clear the camp, he saw the other Essaerist's sheep come down. Two or three of them moved into the camp, sniffing around, looking to make sure there weren't any traps or anyone left behind. Other than the few groaning wounded on the ground, there was nothing.

Valfric looked away as the sheep made quick and efficient work of the couple of people who were left. He felt a wave of rage, fear, and shame roil through him, along with a deep sense of sadness. Yrthorn hadn't been the only one lost today. Others had been, along with so many things that they had gathered.

And while he didn't like Caelbercht, he was someone that he'd grown up with, whom he knew, and having him and his men gone was a loss. All of it had been such a loss.

As they kept moving, Valfric checked behind them, often with his Essaerites looking for pursuit. There was none. The other Essaerist wasn't going to come after them. He had no need to. There was no point in him trying to take or kill all of Valfric's group. No, he had gotten to where he was by being shrewd and smart. His company was already full of war trophies and loot that they had acquired while being mercenaries down in the south. This was just an addition to that.

And for every moment that Essaerist was away from his people was time that they were exposed to attack, something Valfric doubted the other man was willing to do. Their pace slowed some after a few hours, and Valfric rode up next to Ilara, Thraindel, and Aelric.

The latter was looking down, blood on his hands still from Yrthorn.

He looked over at Valfric. "You had to give up the chase of Nefeli, didn't you?"

Valfric looked ahead, feeling that same shame boil in him.

"Yes. Yes, I did."

He felt a hand clap his shoulder. "It was the right thing to do," Aelric said, his anger and rage seeming to be burned off. "If you hadn't pulled your Essaerites, we wouldn't have made it, or if we did, we would have lost so many more. There was no bringing Yrthorn back to life," he said with a sigh.

"I know that," Valfric said, his voice heavy. "I just wish that we could have... I don't know what I wish," he said.

"Taken our anger for our own failures out on that girl?" Aelric asked.

Valfric looked over at him. "I never thought I'd hear something like that from you."

Aelric was looking ahead, his expression blank. He shrugged. "It's true, and you know it's true.

"She did what she did because she was afraid, she was hurt, she'd been tormented, and she hadn't been properly broken and trained," Aelric said, "all the things that we knew would be a problem for someone with their first slave and that we should have taken heed of."

If Valfric was being honest, this was where his shame and guilt were coming from. Not that Nefeli had killed Yrthorn. No, in so many ways, Yrthorn had it coming, and he could see that from Nefeli's perspective. Yes, Valfric believed that Yrthorn had the right to do whatever he wanted, just like he would have the right to do whatever with any animal he owned. But Valfric also respected the fact that if an animal turned against its owner, he would be able to see it from the animal's point of view too. Yes, you still had to put it down, but it didn't mean that you didn't understand why it did what it did, and he understood why Nefeli did what she did.

"Do you think she'll make it?" a voice said from next to him.

Valfric looked over to see Ilara riding next to him.

"She might," Valfric said thoughtfully. "We're only a couple of days away from Lysandrian settlements," he said with a shrug.

"Yeah, that was what I was thinking," Ilara said. She looked down. "I'm sorry, Valfric," she said softly. "I shouldn't have pushed—" she started.

Valfric cut her off. "We all should have done things differently, but so should have Yrthorn. We all warned him and tried to work with him countless times. It didn't help that he had Caelbercht spurring him on. But unfortunately, that's just what happened."

"Yeah, that's just what happened," Ilara said. She glanced back behind her. "And the other Essaerist?"

Valfric shook his head. "That's on Caelbercht. I don't think he would have done anything to us," he said honestly. "Caelbercht picked a fight and lost it."

"Maybe now the others will listen to you," Aelric said with flint in his voice. "This is a hard lesson, but a lesson that they needed. You are the strongest among us, Valfric. You are a leader, you are a fighter, and you are an Essaerist. If you say that another Essaerist is more powerful or could be, and that it's not a good idea to attack them, now they'll listen."

"Hopefully," Valfric said, hopefully.

CHAPTER 11

Fioralba stood at the window, looking out at the orange and pink sky. The sun was just beginning to peek above the horizon, bathing the area in shafts of warm, honeyed light. This was one of Fioralba's favorite things to do: watch the sunrise and enjoy moments of peace and quiet.

Xavieno had left earlier for training, leaving her on her own. While she missed having his warm form in bed when she had gotten up, she was savoring the moment. Her husband was many wonderful things, but quiet and contemplative in the mornings while the sun was rising? *Well, no one is perfect,* she thought.

She breathed in deeply and slowly as she watched the sunrise. With each breath, she felt her Essaeris ebbing and flowing inside her, in tune with her. Their home sat near the edge of a city, overlooking rolling hills where a handful of cows, sheep, and goats grazed in the morning light. The peace of it all made her smile.

As she watched the sun, she reached out with her Essaeris and created two Essaerites with wiry figures that began to brush and comb her hair. This only increased her feeling of relaxation as the Essaerites' fingers moved through her hair, gently pulling it and arranging the strands into place. They began to weave the tresses into a loose braid, and she turned her thoughts to the day.

Mercifully, she didn't have many errands to run, but she decided to get on with them before the day grew warm and the streets became dusty. She turned from the window and flexed her Essaeris again, this time creating a dress. The air shimmered ever so slightly as the soft green fabric came into existence, wrapping her body in its velvety comfort.

The days had grown cooler but were not cold, strictly speaking. It never truly got cold in this section of Lysandrian, but it would get cool, and she enjoyed this time of year. The dresses were warm and comfortable, meals became heartier, and she loved all the colors of the trees and plants.

While flowers generally stopped blooming this time of year, the leaves of the trees turned from blues and greens to gold, reds, and purples. There was something magical about it, and even at night, some of the luminescent trees and plants' colors seemed to shift just a little bit.

She slipped on a pair of sandals with supple leather straps, grabbed her coin purse, and made her way out of her door. Her first stop was going to be the mill. As she exited her home, she walked to a cobbled street that was empty this early in the morning, save for a few merchants and farmers drawing carts laden with goods for the market.

Before her, the mill loomed; its sturdy stone facade shone in the early morning light, casting a sharp shadow across the grounds. Silos dotted the outside of the property, their bellies full of grain waiting to be ground into flour. Fioralba made her way to the door and walked in, the scent of the place hitting her. Flour hung in the air, swirling and dancing about the people as they worked. It reminded her of when she was younger, baking bread with her mother and grandmother.

Men loaded sacks full of flour from the mills. They greeted her as warmly as one could while loading a sack full of flour, and she made her way deeper into the mill. Mills were not unsafe places to be, but the work could be dangerous. The millstones were large and heavy, and if you got caught in one, there was no helping you. As a little girl, she never would have thought of herself as someone who would come into a mill to do any sort of work, but that changed when she became an Essaerist. She didn't work the mills per se, but she provided Essaerites for them.

In particular, she worked on the stones. She walked into a room where two donkeys were connected to poles and walked around in a circle. In the center of the circle were two large stones grinding atop each other, grain going in the center and coming out as flour on the sides. She waved at a man to stop the donkeys. He did so, and the sound of grinding ceased.

She walked up to the millstones and inspected them. Fioralba didn't provide all of the stone. She could, of course; she had the Essaeris to do it, but it would be wasteful. Instead, she provided Essaeris pieces to the stone where the actual milling occurred. She examined the grinding plates that she had created. Essaeris plates had many advantages over regular stone. For example, in the mill she was at, the millstones ran almost all year round and operated seven days a week. Normal stones needed to be serviced every few weeks, and little bits of the stone would get into the flour and make their way into bread.

Fioralba's Essaeris plates also ground down, with little bits ending up in the flour. However, she had it set to release as soon as it moved away from the main plate, leaving the flour free of any pebbles that might have come from it. Her plates were also much more durable and repaired themselves, making it so she only had to check on them every now and then to ensure they were working correctly, and staying in perfect condition to create a steady, even grind.

It saved a considerable amount of time for the mill staff, which meant more money for them and less risk of equipment being damaged or a stone falling on someone. It also meant they could produce a higher quality product, which again meant more money. For Fioralba, it meant a little extra money in her purse and as much flour as she liked.

After checking on the plates, she went back, patted the donkeys, and sent them on their way again to walk in a circle. As they did, she heard the stones grinding again. She found the mill foreman, and he gave her a small amount of coins for the last few days' worth of production. She checked to make sure there weren't any problems that they had noticed and then went on her way.

The sun was rising higher in the sky as she neared the city, and it looked like it was going to be a beautiful day. The cobbled street became more crowded the closer she got to town, and as she entered, she was met by the sights and sounds of the city in full morning swing. She picked up her pace, her relaxation and calm mood replaced by that of someone with errands to run and complete.

She wound around people, making her way toward one of the markets. There, she found carts lined up along the street with merchants selling everything from grains and fruits to weapons and slaves. She started picking her way around some of the food carts, looking at each item, picking up different pieces of fruit and inspecting them. Merchants chattered warmly with her, and she smiled, making small talk with them as she examined the fruit.

She reached out with her Essaeris with each one she picked, feeling the object. This was one of the things she found so useful about being an Essaerist: they could sense how something was created and made. When she'd been learning how to use her abilities, it had started with simple things like a piece of wood or metal, getting a feel for it and then using her Essaeris to recreate it herself. Then feeling what she'd created and comparing it to the original object. It had seemed silly at the time, but it had proven useful as they moved away from wood and metal to more complex things like animals and plants. She could get a feel for them, how they were made, how they worked, and then use her Essaeris to recreate them.

It took practice and time with every object she made, but once you understood the basics, you could do a lot. But you couldn't eat an Essaerite, or more importantly, if you did, you needed to release it before you digested it, or it would become part of you. They'd also been warned that the acids inside the body changed things and broke them down. If your Essaerite was not created fully or correctly, it could break down into items that turned toxic.

The ability to feel food was handy. Fioralba picked up an apple and reached out with her Essaeris, sensing and reading it. Her power ran through the apple, feeling its quality. She could detect any little worms or rotten spots inside the fruit, or how ripe it was, just by holding it and touching it with her power.

She found a few items she wanted and purchased them, placing them in a bag that she created, and then she went back to wandering around the market. She was getting hungry and hadn't had breakfast yet, so she walked over to a cart that she always enjoyed. There was an older woman who sold flatbread, along with cheeses and jams. Fioralba purchased some and continued walking along, eating the bread.

She bought a handful of other items like bread and some wine that she and Xavieno would use later, and then she drifted around, seeing what artisans had built and what fabrics were available. As she walked, she touched everything, feeling it. If she found something new or something she liked, she would hold up the fabric or item and inspect it, using her Essaeris. If it was something she enjoyed, she'd smile and hand the merchant a coin, usually to their confusion. But Fioralba felt bad whenever she found something she liked and planned on recreating it if she didn't pay the original artisan or the merchant who had originally shown it to her. So she gave them a coin and would move on her way. Feeling out items was easier when they were Essaerites that somebody else had created and that individual was open to you learning about their creation.

This had been another foundational technique that Fioralba, Xavieno, and Mariokos had learned along with Biankara as they trained. If one could produce something of high quality, the others could feel it out and learn how to produce the same thing.

As she finished her shopping for the day, she made her way back to her and Xavieno's home to drop off the food she had purchased. The sun was high above her when she made it back to her home, and she thought about what she was going to do for the rest of the day. She smiled to herself, thinking, *Maybe I'll see what Biankara's up to,* she thought.

———

THE SUN WAS ON ITS DESCENT FOR THE DAY AS FIORALBA WALKED UP TO XAVIENO AND Mariokos. The two men stood on the edge of the training grounds, talking to each other. Both had concerned expressions on their faces. In the case of Mariokos, his expression seemed to be concerned only, whereas her husband's was a mix of concern and slight tension from excitement.

As she approached them, they looked over at her, and Xavieno smiled with that tight excitement she had seen in him before. Mariokos's expression was just tight and reserved.

"How was your day, my love?" Xavieno asked as she approached.

She smiled warmly. "It was good," she said, stepping closer to him. She leaned up and kissed him softly on the lips, tasting the salt, sweat, and dirt of the day. He wrapped an arm around her waist.

"How was your day?" she asked.

"It's better now," Xavieno said, kissing her again.

She enjoyed it, and she kissed him back. She looked over at Mariokos. "And your day?"

"Fine," he replied tightly.

She eyed Mariokos and then her husband. "So, which one of you wants to tell me the bad news you heard?"

Xavieno smirked. "What makes you think I have bad news?" he said as he kissed her neck. "Maybe it's excellent news," he added.

She giggled softly as he playfully kissed her neck.

"Don't try to distract me," she said. "I know it's probably not good news because you look concerned and excited, and Mariokos just looks concerned," she said flatly.

Xavieno chuckled, and she saw Mariokos smirk. "Just some news from a merchant, that's all," Mariokos said.

"What's the news?" she asked, enjoying the playfulness in Xavieno's eyes.

He sighed, and she could see that he had been trying to distract her, or more likely, trying to distract himself.

"Just problems up north," Xavieno said.

She looked over at Mariokos. "Care to elaborate?"

Mariokos shot a glance between Fioralba and Xavieno before relenting. "The Gwenthari have been attacking up north. Raiding parties have been hitting settlements and pushing further south."

She shrugged. "So, how is this bad news? They're far away, and there's no way the Gwenthari can do anything to Lysandrian," she said confidently.

"It means that we're probably going to have to deal with it," Xavieno said. "Chances are, if this continues, we're going to war."

"That's the direction this has been heading all along," Mariokos said softly.

"What makes you so sure of that?" Fioralba asked.

Mariokos shrugged. "Simple. Money."

"And how does money come into play?" she asked.

"It costs money when settlements are hit, but also, war can be profitable. The Gwenthari have years of resources that they're sitting on," Mariokos explained.

"Plus, the bastards sacked the capital two hundred years ago," Xavieno commented bitterly.

Mariokos nodded. "Yes, there's that too, but with the Gwenthari attacking more and more and raiding more, the empire will have to act."

Xavieno added, "I've also heard that the Ulfgarath have been weakened over the last few decades and that they aren't the force they once were. It seems that other Gwenthari tribes are attacking them and whittling them down," he remarked.

Mariokos agreed, "There's that too; they're weak and ripe."

Fioralba nodded, feeling a subtle tension rise within her—not that she was particularly worried about the Gwenthari bothering them, but she wasn't looking forward to the prospect of going to war. It wouldn't be horrible for her; she'd be moving with the legions and staying with Xavieno at night, helping out around the camp. But it would mean that the days of relaxing walks to the mill and spending time in the market would be numbered.

"Do you really think it'll come to war?" she asked.

Xavieno shrugged. "Probably. I don't see a way around it, honestly. Some of the reports we've gotten..." he trailed off, shaking his head in disgust.

"That bad?" she asked.

Mariokos shook his head. "That bad," he confirmed. "Some Aristolios woman was found recently," he said. "She spun a tale of the tortures and torments that had happened to her when a Gwenthari raiding party killed her whole family and then took her as a slave."

Fioralba felt her husband tense next to her in disgust. She looked up at him. "What happened?"

He merely shook his head. "The things they did to her," he said, "they're animals."

"Is she going to be okay?" she asked.

The two men shrugged. "We don't know. We just heard about it. It could be bullshit for all we know," Xavieno said, "but I don't think it is."

"I don't think so either," Mariokos replied. "We've seen what the Gwenthari do before and heard the stories. I don't see them changing."

"No, they won't," Xavieno said.

He tried to lighten the mood. "But enough about that. What did you do today, my love?" he asked, looking into her eyes. Part of her wanted to push for more information, but she could tell that Xavieno was done talking about it.

She smiled softly. "I went to the market and stopped by the mill. I'm looking forward to spending an evening with you," she said, wrapping her arms around his neck.

She felt his arms go around her waist, and he grinned. "As am I."

He looked over at Mariokos. "Have a good one. I'll see you in the morning," he said. "I think I have things that I need to tend to now," Xavieno said with a smirk at Fioralba.

She felt her heart do a little flip and flutter. She turned to Mariokos. "Have a good evening, Mariokos," she said as they began to walk away.

CHAPTER 12

The sun was setting, turning the sky to soft oranges and pinks on the horizon. Above it were deep blues, spotted with clouds, which caught brilliant shades of pink and purple as the light illuminated them. The air was mild, and Mariokos breathed in, savoring the scent of dirt, trees, and flowers.

The gardens at Biankara's family estate were always serene and relaxing. He sat atop a cushioned bench, surrounded by trees that were beginning to turn. One of the trees next to him, which normally bore leaves of deep navy blue, was turning to a dark purple, while others on the same tree were shifting to red. Other trees were in various stages of changing, and around him and Biankara, the autumn flowers bloomed. As the sun set, some of the plants began to glow, with light creeping up some of the stems, accompanied by veins and ribbons of light that slowly began to pulse.

The tree nearest them had little lines of violet that began to show themselves, intertwined with lines of deep blue. They wound their way around the branches of the tree, up to the leaves, and a handful of the leaves glowed a soft blue. It was an altogether relaxing scene. He heard a few birds chirping in the trees and even spotted some of them flying from one branch to another as they settled down for the evening.

With his next breath, he caught the scent of the meal on the table before him. He looked at it, seeing a platter with roasted meat accompanied by an assortment of vegetables, breads, and cheeses. Biankara sat across from him, her expression calm as her eyes meandered around the garden. This was one of the places she enjoyed as well.

Tonight, she wore a silk dress that was a rich emerald green. Her long brown hair was arranged atop her head in an intricate weave, with golden pins holding it in place. Mariokos always thought she looked most attractive in moments like this—when she was relaxed and out of the public eye. The colors of the sky and garden seemed to accent her beauty.

He took one of the flagons of wine, pouring a glass for himself and then pouring some for Biankara. This was one of the few places where she never had the slaves close at hand. He could see them off in the distance; with a wave of the hand or a nod of their heads, they would be there to bring them whatever they wanted. But for now, it was just him and Biankara—something that was nice.

She smiled at him softly and thanked him for the wine. They both took a sip, gazing out at the garden. Mariokos turned his attention to some bread, spreading some cheese on it and taking a bite.

"So what's on your mind?" Biankara asked.

"What makes you think there's something on my mind?" Mariokos replied.

She smiled gently. "Because I know you."

He smiled back at her. This was true. He may not have felt passion for Biankara, nor did she for him, but they were friends, and they had been for many years. He looked at her, picking his words carefully, then decided that wasn't his game. She was the politician; he was not.

He sighed softly. "War is coming."

His statement didn't seem to faze or surprise her. Instead, she nodded. "War is coming," she said. "And this has you concerned? Why?"

When Biankara asked why he was concerned, it wasn't the same way Fioralba did. For Fioralba, the prospect of war felt distant and might mean living in camps or having to forgo some of life's pleasures, but she didn't see the stresses and potential dangers of it. Biankara was different. She understood and accepted all those realities.

For Biankara, war was always on the horizon; that's how she'd been raised. Most of the wars had little to do with combat and everything to do with politicking, conversations, contracts, and deals. These were the battles her family engaged in. While her family helped sponsor some legions, the bulk of their wealth had come from being shrewd businesspeople.

"We're going to have to march eventually. I just don't see any other way around it," he commented.

She took a sip of her wine, and he could tell this had been on her mind as well. "Yes, I agree," she said after a few moments. "My father and I were speaking about it earlier today, actually."

She put some meat on her plate, sliced off a piece, speared it, and took a slow, contemplative bite. They both knew what this would mean: Mariokos would be leaving, and the question would be whether Biankara would be leaving as well.

He felt uncomfortable—not out of some sense of fear of losing her, but from the unease of not knowing what someone thought. The discomfort that came with not knowing what was going to happen next and not knowing what the right decisions would be. In many ways, he assumed he and Biankara would end up together. They didn't have a lot of options, and they knew each other, and they made a good team. But that could be months or years away.

Of course, war would change that. "So we need to decide what we are going to be," she finally said after a few moments. She looked at him, her eyes neither hard nor soft or loving, just thoughtful and contemplative.

"Yes, we do," he said, looking down for a moment. "Biankara, do you want this?"

She took another sip of wine, again thoughtful. "Yes," she finally said after a moment. "I think... I do." She sighed. "We don't have passion or love the way Xavieno and Fioralba do, but we are a good team, and we do care about each other," she said honestly.

He nodded; this was true. They were a good team, and they did care about each other. Part of him felt a slight weight lift off him at the same time as another weight came down.

"Yes, we are," he said thoughtfully.

"What is it?" she asked.

He shook his head. "I just never thought I would be proposing out of a sense of timing and convenience."

She smiled tightly and chuckled a little. He looked up at her. She leaned over the table and placed her hand on his. "And for me, that's all a proposal would have ever been," she said, smiling.

"But we have other things to decide before we can make this official or decide to do it at all," she commented.

"And what's that?" he asked.

She sat back in her chair. "The legions, the war, when we think it'll happen, if we think it'll happen, and what our life is going to look like during it," she said. "For one, I'm not thrilled about the idea of living in a war camp."

She raised her hand, stopping him from saying anything. "I'm not trying to imply that I think it's beneath me, because it's not. There are many women of much higher status who do that, but this war is not the only one that I have the potential of fighting or having to deal with," she explained.

He understood. "Your family."

She nodded. "Yes. Or if this moves forward, our family," she remarked. "So that begs the question: how long will the war last, and when do you think you'll be moving out?"

He thought for a moment and took a few sips of wine before answering. "I'm not sure. If we're hearing about it, that means it won't be long before we march if it happens at all."

"Let's pretend it's going to happen," she said. "When do you think it would? You're the military man, not me."

He considered her question, thinking about timelines and what would be needed for the Legion to start moving. "We would move at the beginning of the year," he said after a moment.

"If we are going to war with the Gwenthari, that will mean moving north. Their winters are much harsher than ours, though the areas closest to the Empire aren't, obviously. Still, waiting for the thaw and for spring to come would be the best choice. Plus, the Legion has to be ready and gather supplies," he said, thinking aloud. "We would move out in January or February," he concluded after a few moments.

She nodded. "That's what I was worried about."

"That worries you?" he asked, concerned.

She nodded. "Yes, it does," she sighed. "We can't get married."

A wave of unease washed over him. "Why?"

"It's not enough time for a wedding," she explained.

He felt his anger begin to flare, but she held up a hand. "I'm not saying this to rebuff you. I'm saying that weddings are just as much a battle as anything else for me and mine," she clarified, thoughtful again.

She nodded to herself as if making a decision. "I will accompany you in the camp, but we will not be engaged, and we will not be planning to get married. When the war nears its climax or its end, then we will begin the process of planning a proper wedding that can be used."

Part of him railed against this idea. Getting married was supposed to be about love and being with someone for the rest of your life, not about positioning yourself or maintaining an image in society. He reminded himself that was just his view of the world, and that he would be playing more and more in Biankara's world as they grew older. She was right. Her family would become his, and their wars would become his, even if he didn't fully understand them or thought them silly.

He also reminded himself that his and Biankara's relationship was anything but what he had expected when he was younger. He had envisioned meeting a girl, falling in love, getting married, and living as poor farmers together. His life had changed, and so had Biankara's. If she had to shift her life from what she had planned and known, who was he to refuse to change his views regarding his?

He took a sip of wine and nodded. "Alright, we're in agreement," he said. "Are you sure?"

She appeared thoughtful. "Yes, I'm sure. I don't have to spend all my time in the camps, and maybe this will end quickly or not happen at all," she said, sounding irritated for the first time.

"I'm sorry," he said to her.

She laughed dryly. "There's nothing for you to apologize for. You're not the one causing this stupidity."

He raised an eyebrow. "Stupidity? I'm surprised to hear you say that. Aren't you worried about the dangers in the frontier?"

She shook her head. "This isn't going to be about dangers on the frontier," she said seriously. "This is going to be about wealth. The legions may be billed as here to protect and build the Empire— with the latter being true— but they are far more than protection; they are an engine for the economy, and the Gwenthari have done enough to provide enough excuses for the legions to be deployed," she explained, shaking her head.

"This is about money, make no mistake about it, and power," she declared. "You know that as well as I do," she said with a huff.

He took a bite of food and, after a moment, said, "I know it is, and part of me hates it, but I also understand that's how the world works," he shrugged. "And the Gwenthari are a threat."

"They are, yes, and they will need to be stopped at some point or we'll need to be fortified against them. But this is about something deeper. Mark my words, this is about money. The fact that it will make the Empire safer is just a side benefit," she said.

She huffed. "And I suppose if I'm being fair, if we were already married, or I thought this was going to happen a year from now after we could plan and have a proper marriage, I wouldn't care. I would see the benefits of it, but as it currently complicates things for us, I've decided I'm going to be irritated about it," she said with a grim smile.

He laughed and smiled in return. This was one of the things he liked about Biankara: she could see things from so many different angles. He raised his glass. "Well, here's to being irritated about it right now."

She snorted. "To irritation," she replied, clinking her glass against his.

VALFRIC GRUNTED AS HIS SHIELD WAS KNOCKED INTO HIM. THE FORCE OF THE BLOW NEARLY unseated him from his horse. His breath came out in a whoosh, and he gritted his teeth. He loved it. *Finally, a challenge,* he thought to himself. He pushed the other man's shield with his own, taking the moment to adjust himself in the saddle. For its part, his mount seemed equally engaged.

The two animals bit at each other and reared up, trying to knock the other off balance. Valfric reached down into his Essaeris and created straps that held him better to the saddle. His sword came up just in time to block the man's blade.

This was not going to be a battle where one side completely wiped out the other. He'd thought that's how battles went when he was a child— that men and women fought until the last one standing, but he'd almost never seen that in his life unless one of the sides was unarmed. One side would usually decide they didn't have an advantage or were going to lose, and they'd disengage. At that point, the winning side had to choose whether to pursue their enemy to inflict more casualties or take their spoils and go home.

Valfric was firmly in the camp of the latter. Thraindel and Aelric struggled with this mentality, but they understood. They'd all seen losses turn into wins, and they weren't here to defend their homes and lands. They were here for loot. The opposing side was likewise not there to defend their homes, either. They were trying to protect their spoils of war. If they thought they were about to lose, they'd abandon their belongings and retreat. If Valfric went after them at that point, those same men would go from fighting to save a few carts of objects to fighting for their lives. That changed the game.

Currently, the band Valfric and his group were attacking had mostly encircled themselves on horses, doing a good job of forming a shield wall. Valfric fought what he assumed was their commander. The man was young, with flaming red hair and vibrant blue eyes. He didn't appear afraid or even angry. This man may have been young, but he was a professional. All the men in this group were. They'd come from months or years of fighting and were working as a unified team.

Valfric's wolves ran around, assisting his settlement mates as they struggled against the other group. The fight had begun like so many others. Valfric and his people had charged out of the forest on horseback, attempting to scatter the group. They had managed to catch them completely off guard, which led to a few early wins, but that changed quickly.

Instead of scattering, the men had formed around a handful of carts. They'd abandoned others, which were now being pulled away by Valfric's people. They wouldn't make off with everything the other group had, but what they'd taken was an easy score.

The red-haired man swung his sword at Valfric, who caught the blow with his own sword. The red-haired man lunged in his saddle, and Valfric felt the man push him back. The move would have knocked him off if he hadn't secured himself with the straps. He stayed in the saddle, but the red-haired man drove the pommel of his sword down, striking Valfric on the cheek. He tried to turn away from the blow, but pain exploded in his face as the pommel connected.

His vision swayed for a moment, and then there was a yell and the sound of metal clashing. His vision cleared, and he saw Ilara engaging the man. Valfric backed off and spat blood to the side. He spun, seeing the carts being pulled away. He looked at his people and shouted, "Back!"

Some of the others seemed reluctant to break away from the battle since they were winning, but his main team complied and encouraged the others. Ilara broke from the red-headed man, who didn't break ranks to pursue her. *Professionals,* he reminded himself. His team made sure everyone was backing off before turning to ride away. With a flick of his mind, his wolves nipped at the horses of the other group, lest they decide to attack Valfric's team with their backs turned.

When they had some distance between them and the other group, Valfric turned to Ilara. "Thanks," he said, giving her a grin.

She looked over at him and smirked. "Happy to save you anytime."

He laughed, turning to spit more blood from his mouth.

"Did anything break?" she asked, this time more serious.

He felt his face and winced a little before shaking his head. "No, I don't think so. That was a good hit on his part, though. Ulfgara favors him."

"Yes, she does. That group was competent," she commented.

He grunted in agreement. He wasn't angry about being hit. In fact, he kind of liked it. Usually, Valfric couldn't find anyone who could come anywhere near matching him, but the redhead had. It made him feel good.

"But I figured I had to save you," Ilara said.

He turned to her and raised an eyebrow. "And why is that?"

She shrugged. "Like I said, Aelric is too big. We've been on the road a lot. I need something comfortable."

He threw his head back and laughed. "That again!"

"Always, she's a smart woman," a deep voice called out.

Valfric looked over to see Aelric grinning at them. "Fuck you both," Valfric said good-naturedly.

Aelric laughed again. "That's Ilara's job, not mine."

"Oh, that's not true. What about Thraindel?" Ilara said.

Thraindel piped up. "It's my job to fuck everybody. Sorry, Val, you aren't special," he said with a laugh.

Valfric smiled, enjoying the banter. Even though they hadn't outright won against the other group, it felt good to be challenged, and they still had a decent take.

"We'll need to ride for a while. I don't care to have them try to take back what we've taken from them," Valfric said.

Aelric's face turned serious. "I was thinking the same thing. It's not the same easy pickings as it was at the beginning."

Valfric shook his head. "No. The size of that party was deceiving. Those men were good."

"That they were," Ilara commented.

She looked forward at the others from their settlement as they moved ahead. "They did better today. They're learning."

Valfric nodded once. "They are learning. It's good, and about time."

"Once we reach camp, I'll make sure the wolves are on watch, and I'll leave one of them to keep an eye on that group," he said.

"Good call," Aelric agreed. "I don't think they'll mess with an Essaerist."

Valfric shook his head. "I doubt they will, but they didn't seem overly shocked to see one either."

"No, they weren't," Ilara remarked. "My guess is they've worked with them before."

That thought had run through Valfric's mind as well. The group they had attacked hadn't been thrilled to see an Essaerist, but it wasn't something new to them or something that inspired awe or fear. That either meant they had worked with Essaerists, or they had back in their home settlement. Either way, Valfric knew that gave them an edge that most groups they encountered wouldn't possess. He wouldn't be able to use fear or intimidation if needed. But it also meant the group probably wouldn't pursue them. If they had worked with an Essaerist before or been around them, then they knew Valfric had at least one Essaerite watching to make sure they weren't being pursued. There would be no sneaking up on Valfric and his team.

After a few hours, they came to a stop in a clearing and decided to make camp. Valfric's face felt better, and he dismounted, quickly setting up a tent with three wolves patrolling the perimeter. He kept them close and barked orders to a few of the people, telling them that they were going to need to post watches.

"No getting yourselves drunk and stupid tonight," he said sternly to some of the men. They nodded grimly.

They had learned that lesson the hard way. While Valfric hated knowing they'd lost people from their settlement, at least they had learned it so they wouldn't have to experience it again.

CHAPTER 13

Frost clung to a handful of plants outside Caelwen's cottage, and her breath puffed out in a big plume as she made her way to the woodpile. Logs thunked and knocked together as she picked them up, gathering them under her arm haphazardly. Despite her tunic, the logs sucked the heat from her, and she shivered, causing one to slip. She tried to grab it and almost dropped the others.

"Shit, fuck," she grumbled.

She got the logs situated and made her way inside.

The inside of her home was warm, and the air was pleasantly tinged with the scent of the fire crackling in the fireplace. Next to the fire, her Essaerite stump was finishing making some bread. Caelwen walked in, placed some of the firewood next to the fireplace, took a couple of pieces, and tossed them in. The fire crackled and popped as the new logs landed.

She noticed Treftune on the table nibbling at something. As she got closer, he stuffed all of it in his mouth.

"What are you eating?" she asked, raising an eyebrow.

The little creature swallowed and skittered partway up the wall. Caelwen searched about, trying to figure out what he had stolen. She inspected the table, but there hadn't been any food there. She checked the shelves to see if he had taken anything. Treftune was a talented thief, in Caelwen's opinion. Many of the Essaeris items she had weren't designed for food preservation but to keep the little shit from stealing. Indeed, Treftune's thievery had been one of the driving forces that made her push her powers when she was younger. She'd had the choice of getting better with Essaeris or eating whatever the little critter didn't want.

She looked over at the fire, seeing the stump cooking, and she couldn't see any missing rolls from the bread it was baking. Besides, the stump was rather adept at defending against Treftune's sneaky little paws. She turned back to Treftune. She eyed him and walked up towards him. He gazed back at her, almost in challenge. She focused on his face, seeing crumbs and a bit of jam there. She smirked.

"Who did you steal that from?" she asked.

His paws came out, wiping his face. He wiped away the crumbs and licked his paws, looking up at her like he had done nothing. She smiled.

"One of these days, you're going to steal something from the wrong person," she said, though she didn't mean it.

Treftune had stolen from everybody in the settlement. In fact, it was just assumed that he would steal from you at some point in time. You could try to stop him, or you could even try to chase him away, but generally speaking, you were dealing with one or more of his Essaerites. If you managed to get a hold of one of them, they'd bite you. And if they didn't bite you, you knew that it was a ruse and that there was another Essaerite somewhere in your home, raiding your pantries. It was easier just to let him steal whatever he wanted, in most people's experience.

But Valfglideas were considered good luck, so no one wanted to make him mad. Still, she couldn't help but laugh, wondering who had been had this time.

As she thought about it, she decided it was probably her uncle. Treftune enjoyed tormenting the man, which was something she had a hard time getting irritated with him about. He leaped up on her shoulder and curled around the curve of her neck, and she scratched behind his ear.

The days were starting to grow short and the nights long. It was a time of year that Caelwen both enjoyed and disliked. She enjoyed the downtime and being able to lie about and stay inside, but at the same time, that was what she hated about this time of year as well.

There were things to do, of course, but not as many as when it was summertime and light out. After breakfast, she contented herself with doing things around the cottage and taking care of some odds and ends. It was midday when one of her Essaerites saw something. It was one of the birds that she had orbiting the settlement.

She moved into the bird, seeing what it was seeing. She saw a caravan approaching. Upon closer inspection, the caravan was made entirely of men dressed in the garb of warriors, with shields and swords. Her heart began to pick up for a moment. But as her Essaerite swooped in closer, she started to recognize some of the people. Her heart continued to beat fast, but it wasn't out of fear this time.

She pulled herself back into her body and grinned, looking at Treftune. "Wulfgren is home," she said with a smile.

The Valfglidea chittered and chirped, and Caelwen moved over to the corner where she had set her cloak. She threw it over her shoulders and walked out the door. She began traipsing down the road towards the settlement center, a bounce in her step. She had been looking forward to this day for some time.

As she passed by homes and cottages, she waved at people, letting them know that the men from their settlement were home from war. Others were gathering in the center of the settlement when Caelwen made it there. Her Essaerite was still following the group of men, who were well into town now and almost to the center.

As they got closer, she could see them with her own eyes, noticing that the men were dirty but seemed to be in good spirits. Many of them smiled as they rode in, greeting those on the streets. As they came to the center and stopped, everyone gathered around them, greeting their loved ones or looking for loved ones who were missing.

Caelwen walked forward, seeing a man with flaming red hair and bright blue eyes. He grinned at her and walked up, wrapping his arms around her, picking her up and swinging her around. She laughed and smiled, holding him close.

"Welcome home, Wulfgren," she said as he set her down.

She'd been afraid that he wouldn't come home, that he'd been killed in the war, but here he was, standing in front of her with all of his limbs and what appeared to be all of his fingers.

He looked down at her and smiled. "How are you?"

She smiled back up at him. "I'm doing well. How was the war?"

"It wasn't too bad, all things considered." He turned his gaze back to the caravan. "And we didn't lose too many people," he said, though there was a hint of sadness in his tone. Caelwen peered over his shoulder, seeing that there were some missing members of their settlement. She felt a twinge of sadness for those families who had lost somebody.

"Welcome home, all!" Ilfthandor's voice called out, and everyone turned to Caelwen's uncle. He was wearing a broad smile as he approached the men. They all regarded him warmly, save for her brother, who gave him a quizzical look.

He looked back over at Caelwen. "He's still in charge?"

She smirked. "You knew I wasn't going to challenge him."

"Coward," he commented with a smile.

Ilfthandor walked up to them, clapping his nephew on the shoulder and hugging him. To his credit, her brother played the role back and hugged her uncle closely, appearing to be happy to see him. "How did our men fare in the far-off battles?" Ilfthandor asked.

Wulfgren grinned. "Everyone did well," he said to cheers from the people.

Ilfthandor looked at the caravan, almost disappointed. "Are these the riches you've brought back?"

Caelwen saw her brother grimace.

"Yes, most of them. Unfortunately, we were attacked on the road," he said. "We didn't lose any of our people, but we did lose some of what we made in the war," he said darkly. He glanced over at Caelwen. "They had an Essaerist with them."

She nodded, making a note to ask him about it later.

Ilfthandor brushed it off. "Well, we are glad to have you home."

Caelwen wasn't sure if she believed him or not. After all, Wulfgren had led the war party that had left a few years ago, and now that he was back, he had not only the loyalty of the men who had gone with him but also their families, along with the loyalty of the people that cared for Caelwen and her parents. For Ilfthandor, this could be a difficult time, she realized, and her uncle may not have been extremely happy to see Wulfgren home.

But even though he didn't seem to be happy about the lack of loot they brought with them, part of her wondered if he wasn't secretly pleased with it, as it might make Wulfgren look weak or incompetent. She tried to push the thoughts from her mind and instead focused on the good news of people being home. She greeted everybody from the war party, with many of them giving Treftune little bits of food that they had with them, a few commenting that it was better to give the little Valfglidea food than for him to steal it. She laughed, enjoying how everyone still remembered him.

———

CAELWEN SAT NEXT TO THE FIRE IN HER HOME. ACROSS FROM HER, WULFGREN SAT CLOSE to the flames, warming himself. He looked older than she'd expected. She'd known he'd look older by the time he came home, but there seemed to be more to it than age alone. He'd seen and experienced the world in a way she hadn't.

It was nice to have him back. It felt like a weight had come off of her she hadn't even truly known was there. Wulfgren was the last thread to a carefree time of life when they'd been young and hadn't worried about anything in the world. They hadn't always gotten along. In fact, Caelwen was sure they'd spent more time fighting than playing when they were younger, but that time was gone, and now she trusted him more than anyone else in her life.

"How's it been managing Ilfthandor?" he asked wryly.

She laughed. "He's a cunt, but you knew that already."

"Well, I guess some things don't change, do they?" he mused. "You, on the other hand, have."

She cocked an eyebrow. "How so?"

He gestured to her. "You're so much older than when I left. I know it's only been a few years, but I almost don't recognize you."

She smiled. "I could say the same."

He smirked. "I half expected to come home to find you married."

She laughed. "No husband here."

"Their loss," he commented.

She smiled softly. "Thanks. But I think we both know that isn't true."

His expression softened. "Blight or not, you're a catch. Just because you can't have children doesn't mean you wouldn't be an amazing wife."

She shrugged. "I suppose I do have my talents." He laughed heartily, and she went on. "So what was it like?"

He was thoughtful for a moment. "Like how I thought it would be and also different at the same time. I didn't mind it, if that's what you're wondering. Part of me thought I would. I was worried that the killing would somehow get to me, but it didn't." He stared into the fire. "Losing people is what got to me," he said with a sigh. "But that is the way of these things."

"You seem like you're much wiser now. I think Ilfthandor is intimidated by you," she commented.

"He should be," he said honestly. "While he's been fucking around for the last few years, I've been growing. That said, he's too old for me to challenge. It wouldn't be right. What has our uncle been up to while I've been gone?"

"Scheming mostly, but he's had us conduct a handful of raids," she said.

His eyes widened. "My sweet little sister has been doing raids?" he said sarcastically.

"What makes you think that I was a part of them?" she asked.

Wulfgren snorted. "You're an Essaerist; he'd be a fool not to have you help."

She relented. "Well, you're right. I mostly keep an eye out for trouble. I know you saw that puma out front."

He nodded. Caelwen had been a competent Essaerist when he'd left, but she'd grown a lot in the meantime. She didn't have anyone to teach her growing up, and it had taken her a long time to get the basics under her belt. While her start had been slow, she'd come a long way.

"I saw that thing. How is it?" he asked.

She shrugged. "It's decent, but it's really more there as a guard. If I need to go into battle, I use more advanced ones. I spent a little time with an Essaerist who came through the settlement shortly after you left. He gave me a few pointers that helped me overcome some of the things holding me back. He said that I would grow quickly, and he was right."

Wulfgren nodded in approval. "That's good." He sat back. "I honestly never saw you as a warrior, though. You've always had a lot of fight in you, and I know you can handle yourself."

"It's not what I prefer, but I am decent enough at it," she said. "I'm more like Mom. I focus on healing if I can."

"In my experience, there is more use in that than fighting," he said.

She was thoughtful for a moment.

"What is it?" he asked.

She bit her lip in thought as she fixed her eyes on him. He'd just gotten home, but the raid on the caravan was weighing on her. "You said you were attacked on your way home? And that they had an Essaerist?" she asked instead of answering his question.

"We were. It was a small Ulfgarath raiding party," he said, "and yes, they did have one. That's the only reason they got the drop on us. But they didn't get the most valuable loot we earned in the war," he said, not seeming bothered by it.

He's changed, she thought. There was a time when she very much doubted that something like that wouldn't have bothered him, but now it seemed like he was telling her about a hunting trip.

"Why?" he asked.

"Just curious," she said.

He smiled at her knowingly. "It might have been a few years, but I still know when you're keeping something from me."

She glared at him for a moment. "Fine."

She launched into the story about when the caravan had come into the settlement. He listened, not interjecting, and she could see his expression harden as the story went on. When she was done, she felt like there was a weight off her chest. "I know it's probably nothing, but I have been on alert ever since. Most of the settlements around here didn't like us before that. I'm not sure if they know about what happened or not."

He shook his head. "Ilfthandor is a fucking idiot," he spat. "You were right to help. I know you didn't have much of a choice, but what a fuck-up." He ran his hand through his hair. "Losing Durgard is bad. We need a smith, especially if Ilfthandor has managed to piss off every settlement around us," he said angrily. He shook his head again. "And I'm sure they do know about it. With me and some of the other men gone, I'm sure the only thing that kept this settlement from being raided was you."

She felt a little uneasy. "I'm not that powerful," she said.

"You don't have to be," he said. "No one knows how strong you are, and the fact is that most people think Essaerists are more powerful than they are." He shrugged. "I guess other than the Lysandrian ones."

"What do you mean?" she asked.

"About the Lysandrian ones?" He confirmed.

"Yes, what about them?" she asked.

"They're strong," he said. "We saw and fought alongside some. They were more powerful than most Gwenthari Essaerists. Some of ours were strong, but those were old, and the Lysandrian Essaerists were young. But a lot of us came home. If there are men who have come home from another settlement that fought alongside Essaerists, then they might not be as afraid of you as they were before."

She looked at the fire, feeling her frustration grow. "So Ilfthandor fucked us?"

"He might have," he admitted. "But only time will tell."

She tried to push it from her mind. There was nothing to be done now other than to keep an eye out. "I've kept your cottage in good repair, but there's no food there. Would you like to stay here tonight, or do you want to go home after dinner?"

He smiled warmly. "I've been roughing it for a couple of years. I like the sound of sleeping in my own bed for once."

She returned the smile. "I can only imagine."

Her mind flicked out to the stump. "Well, dinner will be done soon," she said and stood to set the table.

CHAPTER 14

Xavieno felt his legs and lungs burn as he started up the incline. They were nearing the end of their run, and he was looking forward to being finished with it. Sweat poured down his brow and the back of his neck. Weight pressed down on his shoulders in the form of a vest meant to simulate the feel of a fully loaded pack, plus an additional thirty pounds. The vest was hot and oppressive, and sweat trickled down his brow. Xavieno would have questioned if it were only thirty pounds heavier had he not been the one to create it.

Every legionnaire exercised to keep themselves fit and ready to march. When on the march, the legion moved twenty miles a day at a standard pace. At a hard march, they moved twenty-five miles per day. But it wasn't just the march that one had to make it through. Once at the campsite, camp had to be built. That might entail clearing trees and rocks out of the way, along with building any fortifications needed. At a minimum, this involved digging a ditch and erecting a fence, as well as creating roads inside the camp. The next morning, if they were on the march again, they would tear it down and go another twenty or twenty-five miles, then repeat the process.

So, they exercised regularly, pushing themselves harder than they thought they would in the field. Xavieno didn't mind it; he knew he'd be thankful for it at some point in time. But at the end of every run and workout, he was ready to be done, just like he was now.

It didn't help that Geraldox, his sergeant, seemed to know the exact paths and routes to take to ensure they had the shittiest climbs up hills and the most rugged descents back down. He kept their pace steady and fast, the whole squad jogging in unison as if they were marching. Everyone's feet hit the ground simultaneously, and they all jogged silently, keeping a tight formation. Discipline was one of the key tenets of the legions, and Xavieno appreciated this more than anything else.

Geraldox was at the head of the formation. He was older than the rest of the squad and a seasoned combat veteran, about halfway through his twenty-year contract with the legion. With short, bristly black hair and a muscular build, Geraldox wasn't an attractive man. Xavieno wasn't sure how many times Geraldox's nose had been broken over the years, but it was more of a squiggle than a nose at this point. Everything about him looked like he had taken a beating after beating over his life, and Xavieno suspected he had dished out even worse. But he was an extremely good commanding officer, and Xavieno appreciated him.

Geraldox worked hard with each of his men and took their training and status to heart. Xavieno had been an excellent fighter when he joined the legion, but Geraldox had taken him to another level. The same could be said for his discipline and the way he viewed combat and life in the legion in general. He made you live it, breathe it, and love it, while also kicking your ass and making you run up horribly steep hills.

On either side of Xavieno, jogging with the same amount of sweat and determination on their faces, were Isaios and Pandros. He enjoyed both men, and they all got on well together. In combat, it wasn't guaranteed that Xavieno would be in the main ranks of the legion. Chances were, he would be in the back controlling his Essaerites, with these two men stationed near him to keep him safe should he have to focus completely on his Essaerites. Generally, their squad would wait in the back of the third line, waiting to see if they were needed. Given Xavieno hadn't seen much in the way of combat—just a handful of skirmishes— he wondered if that would change if his suspicions about the Gwenthari proved to be true.

He thought about this as they jogged. What would it be like being on the march in an actual war? Yes, there'd be the twenty miles a day, but that didn't mean they would march every day. In fact, they might only march a couple of days and then spend a day or two in camp. If that happened, they would spend their time fortifying the camp, scouting the surrounding area, and, of course, building roads and supply lines to keep the legions moving forward. Like an unstoppable wave cascading up north through the rest of the continent if need be.

They crested a hill, and he could see down to the city and base below. He tried not to get his hopes up. It wasn't uncommon for Geraldox to let them think they were almost home, just to change directions and head up another hill. He'd learned to assume that until he was back in Fioralba's arms in the evening, there was no potential for rest.

He saw Geraldox look back at them with a wicked grin on his face. "You fucks think I'm going to make you turn around and run some more, don't you?" he said, his tone holding the malicious edge that only a sergeant could manage.

They all kept silent, not wanting to bait him. He looked only partially disappointed. "Maybe I should run you more. None of you are bitching yet," he said and grinned again, but he didn't seem to have the heart for it.

"I'm fine," Pandros shouted. "Could go for a little bit longer, couldn't you guys?"

Next to Xavieno, Isaios smiled. "Yeah, I'm not feeling winded at all," he called out.

Geraldox barked a laugh. "Good try. Lucky for you, I have different plans for you guys today," he said with that same wicked grin.

They continued to run, heading down towards the base, and Xavieno had to admit he was having a good time. He was exhausted, yes, but there was something about training that he seemed to love. As they made it back into the base, they saw other squads returning from similar runs or finishing up exercises. Others were still in the middle of whatever physical training their commanding officers had inflicted on them that day. Some men were holding logs as a group and running around; others were doing push-ups, and others were climbing ropes or otherwise pushing themselves in some way, shape, or form.

Geraldox led them to a series of barrels filled with water. He came to a stop, and all the men took time to catch their breaths and take a drink.

"Xavieno, the vests," Geraldox said between hard breaths of his own.

Xavieno reached out, and with a flick of his mind, released the weights and the vests, which all disappeared from his squad mates. As his vest vanished, he felt cool air run across his sweaty tunic, and it felt wonderful.

He took another drink of water, his breath slowing and his heart coming down to a reasonable pace.

Xavieno saw Mariokos approaching them. He nodded as he saw his friend.

"Alessandros wants to see all commanders and Essaerists," Mariokos said as he reached them.

Geraldox grunted his assent, and Xavieno dipped a towel into the water barrel and wiped his brow.

"Do you know what it's about?" he asked.

Mariokos shrugged. "I'm not sure."

Xavieno didn't care for Alessandros, and he wasn't sure that anybody did, but Xavieno's opinion didn't actually matter. So, as they finished up, they made their way over to a central area where Alessandros was standing with a few of his commanders. Xavieno turned to Geraldox.

"Any idea what this is?" he asked.

Geraldox shrugged. "Beats the fuck out of me, but I doubt it's anything good if that prick is the one telling us."

Xavieno smirked. Geraldox kept a pretty tight lip around most of the squad, but Xavieno was different. After all, he was an Essaerist and was technically higher up in the food chain than the rest of the men in his squad. So Geraldox tended to let down his guard a little bit when he was around him.

Everyone gathered around Alessandros. He was middle-aged with shaggy, light brown hair and green eyes. Alessandros looked every part the Aristolios mixed with a soldier. His build was athletic and lean, though Xavieno wasn't sure how much time the man had ever spent in combat, if any at all.

He surveyed the group of men before him, doing a mental tally to make sure that everyone was present.

"I'm going to get right to it," Alessandros said. "We're going to war." He let the statement hang in the air for a moment.

Xavieno wasn't sure if he was expecting to see any reactions from those gathered around, but there weren't any. Everyone knew they would go to war at some point, and those present were all seasoned Legionnaires, all of them in command. They had seen combat many times before. The only exceptions to that were Xavieno and Mariokos. For the others, being told they were going to war was akin to being told that lunch would be served an hour later than normal. It was just part of life.

Still, everyone's eyes seemed hard as they looked at the Major.

Alessandros continued. "We're moving north, up to the frontier. We're going to take it to the Gwenthari. We leave in a couple of months. Start preparing your men, and prepare the Legion to go. This is not going to be a quick expedition, nor is it going to be an easy one," he said, trying to sound like a commander.

It came off all right, in Xavieno's opinion. Alessandros went on, explaining that they would be joining several other Legions moving north. The primary target was going to be the Ulfgarath, the once-mighty people who had sacked the capital of Lysandrian a few hundred years ago. It appeared that Lysandrian was now going to get its revenge.

Xavieno didn't mind the news. He had been waiting for this call since he joined the Legion. Part of him thrilled at the idea. He was looking forward to battle, to testing himself, and to the glories of war. Next to him, Mariokos looked appraising—not apprehensive, just listening, trying to catch all the details.

A few men asked questions about logistics and items that needed to be done. As per usual, Alessandros pawned those questions off on lower-ranking officers. He had given the news he was here to give, but he hadn't gotten the reaction he hoped for. Xavieno could see it in his expression. He wanted to see the men cheer, or be angry, or surprised, or inspired, but that wasn't going to happen. Everyone around were professional soldiers, and there wasn't a single man in the group who respected Alessandros.

But be that as it may, they would follow his orders.

Before dismissing everyone, Alessandros called out, "Essaerists, come and see me."

Xavieno sighed, as did Mariokos next to him. As the rest of the men left, Mariokos and Xavieno approached Alessandros, who appraised them.

"Is this it?" he asked.

Xavieno looked around. "We're the only two Essaerists in this legion," he said.

Alessandros huffed. "What about your women? Xavieno, I know you're married," he said and looked over at Mariokos. "And what about the woman that you're with? Biankara."

Xavieno shrugged. "They're not in the legion. They help the legion, obviously, but they're not in it."

"Should they be part of this meeting?" Mariokos asked.

Alessandros looked thoughtful. "Yes, they should be. Go get them and bring them back to command in an hour."

Xavieno nodded.

Mariokos said, "Alessandros, I will try to get Biankara here, but—"

Alessandros cut him off. "Find a way to get her here. Either she's going with you, or she's not going with you. If she is, her ass needs to be in the meeting. If she's not, then she can go do whatever it is that she was doing before," he said and walked off.

Xavieno saw Mariokos bristle a little bit, and he looked over at his friend as Alessandros walked away.

"He's such an asshole," Mariokos muttered under his breath.

"That he is," Xavieno replied. "Think you'll be able to get Biankara here?"

Mariokos shrugged. "Probably. She'll at least want to find out what's going on, but I don't think she's going to appreciate being talked to the way Alessandros thinks he can talk to people."

Xavieno shrugged. "She is an Essaerist. She has to listen to him, at least for a little while longer."

The women didn't have the same obligations that men did, but they still had some, and Biankara was of an age where she had responsibilities. That said, her family was powerful, and while Alessandros might have thought himself quite the man and leader, Xavieno very much doubted he wanted to deal with Biankara's family. Xavieno patted Mariokos's shoulder.

"I'm gonna go get Fioralba. See you back here in an hour," he said with a wry smile.

Mariokos laughed. "Yeah, hopefully."

As Mariokos walked away, Xavieno turned and called after him, "What? Are you scared to tell Biankara that she has orders?"

Mariokos laughed. "Maybe a little bit," he admitted sheepishly.

Xavieno laughed harder. He wasn't about to tell Mariokos that he was a coward or anything of the sort. Xavieno was scared for Mariokos. He wasn't sure how long his friend would live if he had to tell Biankara that she had orders to come and show up to a meeting.

Xavieno found Fioralba in their home. As he walked in, she looked up, surprised to see him.

"What are you doing home so early?" she asked. Concern crossed her face. "Is everything alright?"

"It's fine," he said, walking into the room. "But I have news." He paused for a moment before adding, "We're going to war with the Gwenthari."

He watched a wave of emotions cross his wife's face. Fioralba knew that war was a distinct possibility, and she had said she didn't necessarily mind the thought of it but wasn't looking forward to being in the camps. Fioralba was talented, smart, compassionate, and wonderful in so many ways, and that's why he loved her. But he knew war could be hard for her. She always expected things to happen to others and not herself or those she cared about, and she detested violence, though she enjoyed that Xavieno was a warrior and appreciated that part of him. She didn't enjoy violence itself; she found it repulsive and tended to shut down around it.

He could see concern crossing her face now with the reality that they were going to war. She would likely see violence. Would Fioralba fight? No, never. That wasn't a woman's place, but it didn't change the fact that she would still witness it. And she would see the aftermath of it.

She took a few breaths and then said, "Okay, so we're going to war." She nodded. "So be it."

He smiled tightly and walked up to her, placing his hands on her shoulders. "It will be fine, love. The Gwenthari are nothing to us."

She smiled tightly. "I know. It's just... it's just not news I was expecting today."

He could understand that.

"There's more," he said.

She raised an eyebrow. "More?"

"Yes," he said. "Alessandros wants to meet with all the Essaerists who are going to be in the Legion, including their spouses or partners. As you're an Essaerist, he wants to meet with you too. We have a meeting in just a little while with him."

She looked taken aback.

"What do you think the meeting is going to be about?" she asked.

He shrugged. "Probably preparing the Legion for battle. We'll leave in a month or two, and there's a lot of work that needs to be done. Equipment that needs to be made, supplies that need arranging, training that has to happen—things of that nature." Xavieno said, "And Essaerists are some of the best when it comes to manufacturing," he commented.

She nodded, understanding. "I see. We're going to need to help with preparations."

This seemed to sit well with her, and Xavieno was happy to see it. Fioralba enjoyed working, and she relished using her abilities to create and accomplish tasks. Where Biankara wouldn't be happy about the prospect of having to use her powers for manual labor or doing mundane tasks to help the Legions, Xavieno knew that Fioralba wouldn't have that problem. She'd relish the work and lose herself in it.

This was a good thing because he suspected there was going to be a lot of it.

She smiled tightly. "Alright. I guess, when's the meeting?"

"We can head there now," he said. "Let me just clean up real quick."

"Of course," she said.

Xavieno reached into his Essaeris and created a bowl of warm water and soap. He released his clothes and washed himself off quickly, wiping away the grime and dust from the road of their morning run. Once he was done, he created a fresh tunic and put it on.

He held his hand out to his wife. "Shall we, my love?"

She smiled warmly.

"We shall," she said lightly.

They walked out the door and through the base. To her credit, Fioralba seemed completely fine right now, and that relaxed Xavieno. He didn't want her to be tense when she met Alessandros for the first time and had to deal with his bullshit. Though a part of him wondered if Alessandros would avoid the bullshit. With the women, he'd probably just give a simple order and be on his way. But he wasn't sure.

Another thing he looked forward to was seeing Biankara with Alessandros. It could be entertaining, and he made a comment about that to Fioralba. She giggled softly.

"Oh, it will be very entertaining if he tries to pull anything with her," she said. "I'm kind of looking forward to the meeting now," she added after a few moments.

Xavieno chuckled. "Yeah, there is something about it, isn't there?"

And there was. There was something about watching Biankara get high and mighty and talk down to someone or lose her temper. It was satisfying to watch in so many ways unless you were on the receiving end of it, which Xavieno had been many, many times since he had met Biankara. But he didn't think today would be one of those days, so instead of not looking forward to seeing her, he was pretty excited about the prospect.

They made it to where Alessandros was stationed. His office was nice, as far as offices in a base could go. He saw Alessandros standing in the room with one of his secretaries as Xavieno and Fioralba entered.

Alessandros looked at them. "Where are the other two?"

"They should be here shortly, sir," Xavieno said.

Alessandros nodded and ignored Xavieno and Fioralba.

A few minutes later, Mariokos came in the door, accompanied by Biankara. In a way, that spoke very highly of Mariokos, that he'd managed to convince her to come down on a whim, but she didn't look happy about it, and Mariokos looked like he had been through the wringer.

As he entered the room, Alessandros looked up at Mariokos and Biankara. "What took you so long?" he demanded.

"Sorry, sir," Mariokos said.

Biankara instantly fired up. "Excuse me," she said. "What took me so long?" Her tone held a level of sternness and condemnation that Xavieno wasn't sure he'd ever heard before.

His eyes flicked over to Alessandros, expecting to see the man puff up, but somehow he seemed to shrink just a little bit. *Coward,* Xavieno thought. Actually, he didn't think Alessandros was a coward for shrinking away from Biankara; he just wanted to see a fight.

Biankara went on. "I am not someone you can simply summon at your whim," she said, stalking into the room. "I understand we're going to war and that you're going to be needing the help of all the Essaerists who are coming along, but you should know that Mariokos and I are not married or even betrothed. I am with him, and I am coming with him, but I am not something for you to command around. Do you understand, Major?" she said, her voice stern and harsh.

Alessandros looked like he was about to puff up, but Biankara's eyes grew sharper and harder, making Alessandros quaver just a little. He didn't respond to her but instead launched into what he had prepared.

"As the four of you know, we're going to war. Not every legion has Essaerists, and I fully expect that ours will take advantage of all of you. Ladies, obviously, you will not be seeing any combat. But that doesn't mean you're not going to assist the Legion when in the field and before we go," he said.

"As I'm sure Mariokos and Xavieno have told you, the Legion's true power lies in logistics," he continued. "As such, we need help with preparations. Other Legions are going to be manufacturing much of the equipment they need, as will we. But since we have Essaerists with us, that speeds up our process. We're going to be producing some of the equipment needed for the other Legions, as well as repairing existing equipment."

"Mariokos and Xavieno, I want you to focus on training with the other soldiers. I know the Essaerites you create can be very handy. I want you to focus on ones that are similar to Barbarians, who have wild, brawler-type fighting styles," Alessandros instructed.

Mariokos and Xavieno nodded.

He looked at the ladies. "For you two, I have a list of items that need to be manufactured and repaired. Is that something you're up to?"

Fioralba nodded. "Yes, sir."

Alessandros looked at Biankara, who nodded. "Yes, we're both extremely competent Essaerists. I'm sure we can build and maintain anything you need."

"Good," Alessandros said. "That's all for now. My secretary will get you the lists of items needed," he said dismissively.

They walked out, and Xavieno had to admit he was a little disappointed. As soon as they were out of earshot from the office, he glanced over at Fioralba, who smirked.

"You know, Biankara, we were hoping for a lot more than what we got," she said.

Biankara chuckled. "I wondered if that's what you two were sharing glances about," she said, turning up her nose a little. "I'm not here for your entertainment," she added, though her voice sounded jovial.

Xavieno laughed. "Well, still, a guy can hope."

Biankara laughed. "Oh, I am sure Alessandros and I are going to have many wonderful conversations during this war," she said, sighing. "He seems like a true asshole," she looked over at Mariokos. "You weren't exaggerating."

"You can tell he's an asshole with just one conversation?" Xavieno asked.

Biankara looked over at him. "I could tell he was an asshole before he opened his mouth," she said, then shrugged. "Thankfully, I'm very skilled in the ways of dealing with assholes, so he shouldn't be too difficult for me to manage. But boys, tell me, is this war going to be bad?"

Xavieno shook his head. "No, we outclass the Gwenthari in every way."

"But we're going into the frontier," Mariokos said. "That's their home turf. Also, we're not going to have the infrastructure we're used to. It's going to be a lot of building as we go."

Xavieno shrugged. "It always is. But they have main supply roads and things of that nature. The Gwenthari may be diminished, but they used to be an advanced society. I'm sure they have plenty of infrastructure."

Mariokos shrugged. "Maybe. But I wouldn't count them out just yet."

Xavieno smiled. "Oh, I'm sure there's going to be some of them that are tough. That I have no doubt. But compared to the legions—"

Mariokos relented. "Fair enough. Compared to the legions, not so much."

Xavieno grinned. "See? There's the spirit."

Mariokos shook his head.

CHAPTER 15
TWENTY YEARS AGO

Valfric could feel his Essaeris just under the surface. He reached out, trying to touch it. The power felt vast to him, almost like the stories he'd been told about the ocean, but despite how big it felt, it was just out of reach. He tried to do as Garethor had instructed. He cleared his mind and tried to reach out to that ocean of power. He grasped it for just a moment, feeling it begin to infuse him. His excitement rose, and his mind buzzed with it. Along with the shift in thoughts went his hold on the power. He felt it slip away.

He huffed.

"Again," an old, craggy voice said from next to him.

Valfric looked over at him. Garethor was ancient, and Valfric was pretty sure that he had been born before the beginning of time, though he had been told on several occasions that if he made comments like that again, he'd get smacked. So he didn't make any comments. But still, that didn't mean that Valfric was wrong. It wasn't possible for someone to be as old-looking as Garethor and not be older than time itself. It just wasn't.

Valfric was inside Garethor's house. Garethor was the settlement's wise man, and Valfric could understand why, as he was older than time itself. The old man was frail and wizened, with deep folds and wrinkles on his face and skin. His hands shook whenever he moved, and Valfric could see his veins underneath his paper-thin skin. His hair was long and gray and thinning on top, and he had a long beard that came down almost to his waist. When Valfric thought about it, Garethor had probably started growing the beard before the beginning of time as well.

Garethor wasn't an Essaerist, but his mother had been, so he was the closest thing to an instructor that Valfric was going to get. Also, he was the settlement's wise man, so it was his responsibility.

"It's not working," Valfric said.

Garethor's head went up and down in a slow nod. "But it almost worked."

Valfric cocked an eyebrow. "How can you know? You can't use Essaeris," he accused.

"Tone," Garethor said, his hand twitching toward his walking stick.

In Valfric's experience, even though Garethor was old and frail, he could manage to hit pretty hard with that stick, so Valfric tried to make his tone more respectful. "How do you know it was working if you can't use Essaeris?" he asked again.

"Because I could see the look on your face, that's how, boy," Garethor said. Though his voice was stern, it had a warmth to it. "Again."

Valfric huffed. He closed his eyes and tried to reach down into the power in himself. This was so frustrating; he hated every minute of it. Not using Essaeris, per se—he was excited about that—but he hated that he hadn't figured it out yet. He should be a master by this point in time, or at least he thought so. Garethor kept reminding him that he was a little boy and that little boys didn't know how to use Essaeris. But Garethor was wrong. Valfric was not a little boy. He might have been small, and he might have been young, but he was a man, and someday he would be a fearsome warrior. He needed to get this figured out.

Valfric concentrated again but was having a hard time feeling the Essaeris.

"Breathe, calm your mind," Garethor said, his voice trying to sound steady and soothing.

Breathe, calm your mind, Valfric thought in a snide tone. He thought he heard something like a stick being grabbed. How did Garethor know what he was thinking? Valfric was pretty sure that Garethor could read minds. He might not be able to use Essaeris like Valfric could, but there was definitely a kind of— "Ouch!" He called out as he felt a stick whack him upside the head.

Valfric held his head and looked over at Garethor. "What was that for?"

"For not paying attention," Garethor said. "Now. Again."

Valfric glared at the old man, huffed, and went back to what he was doing. As he closed his eyes, he thought he heard the smallest of snickers from Garethor, but that wasn't possible because Garethor did not have a sense of humor, because Garethor had been around since before the beginning of time. And when you're that old, you lose your sense of humor. This was something that was known.

Valfric redoubled his effort, and he felt the Essaeris in him again. He breathed in, trying to clear his mind. He felt it begin to infuse him, and instead of letting his excitement get the better of him, he let it well up inside of him. As he felt it build, he thought of what he needed to create. It was simple, really. He was to make a rock.

Valfric thought of the rock and willed his Essaeris to make it. He felt the power zing from him, and there was a little plop in his lap. He opened his eyes, looking at a perfectly smooth rock sitting in his lap. He grinned and picked it up. As he picked up the rock, he could feel his Essaeris in it.

Garethor inspected it and smiled at him. "See, I told you you could do it."

Valfric grinned and tossed the rock in his hand.

"Good, now release it and do it again," Garethor said.

Valfric felt his enthusiasm vanish. He looked over at Garethor. "Again?"

Garethor nodded. "Again."

Valfric huffed. He released the rock, and it vanished. And this was the way of things. For what Valfric was pretty sure was multiple days, weeks, and even years. But Garethor told him it had only been a few hours. But everyone knew that if you were as old as time itself, you didn't recognize time like a normal person. And even though Garethor thought they'd only been there for a few hours working on this, Valfric knew better. Valfric knew that he'd been in here for ten years. And in that time, he'd created three or four rocks. When he thought about it, maybe it hadn't been ten years. Maybe he'd only been in there a year. He thought again. *Yes, a year,* he thought. *I've been in here a year.*

Valfric was saved from having to make another rock as a figure came wandering into the room. It was the Wolxaran that was bonded to Garethor. It was almost the size of a large dog. It had a long bushy tail and sharp features. It was like a cross between a fox and a wolf. Its fur was the same gray-white as Garethor's hair, and it looked over at Valfric with intelligent eyes. They were good luck, of course, and having bonded with one was what made Garethor the Settlement Wise Man. Well, that, and he was older than time. But it was probably mostly because of the Wolxaran, Valfric thought.

It sauntered up to Garethor, demanding attention. Garethor scratched behind its ears and looked down at it warmly. Valfric was pretty sure he had never seen Garethor look at anybody as warmly as he did the Wolxaran, but he could understand that, too. He didn't think Garethor would be alive if it weren't for the beast. Not that people wanted to hurt him. Well, sometimes Valfric kind of wanted to hurt him, but most people didn't. It was because Garethor was too old to do anything.

Valfric suspected he was capable of doing a few things, but he wasn't capable of working a farm or doing most trades. However, the Settlement knew how important Wolxaran were to the gods. So Garethor got leniency. The Wolxaran protected most of the Settlement's farms from other predators and tended to clear out some of the vermin as well. In exchange, people usually paid it with little tidbits, but they also gave Garethor bread and vegetables that they grew.

Valfric knew that the Wolxaran also caught small game that he and Garethor would eat. Garethor had told Valfric that it had been his mother's, and when she had passed, it had come to him, and that someday when he passed away, the Wolxaran would go to someone else.

The animal looked over at Valfric, came up to him, and sniffed the rock that he had in his lap. It seemed to have an approving look in its eyes, but Valfric wasn't actually sure if it was approval or not. He never knew how he felt around the creature. He knew it wouldn't harm him, but still, it was a Wolxaran. They could be dangerous. And he wasn't sure if it liked him or not. He didn't think it hated him, but it never was super friendly to him. His brother, on the other hand, was different. Garethor's Wolxaran seemed to find reasons to go around Valfric's older brother, Gaelrik, and spend time with him.

Garethor said that someday, when he passed, he suspected that the Wolxaran would go to Gaelrik. Valfric reached out tentatively, and the Wolxaran let him pet its long, soft fur a few times before it went and curled up at Garethor's feet. Valfric looked at the animal curiously and then up at Garethor.

"How come it's able to create Essaerites so much easier than me?" he asked.

Garethor looked thoughtful. "We don't know how they create them, other than it's the same Essaeris that you use," he said pensively. He sighed. "I suspect it's just something that they know how to do, like so many wild animals. They know how to do so many things from birth."

Valfric nodded. "Okay."

"But they must not be experts from birth," Garethor said. "After all, juvenile Wolxaran can only produce a couple of versions of themselves, and they're not as good as the adults. I've seen a lot of animals that seem to struggle and learn. I think they just must have much more of a foothold on it than humans do." Garethor looked at Valfric. "You cannot compare yourself to a Wolxaran. And even if you were to, this is not the one to compare yourself to. He was young when my mother bonded with him. Wolxaran are wise, and they're around much longer than humans."

Valfric thought. "Why did he bond with your mother?"

Garethor looked thoughtful and shrugged. "I'm not sure. Some say that if you do good by a Wolxaran, or if you are a good person or are smiled upon by the gods, then when a Wolxaran has pups, one of the litter will come and bond with you or someone from your settlement. Perhaps that's what happened with my mother. Perhaps not. The way she told it was she found him when he was a pup, and she raised him until he was older. But this seems to be the way of the stories. One finds you when they're young. And then once they bond with a human, they stay with people."

"Do they ever leave people?" Valfric asked.

Garethor nodded. "Yes, occasionally. If they don't find anyone worthy in a settlement, they'll stick around for a while, but eventually, they'll leave and go to the wild and join their own kind. When this happens, a settlement knows that they have done something wrong by the gods and that they need to improve."

Valfric nodded, trying to understand. He didn't understand why the gods just didn't tell them what they wanted, but he also knew it really wasn't his place to question the gods. They did what they did for their own reasons.

"What's on your mind?" Garethor asked.

"You're not a warrior," Valfric said. "I mean, maybe you were once, but you're obviously not one now."

Garethor nodded. "Once, I held a sword and a spear, yes, but it was never what I did. But what do you want to know?"

Valfric looked at the animal. "I understand why it chose your mother. She was an Essaerist, and she was a warrior because she was an Essaerist. And part of me can understand why maybe it chose you because you were her son, but I know you've told me that's not always the case. So if you weren't a warrior, why would the Wolxaran choose you?" he asked, genuinely curious.

"Why would it choose only warriors?" Garethor asked and then held up his hand, stopping Valfric from saying anything else. "Warriors are maybe who we sing songs about and who we want to be as we grow older, but that is not all there is. Wolxaran look for strength. They look for power and people who are strong and firm. Sometimes those aren't warriors."

Valfric didn't believe that last part. He understood where a Wolxaran would want someone who was strong and powerful, but that was warriors. They were the strong, and that's why Ulfgara blessed them. Everyone knew that.

"Okay," Valfric said, not wanting to debate it anymore.

A short while later, Valfric was finally set free from his prison. He walked out of Garethor's house and looked around, surprised to see that it hadn't been years since he'd been in there; it appeared to have only been a few hours, just as Garethor had promised. However, as Valfric knew, Garethor could use some sort of magic to stay alive forever, so he could probably mess with time, too.

Valfric trotted down the road back to his home, not particularly looking forward to it. He enjoyed his brother, Gaelrik, but his father was something else. Valfric's mother had been dead for years. She and his brother Gaelrik were examples of why Valfric needed to be a powerful Essaerist and needed to become a great warrior. Valfric had been very young when it had happened. Their father, as per his usual, was with his friends, drunk somewhere in the settlement and passed out. They came in the middle of the night—not his father or his friends, but men from some other settlement. They had come trying to steal animals and people.

Valfric didn't remember much of it, but he did remember flashes. He remembered seeing his mother fight two men who had come into their house. They had been armed and vicious, and he remembered watching Gaelrik. There had always been something not quite right with Gaelrik. He struggled to be around people, he had a hard time speaking, and he didn't understand things, but he was kind and seemed to be loving and always in a good mood, and Valfric had enjoyed him as a kid. Gaelrik didn't do well with lots of shouting or violence or lots of movement.

He remembered Gaelrik screaming and panicking as they'd watched their mother be attacked. One of the men lashed out at him. Valfric didn't know what the man used, but he remembered seeing Gaelrik on the ground holding his leg and arm. The rest was just flashes. He was so young at the time. But the outcome was that the two men were dead. Their mother, though taken off-guard, was no weakling. She was a true warrior, and she was truly strong and powerful. Just like Garethor said the Wolxaran would be attracted to.

She'd killed both men, but in the process, had been wounded herself. Their father didn't come home until mid-morning the next day, though the rest of the settlement had been by. It was just that he hadn't come out of his stupor until then. Valfric remembered watching over the next few days as the wound his mother had taken festered and eventually took her life.

Their father, who'd always talked about what a great warrior he was and would be, turned to drink and claimed that all of those things he was meant to do could never happen now because he had two boys to take care of. Somehow their father had also decided that it was Gaelrik's fault their mother was dead, even though Gaelrik had been very young at the time. Now Gaelrik walked with a limp and couldn't carry anything heavy. He also had problems using his right arm. Valfric now knew that Gaelrik had sustained several broken bones and a few cuts that night that hadn't healed quite right. Apparently, their father decided that it should have been Gaelrik who died, not their mother. And he still held it against Gaelrik.

Valfric didn't think any of them should have died. Valfric thought, if their father was such a powerful warrior, why hadn't he been home to protect his family?

As he neared their cottage, he could see goats running around outside. That was their life now—goats. Valfric didn't really have any problems with goats, other than they smelled bad and they ate everything, and every now and then, one of them would ram into him and knock him over. But that's what goats did, and there was nothing wrong with them. They milked them for milk and cheese, and they would butcher them for meat and hides. It was the life of every farmer, which was fine, except for Valfric's family was supposed to be warriors, weren't they?

As he came up to the house, he saw Gaelrik moving around outside. Gaelrik was a few years older than Valfric and looked up as he was carrying a bundle of wood. He was hobbling towards the house. Valfric couldn't help but smile as he saw Gaelrik grin and drop the wood, waving at him. Valfric trotted up to the house, not wanting Gaelrik to get in trouble, and he found that he was probably too late. Gaelrik's lip was bleeding, and there was a bruise forming on his cheek.

"What happened, Gaelrik?" Valfric asked.

Gaelrik just shook his head, looking down and muttering something that Valfric couldn't make out. That was common. There were only a few words that Gaelrik seemed to actually know, and he didn't use those very often. Normally he made some sort of noise or grunt, or he would laugh or moan or cry, but he didn't speak very often, and when he did, it didn't make sense.

Valfric helped Gaelrik pick up the wood and carry it inside, where they found their father.

"Where the fuck have you been, boy?" his father asked, his voice like stone.

"Over at Garethor's," Valfric reminded him. "Remember? You told me to go this morning."

Their father grunted. "Don't talk back, boy! Your brother already tried that once today."

Valfric doubted Gaelrik tried talking back, but it was clear that their father was already drunk and angry. So it wouldn't do to push it any further.

"Sorry, father," Valfric said.

"So, did you learn anything? Show me," their father said.

Valfric reached inward, feeling his Essaeris, and produced a rock. It was getting much easier for him. He set it on the table.

His father looked at it in disdain. "A rock? That's it? All you're capable of making is a fucking rock?" he roared.

"I'm getting better," Valfric said, his voice flinty.

Their father's head went back in a bellowing laugh. "Getting better? Please, you're pathetic. And here I thought one of my sons would be useful," he said venomously.

Gaelrik made some sort of noise, and their father turned his head, rounding on him.

"What did you say, you worthless piece of shit?" he growled.

Gaelrik cowered, backing away.

"He didn't say anything," Valfric said, stepping between his father and Gaelrik.

He saw fire build in his father's eyes.

"You defy me," he said. His hand went back and started moving towards Valfric.

These things went one of two ways. Valfric could dodge the blow easily. His father was drunk, but if he did that, it would make his father even angrier, which generally led to a worse beating. Or Valfric could stand there and take whatever the slap was, and it would be over. In a few minutes, their father would be on to something else, and in an hour or so, he would leave to go drink with his friends.

So Valfric stood stock still and waited for the blow. It came hard, and Valfric's head wrenched to the side as the back of his father's hand connected with his cheek. It sent him tumbling to the floor, and he saw stars for a moment. He heard Gaelrik make some sort of noise and try to come to Valfric's aid. He saw fear in his brother's eyes, and his father turned on him, hitting him. Gaelrik hit the ground, and his father kicked him once in the belly.

Valfric tried to make it to his feet, but before he could do anything, there was a deep guttural growl from the door. Everyone's head snapped, and there, standing, was Garethor's Wolxaran. It stalked into the room, its hackles raised. Valfric's father looked at it. "What the fuck do you think you are—"

There was another growl from it, this one deep and menacing, its lips curled up, revealing teeth.

Their father looked like he was thinking about taking it on, but then two more Wolxaran walked through the door.

What was his father going to do? There was a very real possibility that all three were not the actual Wolxaran; they were just Essaerites.

One was a match for any sober, competent man. But Valfric's father was not sober or competent. And there weren't one, there were three. They stalked into the room, all of them beginning to growl.

"If you—" his father said, though his voice sounded scared.

But he didn't finish the threat. Because what threat was there to make? If it attacked their father, nothing would happen to Garethor's Wolxaran. After all, Garethor's Wolxaran was bonded to him. It protected the settlement. The only reason it would attack anybody in the settlement is if that person was a danger.

That meant that, as far as the people of the settlement were concerned—whether some of them were happy about it or not—Garethor's Wolxaran could tear Valfric's father limb from limb, and no one would do a thing about it. Their father knew this.

The Wolxaran went and stood around Gaelrik but not Valfric. In a way, this stung, but it also emphasized what Garethor had said earlier: someday it would pick Gaelrik. And in that moment, Valfric was thankful.

Even though Valfric felt weak now, the day would come when he would be strong and powerful. Gaelrik would never have that. But he would never need it with the Wolxaran. It would ensure no one ever harmed him as soon as it was bonded to him.

Their father looked at the Wolxaran for a few moments and then spat on the floor and stomped out.

Valfric sighed, feeling better. He saw the Wolxaran turn around and nuzzle against Gaelrik, who was crying from having been hit but seemed to be soothed by its presence.

Valfric got up and approached his brother, and the Wolxaran let him. He checked to see that Gaelrik had a new cut on his lip.

"Are you okay?" Valfric asked.

Gaelrik's head bobbed up and down a little bit, and Valfric nodded.

"Come on, why don't you get up? Why don't you go lay down." Valfric said, helping his brother up.

The Wolxaran stayed with them as Valfric helped his brother make his way to bed, where he plopped down. Tears streamed down his face, and Valfric felt hate inside himself—hate for what their life had become. And it had all been the result of weakness, he realized.

Had their father been a strong man, their mother would have never, ever been hurt. She wouldn't have had to defend them by herself. It would have been his father and his mother fighting. It would have been an easy fight. Gaelrik would have never been hurt, and while he would have still been different, he would have been able-bodied.

And they would have had a better, happier life. But because of his father's weakness, Gaelrik, who needed protecting, was hurt even more and was always in danger. And their mother was gone.

He gritted his teeth. As Gaelrik began to sleep, Valfric went over by the fire and sat down. He took a deep breath and closed his eyes. "Again," he said under his breath, and he reached down and felt for the Essaeris inside himself.

CHAPTER 16

The workshop was buzzing with activity as Mariokos stepped inside. Tables and workstations were lined up next to each other, each with craftsmen hard at work. His gaze wandered across the room, taking in the equipment and weapons scattered across the workstations.

He navigated around the groups of people, looking for the two he wanted to find. Off in a corner on their own, he found Fioralba and Biankara. Fioralba was hunched over something that, as he got closer, resolved into arrows. Across the table from her was Biankara.

He came up behind Biankara and placed his hands on her hips. "How are you today?" he asked.

Her head snapped over to him, and she smiled after recognizing who had touched her. She turned around and wound her arms around his neck. "I'm doing manufacturing today," she said in a voice that said she wasn't really enjoying herself. "How is your day going?" she inquired, her voice softer.

He gave her a little squeeze. "My day is going well," he said, and it had been.

Most of Mariokos's time had been consumed by training with the rest of the Legion. He had been creating Essaerites that acted as barbarians for the soldiers to train against. He hadn't had to fight them himself, and he didn't think he would need to anytime soon. His effort was being expended in training others, and he was exhausted, as was his Essaeris. But he'd enjoyed it, not the combat so much, but pushing himself for a long period with his powers.

He looked down at what Biankara was working on. "They have you working on spearheads, huh?"

She turned and looked at it, frowning slightly. "Yes, yes, they have us working on arrowheads and spearheads," she said with a slight huff. She picked up one of the spears. "I have to admit, I don't really understand them."

Fioralba poked her head up and smirked. "Oh, the pointy thing on the end is what you stick inside someone," she said like she was trying to be helpful.

Biankara gave Fioralba a playful glare. "I'm aware of that part." She pointed at the head. "But I don't understand why they're the way they are."

Mariokos took the spear from her. He could understand her confusion. When most people thought of a spear, they thought of an oversized arrowhead on the end of a pike. The Legion used those too, but more sparingly. The reality was that the spear he was holding was more of a javelin. The handle was only a few feet long, but the head was over a foot and a half long.

He held it up, explaining it to them. "Well, it's more of a javelin than anything else, but yes, I can see where you'd be confused. The Legion uses a few different types of javelins," he explained. "You can see how long and narrow the head is as it leads to the shaft of wood. This does a few things. One, it adds weight to the head, which can help when it's coming down, giving it more force. But also, once the head," he tapped the tip of the javelin, "goes through a shield, there's no resistance behind it until it gets to the shaft."

He continued, "In the case of the one you're working on right now, it has more of an arrowhead-type shape to it." He traced his finger along the triangular head of the javelin. "When this goes into a shield, for example, it'll be a pain in the ass to pull out. And if they don't pull it out correctly, they run the risk of bending the rest of the javelin's head," he said, pointing along the long rod of metal. "Or, more likely, they'll break the handle and shaft of it. You see, they're not connected very well in these models. After a fight, we can go through and remove them from any dead enemies. But in the heat of battle, it'll be difficult for someone to pull it out without rendering the weapon useless."

"So, that gives you an advantage how? Just in that they can't throw them back at you?" Biankara asked.

Mariokos nodded. "That, but also, when they have something sticking out of their shield, it'll be a lot more unwieldy. Plus, a legionnaire could grab the spear and be able to pull the shield away or otherwise control their opponent. If it gets stuck in flesh, you have a similar situation. We have other javelins that we use."

Mariokos paused, then using his Essaeris, he created one for her to see. "These are less common, but you'll still see them," he said. "Do you see how, instead of having an arrowhead for the tip, it's just a spike?"

Biankara looked at it and nodded.

"This one uses a different kind of metal that tends to be a little bit more flimsy. The idea behind this is that it will bend—in fact, it's almost a guarantee it will bend—which can be a pain getting it out of a shield, but also means they can't throw it back at us. If you're going after targets that have wicker shields or no shielding at all, this can be ideal because it has a very long tip that can go right through someone," he explained.

He created another one; this one had a similar look, but the arrowhead at the end was missing the hooks that would normally prevent it from being easily pulled out. "This is something that you'll see most Legionnaires carry if they're in the main formations. It has a slightly longer handle, and the steel is more rein-forced, which allows it to go through shields but come out of them easily enough. And trust me, they're sharp and effective. They can go through someone's shield, and if that shield is too close to someone's body, the Legionnaire can stab it into the person holding it," he explained.

Biankara nodded. "And here, I thought Xavieno was the only one who paid attention to the weapons," she said with a small chuckle.

He smiled and shrugged. "Hey, what can I say? We all have things to learn."

She was thoughtful as she looked around at the various equipment. "The shields. Do you use the same ones that everyone else does? They look so thin."

"They are thin," he explained, "but they weigh more than you might think. They are around twenty-five pounds, and yeah, they're only a fifth of an inch thick, but that makes a difference. It'll stop most swords and arrows. Believe it or not, our shields are actually heavier than the Gwenthari's generally are. They're bigger too, and we can use them to push people," he said. "But I'll create my own shield if I need one. That means it'll heal if it gets damaged and that I can customize it to whatever I need.

"On that note," he said, reaching out to create a sword, "You've probably seen the short swords that most legionnaires use."

Biankara looked at it.

Mariokos and Biankara really didn't talk about the equipment he used, but he thought this was a good opportunity to discuss it because her question had been telling. She wanted to know what type of shield he used. She wanted to make sure he was safe.

He wanted to help make her feel more comfortable. "Because Essaerists like Xavieno and I create our own weapons, our swords will never dull. We make them so that the grip is exactly what we want, the weight is what we need in the individual swing—everything. My armor and weapons will look the same as everybody else's, but trust me, they're far from it," he said, looking over at Fioralba. "And Xavieno's won't be either. In fact, he's much better at creating these types of Essaerites than I am, and he has much more skill when using them," he reassured her.

Biankara looked thoughtful for a moment. "So, you aren't concerned about any of this?"

He considered the question and then answered honestly. "A little," he admit-ted. "You don't know what's going to happen in combat. There's a very real possibility that I will spend a good amount of my time behind the main lines controlling my Essaerites. But there's a chance that I won't. Also, even if I'm behind those lines, that doesn't mean an arrow, a javelin, or a dart won't get me. There's always a risk," he said. "But it's not going to control me either. And it shouldn't control you."

Biankara looked up at him and smirked. "Oh, nothing controls me. Trust me, dear."

She looked back at the table of equipment that she had Essaerites making.

"What's on your mind?" He asked.

She looked thoughtful. "I just never thought I would see myself doing this," she said honestly.

"What, using Essaerites to assist the Legion?" he asked.

She nodded. "That, and having to prepare for a war, or anything of that sort. Look, I know that Essaerists are here to make lives easier. And I get that. But I just never saw myself standing and watching them in a place like this." She motioned around.

He thought he understood where she was going with it. Growing up, Biankara was never going to be doing any sort of labor. And she wasn't really doing any labor now. Her Essaerites were, and she was inspecting them and otherwise watching them. But she didn't strictly need to be there. She could probably do something else, but it would be frowned upon if she wasn't there supervising her Essaerites as they prepared weapons and equipment for the Legion.

That was going to be the rub of it for this whole situation for her. She would have to be in a spot where she'd have to get her hands dirty. And it was something that Mariokos wasn't sure she was going to be entirely comfortable with.

For Fioralba, the thought of being out in the field and working wasn't something that would bother her. It would be something that would keep her distracted, and she would probably enjoy doing it. In fact, Mariokos was pretty sure that Fioralba would go out of her mind if she were told she had to sit in the middle of the camp and do nothing all day long.

But Biankara was different. For her, any time she had to work on her own was a sign of weakness. Not that she felt that work was below her; it was just that's how she'd been raised. If she had to do something, then she clearly didn't have the resources to have someone else do it for her. And even though that was Essaeris incarnate, he could see where she would still struggle with the concept of it.

Later in the day, he found Biankara in her home. She was lying in a large tub of hot, steaming water. Flower blossoms covered the surface, and as he walked in, he saw several slaves standing by, holding drinks and food. They gave respectful nods to him, and he walked up to the tub, seeing her eyes closed.

"Am I interrupting?" he asked.

She cracked open an eye. "Yes, you are," she said imperiously. "But since you've interrupted me, you may as well stay," she said with a smile.

He laughed and pulled up a chair, sitting next to the tub. "So how was your day in the shop?" he asked, his voice holding mock concern.

He saw the corner of her mouth twitch up. "If you must know, it was grueling and laborious."

Then she got serious. "It was fine," she commented.

"Not something that you enjoy, though," he said.

She looked at him like he was insane. "Of course it's not."

He smiled tightly. "I'm sorry, Biankara."

She looked at him, confused. "What are you sorry for?"

He shrugged. "That you're going into the field and having to do this kind of stuff all the time."

She sat back in the tub and closed her eyes. "You don't have to be sorry. It's what life is. And I appreciate that I'm not being oppressed or anything of that nature." She sighed. "I just don't enjoy that kind of work. I suppose it's going to be an adjustment for me."

He could understand that. It would be quite the adjustment for her.

"Well, is there anything else you'd like to know about the camps and all?" he asked.

She thought for a moment. "Well, I know we won't be staying in regular buildings if we're marching. What will we be staying in? Tents?"

"Yes," he said. "We'll create our own tents, but they hold two people easily enough. Most Legionnaires sleep on straw that they lay on the ground, putting a cloak over it, but we'll be able to create a mattress," he said. "It won't be as bad for us as for most people, but yes, we'll stay in a tent."

"And not a large one, from what you're telling me," she commented.

He laughed. "No, not a large one."

She thought. "And how often will we be on the march?"

"It depends," he said. "If we're moving into an area, we might be marching a lot—probably twenty to twenty-five miles a day. We'll build camp, sleep, then the next day we'll tear down camp and go another twenty or twenty-five miles. We'll stay in some places for a little while, but unless we're going to be in an area for some time, we won't be building wood or stone structures."

"So our days will be spent walking through the frontier or sleeping in a tent," she said.

"That's not true. We'll have to build camp, which requires clearing any forests in the area, building a wall, digging ditches and roads, and then the next day deconstructing all that or burning it down, along with anything else that needs to be built along the way, whether it be bridges or roads," he said, as if giving her good news.

She opened her eyes again and gave him a playful glare. "Right, all that too," she said and smiled.

"And that's why I'm sorry," he said. "Because I know this is nothing that you want to do."

She waved her hand at him dismissively, but he could tell she was doing it just to be nice. "It'll be fine. Besides, I'll have Fioralba to talk to all day long, and I enjoy her company. I'm sure there'll be other spouses or betrothed or people like us that are there as well."

"There'll be a few, and there are merchants that come through along with entertainers. So you won't be at a lack for someone to talk to," he said.

She nodded. "And I suppose I can bring a few slaves with me," she said. As she said it, Mariokos caught the slightest flinch from the two slaves standing nearby out of the corner of his eye. He very much doubted they wanted to join them out in the frontier. Though they were slaves, Mariokos suspected that their lives were far nicer and cushier than those of most free people in the Empire. And while they wouldn't be abused by other legionnaires or bothered out in the field, it wouldn't be anywhere near as comfortable a life as they were living now.

"Yeah, you can bring them," he said, "but we'll have to take care of them and pay for supplies and all that. But, you can bring them if you want."

She glanced at him. "So you wouldn't recommend it?"

He shrugged. "You can if you want; we just have to deal with housing and all that. Some people do it, though."

She was thoughtful, then sighed. "I suppose I can leave most of them here. I mean, after all, that's what Essaerites are supposed to be for, isn't it?" she said, though her tone held a slight edge to it.

"It's what Essaerites are for. But the camps will have slaves that we can use, if you want. Again, it's completely up to you, and it doesn't matter to me what you choose to do. I want you to be as happy as you can be doing this," he said truthfully.

She looked at him, her expression softening. She reached out of the water and placed her hand on top of his. "I know you do, Mariokos, and I cannot tell you how much I appreciate your concern for me," she said with a soft smile. "You're a very good man, you know that?"

He felt himself smile. "Thank you. You're a good woman."

She smirked. "I'm a decent woman, but you're a good man. And I hope this war goes smoothly and uneventfully," she said. Then corrected herself, "Well, I suppose as smoothly and uneventfully as war can go." She sighed. "I still hate the timing of it."

They'd had this conversation a dozen times. They weren't in disagreement about it. Neither one of them preferred the timing of the war, and if Mariokos was being honest, he'd prefer not going to war at all, and he suspected Biankara was the same. But it was the lot they had, and the lot they would live with.

He reached out and kissed her hand. "Enjoy the rest of your bath. I don't want to bother you too much."

She smiled softly. "Thank you. Dinner later?"

He stood and smiled down at her. "I wouldn't dream of missing it."

She laughed lightly and closed her eyes, leaning back in the hot water.

CHAPTER 17

Caelwen was at Wulfgren's cottage, where he was building some sort of cage. Having him home had been nice. She smiled as he tinkered with the cage. It was a foot or so off the ground and fairly large. The roof sloped down, allowing rain and snow to run off.

She turned her attention to a smaller cage that was sitting on the ground. Inside the cage were four fuzzy creatures. He'd brought them back from the war, as had several other warriors.

"So, what are these called again?" she asked.

Wulfgren glanced at her. "Rabbits."

She cocked her head. "They look like hares... but I don't know, different too."

They were different indeed. They were smaller and less lean-looking than hares.

He chuckled. "Yeah, they're similar but different. Shorter legs, ears."

She turned her attention back to him. "And what's your plan with them again? I know you and a few of the other men brought some back."

"We're going to farm them." At a look from her, he added, "The Rothmornians do this, and that's where we learned about it."

"And these are better than hares?" she asked.

He nodded. "Yes, for one, hares are a pain in the ass. Two, you have to catch them or kill them. These things, you don't." He walked over to the cage. "I have two males and two females."

"And they have to be in this cage? That seems like more work. Why are hares not as good, by the way? I don't mind eating them, and I know you don't either," she said.

He gave her a look like she was being dense. "Like I said, these things are easier. The cage is to make sure that nothing gets to them and to keep their bedding dry. They grow fucking fast." He pointed at the rabbits. "Every time those females have a litter, they'll have five to twelve babies."

She raised an eyebrow. "That is a lot of them."

He went on, "and they'll be ready to eat within two to three months, and she can go right back to having more babies. The Rothmornians who taught us how to do this said that if you rotate breeding your females correctly, you'll always have a bunch of these little fuckers in stock. They can breed up to ten to twelve times a year, but they said it was dangerous to do, and that the females could be stressed."

She peered at a rabbit. "Huh. It is a decent size, and I'm sure it's tasty," she said, looking at the rabbit. She assumed that it was probably around five or six pounds, and since she did enjoy hare, she was sure this would be enjoyable as well.

"I bet the pelts are nice, too," she mused.

He grinned. "Very. They're warm too. There's all sorts of stuff you can do with the rabbits."

She sat back and looked at her brother. "Never pictured you to be the farmer type."

He barked a laugh. "Well, I'm not," he said, after a moment. "Part of me wants to say that I am, but I know deep down I'm a warrior. But I figure these will be handy to have around. It'll be good meat, and the furs will fetch a good price, and it doesn't seem like they're that hard to raise."

She smiled. Wulfgren hadn't always been the most pragmatic person she'd known. Caelwen, on the other hand, tended to be, but not her brother. It seemed that being out at war for a couple of years and being on the road had changed some of those mentalities.

"I'm sure you can trade for the pelts and the meat too if you get tired of it," she said.

"That's the plan," he said, "but of course first I have to finish this cage they're going in," he added, giving her a pointed look.

She rolled her eyes and came over to help him. "You know I'm shit at carpentry." Then she added, "but I made all these wonderful tools for you, so I think I've helped."

She picked up a piece of wood and began walking over to a small station she had created that held various chisels and saws. On the table was Treftune. He had been scurrying around, watching them all morning. She gave him a soft smile and scratched his chin.

"So, what do I need to do with this?" she asked, looking over at her brother.

He stood and walked over to her. He started saying something, but one of her Essaerites pulled her attention. The day had been windy, with high gusts kicking around plants and dust along with everything else. She had a handful of Essaerites in the area, but she couldn't use the normal birds of prey that she liked. They weren't able to fly in the wind. Well, she still had them; they just had to go from tree to tree, staying low, and most of the time they couldn't move.

One of them saw something in the forest on the other end of the settlement. She moved into the Essaerite, its vision taking up her own. "I wonder what it saw," she said to herself.

The bird looked down from the tree it was in, and she caught some movement. She looked closer. *Is that a...* she thought, and then she saw it. A horse, and then another horse, and then more. They were moving slowly and quietly through the woods. Atop the horses were men, wearing armor and carrying shields and weapons. She felt her heart race for a moment, trying to see if she could recognize any of them. She surveyed the faces, not recognizing any of the men as they slowly approached the edge of the settlement.

She pulled herself back into her own body. Next to her, Wulfgren appeared frustrated, asking if she had been paying attention to him. Her head snapped over to him. "There's a raiding party heading into town."

His eyes widened. "What?" She could hear stress in his voice as he spoke. "How many?" he asked.

She moved back into the bird. The men were already past. She shook her head. "I can't tell. Maybe half a dozen or a dozen. I'm not sure. I haven't been able to keep my birds high and out in the air because of the wind. They're almost to the edge of the settlement."

As she spoke, she reached down into herself, stoking her Essaeris. Her brother swore and ran into his cottage. She closed her eyes and let power flow out of her. Next to her, one of her pumas appeared, and then another. With each one that she created, she felt a toll on her Essaeris. She didn't have enough at the moment to be able to create the larger animals that she would prefer, but she would be able to create the Essaerite that she could be in to go fight alongside them.

She had another Essaerite at her cottage that she directed out toward where the men would be coming in. It ran from her home. As it did, it bleated the sound of a horn, raising the alarm.

Her brother came crashing out of his cottage. He had a shield and a sword. He ran up to his horse and mounted. She opened her eyes and looked over at him. "West side of town, near Kernvald's. They'll be there soon. I already have one Essaerite on the way. I'll have these two there shortly, and I'll be right behind them."

He took off on his horse, followed by both of Caelwen's Essaerites.

"Shit," she said to herself.

She closed her eyes again and focused on her power. She breathed in and out, trying to stoke the energy inside of herself, feeling it bubble and surge. Out of the corner of her mind, she saw the puma from her cottage nearing where the men would be coming from.

She felt her heart flip in her chest as the puma saw smoke on the horizon. As it got nearer, it could see Kernvald's cottage in flames. Men were at the cottage, and the puma kept running as quickly as it could.

Men were dragging Kernvald's wife on the ground. The puma darted through the high grass. It heard the sound of horses, screaming, and yelling. It burst out of the grass and rushed at a man pulling Kernvald's wife by her hair. The man looked up just in time for the puma to slam into him.

Its teeth sunk into his neck, filling its mouth with blood. Its head jerked back and forth with quick, powerful movements, ripping flesh and breaking the man's neck. It let go of the man and saw a spear coming at it.

Caelwen tried to keep her focus on her Essaeris as it built inside of her. She willed the power to grow fast.

She was back in the puma. There were more spears coming at it. They were long, and the men stayed on their horses. The puma was backing away from them, trying to find a vantage point to attack from. It saw motion from one of the horsemen, and then there was a net in the air.

She pulled back into herself. "Shit!"

Her Essaeris was finally high enough, and she let it surge out of her in a great gush of power and will. Before her, vines appeared, winding around and growing into the form of the Essaerite that she could control from within.

In the back of her mind, she noted that the puma was down, but the other two were almost on-site along with her brother and other people from the settlement. She pushed the fight from her mind and focused completely on the Essaerite before her.

It finished taking shape as the skull and antlers came into existence. She glanced over at Treftune and said, "Go hide."

He chittered his disapproval and leaped onto her shoulder. She didn't have time to fight him, so she let the Essaerite finish encasing her and Treftune. Her eyes closed, and her vision was taken over by that of the Essaerite. She turned and began to move in the direction of the fight.

The Essaerite's legs were long and chewed up the distance quickly. As she ran, she saw people moving toward the smoke on the horizon. She felt rage inside her as she moved. *Fucking wind,* she thought. Had her birds been able to fly like they normally did, they would have had more warning and could have mounted a more effective defense. As it was, she was down one Essaerite.

She saw towering flames as Kernvald's cottage burned. The fighting around the cottage was chaotic. She could see that the people from her settlement were greatly outnumbered. She saw Wulfgren lashing out at two men while her other two pumas protected his rear. He and the others from her settlement were losing, but that was about to change.

She gritted her teeth and ran faster. She closed on the flight like an avalanche. She was completely the Essaerite, and the Essaerite was death and vengeance. She bellowed a war cry that, through the Essaerite, sounded like some monster from stories told around campfires.

Everyone turned their attention to her. She saw Wulfgren's eyes widen in shock as he took her in, and then he grinned wickedly. Others from her settlement had similar looks on their faces. The attackers didn't seem as happy.

A man charged her, his horse rearing up to smash into her. She lifted her right arm, catching the horse's chest as it came down at her. She grunted, feeling the

Essaerite push as it made contact with the horse. Vines in her feet clung and gripped the ground as she pushed the horse back, sending the animal and its rider crashing to the ground.

One of the vines on her back lashed out with a spike. It speared the man in the chest. He cried out, grabbing the vine as the spike sunk into him. She jerked it out and turned to another threat. This one was four men. She grinned inside her Essaerite and swung her left arm, knocking over one horse. She grabbed the man riding it, and she heard him scream as his upper body was crushed and squeezed in her grip. Her fingers wrapped around him like constrictors. Bones snapped and crunched beneath her fingers.

She registered a hit on her shoulder from a sword. She tossed the man she was holding and backhanded the one attacking her. The back of her hand and forearms were covered in long thorns that tore through flesh. The man went down, blood spraying from his arm. She turned to the last man and used the blade on her left arm to take him out.

As he fell, she saw that others in his party were retreating. Around her, more people from her settlement were arriving to assist. She looked over at the burning cottage and saw two bodies.

She felt sadness as she took in the corpses of Kernvald and his wife. They'd been too late to save them.

Caelwen went to remove her helmet when she felt her stump at her cottage raise an alarm. She moved into it just in time to see an axe come down to split it in two. She fought to stay connected to it as she saw two men in her cottage knocking things over.

She saw one grab and kill one of Treftune's Essaerites. He turned to the stump, and she felt her gut clench. Faelric glared down at the stump, then kicked it into the fire.

"They're some at my cottage!" she cried out.

Wulfgren looked at her, anger flashing in his eyes.

She made one of her birds fly. It fought against the wind, but she already knew what it would find. It saw fire licking up the side and roof of her cottage. As it got closer, she saw the two men get on horses and ride into the forest.

Caelwen redirected one of her pumas back to her home, but she knew it was too late, and that there was nothing it could do.

"What is it?" Wulfgren asked.

She let her Essaerite open up, and she stepped out of it.

"My cottage," she said.

He asked, "What about it?"

"They burned it," she groaned.

His head moved to the horizon where smoke was rising. He called out to some of the men, and she waved him off.

"They left," she said.

"How do you know?" he asked.

"'Cause there were just two of them. I knew one of them," she commented.

She felt a mix of emotions just underneath the surface—anger, for one, at her home being burned down, but also sadness because she liked Faelric, and he liked her, and she couldn't fault him at all for what he had just done. But she could fault her uncle. That she could do.

She turned back to Kernvald's cottage, which was still burning. She walked up to Kernvald and his wife. She looked down at the two corpses. Kernvald was covered in blood from a wound on his chest and abdomen. She wasn't sure if it had been quick or not, but she suspected it hadn't been. His wife had a slit across her throat. As soon as Wulfgren and the other men had shown up, she was sure that the attackers had just gone for a quick kill. But it wasn't a completely one-sided fight, she thought as she turned and looked at the people that she had killed, along with a couple that her brother had killed.

"Caelwen, I'm sorry," he said next to her.

She shook her head. "It's fair. He was from the caravan that I told you about."

"I'm still sorry, and no, it wasn't fair. You were just doing what you were told to do," he said with a huff. He changed subjects. "But my, my, hasn't my little sister changed," he said with pride in his voice.

She couldn't help but cock a smile. "Yeah, I did okay today?"

He chuckled. "Okay is an understatement. I've been around plenty of Essaerists now, and most of them would have a hard time holding up against you."

She rolled her eyes. "Thanks, but you don't have to make me feel better."

He shook his head. "I'm not trying to make you feel better." He looked over at her Essaerite. "That thing is fucking terrifying. And the pumas..."

She grimaced. "If I'd had more notice, I'd have been able to create stronger ones. Maybe we wouldn't have had this much of a problem."

A gust of wind blew, and she was reminded that the reason they hadn't had notice was because of the wind. She sighed. "I'm sorry. Normally my birds see things," she started.

He cut her off. "You still gave us more notice than if we wouldn't have had you, and they obviously planned this out. But that's something to figure out another time. Let's see what we can recover from your cottage."

They made their way to her home. By the time they got there, most of the structure had collapsed in on itself and was still burning.

"Caelwen, I'm sorry. I know you lost everything," he said, his voice thick with grief.

She shrugged. "In a way, yes. But in a way, no," she commented. "Most of my belongings were in stone chests that are Essaerites. They're designed to be safe during a fire. Everything I hold dear and valuable is always in those things."

"I suppose that's why you don't seem as upset as I thought you would about your home burning down to the ground," he said. "But still."

"But still," she echoed.

The real loss was going to be for the settlement in the form of all of the herbs and tinctures that she had. They'd been sitting on shelves, and while a few of them might have made it through the fire, most would not have. Even the ones she had encased in glass— the insides would have cooked and burned. But there was nothing to be done for that.

"This is going to be a hard winter. I was already low on herbs, but now?" she said, letting it hang there.

Wulfgren's expression was grim. "We didn't bring many back with us from war."

And why would they have? It wasn't something that most people brought back as a spoil of war, and even if they had, she knew that Wulfgren and the men wouldn't have known what to look for. That was Caelwen's territory and job. But now? Well, now if anyone got sick or hurt, it was going to be hard.

"Do you think they'll come back?" she asked more to herself than to him.

"Yes," Wulfgren said.

She looked at him. "Do you really think so?"

He nodded. "They were targeting your cottage and Kernvald. They waited until you left and then they did what they did," he said, shaking his head. "And we killed more of their men. They'll be back, but again, that's a problem for another day. Not today. Today, we mourn the loss of Kernvald and his wife, and we figure out where in my place you're gonna stay until we build you a new home."

She scoffed. "I'm taking the bed, obviously. You're used to sleeping on the ground. You'll be fine."

He laughed heartily. "Oh, this is going to be entertaining for sure."

She smiled. "We managed to survive each other as children. I'm sure we can survive a winter together."

"That was before you were a powerful Essaerist," he commented.

She chortled. "And before you were good with a sword."

He laughed. "I might be able to hold up for a little while. But still, I don't think I'm going to egg you on like I used to when I was a kid."

She grinned. "Coward."

CHAPTER 18

Little flakes of snow were starting to fall from the gray sky as Caelwen and Wulfgren made their way to Ilfthandor's home. Before them stood a stone house with a thatched roof. Smoke wound its way up into the wintry air from the chimney, and a few animals milled about in a paddock set a ways from the house. Ilfthandor's was one of the few stone dwellings in the settlement and was a mark of his wealth.

Caelwen pushed on the heavy wooden door as they entered. They found their uncle sitting next to the fireplace, warming his hands. Light flickered on the walls and up to the rafters, casting dancing shadows. Ilfthandor turned, regarding them. He knew about the raid, but Caelwen and Wulfgren hadn't spoken to him the day it happened; they had been too preoccupied with dealing with the aftermath.

Ilfthandor's expression was stern. "Just now coming to see me?"

Wulfgren snorted. "Shouldn't it be the other way around? We're the ones who defended the settlement. Where were you in all of this?" he asked, stalking into the room. His voice was hard and carried an edge that Caelwen wasn't used to hearing from her brother, one she suspected he had become all too familiar with during the war.

To Ilfthandor's credit, he didn't flinch. Instead, he scowled slightly and turned back to the fire. "You wanted an old man to fight your battles for you?"

"I wanted an old man not to make it so we had battles to fight," Wulfgren said, going to sit next to the fire. He stared daggers at his uncle.

Ilfthandor glanced at him. "You don't know what I've been doing while you've been out playing for the last few years."

"Playing? Is that what war is now?" Wulfgren asked.

Before Ilfthandor could respond, Caelwen interjected, "Cut the shit,

Ilfthandor. We know why they attacked us, and you know what happened. We don't need to report it to you," she said acidly. "But what we do need is to figure out, is how we're going to make it through the winter."

Ilfthandor eyed her, his haughty expression cracking for a moment. "What concerns do you have about the winter?"

"Well, for one, all of my herbs and tinctures were burned, weren't they? So if people get sick, that's gonna be a problem," she said. "And while I know you don't necessarily care about the people in the settlement, you are going to care if some of the more powerful families have problems over the winter, or if we lose too many people."

"I do care about the people here, if you—" Ilfthandor began.

Caelwen cut him off. "Don't dare give me any shit right now! We need to figure this out."

He glared at her and then looked back at the fire. "The herbs are going to be a problem," he said and sighed. He glanced over at Wulfgren and Caelwen. His voice softened. "I am glad that both of you are okay, and I am sorry for what happened. It's a shame about Kernvald."

"It was a shame that he died," Caelwen agreed. "There's no undoing it now. But winter," she said, redirecting the conversation back to the urgent matter at hand.

Ilfthandor's chair creaked as he sat back. He gazed into the fire contemplatively. "How did they manage to get past you?" he asked, his tone devoid of accusation. He seemed, genuinely curious.

"It was the wind," she said simply. "My birds couldn't fly in it, so they were going from tree to tree whenever there was a pause in gusts. Unfortunately, it allowed the raiders to get closer."

Ilfthandor nodded.

Wulfgren spoke up. "They knew she was an Essaerist, and they knew she used birds." He looked over at his sister. "It's not uncommon, but anybody who's dealt with Essaerists knows there are ways to get around your Essaerites. In this case, they exploited the fact that it was windy."

Ilfthandor grunted. "The bastards had probably been waiting for days or weeks out in the woods, farther than where Caelwen would think to look."

She was surprised to hear that there was no condemnation in his voice. He wasn't blaming her. He wasn't blaming himself either, but he wasn't blaming her, and that was a surprise.

"I would have thought you'd be irate with me right now," she commented.

Ilfthandor shifted his gaze to her, then back to the fire. "No, the reality is we're lucky you found them when you did," he said with a grunt. "If this were a normal settlement," he said, pausing, "well, things could have been worse."

"I have a couple more pumas along the edges of the settlement," Caelwen explained, "but if they know how to evade me, it's going to be difficult for me if they want to come back."

"Oh, they'll be back," Wulfgren remarked. "That I can promise you. The question will be when and how many."

"And how many attempts they'll make," Ilfthandor commented, his expression showing concern.

"And how many attempts they'll make," Wulfgren echoed.

Wulfgren looked over at Caelwen. "Do you have any ideas on how you can keep an eye out?"

She stared into the fire in thought, feeling its warmth on her face and hands. "Yes, I can create some smaller Essaerites, ones like Treftune. It will limit how many Essaerites I can make to assist should someone attack, but I can have them in the trees around the settlement. It will give us something, and it's better than nothing, but still..."

"Then that's what we'll do," Ilfthandor said. "I suppose this means you won't be able to do any foraging for anything."

She gave a slight shrug. "Even if I wanted to, everything's dead now. With the frost we've been having lately, and the snow that's coming, there won't be any herbs left that are worth salvaging."

"And I suppose there are no neighboring settlements that would sell to us," Wulfgren commented.

She saw her uncle flinch slightly at these words. No, there weren't any settlements nearby that would be willing to sell to them. In fact, it was likely that the settlements nearby were now housing the men who had attacked them yesterday. Ilfthandor had managed to make enemies of everyone around them. And now, Caelwen and Wulfgren would have to find a way to protect their settlement through the winter.

"We'll just have to see what we can do then. Thank you for coming by and telling me," Ilfthandor said.

"There's more we need to talk about," Wulfgren said.

Ilfthandor waved him off. "Not now."

Caelwen noticed Wulfgren's jaw tighten, but before he could say anything, she touched his arm and shook her head softly. She had learned long ago that when Ilfthandor was done, he was done. He wouldn't speak about anything again, and if he did, he would be an ass just to be spiteful. There was no point.

Her brother stood, and they walked out of Ilfthandor's house, starting back toward Wulfgren's home. She felt the icy wind moving across her cheeks and through her hair.

She glanced over at her brother. His face was red with anger, and his eyes were hard.

"What are you thinking?" she asked.

He looked over at her quickly and then back to the road. "I think our uncle fucked us and everyone who lives here. It's going to take us a long time to rebuild relationships with those around us, and those relationships are extremely important."

She breathed out. "Yes, yes they are. And I agree it is going to take a long time, once Ilfthandor is no longer in control."

"Yes, once he's no longer in control," Wulfgren said.

But that was going to be another problem. It wasn't as if they could just oust Ilfthandor; that wasn't how it worked. They would need to have enough support from the settlement to do it, and a legitimate claim. As it stood, she wasn't sure they would have enough backing should they make a move for power, nor did they have a legitimate claim. Ilfthandor was an ass, but ordering a raid was his right, and the people in the settlement understood that.

Wulfgren looked thoughtful and sighed. "But not during winter."

She agreed. While Ilfthandor needed to go, there had to be stability, and right now, that wasn't something they had. With Caelwen having lost her home and all of her herbs and tinctures, everyone was on edge. They had been raided, and though the losses had been minor as far as those things went, they had still taken losses. Right now, Caelwen, Wulfgren, and Ilfthandor needed to show a unified front to the rest of the settlement; otherwise, winter could be very long and difficult, and it would have nothing to do with those outside of their community.

So she resigned herself to a long and trying winter.

––––––––

THE TASTE OF THE MEAT COATED VALFRIC'S TONGUE AS HE TOOK A HEARTY BITE, RELISHING its savory warmth. He swallowed and took a drink of Bryndraught. He looked over at Durnara as he set his mug down. Valfric's raiding party had returned that afternoon. They'd been welcomed into the settlement like heroes, everyone excited to see how much loot the group had brought back. He could still see the pride on the faces of those who had gone with him. It had been a good trip overall.

Yes, they had lost some, but some of those they had lost were a hindrance to their settlement, which made the losses easier to accept. That wasn't the case for Yrthorn, but it applied to some of the others. It had also been a very profitable trip, and everyone was going to be fat and happy for the winter, Durnara included.

Durnara regarded him with a look of pride. "You did well. We didn't lose that many, and those who came back seemed to be harder, and to remember what they once were."

That was the hope, wasn't it? That they remembered who their people were, something they had forgotten. They were warriors. They were killers. They were raiders and reapers. That's what they were. That's what the gods had wanted them to be, and that's what Valfric had turned them into. He reminded the people of what they were and of what they were capable of.

He smiled grimly. "Yes, I think they remember now, and hopefully they won't forget again."

"They will, but that's fine, because we'll keep reminding them... How did you lose Yrthorn?" she asked after a moment.

Valfric let out a breath. He knew this would come up. "The slave," he said simply.

"Did you kill her?" Durnara asked.

He shook his head. "No, I would have, but we were attacked by the Essaerist. My wolves were almost to her when the attack happened."

"That's bad luck," she commented, looking disappointed. "Tell me about this Essaerist."

He recounted the encounter they had with the other Essaerist. She listened patiently as he went over everything. When he was done, she asked him to describe any emblems on the shields he had seen from the group the Essaerist was with.

When he finished, she looked thoughtful. "I don't know who they are. Probably Wulfharboria," her voice gritty and irritated. "But at least they didn't make off with much. And it sounds like those they killed needed to be removed from the flock anyway. I hate losing some of our own, even if it's needed."

He agreed.

"So do you want us to stay in for the winter or do you want us to go back out?" he asked.

She shook her head. "Stay in for the winter. There's no reason to risk yourselves in the cold just for spoils that won't be worth it." She smirked reading his expression. "I can tell you don't like that answer. You're welcome to go out on your own if you like."

He chuckled, "I don't think Ilara, Aelric, and Thraindel will go with me if I were to leave now, and it's not that I'm not happy with the answer." He took another drink of Bryndraught and looked around, "I just don't know what to do with myself."

Durnara snorted. "The same thing all of us do during the winter: stay by a fire and stay warm. It might be good for you to, being in one place for a while."

"I've always lived here," he said.

Her eyes rolled. "That's not what I mean. And you know it."

It was his turn to snort. "Fine, we'll stay here." He looked down at his empty plate. "Thank you for dinner."

She nodded, "Of course."

He stood and walked to the door. Before opening it, he felt inside himself, reaching into his Essaeris. He let it ripple out into the form of a long fur cloak that he wrapped around himself. He braced himself and opened the door, stepping out.

The weather had been turning colder and windier with each passing day, and earlier it had started snowing. Now, the same driving wind was accompanied by snow. As he opened the door, he was hit by a blast of cold, the stinging snow hitting his cheeks as he began to walk.

The snow was coming down heavily, and he figured by morning there would be at least a foot of it. Even if he had wanted to leave, there was no sense in traveling and camping in this weather.

By the time he made it home, he was in complete agreement with Durnara. He was going to sit next to the fire and not come out until spring. He opened his door and stepped inside. A small fire was burning in his fireplace, tended to by a Essaerite. He took off his cloak and tossed it outside, releasing it, lest the snow and frost that had clung to it be brought into his home.

He looked around. His home had always been spartan. He hadn't been one for decorations or knickknacks. For all the looting he did, he didn't have much to show for it. He walked up to the fire and grabbed a few pieces of wood, tossing them in and letting the flames build.

All of a sudden, he felt very alone. This had been what Durnara had been talking about. Valfric was always on the road, always out raiding and doing something, and he always had his friends with him. That wasn't the case now. Now he was by himself, which was the worst place to be. He was alone with his thoughts, and he would be all winter. He could probably convince Ilara to come over from time to time, or he could go to her, but she wasn't going to want him around all the time, and he would have to find a way of living with himself.

So he poked and prodded the fire, letting it build up, and then sighed as he watched the coals, wondering how he was going to pass the next several months.

PART TWO

CHAPTER 19

The morning air was cool and crisp, and the sun was starting to turn the horizon into soft shades of orange and pink. High above Mariokos, the sky was still the deepest blue, and in some parts, black. His breath came out before him each time he exhaled, but he knew the day would warm and become nicer. It had been a fairly mild winter, and he'd enjoyed it. It had been just cold enough that hard work seemed a little easier.

The Legion had been working all through the winter, preparing for their eventual departure. That morning, he had moved out of the base along with the rest of the legion. The days of soft beds and being in the same place were about to be over. They were heading to meet up with the rest of the Legions in the city of Dionisio. From there, they'd be marching into the frontier to find and face whatever awaited them.

He checked over his pack several times, making sure he hadn't forgotten anything. He walked over to a cart where Xavieno and Fioralba stood. He smiled at them. Xavieno looked a little groggy, but Fioralba appeared as though she'd just rolled out of bed. She looked over at him, bleary-eyed. He smiled, and she frowned.

"Don't, Mariokos," she said flatly.

"Don't what?" he asked innocently.

"Careful, my friend," Xavieno said warmly. "Don't forget, we'll be sleeping in the same camp tonight, and it'll only be the canvas of a tent separating you from the rest of the world."

Mariokos chuckled. "Are you saying you think I'm in danger from your wife?"

Fioralba tiredly glared at him. "Maybe he is saying that," she said, but she smiled a little and walked over to him. He put his arm around her shoulder. She leaned against him.

"Is it going to be all early mornings like this?" she asked.

Xavieno and Mariokos laughed. "Could be, but probably not," Mariokos said. "We'll have to tear down camp every morning if we're leaving the area."

Mariokos reached down into his Essaeris and created a handful of little wooden containers with lids. Then he created some beads inside them that were the darkest purple. The beads were small, but inside was condensed juice. Xavieno had created some of his own, and the two of them walked over to a barrel filled with water. They ladled water into the containers, watching the beads inside expand as they absorbed it.

The beads were nice. They could absorb the water and make it taste like whatever juice you wanted. They also kept it from evaporating, and if you happened to spill them, it was fine. Mariokos liked that he could walk for a while, pick out one of the beads, pop it in his mouth, enjoy the taste of juice, and keep on moving. It was like taking little sips throughout the day.

"Where's Biankara?" Xavieno asked.

Mariokos shrugged, looking around. "I'm not sure. I'm not surprised she's late, though."

Xavieno chuckled. "Yeah, I'm sure she's not happy. Did she ever decide if she was going to bring slaves or anything else?"

Mariokos grimaced. He wasn't sure what Biankara would bring. While she had been on board with everything at the beginning, that had started to change over the winter. She hadn't enjoyed the extra work, and it seemed the reality of having to rough it for a while had been sinking in. She'd also been balancing the time she spent helping the Legion with doing things for her family. Yes, her age meant that she had to help out the state as well, which was why she was helping the Legion, but she still had other obligations.

In truth, Mariokos didn't envy her. The trip had led to several arguments, with Mariokos constantly having to remind Biankara that she couldn't bring an entire procession of her own. Every night, everything would have to fit inside the Legion's camp.

"Do you think she's going to have, what, fourteen or fifteen wagons?" Xavieno asked with a wry smile.

Mariokos glanced at him and shook his head with a deep sigh. "Hopefully just one, but I wouldn't rule out fifteen or twenty." He had a hard time keeping exasperation out of his voice.

Xavieno clapped his shoulder as they started back over toward Fioralba. When they got back to her, she seemed to be waking up a little more. She was moving around some items in the handcart they were taking, though Mariokos seriously doubted that Fioralba was going to be pulling the cart by hand. Instead, she'd use an Essaerite to do it.

"Are you going to be riding or walking?" Xavieno asked, coming up to his wife.

"I'm going to be walking for the first part, I think," she said. "I think it might help me wake up, but I'm sure I'll spend some time riding as well. Do you think I should create the Essaerites now, or will I have time to create the one that I'll ride on?"

"Do it now," Xavieno said. "Once the legion starts moving, it doesn't stop. Neither will any of the support caravans with it, and you want to stay with everyone."

Mariokos filled in the gaps. "There's a rear guard that will be there once we leave the empire, but it's a good habit to get into. The legion and its support move very close together. Plus, when we're in the field, we'll either be in front of or behind other legions."

She nodded. "So the supply train moves at the same speed as the legion. Alright, well, I guess create them now it is."

Mariokos saw Fioralba close her eyes, and a moment later, a two-legged Essaerite came into being. Its legs were thick, and it had a strange little head. Its back had a hook on it that she could connect the handcart to. It walked forward, and she connected the cart.

Fioralba was always good at coming up with efficient and practical Essaerites, in Mariokos's opinion. She didn't waste her Essaeris and was skilled at portioning out what she needed. She created a similar Essaerite that had a type of seat on it that she was able to climb up on. She tested the seat out and smiled.

"Comfortable?" Xavieno asked.

She grinned. "Very."

While Xavieno and Mariokos wouldn't be showing off their powers, there was no reason for Fioralba not to. In fact, it was almost a good idea for her to be seen as an Essaerist when they were on the road. Once they were out in the frontier, it would make it less likely that any Gwenthari would be willing to attack that part of the supply chain. Everyone knew that Essaerists were nothing to mess with. And in a way, by being obvious about it, it would give her some protection.

Not that Mariokos was concerned about the supply trains.

"How long until we leave?" she asked.

"Soon," Xavieno said, "within the hour." He looked concerned. "Speaking of leaving, are you going to go find Biankara?" he asked Mariokos.

"I can't," Mariokos said, "we can't leave the legion right now."

"I can go find her," Fioralba offered, and Mariokos shook his head.

"No, don't. If she's late, then she's going to be late. She knows where we're heading. I don't want you to fall behind because of Biankara."

He had no desire to make Fioralba's life more difficult than it needed to be, and they would leave soon. He turned his gaze to the horizon; it was lightening more and more as the sun came up. Mariokos went and made sure everything was fine with his squad leader before grabbing his pack.

It was heavy.

While on the march, they didn't wear their full armor; it was impractical. Not only could the armor get damaged, but it was painfully hot. Instead, they generally wore simple tunics with swords strapped to their belts, but in their pack was everything else.

His shield was strapped to his pack, which held all of his armor and weapons. They also carried two long staves that were roughly seven feet long. Every legionnaire carried these staves. At night, they would be part of the wall around the camp. Some of the support carts that came with the legion had more staves, but having each legionnaire bring two of them drastically reduced the number of carts needed for the supply wagons.

In his pack, he also had several days' worth of food and anything else he would need. He slung it over his back, letting the weight settle on his shoulders. He was used to the weight; they trained with more than that every day. So once it came time to actually march, the packs wouldn't feel so heavy.

He looked around and saw a figure approaching the base. He sighed.

"She's finally here," he said to himself.

Biankara was approaching the camp, and he walked up to meet her. As he approached, he noticed that she was in a normal dress and didn't have anyone with her. He resisted the urge to roll his eyes.

As he came up to her, he said, "Please tell me you're bringing more than that. I know I told you to pack light, but I didn't think you'd go this far," he added with a crooked smile.

She gave him a half-hearted smile back, and as he got near her, he felt concern.

"What is it?" he asked her.

She looked up at him. "I'm not going."

He nodded slowly. This was something he had taken into account. He knew there was a chance that Biankara would need to catch up with the rest of the Legion if she had things at home she needed to tend to. He wasn't happy about it, but he understood that it couldn't be avoided. As long as she met up with them at Dionisio, it'd be fine.

He nodded and sighed. "Okay. I understand. How far behind will you be? Do you think you'll be able to meet up with us at Dionisio?"

She looked down and then back up at him.

"I'm not going at all," she said.

He was confused.

"Oh, did something come up?" he asked, unsure of what to say.

She looked at him, and her eyes didn't seem conflicted—more apologetic.

"Yes, some things did come up with my family," she said, "and those things will pull my attention for weeks, or potentially months. But that's not why I'm not going."

"Okay," he said, unsure of what to think. "Why aren't you going?"

"Mariokos, you love me, and I love you, but just as friends," she said.

He felt his gut drop a little. "Biankara, I thought—"

She stopped him. "This isn't right. We aren't right. I'll always care about you, and I know you're always going to care about me, but can you honestly say I'm the person you want to spend the rest of your life with?"

He breathed out. "No, probably not. I don't think so, but I think we'd be happy."

She frowned softly.

"Do you really think we would?" she asked, and before he could respond, she added, "Look, you don't want to be in my world, and I don't want to be in yours, and there's nothing wrong with that. We'll always be close. We'll always be friends, but this isn't for me," she said, waving toward the Legion. "I'm not meant to go and be support for the Legions. It's not where my strengths lie."

He couldn't deny it. Biankara had many other talents, and making him breakfast and dinner while helping to repair equipment for the Legion was probably not among them.

"So that's it," he said. "You don't want to wait until I come home?"

She shook her head. "No, I'm sorry, I don't." She touched his arm. "You will always mean something to me."

He knew it was true, and he held her gaze. "And you will always mean something to me," he said.

"Are you okay?" she asked.

He thought for a moment, feeling down inside himself, and after a moment, he nodded.

"Yeah... yeah, I'll be fine," he said.

"Do you feel heartbroken?" she asked.

He looked at her and smirked.

She smirked back, "See, this wasn't going to work out. I don't feel heartbroken either."

He huffed. She wasn't wrong, and part of him felt relieved that she wasn't heartbroken, while another part of him was sad and relieved at the same time that he wasn't either.

"So what are you going to do while we're gone?" he asked. "You're not going to have Fioralba to hang out with, and you're not going to have me and Xavieno to boss around."

"A great loss to be sure," she said with a laugh. Her voice became softer. "But I dare say I'll have a lot to do. My family does need me. And as an Essaerist, there's more I can do than most."

He knew this was true. Women in Lysandrian society could become powerful, but there were limits. Those limits did not apply to Essaerists. They held a different position in society, and Mariokos knew that for her family, the prospect of losing Biankara for potentially a couple of years would be challenging.

He heard the sound of a horn and turned to look behind them. The Legion was starting to shuffle around, getting into ranks. He turned back to Biankara. She came up to him and gave him a hug. He embraced her tightly.

When they broke, she looked up at him; her face didn't show the sadness of a relationship that had just ended, but rather the sadness of knowing she wouldn't see her friend for some time.

"Please stay safe," she said, meaning it.

He smiled tightly. "I'll do my best. You too."

She smiled and touched his arm before turning to walk away. He watched her go for a minute, then turned and walked back toward the Legion.

He found Xavieno and Fioralba watching him. Fioralba looked sad and disappointed for him, while Xavieno just looked curious.

"She's not coming," Fioralba said.

Mariokos shook his head.

"Is she going to meet us somewhere?" Xavieno asked.

He shook his head again.

"Oh," Xavieno said. "So you guys are done?"

Mariokos nodded.

"Are you okay?" Fioralba asked.

He thought about it for a moment. "Yeah. Yeah, actually, I think I am." And he meant it. His chest seemed to loosen a little, and his breathing became easier. In that moment, deep down inside, he realized that Biankara had been right. They weren't right for each other. They were trying to force something that would have probably broken on the road when she couldn't go home. And now that she was walking away, he suspected that she was starting to feel much lighter as well.

———

AS HORNS BLEW, ORDERS STARTED COMING DOWN TO FORM UP INTO RANKS. XAVIENO kissed Fioralba and walked over to his spot in the formation. His pack was heavy on his back, but he also felt excitement. They were heading to the frontier. This was something that was actually happening. It wasn't going to be skirmishes or slaves rebelling or drills and maneuvers. They were actually marching to war.

The sun was over the horizon by the time they began to move, and Xavieno marched with the rest of his squad, their steps synchronized and their lines even. The legion moved as a giant column, and ahead of them was the open road. When they went into combat, there would be scouting units ahead, but they wouldn't be fighting for some time. They'd spend the next week making their way toward Dionisio, the last city at the edge of the frontier.

From there, it wouldn't take long until they found themselves in the frontier itself, facing the Gwenthari. He wondered what it would be like. He knew the Gwenthari were barbarians, but he wasn't sure what it would actually feel like to fight them. Would they come at them in hordes, like some of the stories said they would? Or would it instead be small bands that they would have to contend with? Part of him hoped for the hordes. He wanted to have stories to tell when he got home and the memories of great battles.

As he marched, he said a quiet prayer to Bellamara, asking her to bless him in battle. He'd made a sacrifice the night before, and while they wouldn't see any action for a while, he thought it best to please her as much as he could.

His mind turned with questions about the Gwenthari lands. The Dionisiana Province where he lived was beautiful. It had rolling hills, fields, and vineyards. Large estates and small towns were dotted throughout. He knew people traveled from all over the empire to see it, and he had always lived there, but the frontier was altogether different. He knew it was predominantly made up of tall mountains and thick forests, wide valleys, and roaring rivers. It was much more mountainous and difficult terrain than his part of the empire. He knew it was colder, too, in the wintertime, and he wondered what that would be like.

In Dionisiana, they had frost a few times throughout the winter, and a couple of times he had seen snowflakes fall from the sky, but he knew in the northern parts of Gwenthari Territory, they received heavy snow and winters could be rough. He wondered what it would be like living and fighting in those conditions, or if the Legion would bed down somewhere for the winter and wait. It was probably going to be the latter, but it would still be an adventure for him.

He was disappointed to find out that Biankara wasn't coming with them, not because she was a talented Essaerist, but more because he enjoyed her company and knew how much Fioralba enjoyed her. And while he didn't necessarily feel bad for Mariokos about their relationship ending, he did feel some pity for him. Mariokos would be much lonelier on the road now, and Xavieno knew that he and Fioralba would try their best to keep him company, but he could see where it would be difficult.

As the day wore on, Xavieno's mind wandered as he let the motion of marching guide him along. They would stop in a few hours and make camp for the night. He knew they'd be stopping at a fort each day and wouldn't need to set up an actual camp as they moved until they reached the frontier. He was thankful for it. He was also grateful that he was near the front of the legion instead of being toward the back where the dust kicked up from the many men marching. He took a few beads from his container and popped them in his mouth, chewing on them. They popped, filling his mouth with juice, and he swallowed.

He also checked his Essaeris, gauging the levels and looking at a handful of scout Essaerites circling the area. Even though they were still in the empire, the Essaerists were ever vigilant. Not that they suspected an attack, but more out of habit. He knew as soon as they were in the frontier, his scouting abilities would be paramount, so he continued to focus on that now.

He walked with only half his mind in his own body as he glanced around through a couple of hawks he had in the area. From their vantage, he could see the wide-open landscape of rolling hills. It was peaceful, and he enjoyed it. The sun was getting warmer, despite it being January, and it felt nice on his back as they moved.

As they crested one of the rolling hills, he saw a town in front of him. He heard men shouting up the line, letting them know that's where they would be making camp for the night. He wanted to quicken his pace, but he didn't. He wasn't tired, and he wasn't even over marching for the day, but there was something about heading into camp that always made him want to go faster and get settled.

As they arrived at their camping spot, they walked through a set of gates that led into a large open area surrounded by walls. Commanders began issuing orders, and Xavieno fell out with the rest of the men, helping to set up camp. For him, this predominantly meant setting up his tent with Fioralba.

He saw her walking up with her Essaerite pulling the handcart. "How was your march?" he asked her.

"Lovely," she said. "We walked for half the day," she replied with a tight smile.

He laughed. "Sorry, my love."

"It's fine," she said. "So where are we camping?"

He showed her where their spot in camp would be, and they both focused their Essaeris, combining it to create their tent. Inside, there was a cot for the two of them to sleep on, and Xavieno set down his gear. He went to check with command to see if there were any watches for the night. There were only a handful.

So he went and found Mariokos, who was nearby. He had already created his tent and seemed to be getting settled in.

"How was the march?" Mariokos asked as Xavieno walked up.

"It was a beautiful day," he said. "How was yours?"

Mariokos shrugged. "It was fine."

"Do you have exciting plans for the night?" Xavieno asked.

Mariokos laughed. "Oh, you know it."

He chuckled. The plans for the evening would be pretty simple going forward: make camp, prepare food, do sentry duty if assigned, go to sleep, wake up the next morning, tear down camp, and do it all over again.

CHAPTER 20
TWENTY YEARS AGO

Valfric felt his Essaeris pulsing inside him, and it rippled out, creating a little metal horse before him. He focused on it, and the horse's head turned to look at him. He instantly got excited. The horse's head turned away and then turned back to him again. Valfric tried to make the horse's head stop, but it started turning back and forth, quicker and quicker, until the horse fell over. Valfric sighed and released it.

"That was better," Garethor remarked.

Valfric looked at him and huffed. "No, it wasn't. It was horrible."

Garethor didn't know what good was. Garethor was too old to know what good was. This was known.

Garethor sighed. "Yes, Valfric, it was. You're making progress. You're still very young."

He wasn't sure that he was very young, but he suspected if someone was as old as Garethor was, anyone would seem very young. So it was understandable.

Valfric closed his eyes and tried again. The horse came back into the world, and this time, Valfric was able to carefully manipulate the head. After a few hours, it walked around a little bit but tended to fall over.

"You're growing," Garethor said again.

Valfric felt agitated. "But I'm not growing very fast," he said. "I don't even know why I need to do this."

Garethor raised an eyebrow. "What do you mean, 'why would you need to do this'? You're an Essaerist. This is what your kind does."

"My kind makes metal horses?" Valfric challenged. "Ouch," he said as Garethor smacked his arm with his walking stick.

"Don't take that tone with me, boy," Garethor said sternly. His expression softened. "Your kind makes metal horses, yes, but they make all sorts of things. What's gotten into you?"

Valfric looked down, thinking he knew exactly what had gotten into him. His father had. Valfric hadn't been making any progress in being an Essaerist, or so his father had said. He thought that it was time for him to stop wasting his time and start putting his efforts into something more productive—like farming, carpentry, or leatherwork.

"My father doesn't think I'm growing," Valfric said.

Garethor scoffed. "Your father's an asshole," he said matter-of-factly.

Valfric's eyes widened, he was surprised. "You think my father's an asshole? Ouch, what was that for?" Valfric said as he was smacked with the stick again.

"Watch your language, boy. I'm an adult," Garethor said, though he seemed to be slightly amused.

He thought for a moment and then added, "I do think your father's an asshole. Just because you aren't creating beasts and weapons and everything else yet doesn't mean that you're not growing," he said with a sigh.

"But I'm not a good Essaerist," Valfric finally admitted.

"Of course, you're not," Garethor said. "And how could you be? You're a little boy. You can't be a good Essaerist until you're much older."

"How much older?" Valfric asked.

Garethor shrugged. "The best ones are very old. As old as me. But there are very many good ones that are much younger, and I suspect you'll be one of those. By the time you're in your teens or twenties, you'll be a force to be reckoned with, trust me."

Valfric wasn't sure that he believed him, but it was a nice sentiment anyway. "I don't even know why it matters. That's so long away," he commented.

Garethor seemed to be lost in thought for a moment. "Well, you come from a very long line of Essaerists."

Valfric looked at him. "No, I don't. Essaerists are born at random."

This was true. You never knew who was going to be born an Essaerist and who wasn't. Parentage didn't play a role. Garethor nodded in agreement but added, "Yes, but Ulfgarath Essaerists are known. They used to be extremely powerful and will be again someday. I'm confident your generation will do that. It is not about blood but legacy."

This piqued Valfric's interest. "What do you mean they used to be very powerful?" He settled himself, facing the old man.

Garethor looked at him and said, "There was a time when Ulfgarath Essaerists were some of the most powerful. Even today, many are very powerful, but they did everything. They were able to make things to till fields, build our cities, and be the most fearsome of warriors."

That last part got Valfric's attention. "They were fearsome warriors?"

Garethor sighed. "I could see where that's what you latched onto. But yes, they were fearsome warriors. There was a time when they were feared by all."

"And what could these warriors make?" Valfric asked.

"They could make whatever they wanted to," Garethor said. "They could create fantastic beasts or any weapons that they desired. Some Essaerists can even create Essaerites that they can walk inside of. That could be you someday."

Valfric looked doubtful. "I don't think I'm going to ever be walking in one of my Essaerites," he said, looking at the metal horse that was next to him.

"Everyone starts somewhere," Garethor said. "My mother did, and she was a very powerful Essaerist."

Valfric looked at him. "Was she a warrior?"

Garethor nodded. "She was. She did many other things, but she was a warrior, yes."

"And did she have an Essaerite that she could be inside?" he asked.

Garethor nodded. "Yes, she did. And she was very skilled. She defended this very settlement many times. Part of the reason why our settlement is as prominent as it is, is because of my mother and Essaerists like her. And Essaerists that will be like you."

Valfric looked thoughtful. "This settlement's really as strong as it is because of your mom?"

"In part, yes," Garethor said. "This settlement is old but was originally founded by my mother when she was younger and some of the others with her. She was able to help with the building of homes and barns."

"And she defended the place?" Valfric asked.

"Yes," Garethor said. "She defended the settlement. But she told me that when she was a little girl, she had a hard time creating anything at all. She didn't think she'd be able to create more than a rock for years. And then," Garethor said, gesturing with his hands around, "this. But she had to work very hard for it, as will you."

Valfric nodded. In his mind, he could see himself clad in armor, defending the settlement. It made him feel good on the inside. He thought of his brother. *Then no one would ever bother us if I was a powerful Essaerist,* he thought to himself.

"So how long do you think it'll take me to get that strong?" Valfric asked.

Garethor shrugged. "I suppose it depends."

"Depends on what?" Valfric asked.

Garethor smiled. "It depends on how many times you try to distract me by asking for stories instead of working on your Essaerites."

Valfric narrowed his eyes but resisted the urge to make a comment that would get him hit by the stick. So instead, he released the metal horse by his side and closed his eyes, focusing on creating another one. *I will be a powerful warrior one day,* he told himself. *And when I am, no one will hurt anybody I care about.*

CHAPTER 21

The march to the fort on the frontier had been a long one, but not necessarily unpleasant. Mariokos had gotten the chance to see some other parts of the Empire. He had never been to the northern regions of Lysandrian before, but he had enjoyed it. They had moved out from the main part of the Empire into new settlements, as they drew ever closer to Gwenthari Territory.

After the last city they had visited, which hardly deserved the name, they entered areas with just villages and forts. To the north lay the frontier; to the south was relatively unsettled land. The area was plagued by Gwenthari raids and constant troubles, and Mariokos wondered how much of their job would involve securing land they already possessed.

They had been camped for a few weeks at the fort, waiting for the last few legions to arrive that would comprise the expeditionary force that would move into Gwenthari territory. The area was dominated by tall trees, some adorned with occasional bioluminescent ribbons that ran up their trunks. They had seen many more animals than he was accustomed to seeing in the Empire as well. They had seen large deer and wolves, along with a host of other animals he had never heard of before. In the Empire, he knew that most large animals had either migrated away or been killed off, replaced by livestock. Still, he had seen plenty of foxes growing up, and the occasional deer, but nothing like what he saw now.

One of the strangest and most interesting animals he had seen since coming north was the Runeantler. One of his hawks, circling the legion, had first spotted them. They were in a group of about eight. Large and with white fur—something that apparently was common in winter—they possessed large antlers atop their heads and had been foraging in the small patches of snow that still clung to the ground. He'd learned that they could change their horns to suit their needs. When he had seen the group, he noticed a bunch of smaller animals circling around them, which he now knew were Essaerites that the Runeantlers were capable of creating. These smaller creatures could forage in tighter, denser areas away from the main group without danger. They would fill their bellies with whatever they collected and then return to the Runeantler to deposit the food. He thought they were amazing creatures, and from what the men at the fort had told him, they were rugged and tough, capable of forming a type of armor on their hides that made hunting them very difficult. He'd been fascinated watching them. While they had encountered other creatures, those were the only ones they had seen that could use Essaeris.

The fort itself was a work in progress, like so many Lysandrian military structures. It had started as a camp on the edge of the frontier, and day by day, hour by hour, the legion tending it had continued to strengthen its defenses and build more infrastructure in the area. The result was a large stone fort with many permanent buildings.

Historically, where the legions chose to make camps tended to be good spots for travel and trade—not out of any sense of trying to build future-proof areas, but rather because those locations were ideal for a large force to stop. Mariokos suspected that, as time went on, this fort would turn into a city, like so many others had. Many settlements in the area had once started as forts. And after the military moved on, the citizens stayed. This fort would be no different.

Already, outside the walls and in nearby areas, other buildings had been constructed by merchants, farmers, and other support personnel who had come in to assist the legion. Their presence created an economy for those living there. The fort provided stability, allowing for trade with the Gwenthari to the north and for the movement of materials to different settlements.

He had been surprised by the number of Gwenthari he'd seen up here. Many were friendly with the Empire, and many of the settlements in the area were Gwenthari settlements that had integrated smoothly with the Empire. The people were so different from what he was used to. They had a wilder feel to them, which he had expected. But what he hadn't expected was their practicality and advancement. He had always been raised with the notion that the Gwenthari were barbarians—stupid and incapable of anything—but that hadn't quite added up for him. After all, at one point in time, the Gwenthari had been the dominant force on the continent, even reaching down far enough to sack the capital of Lysandrian. *How could a stupid force do that?*

What seemed to have happened was that the Gwenthari had stagnated in some way, or they had moved back, or simply stopped progressing as a society. Mariokos wasn't sure. But he also knew that the farther north they went, the more resistance they would face. The Legionnaires at the fort had reported that scouts found settlements in the area banding together to create cohesive fighting units. This hadn't been unexpected, and the Legion had seriously doubted they would only be dealing with one small band after another. While the Ulfgarath were largely being scattered, they had once been a powerful nation, and many of those old ties still remained. Troops had reported encountering large groups of Gwenthari before, and said the fighting had been fierce.

The Legion would be moving out soon, and Mariokos found Xavieno and Fioralba as they finished packing up. He could see Xavieno's excitement, and it was a bit infectious. He smiled as he walked up to them.

"I don't think I've ever seen someone so excited to be walking into rough terrain before," Mariokos said.

Xavieno looked at him and grinned. "In all fairness, how many people have you seen that have been going into rough terrain before?"

Mariokos chuckled. "That's fair."

He approached Fioralba and hugged her. "Are you looking forward to moving on, or are you going to miss the fort?"

She looked thoughtful. "I can't decide, honestly. There are some things I like about the fort, but some things that I don't."

That was something he could empathize with. In so many ways, the fort had all the cons of a city and all the drawbacks of being on the road. He was sure for the people that lived in the area, with each structure built and each improvement made, life became easier. But for the Legion coming in, it felt mostly like being in a city where you still had to camp.

"Yeah, it's not as comfortable as home," Mariokos said.

She shook her head. "That it's not."

Her gaze swept out, surveying the Legion as it prepared to move.

"So what's the plan? Twenty miles today, and then are we at another fort?" she asked, curious.

Mariokos shook his head. "No. This is the last fort. North of here is the frontier. We'll move twenty miles, build a camp. I don't know about the next day, maybe we'll stay in the area for a day or two, but my guess would be that we'll continue to move north," Mariokos said.

Xavieno chimed in. "That's what I'd put money on. Now that we have all the legions together, the expeditionary force will move quickly, I think. From what my understanding is of the area, we're heading into some high mountains, but those mountains will break up every now and then into valleys where there are settlements and cities, along with plenty of farmland."

Mariokos nodded grimly. *Yes, we'll move out of those heavy areas where it's difficult to maneuver quickly,* he thought. He didn't expect any problems on the road for the next few days. The Legion would know if there was a large force in the area, and he found it doubtful given the fort's presence. It shouldn't be hard for this part of the frontier to receive support from the rest of the Empire, but that would change the further north they went.

Mariokos made his way back to his squad as the Legion was forming up to move out. He saw the grizzled form of his sergeant. The man's name was Erastos. His dark brown hair was like bristles on top of his head. His green eyes were sharp, constantly scanning the surroundings. He had a muscular build and always had an aggravated expression. Mariokos could see his jaw clench now as he barked orders at the men in the squad.

He had always found Erastos to be abrasive at best, but he was one of the best commanders there was, and Mariokos respected him. He was also one of the people who most exemplified in the Legion the cross between combat and construction worker. Erastos was brutal on the battlefield, but in Mariokos's opinion, he was even more brutal when it was time to build fortifications or handle anything of that nature.

Erastos's head snapped over to Mariokos. "What the fuck are you going so goddamn slow for?" he bellowed.

Mariokos quickened his pace. "Sorry, sir."

"You better be fucking sorry. We're supposed to be moving out to go kill these fucking barbarians. And what the fuck are you doing? You're fucking wandering around like it's some fucking nice day in the park," Erastos said, his voice rising and his tone becoming increasingly harsh.

Mariokos felt his face flush. "Sorry, sir. I didn't mean to be fucking wandering, sir."

Erastos growled. "Don't use that fucking language with me, soldier!" He turned his attention to other men, barking orders at them.

Mariokos fell in line next to two other men. Helioz had dark eyes and short wavy hair, a smirk plastered across his face as he stood at attention.

"Looks like you pissed someone off this morning," he said with a laugh.

Mariokos rolled his eyes. "Oh, piss off. I bet he yelled at you before me."

Helioz grinned. "He's yelled at me three times so far this morning. I really think he's starting to like me," Helioz commented, glancing at Mariokos.

Mariokos chuckled. "Yeah, no, I definitely think he is. I think it's going well for you. This is going to be a great war."

As he spoke, he could hear Erastos yelling at some man nearby. The only one in the squad who didn't seem to get berated constantly was Luciakos. Luciakos stood on Mariokos's other side. He was of average height, with bright green eyes and dark brown curly hair. He was the kind of man that women fawned over, though Mariokos had never seen him show much interest in anyone. He was soft-spoken and one of the best fighters Mariokos had ever seen. He was even better than Xavieno by a wide margin. Luciakos was also good at listening and otherwise being there when you needed someone to shoot the shit with.

"Did you get yelled at this morning?" Mariokos asked Luciakos.

Luciakos looked over at him and raised an eyebrow. "Would it make you feel better if I said I did?"

Mariokos thought for a moment. "It might make me feel a little better."

Luciakos nodded. "Yeah, sure, I got yelled at this morning."

"You know Luciakos didn't get yelled at," Helioz pointed out. "The sergeant loves him."

"He doesn't love me," Luciakos replied. "I just do my job and follow orders," he said, looking at Helioz. "Maybe if you did that, you wouldn't get yelled at so much."

Helioz snorted. "No, he yells at me because I'm his protégé."

This made Mariokos and Luciakos laugh.

"What the fuck are you assholes laughing at?" a voice bellowed. All three men stood stock-still, at attention.

"Sorry, sir," Mariokos said.

"I'm fucking sorry? Goddamn sorry, pieces of shit," Erastos said, stalking away.

"He's really on a tear this morning," Helioz said under his breath.

"It's because we're marching north today," Luciakos remarked just as quietly. "You know how the sergeant gets."

Mariokos nodded. He did. "And he hates the Gwenthari."

That was an understatement. Nobody was really a fan of the Gwenthari. After all, you weren't going to be fans of people you were about to fight. But the sergeant had a special kind of hatred for them that Mariokos didn't quite understand. Even with the friendly Gwenthari who had been by the fort and those working with the Legion, Erastos had been an asshole to them, threatening to kill no less than fifteen of them since they arrived. Mariokos didn't know what his deal was, and he had no desire to ask any questions about it.

As the Legions finished forming up, the sergeant returned to the squad and took his place in formation. He seemed calmer now and looked over at them.

"Are you men ready for this?" he asked, his voice much more even.

"We are, sir," they all responded.

"Good."

Soon the order came, and the Legion began to move. Mariokos marched in unison with the rest of the troops as they left the fort's gates and headed into the forest. The road they followed was fairly well-defined, and they'd be staying on it for some time. Men talked amongst themselves as they marched, and the sergeant calmed down. Once they were in formation for the day, he seemed to get more relaxed, and even would join in conversation.

"So, Sarge, do you think we'll find anything today?" Helioz asked.

The sergeant looked at him and shook his head. "Nah, I don't think so. Not this close to the fort. Even those barbarians aren't that fucking stupid," he replied, though his tone lacked its usual venom.

And it would be hard to maintain hatred on a day like today. The sun rose higher in the sky, warming them. It was still cold, as it was still January, and their breath puffed out in front of them. But there was a pleasant smell to the air, and Mariokos enjoyed the change of scenery. He looked at his surroundings as they walked, seeing mountains on either side of them, and tall forests. He could hear the occasional bird chirping in the trees or see one flying overhead. They were further back in the legion, so he didn't see any wildlife, if there was any to be seen; all of it would be scared away. Instead, he focused on his hawks that he had in the air as they zoomed about.

"Looking through hawks," he said softly.

Next to him, Helioz and Luciakos moved a little closer, ready to grab Mariokos's elbows should he be coming up on something rough along the road or if he began to move around. Mariokos moved into some of the hawks in the area as they soared above the forest. He typically kept his hawks high, allowing him to see a great distance, but he saw this wasn't going to work here.

"How's the scouting?" Erastos inquired, his voice not holding any abrasiveness whatsoever.

Mariokos returned to his body and looked over at his sergeant, grimacing. "It's going to be difficult in these woods. The tree canopies are dense, and with the mountains, I can't see at a long range if I stay up high."

Erastos grunted. "Yeah, I was worried about that. I heard the other scouts that we have that are normal men have struggles too. These woods are thick, with lots of places for Gwenthari to hide."

"Have ambushes been a problem, sir?" Luciakos asked.

"Yes, from what my understanding is," Erastos replied. "The Gwenthari are good at hiding, and most of them are on horseback. So even if you see them, they can come up on you quickly. But I think a large group will have a hard time."

Luciakos nodded, seeming satisfied. Mariokos brought his hawks closer to the ground and the legion. As they got nearer, they managed to see through the foliage, on a few occasions, he had the birds dip into the trees, scanning for anything of note. Underneath the canopies, the forest floor was dim, and branches were everywhere, making it impossible for the birds to look around. Mariokos had them pop back up above the trees. It was going to be problematic, and he could see where they were going to have to rely heavily on traditional scouts.

"I could maybe create some dogs," Mariokos suggested. "That could be useful."

The sergeant considered this. "I'm not sure about that. That'd take up more of your Essaeris, wouldn't it?"

Mariokos nodded. "Unfortunately, yes, but they have better noses than the hawks do, so they might get a drop on something."

Erastos looked thoughtful. "We'll have to talk to Theoliano about it and see what he says. We might not have a choice, but also, with a group this large, I'm not worried about us being ambushed by smaller groups of Gwenthari," he said. "Keep your hawks doing their thing."

Mariokos nodded and returned to managing his hawks.

The sun was high in the sky when they descended into a small valley. It wasn't large, and Mariokos could see copse of trees scattered throughout. The orders came down that they were to make camp for the night.

The legion moved to where their campsite would be and formed up, waiting for instructions. Mariokos knew his role. He closed his eyes and controlled his breathing, feeling deep inside himself, sensing his power as it grew, ebbed, and flowed. He tuned out the world as he focused on building up his energy.

When setting camp, there were three main tasks that needed to happen. First, a section of the legion would be dedicated to guard duty. Second, a group would set out to forage in the area for food, dry wood to burn, potential threats, and hunting. Lastly, a group of men would construct the camp for the night.

Mariokos was almost always part of this last group, and it was the one he preferred. For most men, it was a toss-up on what duty they would get, but it rarely was for Mariokos. While Xavieno specialized in combat, Mariokos had focused on logistics, which was why he typically received this task. It was no surprise when Erastos called out the order for Mariokos to begin helping with setting up camp.

He opened his eyes and acknowledged the order. Creating a small stool, he sat down. To either side of him were Helioz and Luciakos. This was their role while Mariokos worked focused on his Essaeris.

While unlikely, it was for them to be attacked and for that attack to be able to reach Mariokos, they still stood over him, at least until he was done creating his Essaerites and could start helping them.

Mariokos reached down inside himself, working on creating the first few. A handful of small, humanoid Essaerites came into existence. They had thick arms and legs and carried axes and shovels, along with a few saws. When he finished creating the four of them, he focused on his main Essaerite.

He felt his energy build within, peaking as he stoked it. It rippled outward, and the hulking form of the Essaerite took shape. While Xavieno had focused on creating multiple strong, powerful warriors, Mariokos had directed most of his focus toward a single Essaerite. This one could be changed and altered, depending on the needs, but its basic form remained relatively the same. It had six legs and was roughly the size of an ox, although it didn't have quite the same weight. It was black, and its skin was like hardened leather, and at the front, a large head could be transformed into a couple of different items. Usually, Mariokos configured it with a large set of pincers capable of cutting down and severing almost any tree or likewise grip onto a stump to rip it from the ground. In its current form, it had two large, vertical, spaded blades, resembling elongated shovels. From its rear, an appendage would move dirt out of the way.

This Essaerite was incredibly strong. Such large Essaerites were known as Essaerithons.

It could withstand significant damage, although Mariokos doubted there would be many times when it would actually be attacked, as it was not intended for combat. Still, if the need arose, he could create small hooks on the side where shields could be attached to protect it from harm.

As the Essaerithon took shape, Mariokos opened his eyes to inspect it. It was ugly and utilitarian in every way, shape, and form, and for him, that was what made it beautiful. With a flick of his mind, it moved toward a large tree and began rooting around its base. There was a sound of popping and cracking as the Essaerithon drove its bladed teeth into the ground and ripped, sending the tree crashing down. The smaller Essaerites began running along it, cutting off branches and stripping it bare.

Mariokos shifted the hind end of the Essaerithon, transforming it into a type of clamp, like giant pliers. The Essaerithon turned and gripped the trunk of the tree, wandering off to remove it from the area. He joined the other Essaerites in carrying some of the branches away. All around them, the camp bustled with activity as men worked to set up. After clearing most of the trees, Mariokos directed his Essaerithon onto its main objective.

It approached a man who was one of the engineers for the legion. He had a stake planted in the ground, and Mariokos walked up to him. The man indicated the direction that the trench needed to be dug on either side. He noted the other stakes marking the corners of the camp and nodded in understanding.

He directed the Essaerithon to the corner of the camp, and its long shovels began working their way into the ground. The beginning was always the hardest, but it quickly turned up the ground, and soon it was steadily moving forward into its own trench. The legions all built similar trenches and walls; all of the camps were the same, barring minor details.

In the case of camps that Mariokos was in, the trench was always much deeper than those of other legions, as they were building theirs with men. The Essaerithon dug about five feet deep and expanded the trench to be five feet wide. It moved forward, its enormous shovel teeth coming up and scraping dirt before kicking it behind.

The other Essaerites flung the dirt behind the Essaerithon into the camp as other legionnaires began shoveling it into berms where the staves would be embedded to construct the wall. Mariokos walked alongside the giant Essaerite, listening to the soil being ripped and torn as it moved forward.

The trench was deep and wide, making it difficult for anyone to cross. On the other side, the berm it created was likewise tall, and though the wall formed with the staves wasn't indestructible, it was designed to slow down the enemy should they choose to attack in the dead of night.

If the legion remained in the area for any length of time, they would reinforce the walls and make them more difficult to get through. They'd also expand the trenches as well, but for day one, this was standard protocol.

It took the Essaerithon a couple of hours to create the trench that encircled the camp, but when it was completed, he looked over to see men digging in and constructing the wall around the camp. He then set his other Essaerites to work digging latrines and otherwise fortifying the interior of the camp. Meanwhile, he sent the Essaerithon to the surrounding woods to rip out trees and clear any brush in the way, ensuring the camp would have plenty of visibility. There would be no sneaking up on them.

When he was done, he walked to where his tent would be. Some of his Essaeris had recuperated, and he felt energy bubble up as he created his tent and cot. He tossed his bag inside and stretched his arms above his head. Around him, he could smell campfires starting to burn as men prepared dinner, which consisted of boiled oats and flatbread made on stones around the fire pits.

Mariokos began tending to his own meal, placing some oats in a bowl with water and starting a fire. He took flour from his pack and made a quick dough that he set on a hot plate next to the fire. He tended to his oats, and when they were done, he added in a few spices from his pack and then felt down inside of himself for energy, creating a handful of other tastier items to plop in the oats, along with one of the jams that he had learned how to make over at Biankara's house that he spread onto the flatbread when it was done.

He took a bite of the bread just as Helioz approached. Mariokos created a stool for him to sit on, and he dropped down heavily.

"Did you eat dinner?" Mariokos asked.

Helioz nodded. "I did. The camp looks good," he said, casting his gaze around.

"That it does," Mariokos replied.

As he finished his meal, the sun was starting to set, and the air was growing cold. Sentry duty was announced, and Mariokos was happy to see that he didn't have anything that evening. When it was time to go to bed, he wandered into his tent and released his clothes. He laid down heavily on the cot, and sleep found him quickly.

CHAPTER 22

Fioralba was walking through a wooded glade. The forest floor was soft under her bare feet, with only a few bits of rough ground. The sun warmed her, and around her, she could smell flowers as they bloomed. She peered around the moss-covered trees. It was alien to her in so many ways, but beautiful. There were so many more trees here than in her home, and they reached so high. She could hear the sounds of squirrels and other animals moving in the canopy, and she took a deep breath through her nose, letting the smell of the forest saturate her.

She continued to walk around, exploring as she did. In the distance, she thought she heard something—perhaps the sound of an animal, or maybe it was somebody playing music. It almost sounded like a horn. She kept walking through the forest, the sound growing louder. Yes, it was a horn, she decided. It wasn't a very pretty-sounding horn when she thought about it. It was just a blaring, loud sound.

The noise became louder, and she searched for its source. *Where's the sound coming from?* she thought. Suddenly, she felt something push her. Her eyes flew open. She was in a dark tent with Xavieno. She heard the horn again, along with the sounds of men. Xavieno was moving.

"Shit, that's the alarm," he said, scrambling to his feet and moving out of the cot.

She rolled over, bleary-eyed. "What?"

"It's the alarm!" Xavieno said, crashing out of the tent.

It took her mind a few moments to realize where she was and what he meant by 'the alarm.' She sat up in her cot, her heart starting to beat faster. She reached inside herself, feeling her Essaeris. She created a small glowing ball and set it next to her. It was a deep red, allowing her to maintain her night vision. It cast everything in a bloody light. Outside, she could hear men yelling, and her heart thumped in her chest.

She created clothes and poked her head out of the tent. They were in the center of camp, where Command and the other Aristolios stayed. Around her, there was a flurry of activity as men rushed to their posts. The flickering torch-light drowned out the stars above them, throwing the camp into contrast.

She got out of the tent but then froze. She wasn't sure what to do. She wasn't part of the Legion, and she didn't know how to fight. There was nothing she could do. So instead, she went back into the tent and sat on the cot, unsure of what to think or feel.

The sound of men scrambling around lessened, but she could still hear it off in the distance. She could hear shouting and yelling, but she wasn't sure what was going on. The horn had stopped, and after a time, things seemed to calm down, but she wasn't sure if that was a good or bad thing. She wished she knew what was happening.

Oh, Fioralba, you idiot, she thought to herself. She could see what was going on. All she had to do was try. With a flick of her Essaeris, she created a small owl that took off from the tent and flew overhead. As it circled around, she could see campfires.

They were in neat rows along with the tents. Everything about the camp was neat and orderly. There was a space between the tents and where the wall began. Other fires were there too, lighting up groups of men who sat waiting. Then there was the wall and trench, and beyond that, open space, until another series of torches, and then more space, and then the woods.

What was it? she wondered. Her owl couldn't see anything. But there had to have been something, hadn't there? *They wouldn't call the alarm so many times for no reason,* she thought. So what had it been? She could only wonder.

———

MARIOKOS KNEW THAT WITH HOW LATE IT WAS, HIS EYELIDS SHOULD HAVE BEEN HEAVY with sleep, but they weren't. They were wide open, and his brain was running at full speed. They'd been slowly pushing into Gwenthari territory for the last week, and thus far, they hadn't encountered any resistance. They hadn't even found any settlements, but the legions had still moved with caution.

Then this evening had happened. They had set camp like normal, and Mariokos had just finished his sentry duty and gone to bed when the alert horn sounded. Now he was awake and had created a series of Essaerites. They were all shorter than regular men, standing only four feet tall. They had thick arms, and their hands ended in little appendages that could easily grab javelins. With them, he had also created bundles of javelins. He had another little Essaerite that was perched on top of the wall. It was about the size of a frog and only had eyes. Those eyes could see into the dark night and were searching for anything they could find.

The idea was simple. If the frog saw something, one of the other Essaerites would throw a javelin at it. It had taken him some time to develop this technique, but now the Essaerites were quite accurate when it came to throwing things, even if they didn't have line of sight.

The problem was, the frog wasn't seeing anything. Out past the main wall, there was a line of torches and watchfires. Sentries would watch, and should anything enter the light, they knew to sound the horn. The problem with this tactic, of course, was that it was hard to see past the light from those fires. That problem was compounded by the deep woods, though Mariokos could see the faint glow from some of the trees that had lines running up their bark. He thought he saw a couple of flying creatures that glowed as well, but it wasn't providing enough light in the forest to see if there was anything in it. They'd caught a few glimpses of something in the trees. It appeared to be men on horseback, but they were keeping out of the light.

There were a handful of reports from the other side of camp of horsemen riding out of the treeline to try and take out torches or watchfires, while others shot arrows over the wall. Then they'd dart back into the woods. It wasn't a concerted attack. Mariokos knew it was meant to harass and keep them awake, and it was working.

Out from the forest, he heard an eerie sound, a chant, and then a shrill scream. It made the hair on the back of his neck stand on end, and he reminded himself of what some of the men in the fort had said. They said that the Gwenthari were very good at getting in your head and that they were evil beings that worshiped evil gods. Mariokos wasn't sure about that last part or the part before, but they were certainly doing a good job of getting under his skin and making him feel creeped out.

He held his position, looking through his frog. He had a couple of hawks, but their night vision was worthless, so he wasn't employing them at the moment. He could create owls, but Erastos had been very clear that Mariokos was not to waste any Essaeris. So he had the hawks sitting at his tent, and instead, he looked through the little frog, seeing what was there, and the answer was nothing.

He thought he caught a glimpse of something rustling in the trees, but it didn't turn out to be anything, and even if it had been, it was so far out of range it wouldn't matter.

"So this is how the night's going to go," Luciakos said next to him.

Mariokos pulled back into his own body and looked over at his friend.

"It might," he said, not liking the sound of it.

"I don't think they could make it past the wall, though," Helioz said confidently.

He was probably right. He didn't think it was likely that anyone would try to attack the Legion at night, past what they were doing already. After an hour or so, the call came down for some of the men to go back and sleep, but they were to stay in their full armor.

Mariokos was not one of those men, and even if he had been, he didn't think he would be able to sleep. So instead, he went back to looking through his frog. As he did, his mind wound around as he tried to make sense of the situation they were in. The Gwenthari were barbarians. This he knew, but now he was starting to appreciate it, and he wondered how long they had been marching with the Gwenthari watching them, while the Legion had been none the wiser.

———

THE SKY WAS BEGINNING TO PINK WITH SUNRISE, AND XAVIENO WAS DONE WITH HIS watch. It had been a long night. First, there had been the horn sounding the alarm, and he'd gotten up with everyone else, and then nothing had happened. Then he'd gone back to sleep for a couple of hours and was roused again for his watch.

He'd created his warrior Essaerites, and they stood next to him, ready for whatever came. But Xavieno didn't think anything was going to come. He was pretty sure, in fact, that the Gwenthari had left the area. They'd managed to take out a few of the torches and fires, but Xavieno wasn't sure that a single Gwenthari had been injured in the entire encounter. None of the legion had been either, and he wondered if that wasn't the point.

It wasn't about hurting the legion. It was about pissing them off, keeping them awake, and otherwise trying to get in their heads, while at the same time, the Gwenthari barbarians got the opportunity to have some fun and get a rise out of the legion. They'd pay for that, that was for sure. Xavieno just wasn't sure when they'd be paying for it. There was a very real possibility that it had only been a handful of Gwenthari that had been bugging them in the night; for all the legion knew, it could have been drunkards looking for a good time.

He snorted, thinking about it. That was probably the case, and in a way, that almost made it worse. If it had been a dedicated force looking to probe the weaknesses of the legion, then at least he would have battle to look forward to. But if it was just a few local men trying to annoy the legion, then Xavieno and every other legionnaire had been made fools during the night. Xavieno didn't like the thought of that.

He checked in on a couple of the hawks he had circling the camp. Now that the sun was coming out, they would be able to see. As they did, he had them move down close to the tree line. The valley was socked in with low clouds and fog that clung to the tops of the trees, but that was fine. He needed the hawks low anyway. As they moved along the tree line, he could see patches of mud that had been disturbed by horses. He was surprised at how many tracks he found.

There was another legion camped just a little ways north of them. He could see them easily from one of the gates, and he saw some tracks in between the two camps as well. *Fuck,* he thought to himself. *They were moving between us, and we didn't even know.* That gave him a little pause. *Maybe it wasn't drunks,* he thought.

He had the hawks move around the other camp as well, seeing that they had also lost a few torches and watchfires.

Xavieno heard someone approaching him. He pulled himself back into his own body and looked over at Geraldox.

"What do you see, kid?" Geraldox asked, his voice rough.

"They surrounded us, sir," he said. "I found tracks around our camp and the other camp and in between."

"Can you tell how many?" Geraldox asked.

Xavieno shook his head. "Hard to tell. I'm sure some of the trackers from the legion can figure it out, but I don't have an idea."

Geraldox nodded. "Alright. I guess that answers some questions then."

Xavieno looked at him. "What questions are those?"

Geraldox sighed. "The type of enemy we're dealing with here."

"And what type is that, sir?" Xavieno asked.

"One that's clever," he said. "One that didn't go straight after the legions and go toe-to-toe against us."

Xavieno smirked. "That'd be suicide."

Geraldox chuckled. "Exactly. It's suicide. But at some point, the Gwenthari will be forced into it. Still, I think we can expect things like this to be pretty regular occurrences."

"So do you want owls at night, then?" he asked.

Geraldox huffed. "Yeah, I think we're going to need owls. How do they do during the day?"

Xavieno shrugged. "They do fine. I like the hawks because they're a little bit faster, but honestly, with how dense these trees are, I don't think it's going to matter. The owls are probably going to be a better decision anyway."

Geraldox nodded. "Owls it is, but I only want you to have two of them. I don't want you wasting your Essaeris on scouts. After all, these Gwenthari may be able to harass us, but they're not going to be able to get over the walls of the camp."

Xavieno nodded. "I understand, sir. Two it is."

CHAPTER 23
TWENTY YEARS AGO

Valfric walked back into his settlement, a wide grin on his face. In his left hand, he held two dead hares he had managed to catch. Catching the little creatures hadn't been the part that made him so happy. It was how he had caught them. He wouldn't ever tell Garethor this, but Valfric thought he might be getting better, and it might be Garethor's doing. He had been able to create a snare using his Essaeris, which would lead to them having dinner tonight and tomorrow.

He was also happy because he thought his father would have a hard time complaining about Valfric coming home with dinner, but he was sure his father would find a way.

As he walked through the settlement, he saw people working in the fields and otherwise engaged in daily activities. He smiled, waving at them, and many waved back, a few making comments about the hares.

He walked by Garethor's house, but he didn't care to go in and bother the old man. He thought that the hares might be too tempting for the Wolxaran, so he kept on walking toward his house.

He felt his clothes getting damp with the heavy mist that hung in the air. Or was it cloud? Or was it fog? Valfric could never be sure what it was. People had explained it to him several times, but he thought it was all kind of silly. After all, a cloud was the same as fog and mist, wasn't it? It was gray, fluffy stuff in the sky that made you wet and cold.

Valfric decided that it was a cloud he was in, not fog or mist, because it'd be weird to say that there was fog or mist high in the sky that rain came from, wouldn't it?

As he trudged onto his property, he heard a horse whinny and a loud crash. Then the horse came tearing around the side of the house, a cart being dragged behind it. Instantly, Valfric dropped the hares and jumped out of the way of the panicked animal.

As it dragged the cart, he heard a snap and break of the harnesses. The horse went careening around, kicking and bucking. Following the horse was his father, who was swearing and yelling at it. "You fucking dumb nag," he yelled, waving his arms around.

Valfric didn't think that yelling at the horse was going to get it to calm down, but he also didn't think he should say that to his father. His heart had picked up, but it was starting to calm as he saw the horse move away from the house. As it did, it seemed to calm some.

His father was trudging after it, and Valfric jogged to catch up to him. "I've got it, Father. It's okay. He listens to me."

His father shot him a dagger-like glance. "Where have you been, boy?"

Valfric pointed to where he had dropped the hares. "I was out catching dinner. I've got the horse. Do you mind taking the hares?"

His father grunted. "Fine," he said, and went off to pick up the hares.

Valfric walked up to the horse. It was padding around in the field and still seemed agitated. He held up his hands and spoke soothingly to it. The animal seemed to calm some.

As Valfric approached, he could see sweat along its flanks as it breathed deeply. It seemed a little uneasy as Valfric got closer.

"You're fine, you're fine," he said.

It calmed more, and Valfric walked up to it. The horse's head came down, and Valfric gently stroked its velvety nose and head. "See, you're okay." He stroked its neck.

He stood there for a time with it, calming it down. "Let's go on back, okay?" he said softly. He gently took the rope around its neck and led it back toward the house, speaking to it soothingly the whole time.

As he got nearer, he could see the cart on the ground, and he wondered what had happened. Valfric decided he would get the horse tied up and then see what was going on. As he approached the house, though, he saw a form on the ground.

Valfric let go of the lead and jogged up to the form, gasping. "Gaelrik," he exclaimed. He knelt next to his brother, who was lying on the ground covered in blood. His face was bloody and looked almost broken, and Valfric could see dirt and mud along with blood on his clothes. *He must have been run over by the cart,* he thought.

Valfric tried to shake Gaelrik, who didn't make any sound. He held his ear close to his brother's nose and mouth and heard gurgling. He called for his father, who finally came around the corner.

"What is it?" he asked.

"It's Gaelrik. He's been hurt," Valfric said.

His father came up to him, looked down, and swore. "Shit, go get help," he demanded.

Valfric rose on shaky legs and began running to the only person he thought of who might know what to do. He tumbled onto Garethor's property and into his house. As he barged in, the Wolxaran snapped its head over to him, as did Garethor.

"What do you think you're—" Garethor started and stopped, seeing blood on Valfric. "What is it?" he asked, worried.

"It's Gaelrik. He's been hurt. He's been run over by a cart," Valfric said, terrified.

Garethor got up and moved as quickly as he could over to Valfric's house. Gaelrik was still where Valfric had found him. Garethor approached him, looking down. From behind him, Valfric could hear Garethor's Wolxaran whine softly and pace around.

"What happened?" Garethor asked.

"I don't know. I was coming back. I caught some hares, and the horse came around dragging the cart," Valfric said.

Garethor looked around. "Where is your father?"

Valfric searched around, confused. Where was his father? He called for him and went looking for him. He found him inside the house, skinning the hares.

"What are you doing?" he asked.

His father looked over at him. "Dinner."

" Gaelrik is hurt," Valfric said. "And Garethor is here."

His father sighed and went out.

Garethor looked up at him. "What happened?"

"Cart accident. The boy should have been paying attention," his father said.

Valfric saw anger and disgust cross Garethor's face. "Your son is lying on the ground, and that's what you have to say?"

Valfric had never noticed it before, but Garethor could be rather intimidating. Valfric's father huffed. "He wasn't my son. He was a waste," he said and turned to walk off.

Valfric couldn't believe what he was hearing. He watched his father go and felt traitorous tears in his eyes. He looked back down at Gaelrik and then up at Garethor.

Garethor's expression had gone from hard and angry to soft and sorrowful, and he put his hand on Valfric's shoulder. "I'm sorry."

"You're sorry for what?" Valfric said, glancing back down at his brother. "No. No, that's not what happened."

Garethor's expression remained soft.

"No, no, no, no, no, no, no," Valfric said, feeling himself rip apart on the inside.

He moved over to his brother and shook his shoulders, but Gaelrik didn't move. He put his face back down by his brother's nose and mouth and didn't hear anything. He felt tears running down his face.

"No," he said, "no!"

Out of the corner of his eye, he saw Garethor's Wolxaran come up and curl up next to Gaelrik, resting its head by him. The Wolxaran seemed sad and forlorn.

Valfric sat back on the ground, tears streaming down his face. "No, I'm so sorry."

He felt a hand on his shoulder and looked up to see Garethor. He was surprised to see that Garethor's eyes were shining. "It's not your fault."

"But if I had..." Valfric started.

Garethor shook his head, cutting him off. "It's not your fault."

"Then whose fault is it?" Valfric asked.

Garethor unconsciously glanced toward the house but then looked back at Valfric and shook his head.

"It's no one's fault. It just is," he said, but Valfric knew the truth. He knew whose fault it was. It was his father's—the man who was supposed to be watching over and taking care of his brother.

Valfric gritted his teeth, some of his sorrow and sadness being replaced by anger.

He rested his hand on his dead brother's and then reached over tentatively to scratch behind the Wolxaran's ears. It didn't growl at him or anything. It just looked up at him, sad.

Valfric sat with his brother until the sun had gone down and people from the settlement had come by to take his brother to clean him up and give him a proper burial.

Valfric felt numb. His heart had turned to stone, and that night, when his father was done cooking the hare, Valfric didn't come in to eat it.

He was done with his father. He was done with everything.

CHAPTER 24

The winter had not been a good one for Caelwen and her people. As she had worried, they'd lost several individuals to illnesses that Caelwen was pretty sure she could have prevented had they not lost all of their herbs and tinctures. They'd also endured no less than three attacks on the settlement. None of them had been large, mind you—more just probing, harassing attacks. She had been able to fend them off with relative ease, but she was now in the position of having to keep three of her large cats at all times. She had turned the creatures from black to a snow white that blended in with their surroundings.

The cats orbited around the settlement, seeming to meander, but always in a spot where they could support each other at a moment's notice. She'd had to keep them close to town, which was fine during the wintertime. There wasn't anyone out in the fields, and the livestock was kept close to people's homes, but she knew that would change with the thaw.

She'd also moved to using more owls to patrol the forest. She had the occasional hawk as well, but she found that she needed the owls for the lower light during the winter and in the dense forests. Everybody was on edge, just as they should have been. The only exception to that were the men who had been with Wulfgren when he had been at war. They'd been keeping sentry duty around town, and it seemed to come naturally to them. After all, that's what they'd spent the last few years doing—posting watches and raiding whenever necessary. For them, this was how life should have been. Not being attacked so much, but always being ready for an attack. Still, she could see the stress in the eyes of the men whenever she saw them. Yes, they knew how to keep guard, but they also knew what they were up against. Being attacked in the dead of winter wasn't exactly common.

Things had compounded when Caelwen went to a neighboring community in an attempt to buy herbs and tinctures. She'd been turned away flatly, and it had happened in another settlement. It turned out that Ilfthandor's policy of pissing off every settlement around them was biting them in the ass. No one would work with them or talk to them. In fact, there hadn't been a single caravan or trading party that had come since the caravan she'd helped attack months ago.

The word was out. They were not to be trusted. Further, the word was out that they didn't have a smith, that they were small, and that the only thing keeping them safe was Caelwen and Wulfgren's men, of which he didn't have very many.

She was concerned about the spring and summer. If they could make it for a year or so, she was sure that things would settle down and that they'd be able to rebuild ties with other communities, but they had to make it that long for that to happen. She knew the other settlements wanted to attack them, but they didn't have the courage to do it yet, or the means, or perhaps they were waiting for spring. She didn't know, and she hoped she wouldn't have to find out.

She'd managed to clear the rubble away from her cottage, but she hadn't gotten around to rebuilding it yet. She wouldn't be able to until the spring, and even then it would be difficult with so much of her Essaeris being taken up by defenses. So she'd been forced to stay with her brother. It had its pros and cons. She'd enjoyed having someone to talk to, other than her uncle, but she'd also missed having her own space. In so many ways, they got along well, just acting as the adults they were, and then they'd slip back to their ways as children and bicker and argue over something benign and stupid. But living with him, she could also see the tension in him every time there was an attack. He knew what was coming, probably better than she did.

Her mind reached out to one of the birds in the area. It was circling high above them, taking advantage of the mists that were starting to clear. She sent it in a large circle around the settlement. With each pass, it expanded out, increasing its search radius. It couldn't see very much through the trees, but that was fine. Caelwen didn't need it to see through the trees. She wasn't overly worried about small groups coming at them. Not only would the sentries spot them, but her larger Essaerites would be able to take care of that. No, she was more interested in concerted efforts against them, and the hawks did fine for that.

She had them run up the river, looking on the banks, seeing if they could spot any activity, but they saw none. This wasn't too surprising. She'd have the hawks circle more and more until they reached the edge of other settlements. Then she'd bring them back in and have them do it again.

As the hawk's circle got wider, it approached one of the neighboring settlements, this one much larger than Caelwen's. As it neared, she saw something outside it, and she redirected the hawk. She felt her heart pick up just a smidge. Outside of the town, there was a group of tents. There were a lot of them she could see. As the hawk moved around, she was able to see men, and only men. They had armor, shields, and weapons, and Caelwen felt her gut clench. Were they there to raid the other settlement, she wondered. She had the hawk continue to watch. As it did, she noted people from that settlement talking to the men in the camp.

"Shit, shit, shit," she said to herself.

She was sitting next to the fire in Wulfgren's home. He shifted.

"What is it?" Wulfgren asked, his voice concerned.

"There's a group of men in another settlement. It looks like a lot of tents," she said, her voice holding just as much tension.

"What can you see about them?" he asked.

"It looks like they're warriors," she said, "but I don't think they're there to attack the settlement. People from the settlement are speaking with them."

Wulfgren was silent for a bit, and when he spoke, his voice was hard. "They're here for us. The thaw's starting, and it makes sense—we're ripe. Can you see anything else?"

She watched. "It looks like there are a few more approaching. It's hard to tell, but there's at least fifty of them."

"Fuck," Wulfgren said. "We can hold that, but..."

She pulled into her own body and looked over at her brother. She agreed—they could hold that many off. They had enough people to hold it for one, but they also had Caelwen and her Essaerites. She may not have been as skilled as a Lysandrian Essaerist, but those cats were over three hundred pounds apiece and could shred through flesh in armor. They would be nothing to balk at. The question was, how many assaults could they withstand?

"What should we do?" Caelwen asked, hearing the uncertainty in her own voice.

Wulfgren's expression was thoughtful. "Keep watching them, but we're going to have to talk to Ilfthandor about this."

So she watched. The men did not move that night, and the next day, more arrived. Every time someone else showed up or another party arrived, Caelwen told her brother, who had become more concerned. Finally, on day three, she felt her heart drop.

"There's more approaching," she said in defeat. She pulled herself back into her own body and looked over at her brother. As he saw her expression, she could see his own turn concerned.

"What is it?" he asked.

"There's mountain goats with them," she said.

Wulfgren cocked his head to the side. "Mountain goats?"

She nodded slowly. "Yes, mountain goats."

"And this should matter why?" he asked, confused.

She sat down next to him by the fire and huffed. "Because they're walking alongside them without any problems, and they look perfect and everything else, and they're with a very old man."

Again, Wulfgren still seemed unconcerned. She looked at him as if he were dense.

"He's an Essaerist. Those are Essaerites," she said.

She saw Wulfgren's expression go pale.

"Fuck," he said.

Fuck was right.

"If there's another Essaerist..." she let it hang there.

"Damn it!" Wulfgren shouted, standing up. His face flushed red with anger. "If there's another Essaerist, we can't hold up against this. And if he's old—"

Yes, the being old part was the most concerning for Caelwen as well. It would mean that the man was extremely skilled, and she could only wonder what those goats could do.

"What do we do?" she asked.

"We're going to go talk to Ilfthandor," he said.

———

CAELWEN STOOD IN ILFTHANDOR'S HOUSE AS WULFGREN AND SHE WENT OVER WHAT THEY had found. When they were done, his attention turned to her.

"So what do you want me to do?" he asked, his voice irritated.

Wulfgren scowled. "We need to figure this the fuck out! That's what we need to do. We can't hold that back."

"Please. If you're as good as you and your men claim to be, you should be able to do it with ease." Ilfthandor waved a hand over at Caelwen. "And we have her. So what if they have another Essaerist? We have one of our own."

"They have one that will beat me," Caelwen said. "Ilfthandor, you don't seem to understand. This man is old, and from what I can see, the Essaerites that he has... they look powerful, and he has a lot of them. More than I can produce."

"You're telling me that those cats that you've made aren't capable of taking out a mountain goat?" he said, incredulous.

"I'm sure they're a little bit more than goats," she said. "But that's beside the point. Even if they are just goats, that means he can create other things. Old Essaerists are powerful and skilled. Ilfthandor, I can't beat him, and there are more men than Wulfgren and his men can take. We're not going to be able to hold them off easily."

"So we struggle to hold them off," he said.

Wulfgren shook his head. "You don't seem to be understanding this. We're going to lose. At best, we will lose half of our property. At worst, most of us will die. And who knows what else? Unless we can get support from others who are willing to come to our aid, or at the very least not assist in this, we're going to be fucked. We're ripe for the taking, and these people see it."

"What other option is there? I'm not leaving," Ilfthandor said, looking around. "I can understand that for you, you may not care, because you've been on the road, doing whatever it is you needed to do to make money. But here, I've been building a community. I've been building something great behind me. You wouldn't understand."

Caelwen scoffed. "No, you've been getting yourself rich on the backs of those around you, and irritating literally every other settlement around us. And now, we are in this position because of you," she said, glaring at him. "So unless you have any ideas for making the other settlements happy..."

Ilfthandor's expression was thoughtful. "Perhaps we could broker a deal with one of them."

"What kind of deal do you have in mind?" Wulfgren asked.

Ilfthandor shrugged. "It's hard to say, but we do have some things that we could leverage," he said, glancing over at Caelwen. "Perhaps a marriage could work."

She rolled her eyes. She knew where he was heading with this. Caelwen was high enough up in their settlement that her marrying someone from another settlement could be considered a binding contract. It wasn't something that bothered her, necessarily, but she didn't think this would work.

"Do you really think that's going to work?" she said.

Ilfthandor shrugged. "You're a powerful Essaerist, Caelwen. Don't underestimate your value."

"So your plan is to sell Caelwen in exchange for one of the settlements backing off?" Wulfgren said.

Ilfthandor looked thoughtful. "Do you think it's a bad idea?"

Deep down, Caelwen stopped herself from being irritated and instead thought about what Ilfthandor was saying. Her mind worked through the problem. It wasn't necessarily a bad solution, she decided, and one that she wasn't unwilling to consider. However, it wasn't necessarily a good solution.

"That gets one off our backs," Wulfgren said, "and it also pulls Caelwen away from us. So, yes, you will be able to neutralize maybe one settlement, perhaps even the largest of them, if they would go for it. But, in exchange, you will weaken us, and those others won't necessarily back off. Not to mention, you have an innate ability at making bad-faith deals that everyone knows. I think it more likely that they would accept a union and then turn around and stab you in the back." Then he looked at his sister. "And probably stab her in the back as well."

Ilfthandor was thoughtful for a moment, as if he was planning to argue that, but he couldn't. Because at the end of the day, Wulfgren was right. That's exactly what would happen.

"Well, then you're going to have to figure out how to defend us," Ilfthandor said. "Because those people are coming, whether you like it or not, and it's your job to keep this settlement safe."

Caelwen fired up. "So what, you're going to pawn it off on the rest of us? Not even lift a finger to try to help out?"

"And what would you have me do?" Ilfthandor asked.

She waved around the house. "You have lots of money, Uncle. I'm sure you could find a way."

He scoffed. "That's not going to happen, and it wouldn't work anyway, and you know it. I'm done with this conversation. You're going to figure out how to keep us safe, or we can all get ready for the afterlife. Either way, I'm done with this. Get out."

The two of them walked out of the house, both fuming. As they walked, Wulfgren said, "he's such a fucking idiot. He's going to get us all killed."

"I agree," she said, thinking.

He glanced at her. "What's on your mind?"

She was lost in thought for a few moments. "I'm thinking about how we handle this."

"We've talked about it. We don't have the ability to stop them," he commented.

She shrugged. "Perhaps not, but... But I don't know... leaving is an option." She let it hang there.

"Yes, we could leave," Wulfgren said, "but I wouldn't leave the rest of the people here behind."

"Nor would I," she said. "But either way, the people have a right to know, don't they?"

Wulfgren looked over at her and smirked. "You're going to try to go over his head, so to speak?"

She shrugged. "Perhaps. But even if I'm not going to try to go over his head, we have a threat. And that means we have to talk to the rest of the settlement. Everyone's on edge already, and if we're going to repel this, we're going to need every single able-bodied man and woman if someone comes at us."

He nodded grimly. "I agree."

———

Caelwen stood against the wall as people filed in. They were in the meeting hall in the center of the settlement. Fires burned in the fireplace, and the air was warm and humid as everyone crowded in. The whole town was there, and she saw her uncle come in through the door and glare daggers at her. He walked up to her and spoke softly, so his voice wouldn't carry.

"What the fuck is going on?" he asked.

She glared at him. "We're taking care of it."

"What do you mean, you're taking care of it?"

She rolled her eyes. "What do you think I mean, Ilfthandor? If we're going to have to repel a group this size, everyone needs to know. We have to prepare for it; we can't spring it on them when we get attacked. Not that it's going to matter anyway," she commented.

"And why is it not going to matter?" he said.

"Oh, you'll see," she said.

Wulfgren got up before everyone and shouted at the top of his voice. "Good evening," he said, his voice booming out. Everyone got quiet. Caelwen looked around the room, seeing the gathered people. There was a fair amount of curiosity in their faces, but she could see tension just underneath the curiosity. They knew something bad was about to happen. It was the only reason why everyone would be gathered together.

Wulfgren looked around, taking his time. "I come bearing grim news. There is a force amassing near our border. We believe they mean to come and attack us." There were murmurs from the crowd. She could see her uncle was about to speak, and she placed her hand on his shoulder. "Don't interrupt."

Ilfthandor glared at her, but something in her expression made him still.

"This force that is gathering is large," Wulfgren said. "We've watched it building over the last few days. Among their number is an older Essaerist."

The room had already been silent, but Caelwen felt it go even quieter. She could feel the tension. Eyes darted towards her. The expressions in those eyes were concerned and fearful. "The Essaerist is old," Wulfgren went on, "and very powerful."

"More powerful than me," Caelwen said loudly. "I will not be able to beat him, or if I do, it will take all of my focus and energy."

"And there's more," Wulfgren said. "The men that they've gathered now outnumber everyone in our settlement," he said, letting it sink in.

Next to her, she felt her uncle tense. "Is this true?" he hissed.

She looked over at him. "Yes. I told you their numbers were building. They haven't stopped. As of this afternoon, they had more warriors than we have people in town," she said under her breath.

"So what are we going to do?" someone in the audience asked.

Wulfgren surveyed them. "That's why we're here. All of us will have to fight these people if we're going to survive."

"You mean if we're going to be slaughtered by them?" one of Wulfgren's warriors said.

Wulfgren turned his attention to the man and nodded. "It's very likely, yes. But we might survive. But isn't it better to die as free men and women than to become slaves and property? We are a warrior people, and we shall die warriors' deaths! Ulfgara will welcome us into her halls, and we will hold our heads high in the afterlife," he said, his voice holding all of the power and feeling of a wise man and great leader.

The people in the room shifted, and Caelwen resisted the urge to smirk. It was well and good for Wulfgren to say that. There were many in the crowd who would agree with that sentiment. They'd be willing to die for glory, die for honor. But were they willing to let their wives and their daughters and their sons die? Were they willing to lose their lives for nothing? That was the real question.

Next to her, she heard her uncle shuffling. "There's another option," Ilfthandor said.

Wulfgren turned to their uncle. "Do tell, uncle. Please, let us know. We need your wisdom in this dark hour," he said, laying it on thick. Caelwen had to struggle this time not to roll her eyes. But she knew that Ilfthandor would continue the act. They always had to provide a unified front.

Ilfthandor stepped forward, looking concerned. "There is another option."

"Do tell, uncle," Caelwen said. "Please, how can we avoid so many settlements and so many men coming after us?" she asked pointedly.

He glanced back at her, his eyes tightening for a moment. He gazed out at everyone. "We must leave," he said after a moment.

There were more murmurs from the crowd, and he held up his hands. "Listen to me. I have taken care of this community for many years now. I do not say this lightly. But my niece and my nephew are unfortunately correct. We cannot stop this threat. The settlements around us have been poisoned by this other Essaerist who has come into town."

This was news to Caelwen. She glanced at her brother, wondering how Ilfthandor was planning on spinning this yarn of shit.

"What do you mean?" a man asked. "You mean the people who are upset because you have made bad deals with them?"

Ilfthandor looked at the man like he was stupid, but also in a pitying sort of way. "No, my boy, I wish that was the case. For you see, I have recently learned that this Essaerist has been using dark powers to turn the minds of those in the settlements around us."

Now Caelwen was trying extremely hard not to roll her eyes. It was almost painful to do.

"Dark powers?" someone said.

"Yes," Ilfthandor said.

"As you know, Essaerists are powerful and mysterious beings. And some of the ancient, more powerful ones have other abilities," he said. "This man is no different. He has corrupted the minds of those around us. The only reason why you here haven't felt the corruption is because of the protection of my niece," he said, gesturing at Caelwen. "Her power saves us. Even though she does not have the ability to use these powers yet, her presence here has kept us safe," he said, as if Caelwen were some sort of figure from mythology.

She heard her brother stifle a snort with a soft cough. "Yes, I've heard of this," her brother said, though she could tell he was having a hard time playing the part. She also caught the eye of several of Wulfgren's men, who knew that Wulfgren was completely full of shit, but they'd already gotten all of them on board with the prospect of leaving the settlement. Whatever needed to be done to get everyone else on board was fine with them.

Ilfthandor nodded. "Yes, yes, indeed. I'm sure you did see this in the wars that you fought," he looked back out over the settlement. "My brothers and sisters, we cannot hold this back anymore, I am sorry to say."

"So, what, we just leave our homes?" someone else shouted.

"Yes," Ilfthandor said emphatically, "yes, we do. We will gather what belongings we can, and we will leave. We will head south and away from here. The other Essaerist is looking for our property and our slaves and our possessions, not us. We will travel light."

Before anyone could protest, he said, "I understand this is a great sacrifice. Believe me. I have worked years to build up my home and my property and my wealth, and I'll be leaving all of it behind."

This had been tactfully done, Caelwen realized, by being the most well-off man in town, Ilfthandor saying that he was willing to give it up at all to be safe— no other could argue with him. How could they?

There was more hushed murmuring, and Ilfthandor said, "I am sorry, my brothers and sisters. If you choose not to come with us, that is your choice, but know that doing so will be your end. For everyone else, go home, sleep, think about it. Tomorrow, gather your belongings, and tomorrow as the sun sets, we will leave this place," he said solemnly. "It pains me to do so, and the day will come when perhaps we will take this land back. But for now, we must go south. We must settle somewhere else. We must settle someplace where there is not an evil Essaerist that is bent on taking our property and enslaving us. Good night," he said, dismissing everyone.

The people of the settlement shuffled out of the meeting hall, leaving Caelwen, Wulfgren, and Ilfthandor behind.

Caelwen took in her uncle, waiting for whatever vile venom was about to spew forth from him. But it didn't seem to come.

"You meant that, didn't you?" Wulfgren said surprised.

Ilfthandor looked over at him. "Yes, every word."

"The powerful Essaerist who has dark powers?" Caelwen said sardonically.

Ilfthandor looked at her and rolled his eyes. "Don't be daft, girl. They needed something."

"So what changed your mind?" Wulfgren said.

"You," Ilfthandor said. "Caelwen would at least be taken up by the Essaerist and spend all of her time on that; it would be up to you and the men and women of this settlement to defend themselves. And if there are more of them than there are of us, and they're all warriors." He shook his head. "I may not be happy about it, but I can do math," he said condescendingly. "So tomorrow we leave."

CHAPTER 25

For Caelwen, packing what was left of her life's belongings was relatively easy, as most of her possessions had been burned to the ground along with her house. Still, she had a handful of things that she'd kept in stone chests, which hadn't burned. She took those items and packed them into a cart that she and Wulfgren were taking. He, too, did not have many items, as he had just been home for a short time, but it was still a somber event.

She looked around at her settlement, feeling her heart sag with sorrow. Wulfgren came up next to her. He looked forlorn, but not as much as she was.

"You seem to be handling this well," she said to him.

He shrugged. "I've been living on the road for the last few years. But this does affect me. This was supposed to be the end for me. I was supposed to come home, start a family, start a life, build off of the things that I got during the war."

"But then this all happened," she said.

He shook his head. "It started before this. It started on the road when we were raided, and a lot of my spoils were taken. Then it continued when I got home, yes. But this appears to be what life is. We'll find a place. We'll settle. But we'll be starting all over again," he said with a resigned sigh.

She patted his shoulder. "I'm sorry."

"I'm not grousing," he said. "If anything, most of my sadness comes for you. You've put your whole life into this place."

It was true; she had. But she had never tried to put her life anywhere else, either. Still, the thought of it was sad to her. Her mother and father had been here. They had run the settlement. Her grandparents had done the same. She had a lineage here, going all the way back from the time before the settlement to when the Gwenthari lived in great mountaintop cities and fortresses.

But now, all that heritage was going away.

She finished helping Wulfgren pack up his few belongings and then went over to help some of the other people in the settlement. There were a handful of people who were planning on staying. It hadn't been much of a surprise to her. She hoped that when the raiding party showed up, those people would be able to sue for peace and would be able to at least keep their lives, though she found it unlikely.

But most of the settlement was joining them. Nobody was happy about it, but at the same time, they all felt resigned. Her people were practical, after all.

Lastly, she went to her uncle's house. He was packing up a few items in a cart and had a few slaves with him.

"Are you all packed up, Uncle?" she asked.

He looked over at her. "I suppose so," he said, looking back at his house. "I don't like having to start over again. But there's always opportunity on the road," he said with a shrug.

She was sure that he would find some opportunity out there. But she didn't really care what it was.

When she was done with her rounds, she checked on her hawks, seeing that the group and the other settlement hadn't moved yet. If they knew her settlement was planning on leaving, they weren't acting on it, though she found it unlikely that they would know. And even if they did, they were a few hours away. So, her people had the potential of getting away.

She found her brother again and asked if he needed any help.

"No, I'm fine," he said. "Are you going to keep those Essaerites nearby when we leave?"

She nodded. "I'm going to keep the hawks circling around that area to make sure that no one follows us, but I'm going to keep two of my Essaerites in the back and one out in front of us."

He nodded. "That's a good plan."

"Do you need me to create anything to help with the journey?" she asked.

"No, we have horses for the carts, and everyone's fine right now. On the road, I'm sure we will need something. Someone's cart will break, or something of that nature, and if we can't repair it or buy the parts for it, then you'll need to create them," he said. "But that shouldn't be for a little while, and right now I want you to save your Essaeris in case it's necessary to defend us."

She nodded. This was an area where she was unsure of what to do. She had never left the settlement other than to visit other settlements, and she hadn't gone far. And while she had helped raid and defend, she really didn't have the experience that her brother did. She knew she'd be deferring to him for the rest of their journey, wherever that ended up. She was fine with it, in a way. She trusted Wulfgren, and she knew that he trusted her, and that's what mattered.

"At some point in time, Ilfthandor's going to fuck this whole thing," she said. "He's a cunt."

Wulfgren chuckled dryly. "He is a cunt, and yes, he will, and we'll have to watch him. But maybe this proves to be useful."

She raised an eyebrow. "How is losing our entire settlement possibly useful?"

Wulfgren shrugged. "Because Ilfthandor is going to have a hard time keeping control of power on the road, and we're probably going to end up in some other settlement, which means he's not going to be in charge."

"But neither will we," Caelwen said.

Wulfgren shook his head. "Maybe not, but I'll find a place easy enough. I have warriors that follow me," and he nodded at her, "And you're an Essaerist. You have value. Even if you were an inept one, which you're not, you would have value. So you and I will be fine, but Ilfthandor might have to trudge his own path for the first time in his life."

She smiled. "One can only hope."

As the light began to fail, the people in the settlement gathered in the center of town. Ilfthandor gave them a few bullshit words of sorrow, and the procession of people began to move, heading south. Wulfgren and his warriors stayed on their horses, fully clad in their armor, on the outside of the caravan of people for protection. Caelwen sat atop Wulfgren's cart, making sure that the horse pulling it followed the one in front of it. It wasn't something she strictly needed to pay attention to, which allowed her to move into the minds of the Essaerites that she had in the area.

The hawk near the other settlement did not see any change in activity. The men in the settlement were settling down for the night, building fires and apparently getting out drinks and getting drunk, as she saw a few of them drinking and singing. That was a good sign. She also could get glimpses of the old Essaerist sitting next to a campfire, rubbing his hands together. That too was a good sign. If they could move for a day, they would open up a pretty decent gap, she thought, and they would probably be safe. She moved into some of her other Essaerites, seeing what they were seeing. There was still nothing amiss.

One of her Essaerites looked at the end of the caravan from her settlement as it wound its way into the forest and out of town. Then it turned back and began its patrol again. She opened her eyes and looked down to see Treftune digging through her bag, looking for nuts. She opened up a little pouch and let him have some. He sat next to her, chewing. She scratched behind his ears and ran her fingers along his soft fur. Treftune didn't seem to be bothered, per se, but she did think that the little Valfglidea seemed not as happy as he normally was.

"We'll find a new home," she said to Treftune softly. He looked up at her, his eyes intelligent, and then he went back to eating his nut.

When he was done, he wound up around her neck like a scarf and nuzzled up against her chin. She was grateful for him, and she continued to stroke his fur as her mind went back out into the Essaerites around her.

"We're going to be fine," she said to herself, convincing herself that if she could, everything would be fine.

CHAPTER 26

The legion was almost done with its march for the day. Mariokos marched alongside his squadmates, his mind drifting in and out of his body as it moved into the birds of prey he had in the area. He kept them tight to the legion, the birds moving in a slow, methodical pattern. They struggled to see through the dense foliage of the forest, but they could occasionally catch glimpses of the ground. Thus far, they hadn't found any threats.

What they had seen were more animals. He'd enjoyed observing the different creatures in this part of the land. He found it relaxing—watching herds grazing and seeing the occasional predator stalking those herds. The day was cool and moist, but it didn't have the same mist or fog that had been ever-present for the last few weeks, and he was thankful for it. It was nice to be able to see the sky on occasion, and it allowed the sun to bathe them in its warm rays.

Not that the cool didn't have its benefits too, as it kept him just uncomfortable enough to not get lost in daydreams, lest he get out of formation and receive a tongue-lashing from Erastos. They were crossing a field that wasn't wide enough to make camp but gave them a little bit of room on either side of the road.

A handful of mounted scouts moved away from the column, inspecting the tree line for threats. Mariokos brought his hawks in front of the legion, and they swooped down, scanning the ground around them and soaring over the field. One of them saw something strange on the ground, and he moved into its eyes to see what it had found.

The hawk slowed and circled, still relatively high above but lower than it normally would be. As he looked through its keen eyes, he felt his heart give a little jump in his chest. The hawk moved quickly, and he brought another to join it, scouting out in front of them, confirming what he saw. Rote training took over, and Mariokos took a horn from his belt and put it to his lips, blasting out a warning that there was danger ahead.

As soon as the sound came out of the horn, he felt the tension around him rise, as men instantly heard it. At once, he heard Erastos and Theoliano begin to bark orders, and Mariokos fully pulled himself inside of his body. He turned to see Erastos and Theoliano looking at him.

"There's a large group of Gwenthari ahead of us. They're lying in tall grass," he said, keeping his tone controlled and professional.

He pushed his mind back into the hawk, checking the tree line. He felt his heart pick up.

"There are riders in the trees as well," he said.

Theoliano shouted orders, and Mariokos ran with his squad. As he did, he felt his Essaeris inside of him boiling and bubbling up. It rushed out of him, creating four identical legionnaires in full armor next to him.

As the legion began to move, he could hear horns in the distance. The Gwenthari knew that they had lost the element of surprise. Mariokos dropped his pack with everyone else, grabbing only his shield, a spear, and a sword. His squad quickly formed up into lines that joined the rest of their platoon.

As they did so, the skirmish line ran from the main column of men ahead of the platoons forming up. He heard the roar of men and women, and as he got into formation, he saw Gwenthari running from hidden positions toward the skirmish line.

Theoliano was barking orders that were relayed down through the different sergeants, and Erastos called out orders of his own. Mariokos formed up with the rest of the platoon.

They didn't have time to put on their full armor, but it wouldn't be necessary. All they needed to do was hold the Gwenthari until the platoons and squads behind them could don their armor and relieve them.

Mariokos's warning call was moving down the column of soldiers, down to the legions that were following them. It wouldn't be long now before the entire expeditionary force was moving up to Mariokos and the other legionaries in his group.

The sound of people clashing assaulted Mariokos's ears, and he stood stock-still in formation with the rest of his platoon. He could see the skirmish line engaging with the Gwenthari.

The skirmishers, like the rest of the legion, were not in full armor, something that the Gwenthari didn't have going against them. He saw them with shields and many with chainmail. The assortment of men and women were motley in their appearance. Some had a lot of armor, while others had almost nothing. Their shields varied in size, from large shields like those of the legion to smaller round ones, or others didn't have shields at all.

He also saw the gathered assortment with a whole array of weapons. Some had swords, spears, maces, or axes. He was surprised by how many women he saw in the group. That was something that would be unheard of in Lysandrian culture, but for the barbarian hordes, apparently, their women fought alongside them.

Mariokos had been told this, of course, and had chalked it up to rumor. The rumors had said that the Gwenthari women were just as ferocious, vicious, cunning, and capable as the men. That in battle, you had to watch for them just as much as you did their male counterparts. Mariokos had thought it silly. The prospect of women in combat had seemed laughable to him, but now he was seeing it. The women that he saw with the men showed him that this was not something they had just done on a whim. They knew what they were doing.

None of them showed the fear that Mariokos would have associated with a woman going into combat for the first time. And for a moment, he began to realize what they could potentially be up against. They weren't just up against the men of the settlements and the cities of the Gwenthari. They were up against everyone. The whole of the population was a threat.

He saw the skirmishers engage with the Gwenthari, their own fighting style very similar to that of the barbarians they faced. There wasn't a lot of organization to it, and it was more of a brawl than anything else. But that was the skirmish line's job. They were to distract. They were to cause issues and harass the enemy. They weren't to be professional soldiers.

The professional soldiers were getting ready. Mariokos heard an order from Theoliano, and he called out with the rest of his platoon.

From the tree line, Gwenthari cavalry ran out, charging toward the skirmish line. Mariokos saw two of Xavieno's advanced Essaerites run by. They were tall and gleaming white, like marble, their feet like wolves. They ran unnaturally fast. One of them brought up a shield, crashing into a horse, sending it tumbling over. Another one of the Essaerites lashed out with its sword, killing a man.

The one that had knocked over a horse righted itself, spinning around the other Essaerite, stabbing a blade into a horse, and reaching up to rip the rider off with the other hand. He heard the screams of the animals as they went down, and then he turned and looked forward as the order to march came.

Mariokos began to walk slowly with his unit, taking their time as they approached the fight. Before them, the front lines of men held out their shields, creating a wall. The lines behind them held their shields above them, protecting those in the front and behind with theirs. As they got closer to the fighting, more horns sounded, and the skirmish line began to move back and away.

Mariokos felt his heart beat faster, and he felt nervous. He was competent, but battle was battle, and there were no guarantees. His palms began to sweat a little, and from the tension in the men around him, he knew he wasn't in the minority. Everyone had nerves going into battle unless you were insane.

As the skirmishers moved back, the Gwenthari seemed to recognize that there was a new threat coming. Mariokos could see them grin in happiness and joy. They were enjoying themselves, he realized. They were having fun.

He didn't think that fun was going to last.

Some of the Gwenthari began throwing spears and shooting arrows at the legionnaires. Mariokos heard the arrows and spears hit the shields around him, but they didn't hit the men. The platoon moved, not speaking, just listening for orders. They were a silent tide of death.

As the skirmish line pulled back, the Gwenthari ran toward the walls of platoons. As cavalry came up toward Mariokos's platoon, Theoliano barked an order, and they stopped, holding out spears, keeping the horses from being able to move past them. As horsemen ran along, trying to make the line of soldiers back down, the legionnaires held their place, holding out their spears. When they got close, some men threw javelins at the horses, hitting their flanks and necks, dropping them. As they fell, their Gwenthari riders would get up and back away, almost looking shocked that the legionnaires didn't break rank to kill them.

Theoliano called another order, and they began to move forward again at a walk. He heard a cry of men and women from the Gwenthari lines, and they came running at the platoon. Still, the platoon walked and did not make a sound. As the Gwenthari approached, Mariokos readied himself along the front line with his Essaerites on either side of him. Still, he walked.

At the last moment, a barked order from Theoliano made the legionnaires stop, and they braced themselves for the impact. Mariokos braced himself, and moments later, his shield was hit by one of the Gwenthari. He felt the blow push him back a bit, and he gritted his teeth, holding his position, as his Essaerites did likewise. He pushed back, forcing the man away, and then he parted his shield and lashed out with his spear as the man stumbled backward. The spear caught the man's arm, but Mariokos didn't push his advantage.

They weren't here to win. They were here to hold until other platoons could don their armor and replace them. Mariokos held the line, and the Gwenthari lashed out at him, hitting his shield and the shields of his Essaerites and the men around him. Some threw items at them that he heard bounce off the shields above his head, but still, he held the line, and he didn't make a sound.

The Gwenthari didn't seem to know what to do with the Lysandrian shield wall. They would pulse toward the legion, ramming into it, but not making it move. Mariokos couldn't help but grin. This is what the barbarians were going to be facing. While he was having to come to terms with the knowledge that they'd be fighting every one of the Gwenthari, and not just the men, the Gwenthari were coming to terms with the fact that they were going to have to fight the Lysandrian legions. Legions that were very different from the time when the Gwenthari had sacked the capital hundreds of years ago.

From behind, he heard the sound of men marching, and he grinned again. Platoons of the first line had stopped and fully put on their armor and were in their full regalia. As they neared, sergeants and Theoliano shouted orders, making the new platoon meld into theirs, allowing them to replace the line. When it was his turn, Mariokos moved back, allowing himself to be replaced by a member of the first line.

The man was in heavy armor, and as Mariokos stepped back, his platoon moved further away, still at a march, not breaking rank, as the other soldiers replaced them. Once they were far enough back from the line, Theoliano gave the order, and the men broke formation and jogged to their packs and equipment. Mariokos quickly put on his armor. He could have released the armor and recreated it around himself, but he didn't want to waste the Essaeris, so he put it on like everyone else did. The process didn't take long, and within a few minutes, he was forming back up in formation with the rest of the squad and platoon.

Before him, the battle had changed quickly. The Gwenthari were no longer facing surprised men and skirmishers that did not have proper armor or equipment. Now they were facing the Legion proper, and the Gwenthari didn't seem to be doing well against heavy infantry. He could see the line slowly walking forward, not ever in a rush, just moving forward.

Around him, other platoons were forming up, creating a wall that surrounded the field they were in, allowing the support caravans to move inside the legion's protection. As they did so, he saw members of the skirmish line from other legions coming up to assist. They were in their full armor. Behind them, the rest of the legions would be coming. They wouldn't be taken off guard; they'd be ready for battle.

Mariokos glanced over, seeing Xavieno in concentration as he created more of his advanced Essaerites. He could create up to six, and Mariokos wasn't sure how many he'd created thus far. Xavieno glanced over at him and gave a quick, tight grin. Mariokos couldn't help but return it. He didn't like battle, but now that they were here, there was something exhilarating about it.

He heard a Gwenthari horn, but he couldn't see past the line of men. He moved into one of his hawks, seeing the Gwenthari retreating quickly. Some of them were carrying their wounded and their dead, but, by and large, they were leaving the dead behind. Mariokos was surprised by how many there were. He could see dozens just in the area he had been fighting alone. He wondered how many the Gwenthari had lost. He suspected the legion had lost at least a handful of people from the skirmish line and had a few injured in the main legion, but he suspected that the casualties and wounded were not high.

The legion moved on slowly until finally there was a call for a stop. The men halted, waiting for orders as the Gwenthari ran away.

―――――

AFTER THE SKIRMISH, THE LEGIONS HAD PUSHED ON FURTHER THAN THEY WERE PLANNING for the day before setting camp. Just a small way away from them, well within view, were the walls of a Gwenthari town. By that point, Mariokos had managed to save up enough Essaeris and was able to create his Essaerithon that had helped with trenches and the camps. Now, he stood with Xavieno and Fioralba in one of the command tents.

With them were Theoliano, Alessandros, and the legion's general, Damianello. Mariokos didn't have a lot of interactions with Damianello, and standing next to Damianello was Tangelo. Tangelo was the senator who sponsored the legion. He'd met him on several occasions. Biankara's family knew him, and Mariokos had seen him at a handful of gatherings at her house. Tangelo nodded politely over at Mariokos.

"Good to see you," Tangelo said.

"Likewise, sir," Mariokos replied.

Mariokos caught just the hint of a flinch from Alessandros. Alessandros never liked it when people below him had relationships with people above him, but there wasn't much that Mariokos could do to help that. Damianello looked at the gathered Essaerists.

"Good evening. You're here for a very specific reason. To begin with, Mariokos, good job catching the ambush today," Damianello said, making Mariokos feel a sense of pride. "If you hadn't spotted that, we would have lost more men than we did. As you're all aware, we are on the outskirts of a Gwenthari town. This town is not large by all appearances, but it does have a soil-and-timber wall. We are going to attack and take this town tomorrow."

Mariokos didn't question anything. He just listened, waiting for his part in the plan. Damianello looked at Xavieno.

"Those Essaerites that you used today, I want as many as you have on hand tomorrow," he said.

"Yes, sir," Xavieno nodded.

Then he looked to Fioralba. Damianello smiled softly.

"Fioralba, thank you for your assistance and for assisting your husband in the legions," he said.

"You're welcome, sir," Fioralba replied, unsure.

Damianello smiled softly again. "While we obviously would never send a woman into battle, we do need equipment."

Fioralba nodded. "Whatever you need, sir."

"I would like you to produce as many javelins as you can. We have plenty, but Essaeris javelins are far more effective because it doesn't matter if they get damaged, does it?" Damianello said with a smile.

Mariokos wondered how uncomfortable Fioralba was with this conversation. He didn't think she'd really spoken with the general before.

"It doesn't. Is there a particular type of javelin that you would like? When we were preparing for the war, I remember making three different heads on the javelins," she said.

This seemed to surprise and please Damianello, but Tangelo looked like he had expected nothing else.

Mariokos saw a small smirk grace Tangelo's face for just a moment, and Damianello looked over at Alessandros. "Alessandros, it seems you've been blessed with three talented Essaerists. Good for you," he added.

Damianello turned his attention back to Fioralba. "I'm impressed that you know that, and thank you for asking that question. These are not going to be sticking inside of armor or shields. They'll mostly be going into unarmored men and women," he explained.

To her credit, Fioralba didn't grimace at the comment about unarmored men and women. Instead, she just nodded.

Next, Damianello addressed Mariokos. "And you. I'm going to have you use that monstrosity of an Essaerite that you used to trench and create the camps."

Mariokos nodded. "Yes, sir. Is there something specific that you're going to need it to do? I don't have much Essaeris left, but by morning I should be able to make alterations to it if necessary."

Damianello appeared to ponder the question. "I'm going to have it dig around the wall and bring it down. Will you need to make alterations for that?"

Mariokos paused, in thought.

"Answer, Mariokos," Alessandros nudged.

Damianello raised a hand. "Give the man a moment to think."

After some consideration, Mariokos replied, "I will need to put some shields on top of it. It's fairly rugged, but the Gwenthari could damage it and take it out. So, I'll make sure that it's protected from above." He looked at the town's fortifications with both his hawks and now a few owls. "I don't think the wall is going to be too bad, sir. It's not very thick. My Essaerithon should be able to get through it fairly quickly."

Damianello smiled. "Good. That is all. We'll get started in the morning."

———

MARIOKOS LOOKED AT THE TOWN THROUGH ONE OF HIS ESSAERITES. THE WALL WASN'T very high and wasn't very thick. It wasn't going to take his Essaerithon long to break it down. Several legions were completely surrounding the town, and no one had come out, save for one rider whom the legion sent in to negotiate. The rider had been killed. Now Mariokos waited for the command to attack.

Next to his Essaerithon were some of Xavieno's advanced ones. Their job was simple. They were to cover Mariokos's, should that be necessary. It would also be covered by the skirmishers and other legionnaires as they made a concerted effort on the town. They would come close while Mariokos's Essaerithon did its work.

He could see the forms of men and women's heads poking above the battlements of the town as they waited for the eventual attack. Mariokos felt a small bit of pity for them.

The order came, and the legion began to move. Platoons started moving slowly toward the town, keeping out of range of archers. Mariokos saw arrows fly over, occasionally landing before the ranks of the legion. The legion set up a small ballista that they fired over the walls. Skirmishers would run forward, some carrying the javelins that Fioralba had made the night before and hurling them at the people on the wall or just over it.

As they did so, Mariokos's Essaerithon began to move forward. It was covered in shields that Mariokos had created. They were slightly heavier than the shields that normal men carried, but he wasn't worried about it being weighed down. It didn't need to move quickly. It just needed to be protected.

As it came near the wall, the shields were hit by a few arrows, but nothing that was able to make it through. He was more concerned about rocks, but he didn't think it likely that the people in the town would have enough rocks heavy enough to do any damage. Though, the Essaerithon registered some rocks hitting its shielding. Still, it plodded on closer to the wall.

They'd chosen not to have it attack the gate but rather a section next to it, so once the wall came down, the gate would come with it, creating a larger opening for the legionnaires to stream through. As the Essaerithon reached the base of the wall, its giant teeth began to dig.

Mariokos was fully in the Essaerithon and perceived the world through it as if he were it. Above him, the shields on his body were peppered with arrows and rocks, but it didn't bother him. Teeth dug into dirt and wood, ripping and turning it. There were loud pops as rope and wood broke. Still, the Essaerithon continued to chew through the ground and wall. It cleared away material, kicking it behind it. The wall shuddered.

The sound of panicked men and women could be heard. They knew they couldn't stop it. The wall would come down, and then the tide of legionnaires would crash over them like a wave. There was a loud crack as supports broke, and the wall shifted. Mariokos came back into himself and waved to command, who in turn blew a horn.

Men from the skirmish line rushed forward, throwing ropes with hooks over the wall and wrapping the ends around Mariokos's Essaerithon. It pulled the ropes tight. On the walls, the Gwenthari quickly worked to cut the ropes, but Xavieno's Essaerites shot them with arrows.

The Essaerithon heaved, and the wall groaned as the timbers broke and cracked. Then a section came falling forward. As it did, it took the gate with it, falling flat on the ground. On the other side of the wall were hundreds of Gwenthari. They came storming out, all converging on Mariokos's Essaerithon. It quickly registered that it was being hit by axes, swords, and hammers. It wasn't designed to fight, and he didn't even attempt to make it try. Instead, he just had it slowly back away in hopes that he could salvage some of it for that night.

After a moment or two, he realized it was a lost cause, and he released the Essaerithon. As it vanished from sight, the Gwenthari turned their attention to the slowly approaching Lysandrian legion. Mariokos's fight for the day was done. He had used all of his energy on the Essaerithon and wouldn't be expected to fight anymore, so he breathed deeply and watched as the legion pressed forward.

It hit the ranks of Gwenthari warriors, and the legion's line stopped for a time, but only for a short time. Soon the legion was moving forward again, and within no time, they were moving through the gap in the wall. Mariokos heard the sound of fighting move inside the town, and then he began to see smoke rise behind the walls as homes and buildings were set on fire.

The legion began to move in earnest now, with other units moving up to the opening of the wall and pouring in. In no time at all, the legion had stopped moving in an orderly fashion, and men just poured through the wall like a dam that had burst.

There would be no order to stop. There would be no surrender. The town was going to fall, and the Legion was going to raze it.

————

Hours after the wall had come down, Mariokos walked through the gap that his Essaerithon had created. Around him were burning buildings or their remnants. Bodies were strewn about. Many of them had died in battle. Some of the people were still alive. He could see them bound and bloodied. Men were putting slave collars around their necks, though the collars were missing the glass beads that were common. Instead, they just had metal. These people were yet to have been sold or assigned.

He could hear screams and moans from other parts of the town as homes tried to hold out, or as the legionnaires enjoyed the spoils of war. The smell of burning flesh hung in the air, and it made him recoil. As he walked through the town with the rest of his squad, he took in the aftermath.

There would be many winnings from the day, and he could see legionnaires gathering belongings and items, piling them up so that the Legion could distribute them appropriately.

He watched as legionnaires toyed with individuals from the town. One caught his eye as he watched a man who was dressed as one of the warriors. He was being held down by a few of the legionnaires. He was screaming and begging, watching as a few men butchered his family. Mariokos turned away from it.

This is war. This is what happens, he thought. It didn't matter that he didn't care for it. It was what it was. It was all war had ever been and ever would be.

He saw another section of town where people were being rounded up. They appeared to mostly be the old and infirm. Legionnaires were making quick work of dispatching the people. There'd be no one left from this town by the time the Legion left. All those that were living would be slaves. All of their property and belongings, gone.

He also saw groups of foreign slaves. Those that appeared to be Lysandrian were being freed and questioned. If they had been free peoples before, they would be again. But there weren't many. Most of the slaves appeared to be other Gwenthari or mixes of Lysandrian and Gwenthari people. For those, their life wouldn't change much, he thought.

But then he amended that assumption. The reality of it was, though in the moment Mariokos thought the scene was barbaric and uncivilized, he knew that it was commonplace. But that the aftermath, that the lives of the slaves would be far different. Slaves of the Lysandrians had far better lives than those of the Gwenthari. They had some rights. Not many, but some.

So at least there's that, Mariokos thought, though it was a sad comfort.

Still, today would be a sad day for the people of this town. Their lives would never be the same. And for Mariokos, the reality of war was beginning to set in. This was what life was going to be for the foreseeable future.

CHAPTER 27

Hroldenfell was located in the heart of the Faelridge Mountain Range. It sat atop a hill that looked out over the smaller ones in the area. There weren't many connecting valleys or river deltas. It wasn't an ideal place for agriculture, but it did provide a strategic stronghold for the Ulfgarath. Valfric had always enjoyed coming to the city. It was surrounded by a high curtain wall that overlooked the mountain slopes, able to see any enemy army or force approaching. The city itself was bustling with inns, brothels, and places to trade.

He'd come to trade and sell many of the wares they had taken while raiding the year before. Valfric was all too happy to be out of the settlement and in Hroldenfell. It had been a long winter for him, and he hated being alone. Hroldenfell had many distractions that helped him overcome the loneliness and boredom of winter.

He, Thraindel, and Aelric had spent several days fucking and drinking themselves silly at some of the brothels. Valfric came downstairs from one of the rooms, seeing Thraindel sitting at one of the tables, holding a mug of Bryndraught. Valfric sat down heavily on a chair, covered in sweat, exhausted but happy with everything good in the world.

He grabbed a mug of Bryndraught and took a long pull from it before setting it down. Thraindel grinned at him.

"You look like you're tired," Thraindel said with a grin.

Valfric smiled back. "Very," he said, and he was.

The brothel was busy, as people were emerging from their homes after winter and coming into the city to trade and socialize. He could hear the sounds of laughter and conversation. As he peered around, he saw groups of people huddled around fires, and women walking around topless or completely nude.

He smiled. Thraindel looked like the picture of happiness, and Valfric wasn't sure if there was a place Thraindel liked more than a brothel. Maybe the battlefield, but a brothel would be a close second.

"So what have you been up to?" Valfric asked, taking another drink. "I'm surprised to see you at the table."

Thraindel laughed. "We all have limits, my friend. I'm just saving myself for the right one." He smiled at the various women as they walked by. Then he looked back at Valfric and leaned over the table. "But I have been talking with people."

Valfric raised an eyebrow. "Anything interesting?"

The other reason they were in Hroldenfell was to find out the news. It had been a couple of months they had been stuck in their settlement, with little in the way of caravans coming through. Part of coming to a place like Hroldenfell was finding out what was going on in the rest of the world.

Thraindel took a drink of his Bryndraught. "It appears Lysandrian is on the move."

Valfric laughed. "What do you mean they're on the move? And what the fuck does that matter to us?"

Thraindel smirked. "I mean that a few weeks ago, five legions left Dionisio, headed north."

This piqued Valfric's interest; he leaned forward, listening. "Heading north, huh?"

Thraindel nodded. "Yes, they went to a fort where one legion stayed. Four legions have now moved into Ulfgarath territory; they're being led by Feliciano himself."

Valfric thought, trying to roll the name over in his head. "I'm not sure I've heard of him," he finally said after a moment.

Thraindel took a drink. "Yes, you have."

Valfric thought about it. "No, I fucking haven't. Who's Feliciano?"

Thraindel rolled his eyes. "Feliciano, Lysandrian's emperor?" he said, as if Valfric were stupid—and in a way, he was.

As soon as Thraindel said the title, it hit Valfric like an ox. "No shit, the emperor's coming up into Gwenthari territory," Valfric said, feeling excitement bubble inside him.

Thraindel grinned. "With four legions behind him, how many men is that?" he mused to himself.

Valfric thought. "It has to be thousands," he said, his excitement building. It was happening; it was finally happening. The Ulfgarath were going to be reminded of who and what they were.

In so many ways, it was what they had been hoping for when they had been raiding the Lysandrian lands. It had been about this. It had been about putting his people back on top. And now, Lysandrian knew what was coming for them.

Valfric took another deep drink of his Bryndraught. "Fucking cunts are about to learn what's what."

Thraindel nodded. "That they are. So, what's the plan?"

Valfric laughed. "What do you mean, what's the plan? I just found out about this!"

But he didn't disagree. Now that Lysandrian was on the move, the Ulfgarath would need to respond. He thought for a moment and shook his head.

"Four legions. Fuck. That has to be what? Twenty thousand men. It's going to be glorious," Valfric said. "Can you imagine what the battles are going to be like?"

Thraindel laughed. "You mean the slaughters. We're going to send that Lysandrian prick back to his capital with his tail between his legs. Or his head in a box."

Valfric grinned. Yes, this was going to be very good. Once the other Gwenthari peoples watched the Ulfgarath put Lysandrian in its place, they'd remember who they were dealing with. They'd remember why the Ulfgarath were feared and respected. And they wouldn't fuck with them ever again.

Valfric also knew his people would remember what they were, and would go from being the ones who were being fucked with to the ones fucking with others. It was going to be amazing! It was everything their ancestors had done and created them to be. He could almost see the gods smiling down on them as the Ulfgarath people took their rightful place back in the world.

"When we get back home, Durnara will be happy to know this," Valfric said.

"That she will," Thraindel said. "So will Aelric and Ilara. They're going to be excited for this."

That they would, Valfric realized. This would create so many wonderful opportunities for them, and Valfric wondered when Durnara would send them to join other Ulfgarath groups as they decimated the Lysandrian legions. He hoped it wouldn't take her long to send them.

"So do we know where they are?" Valfric asked.

"It's hard to tell," Thraindel said. "I'm just catching little bits of information about it, but it sounds like the main force split off after encountering a small town."

"A small town," Valfric commented. "I'm sure they were surprised by what they met there."

For a moment, Thraindel's enthusiasm slipped a little, and he grimaced.

"What?" Valfric asked.

Thraindel shook his head. "From what I understand of what happened, it was the other way around. It was a small town, and the whole of the army was there, all four legions."

Valfric felt a small pit form in his gut. "Did they lose?"

"They lost within hours," Thraindel explained.

Valfric sat back and shook his head. "No way they lost within hours. That's not possible, especially not if they saw the legion coming."

Thraindel shrugged noncommittally. "That's what I was told, but I don't know if it's true or not. It's all second-hand accounts, isn't it?"

Valfric thought, and then decided maybe it was good if they'd lost that quickly.

"Well, that'll be good then if the Lysandrians went through a town that fast. It'll show people up here how mad they need to be and that they need to put the Lysandrians in their place quickly. Plus, it'll make the legions cocky," he said, deciding that one town wasn't going to be an indicator of anything.

"I agree," Thraindel said. "A small town against any force that large isn't gonna stand a chance, but once they get into Ulfgarath proper, it's going to be different."

Valfric agreed. "Yes, different is going to be an understatement." He smacked the table. "Fuck, this is a great day," he said, excited. He took another long drink. "Well, it sounds like we better enjoy ourselves before we go home because we're going to have a lot of work to do."

Thraindel grinned and looked over at a red-haired woman who was walking by. He reached out and took the woman's left wrist. She turned to him and smiled.

"You know what, Valfric, you're right," Thraindel said. "I best get on that."

He stood and picked up the woman, draping her over his shoulder. She laughed and giggled as he walked away. Valfric chuckled and took another drink of his Bryndraught, then decided to order dinner. It was time to celebrate, and he fully intended to do so.

Caelwen woke under the warm weight of furs. She shifted in her cocoon of warmth, trying to decide if she wanted to start the day or not. In general, the answer was no; she didn't want to start the day. She wanted to stay in the nice warm furs and not have to deal with whatever the day held. But duty called, and her mind flicked out to the Essaerites that she had.

She had three large pumas the color of mud patrolling the area around their camp. The snow had turned to mud, which was slowing things down. She had originally kept the pumas black like she normally did, but they just got covered in mud, and she decided that it was better that people didn't notice them, as opposed to knowing that there was an Essaerist around.

She also checked on a couple of the small birds. They'd been orbiting around and hadn't seen anything amiss. They were surrounded by woods and had been for a couple of days. Wulfgren's earlier assumption that they would be able to find someplace to settle easily had been wrong. They had found many settlements, but none looking for new members.

In a way, it shouldn't have been surprising. After all, they were deep in Ulfgarath territory. Had they been in Wulfharboria, perhaps it would have been different, but the Ulfgarath were wary of the Wulfharboria after the last few decades of encroachment from her people. So they continued to travel south, looking for a new place.

They'd also found that many were willing to take advantage of a group of people without a place to stay. They had traded many of the few belongings they had brought with them, but Caelwen and Wulfgren had also found that there were many settlements more than happy to try and raid a caravan of their size, hence another reason why Caelwen had moved over to keeping her Essaerites more hidden.

It's not that Essaerites didn't make a wonderful deterrent, because they did, but she'd also found that people would just find ways of getting around the Essaerites. After all, she could only spare so much Essaeris to protect her people. So now, her cats stayed on the periphery of the group, and her settlements stayed close together. At night and during the day, it made for slow moving, but it was the best way.

She decided to get up. She got up and began tending to breakfast. Outside of the tent, the air was chill and filled with the scent of campfires that had been slowly dwindling throughout the night. A few sputtered and crackled next to her, while others were starting to build as people woke up and put fresh logs on the fires.

Caelwen did the same, putting some logs on the fire in front of her tent, watching as the flames started to lick up the new wood, casting a nice warm glow. She held out her hands, warming them, and took in her surroundings.

The forest they were in would be beautiful, normally, and part of Caelwen did think it was, but it wasn't her home, and while the trees and animals were beautiful, she knew they were dangerous as well. She didn't know where things could hide or were hiding, what meant her ill will, and what was a friend, so she distrusted everything.

It seemed this was also the policy that Treftune had, because he hadn't gone more than a few feet away from her since they had left the settlement. Even his Essaerites seemed to stay relatively close until they had been in an area for a day or so. Then they would venture out, trying to forage.

Partway through boiling some oats for breakfast, she heard Wulfgren clomping up next to her. He sat down on a log beside her, and she ladled some oats into a bowl for him.

"Morning," she said.

He grunted his reply.

"How'd you sleep?" she asked.

"Fine. I don't mind sleeping on the road anymore," he commented. "But I can tell a lot of these people aren't used to it," he said, looking around at the members of their community.

It was true. Members had been getting more afraid with each day that passed, and with each settlement they passed that was not looking for newcomers. People were on edge, and she could understand why. They didn't have a home, they didn't have a future, and, by and large, they were being hunted.

What would become of them?

They were also disturbed by the news they had heard. In the last few settlements they had been in, they heard rumors that Lysandrian forces had moved from Lysandrian into Gwenthari territory. They appeared to be focusing on the Ulfgarath, but there were plenty of Wulfharboria settlements in the Ulfgarath lands, and so part of her was concerned.

For his part, this seemed to almost comfort Wulfgren. When he had been a mercenary, he had fought with some of the Lysandrian legions. They had hired him, and as he had pointed out, the Wulfharborias had a long history of working with Lysandrian, and that there could be some opportunity there.

This was something that her uncle seemed to agree with. Ilfthandor had latched onto the idea of the Lysandrians looking for Wulfharborias to help out their legions as soon as Wulfgren brought it up. She could understand. Ilfthandor had lost a lot and would be looking for other ways of building wealth again, but she wasn't sure what their people could offer. After all, they were without a home and were just a motley crew. Yes, they had men that could fight, that could potentially go and work for the legions, but what would happen with the rest of the settlement? They would need lands and places to settle, and Caelwen wasn't sure that the Lysandrians would want them in their territory, but maybe they would.

"Anything pop last night?" Wulfgren asked after a few moments.

She shook her head. "Nothing that woke me anyway," she commented. "I haven't seen anybody else in a little while, but I know there are some settlements coming up ahead. Some of them are small, but a lot of them are medium-sized."

He looked thoughtful. "I guess we'll find out how friendly they are."

She wasn't so hopeful. "I'm pretty sure they're going to tell us to fuck off. And here, I thought you said because I was an Essaerist that we'd be welcomed with open arms."

He laughed. "Yeah, I guess I was wrong about that, wasn't I?" he said, and he had been. If anything, it had been the opposite. Small and medium-sized settlements had been concerned by Caelwen. After all, not only was her settlement representing a large amount of newcomers, but also, with her, a large amount of power. That had the potential to change dynamics in most settlements, and Ilfthandor hadn't found a way of talking them out of it.

To her uncle's credit, Caelwen had been surprised by him. Now that he was in the position of having to make good-faith agreements, he had done a very good job of negotiating and haggling everywhere they went, and part of her wondered if they would be destitute if it hadn't been for Ilfthandor's clever negotiations.

Of course, another part of her reminded her that they wouldn't be in this situation if Ilfthandor's propensity to make bad-faith deals or to think only of himself had stayed in check. Still, he was an asset now, and she had to give credit where it was due.

Once they were done with breakfast and the rest of the settlement was awake, they broke down camp and began moving again. Caelwen walked next to the cart that Wulfgren had, looking around the forest around her. As she walked, it helped to clear her mind and make her feel better about their current situation.

As they got further south, she suspected that there would be opportunities for them, and if not, then they would have to move west. And worst comes to worst, they would move north, but they would need to have a wide margin between them and the area they use to live in before they could move north, and Caelwen didn't really want to go that direction.

There had been a reason why the Wulfharborias had been moving south for the last couple of generations, and it wasn't because the north was full of fertile land; it was because it was the opposite.

CHAPTER 28
TEN YEARS AGO

Valfric felt his Essaeris flex and boil inside him. Along with the Essaeris, his emotions roiled and boiled as well. Fear, excitement, anger, joy—all of them were present, all of them screaming and begging for his attention. His heart hammered, and sweat poured down his brow and neck. He lashed out with his sword. It clanged against the sword of a man with red hair and blue eyes, sending a shock down his arm and into his body. The other man grunted and swung at him, and Valfric blocked the blow.

The Wulfharboria man was large, with a long beard. He was muscular and wore chainmail armor and a dented, tarnished helm. Valfric gritted his teeth and tried to hit the man with his shield, pushing him back to create a gap to work with. His blade moved back and forth with the other man's, creating a din that flowed into the chaos of the other fights all around him.

When the alarm had been raised, Valfric had instantly sprung into motion with Aelric, feeling excited and terrified all at the same time. Wulfharboria raiders were at their settlement, trying to raid and pillage what they could, but Valfric wasn't having it, nor were the others from his settlement.

Behind him, tending to other Wulfharboria, were two of Valfric's Essaerites. They were large wolves with sharp teeth and powerful jaws. They ripped through the men, jerking their heads and thrashing the men about. Valfric could sense the blood in their mouths and hear the screams in their ears. It was thrilling and invigorating—everything he was born to do and be.

The man he was fighting came at him, and Valfric parried the blow, taking the opportunity to knock the man back with his shield. The man stumbled, and Valfric lashed out with his sword, feeling it connect with the man's neck. The blade jerked in the man's spine, and Valfric gave it a great yank as it came out, partially severing the head. Blood gushed out, coating the blade and spraying Valfric's shield and face. It was wonderful. It was amazing. It was terrifying.

He turned to the next adversary and began his work. He was knocked back, falling on his ass. He rolled, trying to right himself, but the man was on him, about to cut him down, when one of Valfric's wolves came in and latched onto the man's back, sending him rolling. Valfric raised himself from the ground and stabbed the man, then turned to another.

Next to him, Aelric was handling two men all on his own, and Valfric felt his thrill and excitement surge alongside him. This is what they were. This is what he had always wanted, he thought.

Men screamed and yelled in pain, anger, or death, and Valfric reveled in all of it. He moved from foe to foe, sometimes killing, but oftentimes just wounding or pushing someone back. His arm burned where he had been cut, but the wound was not so bad as to stop him from fighting, though a part of his mind wondered how bad the cut would feel once the excitement from the battle was over. His ribs also hurt from where he had been hit by a mace, but he had taken care of that problem. The warrior who had hit him was now missing his arm.

Most of the Wulfharboria had come in on horseback, but a few had been on foot. Those had been the ones that Aelric and Valfric had tended to. They were starting to thin now, and the rest of the settlement was arriving with more warriors and horses to push back the Wulfharboria. The fight would be over soon, and with it, so would Valfric's excitement, but still, he had been here. They had known that there was a chance they would be raided for several days. They'd found things in the woods indicating that there was a small force in the area.

Valfric had been surprised, nonetheless, when he heard the alarm raised, but now that it was happening, all he could do was focus on the moment. As the men started to back away from his settlement, he felt his heart continue to hammer, and he breathed hard, but he felt the fatigue now. They hadn't been fighting very long, but it felt like it had been an eternity. As the men ran off into the woods, Valfric crouched over, holding his knees, breathing hard.

As he calmed down, Aelric came and clapped him on the shoulder. "That was something else, wasn't it?"

"Ulfgara, it was fucking great!" Valfric said.

He joined a few other people as they poked around the bodies of the people that had attacked them and looked at those in their own settlement who had been hurt or killed. As he wandered around looking at the dead, he noticed a cottage that his father frequented. As he approached the cottage, there was blood on the ground. There appeared to be damage to the cottage.

When he walked inside, he found a group of men lying on the floor in their own blood. Next to them were knocked-over jugs of Bryndraught and mead. Its scent was heavy in the air, along with the smell of blood. In the middle of the group was his father. Valfric looked down at the man, part of him unable to register what he was seeing. His father's throat had been slit, as had the other men's. The damage to the cottage appeared to be from it being ransacked for valuables.

Aelric came into the room and looked down. "Fuck."

Fuck was right, Valfric thought. He knelt down next to the men, shocked at what he was seeing. They were cold, and their skin was grey and clammy.

"All of their throats were slit," Aelric said, kneeling next to another man and looking over at Valfric. "What do you think that means?"

Valfric looked down at the bodies. "It means that they were all passed out when the raiders came in."

It was the only explanation; otherwise, there would have been more signs of a struggle. Instead, the raiding Wulfharboria would have come in and seen a group of men passed out drunk. It had probably only taken them a few moments to slit the throats of those in the room and then go on their way with whatever they wanted.

Valfric felt sick—not at the sight of his father dead. For some reason, that seemed almost right to him. But sick that it had happened, that people had been able to come into the homes of those in his settlement and kill them without so much as those people lifting a finger. How weak were they? *How pathetic were they that this was able to happen to them,* Valfric thought.

It wouldn't have happened to him. It couldn't have. He would have put up a fight. He never lost so much control as to pass out from drinking, but for his father, that had been a daily occurrence for years.

He looked down at the man, feeling a sense of disappointment and hatred rise inside him. If his father had been the man that a man was supposed to be—if he had been a warrior, if he had been strong—then he would have been alive. But if his father had been the man that men were supposed to be, Valfric's mother would have never died, and his brother would have never died for that matter either.

He shook his head and walked out, Aelric behind him.

"Are you okay?" Aelric asked.

Valfric looked back, fighting back traitorous angry tears that filled his eyes. Aelric's expression softened, and he touched his arm.

"I'm not sad," he said. "I'm angry, and I'm disgusted!"

Aelric seemed confused only for a moment, and then he nodded.

"Alright. Alright, then. I'll be angry and disgusted with you," he said.

CHAPTER 29

Emperor Feliciano had five legions behind him when he made it to the edge of the frontier: Aeterna, Fortitudinis, Aquilae, Vindicis, and Gladii. Fortitudinis stayed at the fort at the edge of the frontier, while the other four legions moved north into Gwenthari territory. They had entered the territory of the Ulfgarath. The once-proud Gwenthari nation had long ago fallen into fractured settlements and cities, having been picked at by both the Valfarans and the Wulfharboria. While it had lost much of its greatness and many of its peoples had been pushed around, the cities were still strong. Up to this point, the legions hadn't faced any serious resistance. They had found a few towns and settlements, but nothing that the legions weren't able to handle easily.

Now the forces had split as they prepared for the first major offensive of their campaign. Feliciano had taken with him Aeterna and Vindicis, pushing north towards the city of Hroldenfell. Moving to the west was Gladii, and to the east was Aeterna, which was the legion that Mariokos and Xavieno were members of. Aeterna's objective was similar to Gladii's: to move out and flank Hroldenfell, cutting off any supplies that it might receive from neighboring towns, cities, and settlements. It was also to ensure that the city didn't have any escape routes.

While the Ulfgarath had not formed a cohesive fighting unit yet, that would change as the legions moved deeper into their territory. Areas would be forced to coalesce and overcome previous ill will or grudges in order to defend themselves. The best way to dissuade people from doing this was to show them that there was no chance of success and to prevent them from having the opportunity to do it in the first place. Thus, the march towards Hroldenfell.

From there, the rest of the territory would open up to the legion. As they moved to the east and north, Fortitudinis, stationed at the fort, worked to build supply lines behind the main legions. Conversely, both Gladii and Aeterna had been doing likewise, building supply routes back towards the main front. But the legions had moved quickly to cut off any support that Hroldenfell might receive. This had resulted in raiding parties hitting supply lines as they moved back towards Lysandrian territory. It wasn't something that was unexpected, nor could it be completely stopped. Traveling in a war-torn area was dangerous no matter what. Caravans had guards with them, but they were still susceptible. And the legions could only move as fast as their supply lines allowed. Losing those lines could be a death sentence for a force in another territory.

Thus, that had necessitated Mariokos's current assignment. His battalion, along with several others, were working their way back through Gwenthari territory in scouting parties, looking for any potential threats and ambushes.

If they found them, they took them out. If they didn't find anything, their presence alone showed locals that it wasn't wise to mess with the legions. Many of the settlements, and even towns that they had come to, had capitulated without so much as resisting at all. At first, Mariokos was surprised by this. But the more he thought about it, the more it made sense. Everything they had come upon had been small. Even if the Lysandrian armies had no training whatsoever, they would be able to easily overrun the groups of people. It made sense. They'd capitulate and agree to whatever the legions wanted. Then, once the legions moved on, they would raid supply trains and otherwise harass them. It wasn't so much that they were trying to take the legions out; it was just opportunistic. Seeing squads and platoons of soldiers moving about tended to dissuade that kind of behavior.

Mariokos's platoon was working on the northeast edge of their area of influence. He was presently with his squad, and he had created ten Essaeris legionnaires to accompany them, giving them a force of twenty. It wasn't a large force, but it was certainly something to be reckoned with. They were working through dense woods that were bordered by the occasional open area. For the most part, they stuck to the woods. The trees around them stood tall above their heads, and Mariokos could hear the sounds of birds and squirrels as they moved through the branches above them. Plants were starting to come to life as the land warmed with spring's fast approach, giving the air a mossy, moist scent that he found relaxing.

Their footsteps were soft and muffled as they walked across the soft ground. The dense foliage made it hard to see anything around them. For Mariokos, there were the added issues that he didn't have any Essaerites that could give them any real scouting advantage. The trees made it almost impossible. While he could have created a few small scouts in the forms of animals, they would be almost useless as they'd only be able to move as fast as Mariokos's squad, which would have pulled away Essaeris that could be used to create legionnaires—legionnaires that might be necessary. Thus, they went traipsing through the forest like normal men.

Next to him, Helioz and Luciakos kept a keen watch, their heads on swivels. Erastos moved near them as well. Their formation was loose. They could clump together quickly if need be, but in this type of terrain and forest, shield walls would be difficult to employ, and it was one of the few times the large shields that the legions favored were detrimental. Thankfully they hadn't seen anyone in some time, and he very much doubted that anybody was going to attack a squad of twenty.

Sunlight shone down like pillars from the canopy above them. The honey-golden light had little bugs flying through it and bits of debris floating around the forest. It was an altogether pleasant sort of scene. Whenever someone stepped on a twig or a branch, the sound only traveled for a bit before being muffled by the foliage around them. In this, they knew anyone could easily sneak up on them.

Conversely, Mariokos and his group could easily sneak up on someone else. This again made him feel confident that they were not going to see any hostiles in the area. Setting up a trap in this type of area would be easy, but one had to assume that someone would be walking through to spring the trap, and there was nothing to indicate that this area had any value. So the men moved on, speaking in hushed whispers.

The forest was beginning to clear, and they found themselves in a hilly area that was still full of trees, but a small, rough-worn road wound through it. As they began walking up the road, Mariokos wondered if they would be heading towards a settlement or town, though they had found just as many roads in the area that led to abandoned, dilapidated settlements and towns that looked like they hadn't been lived in for years.

As they moved, Erastos held up his hand. "Hold," he said. Everyone stopped and listened. Mariokos could hear it now. There was a slight murmur of voices, and he could hear the sound of wheels on the ground and horses' hooves clomping.

"Form up," Erastos ordered.

They did so. All the men formed a tight group, with Mariokos's Essaerite legionnaires making up the outside of the formation. "Move slowly," Erastos said. They began to march in formation, moving slowly, and as they came around the corner, they noticed that the sound of movement and voices had stopped.

As they approached another little hill, Mariokos saw it first. "Hold," he said. The entire group stopped and looked ahead of them. They were close. Mariokos could make out the forms of figures in the forest. Off to the sides of the road, there were many of them. They slowly approached, not making a sound. He could see that it was mostly men. They had shields with them but weren't wearing any chainmail or armor. Some of them had swords at their sides, while others had cudgels, axes, and other weapons. But the concerning part wasn't so much the men as it was the woman at the head of their group.

Mariokos looked at her. Her hair was a bright red, framing a face with skin so white and pale it almost glowed. Her eyes were a vibrant blue that pierced through him. Her body was wrapped in vines and branches. Atop her head was what looked like a deer skull, with antlers coming out of it. She was breathtakingly and devastatingly beautiful. Mariokos wasn't sure if he'd ever seen anyone so beautiful before in his life, while simultaneously he was unsure if he had ever seen anything as disquieting as her wrapped in vines and branches. Next to her was a man who was taller than she was, with the same red hair and vibrant eyes. He had a shield with a sword at his side, he looked like a man who had seen a lot of combat.

Erastos grunted. "Fuck. We've been ambushed."

Mariokos couldn't disagree, but at the same time, he was having a hard time understanding why the Gwenthari in front of them were not attacking. Also, they were Wulfharboria, not Ulfgarath. While he knew that most of the members of the Legion didn't see a difference between the types of Gwenthari, Mariokos knew that their differences couldn't be more drastic.

At a barked order from Erastos, they all formed a quick shield wall and held out spears. The Gwenthari murmured, holding their shields out in front of them, drawing weapons. The beautiful, terrible woman in front of them narrowed her eyes, and the helm moved down, covering her face. Its eyes glowed green. From the sides, Mariokos heard the sound of movement, and he glanced over.

"Fuck," he said, "we're surrounded."

Erastos shot a glance at him. "What do you mean?"

"Look to the right and to the left. They're in the trees, not people." On either side of them were large pumas, or creatures that looked like pumas, by and large. Their fur was a deep chocolate brown mixed with green that blended into the foliage perfectly. He could see one of them lift its lip, its teeth all metal. Mariokos felt his heart pump a little faster. There was scurrying before them, and a man with gray hair and a gray beard came out.

"Stop, stop!" he shouted, holding up his hands, one pointed at his own people, the other at Mariokos and his group. "Stop," he bellowed again.

"We mean you no harm," the old man said.

"Bullshit," Erastos grunted.

Mariokos could see the man's eyes moving back and forth, not in fear, but calculation, trying to figure out how they were either going to retreat from this or how they were going to scare the Gwenthari away.

"I mean it, we mean you no harm," the old man said.

"He's telling the truth." The man next to the Essaerist said, "We are not here to harm you." He looked over at the woman. "Caelwen. Maybe help with this."

The woman looked at the man next to her. He could almost feel her resistance, but eventually, he saw her shoulders go down a little bit, and the skull removed itself from her face, revealing the beautiful woman below.

"See, we are not here to harm you," the old man said. "We would like to join you. We would like to enter your employ."

Mariokos heard Erastos snort, and he could see that Erastos was about to give the order to attack. Mariokos spoke under his breath, "Erastos, I don't think they're lying."

Erastos looked at him. "How the fuck could you know that?"

Mariokos eyed both the Essaerites that he could see on either side of them. "Because they could kill us if they wanted to. They also could have used those cats before we knew they were there."

Next to him, Helioz hissed, "You could take out those Essaerites."

Mariokos nodded softly. "Yes, I could, and my legionaries will if they attack us, but even if they didn't have Essaerites, look at how many of them there are. They would win, even without an Essaerist, but with an Essaerist, I'll be engaged, and just by sheer force of numbers..." Mariokos said, letting it hang there.

He saw Erastos's face relax some. "They would win, and they know it." He sighed and gave the order to stand down.

The legionaries lowered their shield wall, and Erastos stepped forward. He glanced at Mariokos. "I want you with me."

Mariokos walked with Erastos as the old man, the Essaerist, and the other man approached them. Once they were a few feet apart, Erastos said, "My name is Erastos; this here is Mariokos. Who are you?"

The old man touched his chest. "I am Ilfthandor; this is my nephew, Wulfgren, and my niece, Caelwen."

Caelwen was looking at Mariokos, appraising him, but not in a way that felt predatory; it was calculating and curious. Mariokos couldn't help but do the same, and part of him was thankful that he had the excuse of that he should be paying attention to another Essaerist instead of the fact that he was looking at a woman who, by her appearance alone, made him feel like he was a boy again in front of the town's prettiest girl.

She could fucking kill you, Mariokos thought to himself, and she could. She was an Essaerist. From what they had been told, the Gwenthari Essaerists were nowhere near as skilled as those of Lysandrian, but that didn't change the fact that the woman in front of them was deadly. She could kill him. It could be a challenge, but she was capable of it. Though Mariokos suspected that he would have the upper hand and that he would be able to take her in single combat. Still, that wasn't the point. The point was that she was dangerous, but that somehow made her even more beautiful. He tried not to let his face show it, but she had a small smirk that touched the corners of her lips as she looked at him, and he wondered if she had seen through him or if she was thinking the same.

"We see you have an Essaerist, too," Ilfthandor said. "Which of your number is it?"

The woman spoke. "It's him," she said, looking directly at Mariokos. Her uncle looked over at her, raising an eyebrow. She glanced at her uncle and shrugged. "It's him."

Mariokos couldn't help but smile. "How'd you know?"

Erastos gave him a dirty look.

She shrugged. "We know our own, don't we?" she said.

"That we do," Mariokos said. She knew what he was, which meant she knew he was just as capable of killing her as she was of killing him.

The man, Ilfthandor, seemed confused for a moment, but then went back to what he had been saying to Erastos before. "We would like to work with you. Some of the men in our settlement have worked for Lysandrian legions before. My nephew, for example, has recently come back from a conflict you had in the southeast."

Erastos looked at the man, Wulfgren. "Is that true?"

Wulfgren nodded. "Yes," he said. "I fought with the Praetoria Legion down there."

This seemed to satisfy Erastos. Praetoria had been recently involved in an engagement in the southeast, and from Mariokos's understanding, that Legion had never been outside of the region. It was unlikely that anyone from a northern area would know about the Legion unless they had seen it. And it wasn't uncommon for the Legions to hire mercenaries from northern lands. Their cavalry was wonderful, and he knew that the Empire had the best luck with mercenaries from Wulfharboria.

"They are Wulfharboria," Mariokos said under his breath.

"And how do you know that?" Erastos asked quizzically.

"The red hair," Mariokos said.

Erastos seemed to look like he was conceding a point. "Yeah, I've heard that."

"So why do you want to join the Legion?" Erastos asked.

Ilfthandor looked grateful. "We've been driven from our homes and need a new one. We thought working with the Legions would be a good way to start."

"So you're looking for a handout," Erastos said.

Ilfthandor shook his head. "No, not a handout. Employment. Is that something you're interested in?"

Erastos shook his head. "Not my call to make. But," he said, looking around, "I suppose if you meant us harm, you could have done it."

"But we didn't," Wulfgren said.

"But you didn't," Erastos echoed. "We can take you back to our Legion, but I can't make you any promises from there."

This seemed to give the group pause, but Ilfthandor said, "We completely understand. Thank you for your consideration."

Erastos nodded. "Right, well, I suppose we should head back then. How many of you are there?"

"There's a lot of us," Caelwen said. "But we've been packing light so we can move quickly."

"Is there a reason we should move quickly?" Mariokos asked.

She glanced at him, appraising him again. "We have seen groups following us on a few occasions. A caravan like ours out in the open— it's tempting," she commented.

"We don't know if there's anyone following us now," Wulfgren said, "but it's possible. Especially this close to the front."

Erastos looked at him. "What makes you so sure you're close to the front?"

Wulfgren looked at the men behind Erastos and Mariokos. "Because you're a scouting party. And that tells me that the Legion's close. Maybe not the main Legion that's fighting in this area, but a Legion nonetheless. And you're always at the front. Don't tell me. The supply train's getting hit?"

For the first time, Erastos looked almost impressed. "Clever. How do I know you're not one of the ones attacking the supply trains?"

Wulfgren looked behind himself. "With this many children and elderly," he said, shaking his head, "I can't leave them alone; it's too dangerous in these parts."

Erastos looked back at the gathering of people. "I suppose it is. Well, very well then. We'll head back to the Legion. Again, no promises."

———

CAELWEN WATCHED AS THE LEGIONNAIRES WENT BACK AND TALKED AMONGST THEMSELVES. She looked over at her uncle.

"Do you trust them?" she asked.

"Maybe. Maybe not," Ilfthandor said. "It's hard to tell. This is one unit. They hardly speak for their whole command."

She looked over at her brother, who shrugged. "It's true. I don't like the part about no promises. But in my experience, Lysandrian command is very level-headed, and they think strategically."

"So do you think they'll go for it?" she asked.

Wulfgren shrugged. "I don't see a reason why they wouldn't. We have good fighters with us, and they'll be interested in that for this campaign. So, yes, I think they will."

He looked back at the rest of the settlement. "Now what they'll do with them, I'm not sure."

"If you think I'm going to let my people be enslaved," Ilfthandor said.

Wulfgren snorted softly. "I know you would do it in a heartbeat, but I wouldn't be worried about that. It's not exactly like the Legion will be able to make a deal with some of us and say, by the way, we're enslaving the rest of your people. No, at worst, they'll send them on their way. But it'll be behind the front lines."

He looked over at his sister, and Caelwen cocked an eyebrow. "What?"

"Release most of that suit that you're in," he said.

"Why would I do that?" she asked.

"Because they are trusting us because they know they don't have a choice. We could have killed them if we wanted to. Now we need to show them that we are going to give them trust, not because we have to, but because we want to," he said.

The Commander, Erastos, and Mariokos were coming back. Caelwen looked over at Mariokos. His skin was olive, and his eyes were deep green. She saw brown hair sticking out from under parts of his helmet. She was intrigued as she looked at him. She hadn't seen any Lysandrians before, and while they all had a similar appearance, she enjoyed how this one looked. He was attractive, and he held himself with confidence, but not cockiness. She liked that.

As he and Erastos approached, she also looked at the other man. Erastos, on the other hand, looked to be older than Mariokos. She could see hardness and distrust in his eyes. It was probably why he was in leadership.

"Alright, we'll start heading back now," Erastos said. He glanced over at Caelwen. "I'm going to have to insist that you accompany my Essaerist."

Caelwen raised an eyebrow. Mariokos stepped forward. "This is standard. You're an Essaerist. You pose a threat."

She sighed a little. "You're an Essaerist, and you pose a threat."

Mariokos smiled, and she rather enjoyed the look on his face.

"Two threats make something safe, don't they?" he said, trying to lighten the tension.

She almost smiled, but controlled herself. Instead, she just glanced over at her brother, who nodded softly. "Fine. I will go with you," she said, walking up to Mariokos.

Her brother and uncle went to rouse the rest of their settlement, leaving her alone with Mariokos. She stood close to him. He was taller than she was, but not as tall as she would have expected. In her mind, the Lysandrians were either very tall and menacing or rather short and not threatening. Instead, they appeared just to be men, though to their credit, she noticed that all of them held themselves with poise and control. Their arms were all muscular and chiseled, and their faces held keen gazes as they watched her people move about.

They began to walk with the legionnaires in the lead, Mariokos looked over at her.

"How many Essaerites do you have in the area?" he asked her.

"A few," she said. She could tell he resisted the urge to roll his eyes. She smiled softly and saw his eyes widen for just a moment.

"Those pumas that you saw? I have one more at the rear. And then I also have a couple of hawks in the area, for all the good they're doing, with how dense this forest is." She grumbled.

He nodded and looked forward as they walked. "Yes, they don't seem to do very much for scouting, do they?"

She huffed. "No, they're absolute shit for it. But I'm glad to hear that others are having problems with it, too," she commented, smiling tightly.

"Yes, it's been difficult, but they do find some things." He looked over at her. "Have you found anything useful for looking around?"

She shrugged. "Smaller animals, but not while on the move."

From inside her tunic, Treftune popped his head out.

He smiled. "Is that an Essaerite?"

She shook her head. "No. And if he was, he'd be the least wieldy and controllable Essaerite I've ever had."

As if to prove the point, Treftune looked keenly at Mariokos. He smiled at him, and Treftune leapt off her shoulder and onto his, scrambling up on top of his helmet.

"Whoa, what—" he started. He made to grab at Treftune, who just scurried out of the way and then went down his back and along his side.

"What the—?" he started.

"He won't hurt you. Treftune, cut it out. You're being rude," she said. Treftune chitted at her, and he jumped onto her shoulder.

"You're gonna get us killed," she said to him sternly.

She heard Mariokos chuckle. "That thing is interesting."

She smirked and held out her hand. "Drop it," she said. Mariokos looked confused. Treftune glared at her. "Drop it," she said to the Valfglidea sternly. It spat out something onto her hand. It was purple and round like a bead.

"How did he..." Mariokos started patting his side. She handed him whatever the bead was.

"They're thieves," she said. "Cute thieves, but thieves," she commented. Treftune chirped, and she glowered at him. Mariokos bounced the bead in his hand and smiled, then held it out to the little Valfglidea. "You can have it; they're just water." Treftune took it and chewed on it. Then he jumped back on Mariokos and began to scurry around him again. To his credit, Mariokos didn't seem put out.

"What are they?" he asked.

"They're called Valfglideas," she said.

"Oh, I think I've heard of these," he said. "I heard they're rare."

She smiled. "Not so rare. Just very good at hiding and very good at stealing. They can also use Essaeris."

He looked at her. "Really?"

"Yes, they can change their fur, their teeth, and they can create other versions of themselves. That's why they seem so rare. You never actually see them. If you see anything, you might see their Essaerites," she said.

"That's fascinating," he said.

She laughed as she watched Treftune scurry around on him. In her experience, Treftune was a far better judge of character than any human she'd ever met.

"So how long have you been traveling?" Mariokos asked.

"A while," she said. "We've had some trouble with some of the settlements that were near us," she commented. "And they had an Essaerist."

He nodded. "Not one you wanted to tend to?"

She grimaced. "He's ancient."

Mariokos looked confused. "Okay."

"So, he's powerful," she said, as if Mariokos was dense.

It was his turn to give her a look, as if she were the one being stupid.

"Why would his age have anything to do with his ability?" Mariokos asked, confusion evident in his voice. Then, realization seemed to dawn on him. "Oh, interesting."

She raised an eyebrow. "Interesting?"

Mariokos's face was apologetic. "I'm sorry; I don't mean to be rude. We heard that foreign Essaerists don't have the same training that Lysandrian ones do," he explained.

"And that would matter how?" she asked.

He shrugged. "Simple. By the time I joined the Legion, I was just as powerful as any other Essaerist in the rest of the empire. Age has almost no impact on it."

For a moment, she didn't believe him, but then she remembered a conversation she'd had with her brother, where he had said that the Lysandrian Essaerists were all very powerful. Perhaps this was why. She sighed.

"Well, at any rate, he's stronger than me, and they outnumbered us, so here we are," she said, gesturing at the road before her.

"I'm sorry about that," Mariokos said, then added, "You look surprised to hear me say that."

"I am a little. You're here invading, aren't you? I'm surprised to hear that you're sorry that someone was driven out of their home," she said. "Sorry."

He didn't look offended.

"No need to apologize; you're right in so many ways, though we're not here to drive people out of their homes, by and large. But we're also here dealing with the Ulfgarath, not the Wulfharboria," he said.

She cocked a smile. "So you know the difference between Gwenthari, I see. I take it your commander doesn't."

"Oh, he does," Mariokos said. "He just doesn't appreciate it."

"And you do?" she asked.

"I do," he confirmed. "Yes, both the Ulfgarath and Wulfharboria are Gwenthari; however, they're different nations and different peoples. And I know a lot of Wulfharboria have fought with the legions. Like that man with you."

"Wulfgren," she corrected.

"Yes, Wulfgren. Your brother, right?" he asked.

"Yes," she confirmed.

"So, do you think my people are going to be in trouble when we get back to your legion?" she asked seriously.

Mariokos looked thoughtful. "I don't know, and I can't speak for the legion; however, I do know that we're always hiring mercenaries, and from what little I've seen, it looks like you have some men that look capable. Clearly, your brother is, but I don't know about the rest of what you have. Perhaps the legion goes for it; perhaps it doesn't. But I don't think you're necessarily in danger."

"Does me being an Essaerist sweeten the pot?" she asked.

He looked thoughtful. "How do you mean?"

She gave him another look like he was stupid. "You saw the Essaerites that I created. Those pumas are nothing small to deal with. Each one of them is three hundred pounds, and their mouths and teeth are metal."

"Oh, I have no doubt they're tough, but in my experience, the legion doesn't tend to have women in combat," he said. He held up his hand. "I know for the Gwenthari it's different. Perhaps in some auxiliary form, maybe, but also with you being an Essaerist, maybe they would want you in combat. Do you really want to fight for the legions?"

She looked thoughtful. Then she glanced back at her settlement behind her. "If it means that they have a better future, then I suppose I would."

He shrugged. "Then maybe they'll allow you to; I don't know." They kept walking, approaching a clearing that the road wound through. "But we'll find out soon enough, either way."

She nodded. "That we will."

CHAPTER 30

As Lysandrian forces moved north, Valfric hadn't been surprised to hear of settlements and towns being displaced. This, along with Wulfharboria mercenary groups heading to work for the legions, had caused a fair amount of panic and chaos. He hadn't been shocked when Durnara told him that it was time to go raiding again. Not only was spring coming and would soon be in full swing, but there were lots of people on the roads, which meant plenty of opportunity. Likewise, there were a lot of people who had scores to settle and were looking for chances to move up in life, which made recruitment relatively easy.

It hadn't been difficult to find people willing to join Valfric when he'd been in Hroldenfell. Since then, his little team and those from his settlements had managed to pick up several other small groups, making for a decent-sized raiding party—not large enough to take on any of the legions by any stretch of the imagination, but more than enough to handle most supply caravans.

That wasn't to say that Lysandrian supply caravans didn't have protection. Most of them had guards, or at least the ones that were official did. The legions needed everything from food to equipment to entertainment, along with selling whatever they managed to steal from Valfric's people.

However, not all of the caravans came with guards. Sometimes small groups would be separated from larger ones, or individual merchants or small merchant chains would try to make journeys on their own. Occasionally they had a little protection with them, but usually not much. This made for relatively easy pickings for Valfric and his team.

They would find a group, hit it hard and fast, taking whatever they could and burning whatever they couldn't. Then they'd leave. They were far from being the only ones doing this. He knew that many other Gwenthari raiding parties were out there doing likewise.

While Valfric and his team had seen a few of them, there hadn't been any issues between the groups. After all, why get in a fight with somebody who could potentially resist you when there were so many easy targets elsewhere? And why go against your own?

Valfric had been loving it, as had Aelric, Thraindel, and Ilara. He wasn't sure he'd had this much fun in a long time, which was surprising because he had really enjoyed attacking the Wulfharborias as they'd come back from war. But this seemed to be more enjoyable for some reason. Perhaps it was because of how arrogant he found the Lysandrians to be, thinking they could come into Ulfgarath territory and take whatever they wanted without any repercussions. It was arrogance on a level that Valfric could hardly comprehend, but he was helping the Lysandrians to figure out exactly what it was they were doing and the cost of doing it.

There had also been the added excitement that Valfric had to actually try to scout. He always scouted to an extent, but now it was more important. Since they had begun their campaign of disrupting the Lysandrian supply lines, one of the legions nearby had stopped and begun sending men back to secure those supply lines and otherwise fortify and rebuild roads. It meant that Valfric had to keep his wits about him because he wasn't the only one hunting in the area.

Valfric checked in on his Essaerites. They'd been tracking a large group for the last few days. The caravan had been moving southwest. At first, Valfric wondered if it were people heading toward Hroldenfell to help the fight against the Lysandrians, but they had found that it was Wulfharboria. They had been slowly catching up to the group, and even though it was large, Valfric and his group thought it could be easy pickings. It appeared to be almost an entire settlement's worth of people. With them, they had carts full of belongings and lots of livestock.

He had a hawk following them from a distance. There was another problem that was going to come with this settlement: they had an Essaerist with them. The group had entered a clearing and was walking along a road. He had the hawk swoop about, checking on them. Valfric and his people were set up almost perfectly. The group would be passing by them soon, and when they did, he would use his Essaerites to engage the other Essaerist's Essaerites, and then the rest of his party would be able to run out, take carts and livestock, and be out of the area.

Next to him in the trees, Ilara shifted. "Are they coming?"

Valfric nodded. "Yes, I see the back of the caravan with my hawks now. I'm trying to find the other Essaerist's Essaerites, though." This would be something that he would need to time. He would need to engage the other Essaerites and make sure he didn't miss any of them if this was to go off without a hitch.

"And you're sure you can do this?" Aelric asked.

Valfric grinned. "Yes, she looks like she's younger than me and she's having to protect an entire caravan's worth of people," Valfric said, referring to the Essaerist he had seen. He had watched her, and she did appear to be competent, but she was younger than he and stretched thin. So far, he had found three large Essaerites, all of them in the form of large cats. They kept fairly tight with the rest of the settlement, which gave him a pretty high degree of certainty that they would be able to sneak up on them.

The caravan had been moving through the forest, which was difficult to scout with anything other than ground animals, and even then there could be some difficulties. So he didn't think that she had any hawks or owls in the area, and if she did, he highly doubted that she would be able to find everything. As his hawk moved forward, he kept it above the caravan and slightly away lest she figure out that they had something following them. But what gave him pause was as it came to the front; he saw some new figures.

"Fuck," Valfric said under his breath.

"What is it?" Thraindel asked.

"Lysandrians," Valfric said, his voice hard with anger. Near the front of the group, he saw them. It looked to be about two squads' worth of legionnaires. They were walking in front of the Wulfharborias, and just a little ways back from the main group of Lysandrians was a Lysandrian man walking with the settlement's Essaerist. He saw them talking and conversing with each other, and he felt a pit of rage in his gut.

"Fucking traitors," Valfric said under his breath. Everyone knew that the Wulfharborias were traitors. They had betrayed their own kind in so many ways. First, when they had joined some of the Lysandrian legions in wars down south as mercenaries. But mostly, when they had helped attack the Ulfgarath. Given the Valfarans had done that as well.

But still, there was something that just bothered Valfric as he saw the Lysandrian man walking with the Wulfharboria woman. It was one thing when Gwenthari were attacking other Gwenthari, but to go outside to do what they had done, that was unacceptable. The Wulfharborias had been encroaching more and more into Ulfgarath lands over the last few generations.

Well, Valfric was going to help get a little revenge for that now.

"Are we still attacking?" Aelric asked.

Valfric nodded once. "Bet your fucking ass we are. There's only twenty of the legion. We can get them distracted and maybe even take out some of them, and we're definitely going to kill that fucking Essaerist if we can."

He had zero desire for an Essaerist, no matter how young she was, to join the Lysandrian legions to help them try and take Ulfgarath lands. But it did require that they change their plans a bit. Now, instead of the quick smash-and-grab job they had been planning, they would need to focus their attention on the Essaerist and the Lysandrians while the rest of the group tried to steal what they could.

"So what are we going to do then?" Aelric asked.

Valfric thought. "Most of the teams are still going to do whatever they were going to do before. We can't communicate with them anyway." They had groups coming up from behind the rest of the caravan. In many ways, this wouldn't be different for them; it would just be different for Valfric and his small team.

Now, instead of predominantly harassing, they would have a target. Their first target was going to be the Lysandrian commander, who was walking with the Essaerist. That would be important. Then they would deal with the Essaerist, if they could. Part of his mind realized that it would be difficult to take her out. She would have the protection of her whole settlement, but it was still doable. He reassessed his plan. *The Essaerist first before her people can protect her, then the commander,* he thought.

———

Mariokos walked next to Caelwen, unable to deny that he found the other Essaerist fascinating and captivating. He also found her Essaerites equally interesting. She was eyeing one of his that was walking in front of them.

"That's an Essaerite, right?" she asked.

He nodded. "Yep, it is."

She looked thoughtful. "They look almost just like you, but not," she said, confused. "Are you trying to get them to confuse somebody?"

Mariokos smiled. "No, not necessarily. From a distance, these will be almost indistinguishable from a regular legionnaire. But up close, obviously, they don't pass the test," he admitted.

And it was true. The legionnaires that he used had the same color of skin that he did, but they were missing hairs on the arm or had minor details that you would see on someone's skin.

"So why do you make them?" she asked.

"It's simple. They fight just like the legion does. They mix in well with the rest of the legion, and we work well together. It's pretty common for Lysandrian Essaerists to be able to do this. In fact, it's a requirement," he said.

She nodded.

"How about yours? They look fascinating," he said.

She smiled tightly. "Yes, they have their purposes, for sure."

He noted that it didn't sound like she was exactly happy to have them. "They have their purposes?" he asked with a crooked smile.

She looked over at him, her eyes widening for a moment. "Yes. Sorry—No, they have their purposes, and they've been very useful. I just don't like having all my power tied up in creations whose only real purpose is to destroy everything around them," she admitted.

"I can understand that," he said.

She raised an eyebrow. "Can you?"

"Yeah, I can. These Essaerites have their place," Mariokos said, gesturing towards the legionnaire ones, "but predominantly they're here for war. Yes, they can do everything else that a legionnaire can, and that's part of the reason why we make them. They can help us with construction or any other tasks around a base, but basically they're here in case they're needed for combat."

He was about to say something else when he saw her eyes widen. "Shit, we're about to be attacked."

He was confused for only a moment before one of his own Essaerites noted the fast approach of four very large wolves being followed by people on horseback. Training instantly kicked in, and Mariokos barked, "Attack! Essaerites!" he shouted.

With rote motion, the legionnaires instantly stopped, and Erastos began to bark orders. Mariokos turned to the tree line, seeing the four animals come barreling out of the woods towards them. Their mouths were open, their teeth flashing.

His legionnaires moved to get in the way, but the wolves were too fast; they moved past them and were heading right for Mariokos. Except in that moment, Mariokos realized they weren't heading for him. They were heading for Caelwen. He gritted his teeth and stepped in front of their path, swinging his shield up; one of the wolves jumped, smashing into him.

The weight of the animal knocked him back, and he heard the shield crunch. He turned, redirecting the momentum, sending the animal sprawling on the ground. Mariokos stumbled, falling. He released his shield, and his hand caught him.

He rolled to get up, and he saw another one of the wolves change direction and dart towards him. It jumped at him, its mouth opening, and was hit by one of Caelwen's large pumas. Its jaws wrapped around the shoulder of the wolf, and they rolled on the hard-packed dirt of the road.

The puma shook its head back and forth, shaking the wolf. Two other wolves changed direction, going after the puma, latching onto it. Mariokos felt his Essaeris inside of him, and he reached out, creating a dart that was wrapped in silvery cord. He threw it, hitting one of the wolves, and the cord snaked out, coiling around it. The wolf bit at it, but it was too late. The cord began to tighten itself, a little ratchet on the top of it clicking away.

With each ratchet, it clamped tighter around the wolf. He heard a bone crack, and Mariokos was on his feet. He created a spear in his hand and jabbed it through one of the other wolves before it could take out Caelwen's puma. The spearhead cut through flesh and fur, and the Essaerite bit at it. Mariokos drew out his sword and removed the animal's head.

A moment later, Caelwen's Essaerite finished with the original wolf that had been attacking. The legionaries were fully formed up now, making a shield wall. Mariokos turned to Caelwen, seeing that she was being wrapped in vines.

"How long do you need?" he asked.

"Not long," she breathed.

He nodded and created another shield.

———

CAELWEN FELT HER HEART BEGIN TO HAMMER AS SHE WATCHED HER PUMA TWISTING ON THE ground with three of the other Essaerist's Essaerites. She saw Mariokos's hand move out as he threw a dart coiled in silvery cord. She watched it sneak around one of the wolves, constricting, breaking its bones.

Deep inside herself, she felt her Essaeris burning like a fire wanting to explode out of her. She began letting it come out. Vines began to sneak around her legs, feet, and arms.

She watched as Mariokos was up now, dispatching one of the other wolves, her puma finishing with the other. Three Essaerites lay defeated in a matter of moments. She realized all of hers were still up, and the legionaries were forming a shield wall at the front of the caravan.

The sounds of battle grew more clamorous around her. She could hear people shouting and screaming. Mariokos turned back to her, asking her how much time she needed.

She concentrated deeply, focused on creating her Essaerite, watching in awe as the legionaries formed up. Men and women, clad in armor and shields, emerged from the forest. They rode around her settlement as her people formed up into a protective ball.

Still, her Essaeris was working. It took time for her to create this Essaerite, and while it had been needed, she kicked herself for the necessity of having to release it earlier when they had encountered the Lysandrians.

The attackers had blonde hair and blue eyes. She suspected they were Ulfgarath, as it was rare for the Valfarans to be in this area. They swung their shields and clubs at the shield wall, but the Lysandrians held steadfast. It was an impressive and formidable sight.

Others came spilling out on foot, and they ran at the settlement and Lysandrians. She watched as they smashed into the Lysandrian shield wall.

Mariokos was part of the wall, and she saw him and his Essaerites push back with their shields, pushing people over. The Essaerites worked in a flash, their spears and blades coming out, cutting people down before reforming the wall. Then they repeated the process. It was awe-inspiring.

At first, when she'd seen the Essaerites, they'd seemed silly and pointless, but now, seeing them work, she understood. They augmented the men around them, and the formation worked together perfectly. She watched as Mariokos worked with them. The Essaerites would anticipate each other's reactions and act appropriately. The Gwenthari attacking them stood almost no chance.

She saw two more Essaerites come into existence. They were short, with spindly limbs. They began collecting javelins from some of the gathered legionnaires, and Mariokos created more javelins. She was confused for a moment until she saw one of the little Essaerites jump in the air and then throw a javelin. It struck a man on a horse, knocking him off.

Another one of the little things jumped in the air, clearing the tops of the men fighting before it, and then threw its javelin. It too struck home.

She felt her Essaeris surge inside of her, and she let it roll out, completing the

Essaerite. She grew as its legs formed, and the skull helmet came down, its eyes glowing.

"I'm ready," she yelled.

Mariokos turned and nodded, and Caelwen plowed forward. The Essaerite legionnaires before her parted like water, and she saw the startled look of a man as she came out. She swung her arm, sending the man flying.

A horse was coming at her, and her vine tentacles on her back lashed out and threw a spike, embedding it in the chest of the horse, which dropped. She swung at another man, cutting him in half, and the group began to back away.

———

VALFRIC FELT SHOCK RUNNING THROUGH HIM. NEVER IN ALL HIS LIFE HAD HE LOST THREE Essaerites that quickly. It had been over in a moment. He hadn't even realized that the Lysandrian man was an Essaerist as well. From a distance, his legionnaires looked just like regular men, but once he'd gotten up close, it was obvious as day that they were Essaerites. Three of his wolves were down, and his whole group was engaged.

And now, they were terribly outnumbered. The settlement had formed up and was defending themselves admirably, while the Lysandrians at the front were ripping their way through warriors.

And now he had two Essaerists that he had to deal with. His gambit for going after the woman had failed, and now she was in an Essaerite that wrapped her body with wood, thorns, and vines. She stood tall above all the men in the area and was a terrifying sight to behold. Her skull helmet with the antlers coming off of it was frightening, and he watched as she swung her hand out, taking out men and horses.

He'd been wrong about her too. She was young, but she was clearly very capable. And he had no doubt that the Lysandrian Essaerist was equally, if not more, capable.

He yelled to Aelric, Ilara, and Thraindel, "Retreat! Retreat! We need to get back!"

They seemed to have already figured that out. They were disengaging from their enemies and backing away. Everyone was backing away now, and Valfric realized they were going to have to leave people behind if they wanted to live. People were running on foot, but now others from the settlement on horses were coming up and cutting them down as some of the Lysandrians' Essaerites jumped in the air and threw javelins at them.

Valfric had one wolf left that he used to harass the people as Thraindel, Ilara, and Aelric formed up with him. They rode into the forest with a few other members of their raiding party.

He looked back. "How many did we lose?" he said, seeing Aelric covered in blood, though he didn't know if it was his own or not.

"Hard to tell. A lot," Aelric said, his voice full of stress. And they had lost a lot.

He was sure most of their raiding party had been killed. They'd been counting on being able to take out the Essaerist and then scattering the others and using his wolves to harass. It hadn't been that way at all.

And the legionnaires. Valfric couldn't believe what he saw with them. They hadn't flinched at all. They'd held their wall and worked in perfect harmony, even the human ones. But the Essaerite ones had been the worst. It had been almost instant death for anyone attacking them.

His wolf was behind him and looked back, seeing that two of the other Essaerist's Essaerites were fast approaching. Valfric drove himself faster.

"Come on, we're being followed," he said.

He saw fear flash in his friends' faces for a moment, and they began coaxing the horses to run faster. The cats were catching up, and Valfric turned his one remaining wolf around to engage them, to give them time. It turned and barreled into one of the pumas, which rolled on the ground with it. The other continued to chase them.

Shit, Valfric thought, as the horses ran faster.

He felt down inside of himself, feeling for Essaeris. As they passed a tree, he tried to create a net to catch the other Essaerite. It did so, but only seemed to slow it down. Still, the gap was opening. His last wolf was down now and was completely shredded.

Fuck, I have nothing left to protect us, he realized.

But the horses kept charging through the trees until they made it out the other side and were in an open valley where they were able to pick up speed. Valfric looked behind himself, seeing the Essaerite come out of the tree line, but it slowed and came to a stop. He spurred the horses on, faster and faster. There was only a handful of other people left with them as they kept moving.

He didn't stop the horses running for what felt like hours, but eventually, the horses stopped, their flanks covered in sweat. Valfric was also panting, his heart still thundering in his chest. The others gathered around them. There were only a handful left, and he noticed that some of those were wounded.

"Fuck, are we still being followed?" Aelric asked between breaths.

Valfric shook his head. "No, I don't think so; it stopped."

He looked up at the sky, searching for any other signs of life, hawks, or any other birds that might be Essaerites tracking them. His own had found that the group they had attacked was now moving again, and it appeared that both the other Essaerist's Essaerites were back with them.

"I don't think they're going to pursue us anymore," he said.

"What the fuck was that?" Ilara asked. "Were there two Essaerists?"

Valfric nodded. "Yes, one of them was Lysandrian. I didn't," he stammered, "I didn't know."

She didn't look angry with him, just afraid. Valfric looked at his other friends. They shared similar expressions of fear. It wasn't something they were used to feeling; usually, they were the ones who made others feel afraid. But today had been different. Maybe it had been good. Perhaps if they had attacked and been in a worse spot, the Lysandrian Essaerist could have done more to them, or perhaps not.

Either way, Valfric realized that the days of easy picking and easy raiding were far, far behind them. And now, he realized with a bit of concern that the real war was beginning.

CHAPTER 31

Mariokos worked to calm himself as soon as the fighting was over. He'd been impressed with Caelwen. Her pumas were incredibly effective and had made quick work of both men and the other Essaerist's wolves. He also owed her his life. Yes, he had been moving to block one of the Essaerites from attacking her, but she didn't have to save him, especially since she didn't know him, and that counted for something.

The two of them had done something for each other during battle, protecting one another, and in a way that built a bond—a bond that was far deeper than you got when you first met somebody.

He'd also been impressed by her Essaerithon. It was terrifying and powerful. It had ripped through the other Gwenthari when they attacked, and while it took her some time to create, it was well worth it.

She came walking up to him in that Essaerite. The skull helmet came back, revealing her face. He could see stress etched into her expression, but she seemed to be keeping it under control.

Erastos was barking out orders to the rest of the men in his squad, and Mariokos turned to him.

"Check the area," Erastos said.

Mariokos closed his eyes, and his mind went into some of the birds he had above them. He could see that the people who had attacked them were running away—well, those that were left. What had been a fairly well-planned ambush had completely backfired on the attacking force.

Mariokos could only make out maybe eight or nine of the group left, and a few of those appeared to be wounded. They were galloping hard away from them now, and Mariokos could make out two of Caelwen's Essaerites chasing them down.

He looked over at her. "Are you going to run them down?"

She was almost up to him now. "If they slow down, yes. But otherwise, no," she admitted. "Those pumas are fast, but they're not as fast as a horse."

Mariokos acknowledged with a nod and turned to Erastos. "It appears those that are left are running away."

Erastos nodded grimly and shouted an order for everyone else to check the dead. They began doing so, and Mariokos had some of his Essaerites move to the periphery of the group to keep watch, lest there were others in the forest. Mariokos's head moved around, scanning the area.

"How did your people do?" he asked, seeing Ilfthandor and Wulfgren coming up to them. Wulfgren was covered in blood, though it didn't appear to be his. For his part, Ilfthandor looked like he hadn't seen any action at all. It wasn't exactly surprising; the man was old, and Mariokos very much doubted he spent much time in combat.

Wulfgren's face was hard and controlled, like someone who had seen a lot of this in his life. "We fared alright. They tried to come at the rear," he explained. "My guess is that they were here to try to take the last few carts from our caravan."

"So, why did they come after us up here in the front?" Caelwen asked.

"Simple. We were the biggest threat," Mariokos said. "But they weren't just coming for us," he said, looking at her. "They were going after you."

This seemed to take her by surprise. Her brother answered, "Makes sense. It was pretty obvious that Caelwen is an Essaerist. And since they had an Essaerist with them," he said, then shrugged.

Mariokos agreed. "She was the biggest threat they could see. There's no way they could have known that I was one too," he said, smirking.

"See? Another benefit of using the Legionnaires," he said.

Her expression of concern broke for a moment, and she snorted a laugh. "I suppose I can see that."

She sighed. "Thank you."

"For what?" he asked.

"You stepped in front of that Essaerite. It would have attacked me if not. I would have died," she said.

"You're welcome, and thank you for saving me, too," he said.

"Of course," she replied.

"So what now?" Wulfgren asked.

It was Erastos who spoke as he came up to them. "Now we head back to our camp, just like we were doing before."

"You aren't concerned my people were in on this in some way?" Wulfgren asked.

Erastos looked at the other man, calculating for a moment, and then shook his head. "No, I don't. Some of yours got injured. This was a botched attack. That said, you should know that when we get back to camp, it's not going to be all love and kisses," he said. "You're a potential threat to the Legion."

This didn't seem to surprise Wulfgren in the least bit, but Ilfthandor and Caelwen did look surprised by it. Wulfgren looked at them. "They don't know that we're not a threat. So, we'll be kept under guard when we get back to the Legion until we're able to negotiate terms or come up with some other arrangement."

Then he looked over at Erastos. "Am I correct?"

"Yes," Erastos said frankly. "That's pretty much the long and short of it. So, let's get moving. I don't want to be out here once the sun goes down."

Ilfthandor and Wulfgren began issuing orders to their people, and Erastos did the same to the rest of the Legionnaires. Mariokos stayed with Caelwen.

"So, are you going to stay with me the entire time?" she asked.

He grimaced a little. "Yeah, sorry about that. You are an Essaerist."

"Even though we saved each other's lives," she said, with a slight smile at the corner of her mouth.

Atheonis, how he shouldn't like how that smile looked.

"Yep, sorry," he said.

She seemed to think for a moment. "Well, I suppose there are worse traveling partners to have."

It wasn't exactly a compliment, but that part of his mind that had never made it past twelve or thirteen years old took it as a compliment. A beautiful woman said something that could be interpreted as being nice about him. He tried not to grin.

They began to walk, moving back towards the camp. Mariokos didn't make conversation with her this time. Instead, he paid attention to his Essaerites, checking the area. She seemed to be doing likewise, but he could still see her relax after a short time as they walked together.

CAELWEN WAS GETTING ANXIOUS FOR THEIR JOURNEY TO BE DONE. IT HADN'T TAKEN THEM long for the road that they were on to connect with another larger one that would lead them to the Legion. All around her, things were different, though. She could see it. The road that they were on was far nicer than any road she had seen in or outside a settlement. Occasionally they would pass groups of Lysandrian legionnaires working on the roads, and she looked at them curiously.

"Why are the roads so nice?" she asked Mariokos.

"We improve and build them up as we move through," Mariokos said.

"Why?" she asked.

He shrugged. "Because roads are important. They're useful for moving supplies, goods, and people. So we improve them." Reading the look of confusion on her face, he added, "Look at it this way: the army can't move ahead without them."

"Alright," she said, not really sure she completely understood what he was getting at.

After a while, in the distance, she saw what almost looked like the walls of a city, but not at the same time. They were made out of wood, but they weren't tall like a city's or town's wall. After a moment, she realized that it was the Lysandrian base.

They were coming down a slight hill, and she took it in. All around it was a deep ditch that had spikes sticking out of it, and there were gates that were manned. She saw legionnaires moving around it, working on it.

"Are you building a city out here?" she asked Mariokos, confused.

He shook his head. "No, it's just a camp."

"Just a camp?" she said.

He grinned. "Just a camp," he said, "given this one's been here for a little while. So, it's a little bit more built up. But yes," he said with pride.

She supposed she understood his pride; it didn't look like a camp to her. To her, a camp was a loose collection of tents, with animals tied up somewhere. This was far from that. The wall was even-looking; all of the spikes that were making up its exterior were the same height, and it ran straight. The road coming up to it looked to be as if it was purpose-built for going into the camp.

As they neared, a group of horsemen came out, riding up to them. Erastos held up his hand, and everyone stopped. The horses came up and talked to Erastos, with men looking over at Mariokos and Caelwen.

"Erastos is letting them know what's going on," Mariokos said to her, trying to keep his tone comforting. But she could hear a slight edge to it as well.

After a few moments, the horsemen rode back into the camp, and Erastos came back.

"Alright," he said, "they're going to set you up with an area outside of the camp tonight. You will be under guard, but again, this is standard procedure," Erastos said, as if he was trying to make sure not to create a situation. He looked over at Caelwen, Ilfthandor, and Wulfgren.

"The three of you will need to come into the camp, though," he said, and then paused, looking over at Caelwen. "I assume you're a decision-maker for this group, aren't you?"

Ilfthandor shook his head. "No, she's not. I am, but they are my family."

Wulfgren looked like he was about to say something, but Erastos nodded and turned around.

"Very well, then. I still want the three of you to come in. There's no way I'm letting an Essaerist go unchecked," he said.

As they started to walk, Caelwen hung back a little bit to talk to her uncle.

"What are you getting at?" she asked him softly.

Ilfthandor gave her a stern look. "Girl, this is not the time. We need to make a deal with these people, and you two need to keep your mouths shut."

She shared a glance with her brother. It appeared the old Ilfthandor was back. Now that he had an opportunity to further himself in some way, Caelwen had no doubt that that was exactly what he was planning on doing.

Ilfthandor told the rest of the settlement that they were going to be going to a camp outside of the main camp. There were some grumbles, but people didn't seem to expect anything otherwise.

Erastos and the rest of the Legionnaires led them to where this camp was going to be, and as everyone else was setting up their tents, he came up to Caelwen, Ilfthandor, and Wulfgren. "Let's go in."

She felt uneasy for the first time, and they began to move towards the camp. Just past the main gate, she was able to see rows and rows of tents. They were displayed neatly, with small paths in between them. There were fire pits built, where men either cooked or worked, and she was surprised to see other areas where it appeared there were merchants or grounds to practice on.

As they moved through the camp, it felt more and more to her like a very well-organized city, and less like some place to sleep at night.

She looked over at her brother. "This doesn't seem like much of a camp to me," she said softly.

He smiled tightly. "It is," he said. His eyes looked around knowingly. "The Lysandrian camps aren't like what we would consider one to be. And, in case you're curious, when they go on the march again, they'll tear this place down, and every night they'll build another one just like it."

Her eyes widened a bit. "Every night?"

He nodded. "Every night. And the longer they're in a place, the more advanced the camps get."

He went on, "If we're still here in a month, this place will have stone walls."

"So then they'd make it permanent?" she asked.

He shook his head. "Not necessarily. They still might rip it down when they moved," he said, trying to explain the Lysandrian legions. "There's a reason they do as well as they do. And I know that every Gwenthari thinks that they can lick the Lysandrians, but they can't," Wulfgren said. "Nobody can. Maybe a few hundred years ago, but not now."

They were led to a large tent in the center of the camp. As they neared it, they saw many other legionaries. All of their eyes were hard as they watched the newcomers. Next to her, Mariokos moved in a relaxed, yet controlled manner. This was his home, but he also realized that he was supposed to watch and guard her—not for her own safety, necessarily, but for the safety of those around him.

It was an odd sort of feeling for Caelwen. She knew others saw her as a threat, but she had never been in a place where that knowledge was so acutely known to those around her.

As they approached the tent, there was another man standing out front who walked up to Mariokos. He clasped hands with him.

"Mariokos," he said.

"Xavieno," Mariokos replied. He gestured over to Caelwen. "This is Caelwen, the Essaerist."

"Really?" Xavieno said.

Mariokos nodded. "Yes, she is."

She looked at Xavieno, trying to gauge him. He held himself with a great deal of confidence. His jawline was firm, and his expression confident. He was a very attractive man, and she suspected that he knew that. His eyes moved up and down her, but not in the way that most men's did; it was in the way of someone who was calculating a threat. She could respect that.

Ilfthandor was brought into the tent, leaving Wulfgren and Caelwen outside. She didn't like that at all, and she glanced over at her brother, but there was nothing that she could do or say at this point. Instead, she stood with Mariokos and the other Legionnaires, who all watched her with distrust.

"So, you encountered another group," she heard Xavieno saying softly.

Mariokos nodded. "Yeah, actually, this one over here," he said, nodding to Caelwen, "saved my life."

Xavieno looked over at her and seemed to regard her differently. His expression softened some. "I mean, well — you were never that good of a fighter," he said.

Mariokos snorted. "Thanks, I appreciate that."

Xavieno smiled tightly, and then, to Caelwen, said, "Thank you for saving my friend."

She smiled softly and nodded. "My pleasure, and he saved my life as well."

Somehow this seemed to make Xavieno warm to her more. "Oh, well, doesn't that change everything then? Now you two are comrades in arms," Xavieno said.

Mariokos chuckled, and Xavieno said, "So, I take it you're replacing me. You're going to be running off with the Gwenthari now, drinking with them and fighting with them, and all that."

Mariokos rolled his eyes and was about to say something when a Legionnaire came out and called Caelwen in. She glanced over at Mariokos and then walked into the tent.

The inside of the tent was warm and well-lit. She saw a group of Legionnaires sitting on one side of the tent and her uncle standing on the other. She came up and stood next to him.

A man in front of her eyed her. Then he said to Ilfthandor, "This is your niece?"

Ilfthandor nodded. "Yes, this is my niece, Caelwen. She is an Essaerist, as I told you."

The man nodded and stood up, appraising her. "My name is Damianello. I am the general of this legion."

His voice held a tone of command to it, and he held himself in the way that she suspected her uncle thought he held himself—in confidence and with command. Here before her was a man who was extremely good at everything that he did and was a man that was used to getting his way.

She nodded at him. "It's good to meet you," she said. He gave a quick nod.

"So your men will fight for our legion, and in exchange, we will give you lands to settle in," Damianello said to Ilfthandor.

He nodded. "Yes, that is the deal." Then, he gestured at Caelwen and added,

"And as is our way, Caelwen here will marry one of your leaders to cement the contract."

She felt her heart give a little kick. She was to do what? She looked over at him and tried not to glare. He smiled.

"Oh, don't be shy, my dear," Ilfthandor said, trying to sound warm. He turned back to Damianello. "She will make one of your commanders a very good wife. As you can see, not only is she an Essaerist, but she is young and beautiful."

She was resisting the urge to create a dagger to stab her uncle with, though part of her knew that this was always a possibility. She was in the leading family of her settlement, and deals like this weren't uncommon. Still, she would have preferred to have been consulted before being sold off.

And while part of her wanted to say this, wanted to protest, she knew that the moment she did, her settlement would look not only weak but like they were trying to make a deal in bad faith. And all that would do was lead to her and her people being killed and enslaved. So instead, she looked over at Damianello, who was eyeing her.

"Yes, I look forward to marrying one of your men," she said, her voice a little halting.

This seemed to please him in a way. And he was about to speak when she made a realization. Ilfthandor was trying to make a bad-faith deal. The man in front of her, who was about to marry her off to somebody, or was going to marry her himself, had no idea what he was actually getting into.

She spluttered, "But sir, I think there's something you should know."

Damianello's eyes fixed on her and narrowed a little bit.

"And, what's that, girl?" he said.

She felt her cheeks flush red. "I cannot bear any children," she said. "The blight got me when I was younger."

Damianello glanced over at Ilfthandor, who spluttered, "But she'd be a wonderful wife, and it's hard to tell if the blight actually took hold, you see."

Damianello held up his hand. "It's fine. I don't care if she can breed or not. A deal's a deal, and this is a good contract. And while it might be your people's way to marry somebody off to seal a deal, Lysandrian has her own way of doing things, and her own way of handling things," he said. "But I respect your traditions, so she is ours now. Your warriors will fight with us for no less than two years, and the rest of your settlement will be given lands where you can go and make a life. I recommend you follow Lysandrian law if you want to do well."

The words, "she's ours now," stuck like ice in her chest. She'd been sold. In that moment, she realized it. She'd been sold.

———

MARIOKOS WAS STANDING NEXT TO XAVIENO WHEN A SOLDIER CAME OUT AND SUMMONED them into the tent. They came in, and Mariokos looked over at the gathered group of men. Off to the side, he saw Ilfthandor, who looked slightly concerned, and Caelwen, who looked pale.

Damianello spoke to Mariokos, "We have a matter we need your help with."

Mariokos nodded. "Yes, sir, what is it?"

Damianello looked to Mariokos, then to Caelwen, and then to her uncle and back to Mariokos. "We have reached a deal with these people for them to work for the legion. One of their stipulations is that there is a marriage to cement the deal." Damianello turned his attention to Ilfthandor. "For someone like your niece to marry a ranking member of another group to cement a contract might be common in your culture—but Lysandrian has traditions as well. And in our tradition, Essaerists do not marry normal people. They only marry Essaerists."

Mariokos felt confused, and Ilfthandor looked like he was about to speak, but Damianello held up his hand. "This is the way of it. I know that not honoring your ways will be seen as the legions making a bad-faith deal, but your people want to be part of the empire, which means respecting our traditions as well. Mariokos is an Aristolios, which is the highest class in our society. By marrying him, Caelwen will likewise be Aristolios."

Mariokos felt his gut fall out from him. By marrying him?

"Sir, I'm..." he started.

"Confused, yes," Damianello said. He held Mariokos's gaze. "You are not promised to anyone, are you?"

"No, sir," he said.

Damianello nodded slowly. "Mariokos, you are an Aristolios. I cannot make you marry this woman, but I am asking you to. She is willing, and this isn't so different than a situation I understand you were in prior to our campaign."

Mariokos was only slightly surprised that Damianello knew about him and Biankara. But he'd felt so much better after things with her had been broken off, and now he was in a spot of being with someone he didn't even know. He looked over at Caelwen. He'd enjoyed their conversation, but that was hardly a test for a marriage. She looked back at him, her expression seeming to calm since he'd walked in. He could say no, but then what? *There will be problems*, he thought. Problems that would probably fall on Caelwen and her people.

He looked into her vivid blue eyes and seemed to calm a little. Caelwen had saved him without a moment's hesitation. From under her tunic, he saw Treftune looking at him intently. For some reason, seeing the little creature look at him made him feel better. He took in a quick breath and looked back to Damianello.

"Yes, sir, I am willing," he said, surprised by the confidence in his own voice.

Damianello seemed to relax at his words. "Thank you, Mariokos. I am sorry that our present circumstances will not allow for a wedding befitting an Aristolios." He turned to Ilfthandor. "It is done."

Damianello smiled. "Congratulations on your new marriage. I will have the paperwork taken care of. Now we have business to attend to," he said in dismissal to everyone.

"Yes, sir," Mariokos said. He led Caelwen, Ilfthandor, and Wulfgren out of the tent.

Mariokos's mind was still reeling, and he looked over to Caelwen, who also looked like she didn't know what to think. Ilfthandor looked put out for some reason.

Wulfgren was approaching them. "What's wrong?" he asked his sister.

"I'm not sure there is anything wrong," she said after a moment. "But I'm married to Mariokos now."

Wulfgren looked over at Mariokos, and then back at her, confused. "Our uncle made a deal," she said.

Ilfthandor rounded on her. "Girl, what are you—"

Xavieno cut him off. "Maybe this isn't the place to have that discussion. And besides, Caelwen here is a ranking member of Lysandrian society now. I wouldn't want to make her mad." He slapped Mariokos on the shoulder. "Buddy, you with me?"

Mariokos nodded. "Uh, yes, I'm with you," he said, his mind reeling as reality was setting in.

There was no way this was real. This hadn't just happened.

They began to walk, and Xavieno said to Ilfthandor and Wulfgren, "You will have to go to your camp, but I'm sure the legion will be by with a contract at some point. As we're on the same team now, welcome to the legion," he said, holding out his hand to Wulfgren.

Wulfgren took it. "Thank you." He looked over at his sister. "Will you be alright?"

"I'll be fine—I will come by and get some of my things in a bit," she said and then looked at Mariokos. "Can I do that? Or am I staying with my people?"

He nodded. "Yes, of course you can. We have a tent, but we have some room for a few things in camp," he felt his face heat up. "Sorry we don't have a lot of room on the march."

What a horrible way to start a relationship. To his surprise, she laughed. "Well, I guess it's good my home was burned to the ground. I don't have many belongings."

"I'm so sorry..." he started.

She looked at him, her expression softening. "It's fine. It made leaving easier for me." She turned to Wulfgren. "I will be by when I can."

Mariokos watched as Wulfgren and Ilfthandor walked off, leaving him with Caelwen and Xavieno. The latter turned to them. He smiled.

"Look, I know this is a shock to both of you, but Mariokos here is one of the most amazing people I've ever met. He's going to be a great husband," Xavieno said.

And then he turned and looked at his friend and smiled.

"And now you don't have to go through the whole war without a wife," he said. He slapped Mariokos's shoulder again. "Fioralba is going to love this," he said, walking off. "I can't wait to tell her!"

Mariokos watched his friend walk away and scowled at him. Then he looked back to Caelwen, unsure of what to say or do.

"Um," he said.

"Do you want to show me which tent is ours?" she asked.

He nodded. This he could get his head around—practical matters. These were things that he excelled at.

"Right, yes, our tent," he said, tumbling over his own words. He guided her over to the area his squad was in.

Erastos looked up when he came over, as did Helioz and Luciakos.

"So?" Erastos asked.

"So I'm married now," Mariokos said.

Helioz barked a laugh, and Luciakos looked incredulous at them.

"Who are you married to?" he asked.

Caelwen nodded and spoke softly, "Me."

Erastos seemed to look irritated and grumbled something before walking off, but Helioz and Luciakos just seemed amused. They tilted their heads towards her.

Helioz laughed again. "How'd that happen?"

"Damianello made a deal," Mariokos said.

Helioz seemed to lose it.

"Can he even do that with an Aristolios?" Luciakos asked.

"Oh, I agreed to it," Mariokos said.

Helioz controlled his laughing and eyed Caelwen, "I'm sure you did. What a shock."

Luciakos smacked Helioz. "Well, welcome to the Legion," he said to Caelwen.

Mariokos shook his head, "Come on, we're over here," he said to Caelwen, leading them away from his squad.

CHAPTER 32

After making his awkward introductions with his squad, Mariokos took Caelwen over to his tent. It was a little separated from the rest of the squad, which all slept together, but Essaerist slept on their own, in their own tents, as they were part of the Legion, but not legionaries in some of the stricter senses of the term. For one, their terms were significantly shorter, and two, they had many more freedoms than the normal legionnaire did. They were also located near the other Aristolios in the camp. It wasn't to say that the tent was fancy or ostentatious in any way. It was small, but it comfortably held two people, along with a couple of packs.

"This is our tent," he said as they arrived.

Caelwen looked at it, her eyes moving over the smooth cream-colored fabric. "It looks nice," she said after a moment.

He wasn't sure if she was being honest or not, but he thought she was. He obviously didn't know this woman—well, he didn't know his wife, he should amend— but she didn't seem to be somebody who employed much in the way of subterfuge, and Mariokos was pretty confident that what you saw with Caelwen was what you got.

"Thanks, it's nicer than most, I'll admit," he said, and it was true.

Mariokos, like all Essaerist, created everything for his camp every night. It was standard procedure for them. He walked to the opening and opened the flap. Caelwen poked her head inside.

The inside of the tent was tall enough to stand in if you were in the center; the fabric sloped down on either side, going to the ground. In the center of the tent was a cot that Mariokos normally slept on. He would need to widen it for Caelwen and him to share. The ground was covered in a tight straw weave.

This was one of the areas that made the tent unusual compared to those in the rest of the Legion—that it had a floor, so to speak. Not a good one or a permanent one, but something covering the ground other than straw that the men would sleep on. This too was standard procedure.

Caelwen was inspecting the mattress. She reached out and pressed down on it.

"It's soft," she said, surprised.

He smiled. "Did you think it wouldn't be? And is that a problem?" he asked, wondering if that was going to be an issue for her.

She shook her head but didn't look disappointed. Instead, she looked pleased. "No, it's great. I haven't slept on anything more than the ground or on a cart for a while." But she still looked confused. "You carry this around with you everywhere?"

He shook his head. "No, I create it every time I set camp."

She looked over at him and cocked her head. "You mean with Essaeris?" she confirmed.

"Yeah, with Essaeris," he replied.

"Every night?" she said.

"Every night," he echoed, "well, unless we've been in camp for a while. Why does that surprise you so much?"

She shrugged. "It just seems like a waste of Essaeris," she said, and then added, "Sorry, I'm not trying to be difficult. I'm thankful for a soft mattress. I'm just surprised, is all. I would have thought the army would have been more... efficient."

He smiled. "We are, but this is standard procedure for all Essaerists."

It made him wonder where this line of thought was coming from, and he asked, "You don't create stuff. You said you just slept on the ground or in a cart every night."

"No, I didn't create anything to sleep on." She gave a shrug. "I guess sometimes some blankets or some furs, but not much, no. I just don't want to put that much Essaeris into it," she admitted.

"And you're surprised that we do," Mariokos mused. "Do you have anything that you create every day or almost every day? Something simple like clothes or, well, bedding?" he said, searching for examples.

She shook her head. "I mean, I have some bowls and things of that nature, and there are things that I create regularly, but not almost daily."

He nodded. "But those things that you create regularly, they've gotten easier for you, right?"

She nodded. "Of course."

He smiled. "And this is why we create our tent and our bed every day," he said, gesturing around. "It's something that we learn when we're in training. For me, creating this takes no energy whatsoever. The Essaeris needed is almost laughable," he said, explaining.

"Okay, I guess that makes sense," she said. "The more you create something, the less Essaeris it takes to create and sustain. I suppose I could see that where it's not really a problem."

He shook his head. "It's not about the Essaeris that it takes to create and sustain it, necessarily." He touched the fabric of the tent. "That makes this fabric easier for me to create." He touched one of the wooden poles. "And wood," he said. He saw her look around.

"And all the base materials for everything inside of here," she said, as if she was starting to understand.

She looked down, seeing a metal bowl. "Metal, not wood."

"Correct. Wooden bowls are pretty standard in the Legion. They're lighter to carry around, and they don't rust, and they're easier to make," he said. "But creating a metal bowl and plate every meal..."

"Means making everything else out of metal easier and takes less Essaeris," she said, as if she was having an epiphany.

He smiled. "Exactly."

She looked at him, her eyes moving up and down him. "And your clothes and armor?"

He nodded. "Yes, everything. I create everything when I need it." He ran his hand down his tunic, his hand stopping at a stain. "Even the stains."

Her head cocked to the side again. "But it looks like an old stain." Her eyes went up to his. "Why would you do that?"

He gave a shrug. "It's variations in the Essaerite. It also helps me blend in more if I were to be out and about and not have any Essaerites with me. But again, adding in that little bit of complexity..."

"Makes it easier to do more," she said, finishing.

He smiled. "Exactly." He breathed out. "Well, we should probably go to your camp. Well, not your camp, I should say," he amended. "We should go to your settlement's camp. I'm sure you have some belongings that you would like to get."

Her head bobbed quickly. "Yes, thank you. And thank you for showing me around."

"Of course. This is your home now, too," he said awkwardly.

She smiled tightly.

"I'm sorry, I know," he started.

She shook her head, cutting him off. "This is awkward," she said, looking at him.

She reached out and placed her hand on his arm. "But it has to get better, right?" she said, and smiled.

Bellisara, you outdid yourself when you made her smile, he thought.

Mariokos felt himself smile. "I don't think it could get too much worse."

She laughed. "Well, now I suspect it will, won't it?"

What she was getting at hit him, and he flushed a bit. "I suppose it will."

He led her out of his tent, and they began walking through the camp. Before they had been attacked, talking to her had seemed effortless, but now it wasn't. He was reminded of what Damianello had said about Mariokos and Biankara. Theirs was a relationship out of necessity in many ways, and he'd been prepared to make it work. He glanced over at Caelwen. Talking to her had been easier in some ways than with Biankara; also, unlike Biankara, he did feel a strong attraction to Caelwen. It wasn't just that she was attractive; there was something about how she spoke and moved.

You don't know anything about her, Mariokos, he reminded himself.

They were making their way to the edge of the camp. *So change that,* he thought. He saw Treftune perched on her shoulder, watching him. He reached into a pouch and pulled out another water bead. Treftune jumped off her and onto his shoulder. His soft fur ran against his neck, and he couldn't help but chuckle.

"Careful," Caelwen said.

"Will he bite me?" he asked.

Treftune took the bead of water. She looked over at the animal with a fond smile.

"Yes, but he doesn't bite much and not hard. But you need to be careful because he's training you," she said with a smirk.

Treftune was sniffing around Mariokos's face and head; he reached up, and the little Valfglidea rubbed his head and face on his hand. He smiled, "Seems like there are worse things to be trained by." Treftune chittered and wound around his neck.

Caelwen was watching intently. "Everything alright?" Mariokos asked.

She thought for a moment, "Yes, it is..." she composed her thoughts, "Treftune is the best judge of character I've ever met, and he likes you. In fact, he seems to like you a lot." She thought for a moment. She was about to speak but didn't.

"Tell me," he said.

For some reason, he wanted to know everything that went through this woman's head. She glanced ahead for a moment and then back to him. "I was thinking about how awkward this is but that it shouldn't be."

"I see. Have you been married to a stranger before?" he asked with a smile.

She smirked, "No, I haven't. But I've had lovers."

"As have I," he admitted.

This seemed to make her relax some. "Was it awkward with them?"

He blew out a breath, "A few times, but no, normally it wasn't, but I also wasn't married to them."

"That's fair." She chewed on her lip. "If I'd met you at any other time, I would have found you attractive and enjoyable to talk to," she glanced over at Treftune. "And just even on that, I would have taken you home, but with how Treftune is treating you, I would have thought I might have found someone special."

Mariokos felt his face flush a bit at her words, and his stomach did a little flip. "Yeah, I would have probably thought the same thing," he laughed. "Well, if I'd had the courage to talk to you," he admitted.

She laughed, "Tell me more about that."

He laughed again, "Well, you're beautiful. It would have taken me a bit to build up the guts to do it." He ran his hand through his hair and shook his head, "I. No."

"Say it," she said.

He smirked, "Xavieno would have made me. I promise I'm not awkward or strange. I just don't always do well with flirting. But after I was comfortable with you, I would have felt the same way."

She nodded and smiled. The golden light of the setting sun caught in her hair, and she looked up at him with mischievous eyes, "Tell me more about me being beautiful."

He laughed heartily. He glanced at her and back ahead. "Your eyes."

"My eyes?" she said.

He nodded, "When I saw them, I was struck by them."

She smiled and bit her lip. He loved that but didn't say anything.

"This feels better," she said.

"It does," he said.

Treftune chittered, and Mariokos handed him another bead. Again, she was watching.

"What?" he asked.

She thought to herself for a moment and then moved closer to him. His heart gave a little flip, and he reached out and took her hand. Her fingers wove through his, her skin soft and warm. With the touch, he felt his nerves calm.

"I think we will do alright," she said.

He smiled, "I do too."

They walked through the camp to one of the gates and passed some sentry units. As they got out, he was met by a few of his Essaerites that looked like legionaries.

Caelwen glanced over at them.

"I figured you might need some help carrying some things back, and they're not doing anything else," he said. "Also, I'll put a few of them around your settlement to keep sentry duty."

She smiled tightly. "I have some Essaerites in the area, too. I've been keeping them away from the camp and hidden. Will that be a problem?"

He was thoughtful. "It could be, but maybe not. Those Essaerites of yours were very useful, but the Legion doesn't know about them, necessarily," he said, thinking to himself. "How many do you have?"

"Three," she said.

He nodded. "I'll have three of my legionary Essaerites walk out into the woods, and you can have your Essaerites go up to them. My legionary ones will bring yours back towards the camp, which will tell the other legionaries in the Legion that those Essaerites are safe. Then they should be fine to hang out in your settlement for the evening, or you can bring them into the camp if you'd like," he said.

"Thank you. I'll keep them with my people. But will I need to not have them?" she asked.

He could tell she sounded a little sad, but also semi-hopeful. He shook his head. "It'll be up to you. The Legion just has to know what they are, so that way they're not surprised by them. That's part of the reason why my Essaerites look like legionaries. It's something that they're trained to see, so that way they're not alarmed by them."

"That makes sense," she said. "And I suppose merchants are used to seeing them, too."

He nodded. "Exactly. Everyone knows what they are, but I think yours will be very useful. We'll find a way to work them in if you want to keep them around," he said, and smiled.

They were at her settlement's camp now, and Mariokos looked around, seeing the assortment of tents around carts. People were trying to make fires and cook meals for the night. They all looked up at Caelwen and smiled. He could tell that she was respected by her people, which meant something. He knew that many in Lysandrian saw the Gwenthari as being barbarians in so many ways, but Mariokos didn't hold that view. Yes, they were different than Lysandrians, but that didn't mean that they were barbarians. Some of them were barbaric, yes, and some of them were unrefined, but he had seen others that were very refined and calculating, and those that had been working and fighting with the Legions had been respectable enough, more respectable than many of those in the Legions.

They made it to the center of the camp, where Mariokos saw Ilfthandor and Wulfgren. They walked up to them, and he noticed that Caelwen tensed a little bit as her uncle approached.

I wonder what that's about, Mariokos thought.

Ilfthandor was holding a rolled-up piece of paper. "Well, I suppose we're officially part of the Empire now. They gave us this contract," he said, holding it out to Caelwen.

She glanced over at Wulfgren. "I read part of it," he said, "but I don't understand everything."

Caelwen unrolled it and began reading, taking her time. Mariokos looked over her shoulder, reading through the contract, and then he looked up at Wulfgren and Ilfthandor.

"You don't read, I take it," he said.

Ilfthandor scowled at Mariokos, but Wulfgren said, "I read some, but not as well as my sister does. It was something our mother wanted us to do." He looked over at Ilfthandor. "His reading's not as good as mine."

"Our society has little use for the written word," Ilfthandor said, almost a little pompously.

Mariokos nodded.

"Well, Lysandrian society puts a lot of value on it," he said. "And according to this document, you're Lysandrians now."

Caelwen handed him the paper. "My reading is far better than my brother's and uncle's, but I suspect it's not as good as yours. What does it say?"

"If the Legion was looking to make a bad faith agreement with us, I'm sure your new husband would join them," Ilfthandor said. And then he looked over at Mariokos. "Not that I think they're trying to make a bad-faith agreement."

Mariokos smiled tightly. "No, they aren't trying to. And for your information, when it comes to Lysandrian society, our spouses are who we're supposed to be the most loyal to," he said. "So since Caelwen is my wife, and you are her family, well, I'm not going to betray her."

He read over the document. "And it doesn't look like the Empire is looking to betray you either. It's pretty standard, honestly. It looks like your whole settlement will be joining the Legion and fighting with us for," he paused and read down, "it looks like for two years. And at some point, you'll be settled somewhere," Mariokos said. "Pretty standard."

"Will we always be outside of the camp like this?" Wulfgren asked.

Mariokos shook his head. "No, you won't. When we move on, the next camp will have room for your people. And that should happen in the next couple of days," he said. "We've been here for a while, so it's time for the Legion to begin moving again."

Wulfgren nodded like he expected no less.

Mariokos opened his mouth to speak again when he heard a horn from inside the camp. Ilfthandor looked over at it, but Wulfgren seemed to be expecting it.

Mariokos looked over at Caelwen, "It's time for us to head back into camp. I'm sorry I thought we had more time."

"It's fine," she said to Mariokos and then to her uncle and brother. "I'll be back tomorrow."

Mariokos began to lead Caelwen back up towards the camp. As they made it to the entrance, he saw a few sentries coming out to stand guard for the night, while others were grabbing torches and piles of wood to set up watch fires around the outside of the camp.

"You're very secure here, aren't you?" Caelwen pointed out.

He smiled. "It is an army on the move."

"I suppose," she commented.

She looked forward, and he felt a moment of awkwardness again. Then she said, "Do you have any ceremonies or anything that you and we need to do?"

He was thoughtful. "I was going to ask you something similar. I don't know of many foreign and Lysandrian marriages. I know they're a thing, but I just don't know anybody."

She nodded. "I haven't either," she said with a chuckle. "But do you have any traditions that I'm supposed to follow now that I'm Lysandrian?"

He was thoughtful. "There are traditions, yes, but they're more with family and friends. But as far as the Legion is concerned, we're married. If we had people around, we would do a ceremony, perhaps, but with you not knowing anybody here and it all being soldiers and my family not being here... But we can do something if you'd like. What would you normally do?"

"Normally, there's a feast and a ceremony," she said, "but our relationship and marriage was born out of a contract. So the feast is more to celebrate the contract, and the ceremony would be similar to what you're describing. And I don't know if I care about that," she said honestly.

His mind flashed with conversations like this with Biankara. Oh, how Caelwen was different. With Biankara, they had talked about their wedding in detail. There would be so much pageantry behind it, but it appeared that Caelwen didn't care about that, and Mariokos didn't either. It made him think for a moment as they walked.

"How about this?" he said. "When we're ready, we can say some things to each other."

Caelwen looked thoughtful, and he saw a smile touch her lips.

"That's fine with me," she said.

They were almost back to his tent now, and all around them there were fires burning as men cooked for the night. He walked up to the tent and began pulling out pots and rations of food.

Caelwen looked around. "Do you need any help? I don't know what the role of a Lysandrian woman is."

"They tend to be more domestic, I think, than the Gwenthari variety," Mariokos admitted, "but it doesn't matter necessarily to me. I'm used to making dinner, but you're welcome to help. Maybe you could build the fire?"

She nodded and began building a fire. He watched her for a time as he prepared ingredients for dinner. He put some oats in a bowl with some water and set it next to the fire to boil.

"I'm sorry. We tend not to eat heavy dinners," he said. "Or lunches or breakfasts," he admitted.

She smiled. "I guess that's good to know."

She cocked an eyebrow. "So you said that you think Lysandrian women are more domestic than Gwenthari?"

He nodded. "Yes, they tend to take care of things around the home or in camp. For example, normally you would take care of the tent and cooking and things of that nature."

He watched her, and she nodded after a moment. "That seems easy enough. Am I going to be expected to fight?"

"I don't know," he said honestly. "You're an Essaerist, but that doesn't mean that you have to fight. Lysandrian women don't."

She looked thoughtful. "Well, I may be Lysandrian now, but I'm still Gwenthari. Gwenthari women fight," she said. "Not that I'm asking to, but I'm telling you that I'm willing."

"I understand, and thank you. We can talk about it more over the next few days. I'm sure both of us are going to have a lot to learn," he said.

She smiled and laughed. "I think that's a pretty safe assumption."

They ate dinner in relative silence. Every now and then, Treftune would pop out from somewhere in Mariokos's tent and come over to Caelwen or him. He reached down, scratching behind the creature's ears. Mariokos liked him.

At one point, he heard some grumbling from a tent next to him, and he saw what must have been one of Treftune's Essaerites come out, its mouth full. It ran over into Mariokos and Caelwen's tent.

Mariokos looked at Caelwen, and she scowled down at the Valfglidea. "Don't steal," she said. The animal looked up at her and chitted something. Mariokos couldn't help but smirk.

"He does seem to like stealing," he said.

She huffed. "Yes, he does."

He heard more grumbling from the tent over. "What do they normally take?"

She sighed. "Usually food, but other things, anything shiny they might go for. I'm sorry if this causes problems."

He couldn't help but smirk. "Oh, I'm totally fine if he steals from people in my squad. In fact, this could be entertaining."

Then after a moment, he said, "Would there be any chance we could teach him how to steal from someone else?"

She looked at him confused. "Who would you want him to steal from?"

Mariokos just smirked. "I don't know. There might be a couple of people."

CHAPTER 33

Caelwen was half-lying on the form of a sleeping Mariokos, when the sound of a loud horn woke her, making her eyes fly open. At once, her heart raced in her chest. She stirred, looking to the tent flap. She felt Mariokos shift, and the horn sounded again. *Are we under attack?*

She patted his chest. "Wake up."

He groaned, and his eyes flickered open.

"Wake up!" she said more urgently.

He studied her face. "What's wrong?"

She felt his arm tighten around her waist, pulling her close. "Don't you hear the horn?" she said. "Are we under attack?"

Mariokos appeared confused for a moment. Then he groaned. "It's morning already."

"What do you mean it's morning already?" she asked.

"That's the horn to wake up and start the day," Mariokos said with a great yawn.

It was the what? She stared at him. "There's a horn in the morning to wake us up?"

He looked over at her, and she felt his hand move up and down her back. "Sorry if it startled you. I should have warned you."

She settled back down into his arms, her mind drifting to the night before. But she pushed it from her thoughts; there were more urgent matters at hand.

"Do they do that every morning?" she asked.

He nodded. "Yep, every morning. It's what they wake us up with." Then, reading her expression, he asked, "Something wrong?"

"Every morning," she confirmed, her tone flat.

He made an apologetic smile that she found rather cute and endearing. "Sorry," he said.

She groaned. "Is it late in the morning?"

"No, it's usually around sunrise," he said.

"Around sunrise?" She gaped.

She rolled over onto her back and heard him chuckle.

"You find this amusing?" she asked.

He rolled onto his side and put his arm over her. "I mean, I don't *not* find it amusing," he said, then added, "you get used to it, trust me."

She glared at him. "I doubt it."

She lifted her gaze to the tent above them and huffed. "So, I suppose there's some sort of drill or something in the morning?"

She saw him cock a smile. "See, you're learning the Legion quickly. You haven't even been here a whole day yet, and you know how this goes."

She snorted. "After seeing this camp last night and all of you when we were attacked yesterday, it gave me a bit of an idea. Plus, Wulfgren told me a little bit about what it's like being around the Legions when he worked with them down south." She felt her irritation rise. "He didn't say anything about being woken up by a horn every day, though."

He nodded. "Yeah, I'm sure he gave you a bit of an idea, but today should be pretty easy. I'm technically off. It's a personal day for me. It worked out well that we got married yesterday."

She looked at him. "Would they not have given you the day off if it wasn't your normal day off?"

He laughed. "I don't think they would have, no," he admitted.

"There'll be roll call soon, even though it's my day off, I have to get ready. Though I'd much rather stay in bed with you," he said, looking down at her.

She felt her heart flutter a little bit. At least that had been nice. Once all the awkwardness had been pushed aside for the moment, she'd been able to enjoy herself, which was something she hadn't entirely been expecting. Not that she had thought that Mariokos would be a poor lover or that he was even a bad person, but rather, if she'd been sold off for one of her uncle's worthless contracts, she didn't expect it to go even remotely well for her. But thus far, it had.

She reminded herself that it hadn't even been a day yet and to give it time before she counted herself lucky, but she smiled up at him. His brown hair was disheveled, and it made his face look even kinder than it already did. It almost made up for someone waking her from a dead sleep with a horn.

"So, don't tell me. I bet I can figure this out. We're going to have boiled oats for breakfast," she said.

He grinned. "You've got it! But we usually put honey or figs in there, and we make some bread."

She smiled. "I'm surprised you have luxuries like fruit and honey."

He grimaced. "You and I do," he said, then explained, "I use Essaeris to create them."

She was confused for a moment, then a little concerned. "You know you shouldn't eat Essaeris, right?"

He nodded. "Oh, I know. I set it to go away once it's in my stomach or have been in my mouth for a while. You'll find it's pretty common for Essaerists to do. Again, it's part of our training. It makes the food much more enjoyable. But no, I never actually fully eat anything that I create. Do you not do things like that?"

"I've honestly never thought to," she said. She was starting to wonder how far behind she was compared to the Essaerists of Lysandrian.

Her brother had told her that they were advanced and that they were trained by the government. She was starting to appreciate now that that might be a bigger deal than she thought.

She looked at Mariokos. "Can you teach me how to do that? Is it something that I should know how to do?"

He shrugged. "I do think it's something that you should know how to do. But that's just because I think every Essaerist should have certain baseline knowledge," he said honestly. "I can work with you on it. So will Xavieno and Fioralba. But have you worked on creating Essaerites where you release them on predefined conditions?"

She thought for a moment. "I can do it, yes, but I suspect that I'm going to need to get better at it." She felt a little forlorn, and he reached out and touched her shoulder.

"Don't be upset," he said. "We'll get you up to speed."

She looked at him. "I'm not upset, I'm just..." She was at a loss for words. "Starting to appreciate how lacking I am."

He nodded in understanding. "Everyone starts somewhere," he reassured her. "Besides, you'll pick it up in no time." His confidence in her abilities made her smile, and she found herself eager to learn.

She saw concern on his face.

"And you're not lacking," he said honestly. "You just didn't have the same training that we did. It's not that yours was better or worse."

She chuckled. "I didn't have any training," she said, then amended, "Well, I did a little bit, but it was a week or two at the most and some foundational stuff."

He looked at her, surprised. "You weren't trained at all?"

She shook her head. "No. Almost no Gwenthari Essaerists are. Some of the ones around larger cities are, but otherwise we don't get any training," she said, feeling embarrassed.

She saw him looking at her, a look of amazement on his face. She felt her face flush with irritation and humiliation. "I said, I'm sorry for lacking."

He shook his head. "No, don't—don't get me wrong — if you haven't been trained — and those pumas..." his voice trailed off.

"What about them?" she asked, offended.

He held up his hand. "I'm sorry. I'm not doing this right. You're amazing."

She was taken aback. "I'm amazing for not being trained and not being as good as you?" She felt her irritation start to rise.

He shook his head and laughed. "Look, I don't know if you're as good as me or not. I suspect there are some areas where I'm a lot more advanced than you, but when it comes to figuring things out, I'm going to go out on a limb and say you're a whole lot better than I am—or any Essaerist that I've ever met," he said, sounding honest. "You figured all that out on your own. I had to learn it in classes and from dedicated instructors. You figured it out. And that is amazing!"

She wasn't sure if she believed him or not, but she couldn't hear any deceit in his voice. He shook his head and chuckled again. "Atheonis, and those things. And you figured that out on your own." He ran his hand through his hair, and she found that she really enjoyed the gesture.

She raised her eyebrow. "Who is Atheonis?"

"Sorry, you probably don't know our gods. Atheonis is the god of wisdom; he's the king of the gods." He ran his hand through his hair again. "If we're able to work with you... fuck, you're going to be a monster," he said and smiled.

He thought for a moment. "Do the Gwenthari believe in a god of wisdom? I've heard some people say the name Ulfgara."

It was going to be interesting learning about Lysandrian culture and gods. "Ulfgara is the goddess of war. But yes, we do have a god of wisdom; he is Thrain." She explained, "He is also the god of leadership; he is old-looking with a long beard, and his eyes see all and are molten gold."

Mariokos was thoughtful for a moment. "Atheonis has eyes of deepest blue like sapphires, and he too leads." Mariokos looked down and then back to her. "Do you follow a certain god? In Lysandrian culture, people will dedicate themselves to a god. For example, I follow Corianthus, the god of the harvest."

She felt a soft smile touch her lips. "Many of us do, yes. Many want to enter Ulfgara's halls in the afterlife."

"Do you want to enter her halls?" he asked.

She shook her head. "No. I'm drawn to Caelith, the goddess of nature and growth. My parents named me after her. When the day comes, I want to wander her forests and glades and watch as she makes the world grow."

He placed his hands gently on her hips and kissed her. "That sounds beautiful."

She held his gaze and rolled on her side to lean into him. "Thank you, and Corianthus sounds wonderful too," she smiled. "I am happy that neither of us feels connected to a god of war."

He kissed her again, and her hands slid up his chest. "I was just thinking the same thing. For us, the goddess of war is Bellamara; you will hear her name often in the Legion."

There was the sound of a horn outside.

"Alright, we need to get up for roll call, or at least I do, I should say." He stood, and she rather enjoyed the sight of him, but then a moment later, a tunic came into existence covering him. Then there was a belt that he wrapped around his waist. He glanced down at her with a longing sort of expression in his eyes that she had to admit she found very enjoyable.

She stood, and her arms went around his neck. Then he smiled and kissed her. "No more awkwardness."

She smiled. "No more awkwardness." She was thoughtful for a moment. Then she said, "Should I create my clothes too?"

He shrugged. "If you want to. It's probably good for you too. Here, do this," he said after a moment.

He placed her hand on his tunic, and she could feel his Essaeris all of a sudden, almost like it wanted to talk with her. Her eyes widened a bit, and he smiled.

"I figured you hadn't experienced this before," he said.

She stared at him, amazed. "I can feel your Essaeris."

He nodded. "Yes, you can. If you've never been around any other Essaerists, I could see where this is something that's new for you. Relax and feel with your Essaeris as well."

She closed her eyes and did so. As she did, she could feel his power—almost in an inviting sort of way. She let her abilities touch his, and it was almost like there was a conversation between them. She could suddenly feel his tunic—not the fabric, but the Essaeris that made it. Her eyes opened again, and she looked at him in amazement.

"I can," she started.

He smiled. "Now make it," he said, his voice soft and comforting.

She nodded. Her heart was picking up a little bit, though it had nothing to do with alarm or longing. It was excitement. It was the feeling of advancement. She felt her power inside of her, and then a moment later it came out in a rush, creating a tunic around her that was similar to Mariokos's. The fabric was soft and had a weave that was slightly different from what she was used to. She ran her hand down it.

He gently took her hand and moved it to his belt. "Again," he said.

Again, there was that strange sensation of his power touching hers, and then a moment later she created her own belt and wrapped it around herself. He smiled, his expression showing pride.

"That took me a week to figure out how to do," he said.

"How to make a tunic?" she asked.

"No. How to even begin to communicate with somebody else's Essaeris," he said. "I guess it makes sense; you've been creating things for a long time. But still, I'd be lying if I said I wasn't just a little bit jealous that you picked up on it on your first try.

"Come on," he said. He gently took her hand, and they walked outside of the tent. Around her, she could smell fires burning while men made breakfast. Others were greeting everybody, and she saw that everyone was standing outside their tents.

Roll call, she realized.

After they were counted and had breakfast, Mariokos took her hand and said, "I have some people I want you to meet." He led her over to another tent, where she saw the man they had talked to the day before. Xavieno was his name, she remembered.

With Xavieno was a short woman with the same olive skin that all the Lysandrians had. Her hair was long and brown, and her eyes were deep green. She was altogether very beautiful. She smiled at Mariokos and then walked up to them.

She peered over at Caelwen, her expression calculating and welcoming.

Xavieno came over and joined them. Mariokos put his arm around Caelwen.

"Caelwen, this is Fioralba, Xavieno's wife. Fioralba, this is Caelwen," he said, and she cut him off.

Fioralba smiled broadly. "Your wife." She reached out and took Caelwen's hand. The other woman's skin was soft and warm, and Fioralba looked her in the eyes.

"Welcome to the Legion. Xavieno told me you're an Essaerist—obviously since you're married to an Essaerist," Fioralba said. "I hope your evening with Mariokos wasn't—" Fioralba started, biting her lip and glancing over at Mariokos, then she looked back at Caelwen, slightly apologetic. "—too unpleasant."

Caelwen heard Xavieno snort a laugh, and next to her, Mariokos sighed.

"Really, Fioralba?" Mariokos said.

Fioralba looked over at Mariokos and then back to Caelwen. "I know this is not going to be easy, but you might be able to teach him. I hear some men learn —and if you try hard, he might actually learn how to please a woman someday."

Caelwen couldn't help but laugh; she felt her cheeks flushing red. She looked over at Mariokos. "I like her."

Mariokos rolled his eyes. "Of course you do."

Fioralba smiled and let go of Caelwen's hands. "But seriously, welcome to the Legion and welcome to our little family," she said as Xavieno put his arm around her.

"And I heard about your Essaerites," Fioralba said.

Caelwen smiled. "Yes, thank you. I'm happy to be here. And what about them?"

Xavieno smiled. "I saw them with Mariokos's when they came back in. They're pretty impressive."

She felt Mariokos pull her a little bit closer.

"Oh, they're nothing," he said, and she looked over at Mariokos, surprised and a little hurt.

"She has no training at all, and she created those," Mariokos said to Fioralba and Xavieno. Both of them looked at her, eyes wide.

"She did that without any training?" Xavieno asked, dumbfounded.

Fioralba smiled. "Talented, I see."

It took Caelwen a moment to realize that Mariokos was bragging about her, that he was proud of her. She was surprised to feel a bloom of pride in her chest.

He wasn't saying it to move ahead or as some sort of manipulation, like her uncle would do the few times that he ever spoke highly of her. Mariokos was talking about her because he was genuinely proud and impressed by her.

"There's more," Mariokos said. "She's never been around other Essaerists before."

"This tunic," he said, glancing down at Caelwen.

Fioralba looked up. "You mean, she copied?"

Mariokos nodded. Xavieno grinned.

"Very talented indeed." Fioralba smiled, her expression showing how impressed she was.

Caelwen couldn't help but smile.

"My, my, my, didn't our little Mariokos land in it?" Fioralba said.

Caelwen smiled more.

"I really did," Mariokos said, and she was happy to hear the earnestness in his voice. "I thought I would introduce her and then show her around the camp and maybe give her an idea of Lysandrian society."

Fioralba's expression got serious. "That's probably a good idea. You came with your whole settlement, correct?"

Caelwen nodded. "Yeah, we were driven out of our homes," she said, and she saw Fioralba look sad.

"I'm sorry. It wasn't the Legion, was it?" Fioralba asked.

Caelwen shook her head quickly. "No, no, it was other settlements, but thank you," Caelwen thought. "On that note, what will happen with my settlement? I know you said at some point they'll get lands to settle in and that they were citizens, but I don't really understand that, I don't think."

"That's completely understandable," Xavieno said. "Well, first you need to understand Lysandrian society, and where your family—or settlement, I should say—falls into that."

He looked over at Mariokos. "What was decided with them?"

"Well, they are to serve with the Legion, and they will be living with us during that time, obviously, but after that point in time, they're citizens," he said. "They're coming in as Subaltero."

Xavieno nodded. Caelwen looked over at Mariokos. "Subaltero?"

"Yes," Fioralba said. "There are different levels to free people in Lysandrian society, but there are different rights and different—how do I put this—privileges that different levels of society have."

Mariokos took over. "At the bottom of our society, or I should say of free citizens, are Subalteros. There are slaves beneath them, but for now, let's not talk about slaves. So you have Subalteros. Then, you have Citizano. Citizanos make up a good majority of Lysandrian society. They can vote, they can own land; they are higher up than Subalteros. And at the top, there's Aristolios."

Xavieno spoke. "You're an Aristolios, just by virtue of being an Essaerist, and also that you're married to Mariokos. Mariokos is an Aristolios, and because you married him."

Caelwen nodded, trying to wrap her mind around the new social structure. "And those of my settlement, you said they're Subaltero?"

Fioralba nodded. "Yes, it sounds like they're Subaltero." She looked over at Mariokos. "But she has a brother."

Mariokos nodded. "Yes, your brother Wulfgren, he's Citizano."

Caelwen cocked an eyebrow. "My brother is higher than the rest of the settlement?"

Mariokos nodded.

"Yes. Because he's your brother. When you became an Aristolios, he was moved to being a Citizano.

"I know it doesn't make sense, but when someone is an Essaerist and they become an Aristolios, or even if they just become an Aristolios from any of the other classes, their family will usually move up. They can only move up to Citizano, though. They can't move up to Aristolios without actually joining the class either through marriage or by being an Essaerist or by legally being promoted. But yes, your brother is a Citizano," he explained.

She couldn't help but smirk. "So are you telling me that my brother is ahead of my uncle, even though my uncle was the head of our settlement?"

"Yes. Do you find that amusing?" Mariokos asked, confused.

She grinned. "I do find that amusing, yes. Very amusing. And I know Wulfgren will, too. But Ilfthandor?" she smiled broadly, feeling true happiness. "He's not going to."

But then she remembered something else they said. "Slaves," she said. "I know you have them. We do, too, obviously. Both Gwenthari and Lysandrians have slaves, but I've seen, I think, a few around here. They have the collars around their necks, like ours do, but they also have glass on them. Is that just for decoration?"

Xavieno shook his head. "No, it's not. We do have slaves like you do, though I do think that there's probably some differences in their rights. But the glass is important."

Fioralba went on. "You'll see three different types of glass on the collars of some of our slaves. Or occasionally, you'll see one that doesn't have any glass on their collar at all. If you see that, that means they haven't been bought by anyone yet. Or they're like the lowest of the low. Sometimes when someone is sentenced to execution, they'll be made what's called an iron slave, which means that they don't have any glass on their collar. All of society owns them and can do literally whatever they want with them."

Mariokos continued, "If you see red glass on a collar, which you've probably seen a lot of here, that means that the slave is owned by an organization. In this case, it'll be the Legion. Anybody who's in the Legion can use that slave as the owner sees fit. In this case, because it's the Legion, the sponsor of this Legion is our Senator, so they're kind of his property," Mariokos said. "But the rights that they have are based on being his property, so you can't treat them like you would an iron slave. I don't know if that's similar or not to how Gwenthari society is."

She thought. "In Gwenthari society, there are certain baselines that you can do with any slave, and treatment and requests that you can make. But then some things go over to the owner," she said. "For example, you can't kill a random slave. That would be destroying somebody else's property. But owners can do whatever they want with their slaves."

Mariokos nodded. "Similar-ish here, but not quite. For example, even owners cannot kill their slaves, and there are rules for how they can be treated. You will see ones that have green pieces of glass in their collars. They're owned by Citizanos, and not by an organization.

"And then there are those that have blue glass in their collar. Those are slaves that are owned by Aristolios. And as such, when it comes to being a slave, they have it the best. And actually, an Aristolios slave does have more rights than a Subaltero does, though they can't vote or own property or any of that. If you see anybody in the Legion who has red, because you're a part of the Legion, you can ask them to help you with work or to do things around the camp. But that's it. That's all the Legion allows with its slaves. If you see blue or green glass..."

"I can't ask them to do anything," Caelwen said.

Mariokos smiled. "Not necessarily. Green you can ask some things of, but blue you cannot, because someone who has blue glass is owned by somebody at the same rank as you."

She felt her head spinning a little bit. "It seems that Lysandrian society is far different and more complex than that of Gwenthari," she shook her head. "I just won't bother any of them. But thank you for explaining it to me."

She felt Mariokos give her a little squeeze, and Xavieno and Fioralba smiled. "Of course, it can take a bit to get used to."

And then Caelwen asked, "Do any of you own any?"

Mariokos shook his head. "No. None of us do, but we're also Essaerists."

She cocked an eyebrow. "Do Essaerists not own them? In Gwenthari society, Essaerists can own slaves, but my guess is they can't in Lysandrian."

Xavieno shook his head. "We can. We just don't see it very much when it comes to Essaerists. You see, for all of us, none of us were Aristolios when we were born, but once we became Essaerists, we were. Most Citizanos and Subalteros don't own any slaves. Well, Subalteros can't, but you won't see many Citizanos who do. And we can create Essaerites to do whatever we want, so none of us really have the desire for them," he said with a shrug.

Caelwen nodded. "There's not a lot of use for them," she said.

Xavieno nodded, and Mariokos gave her another squeeze. "Come on, let me show you around the camp. There'll be lots of opportunities for you to get confused by Lysandrian society," he said with a smile.

She chuckled. "Oh, of that, I'm sure I will."

CHAPTER 34

There were things that Caelwen just knew. Deep down inside, down in her bones, there was knowledge she had that she didn't have to work for. It was always there and would always be there. She knew this to be true. Everybody had knowledge like this. Like the knowledge that she had now, that she hated whoever the fuck it was who blew the horn in the morning to wake up the Legion. She didn't know if it was the same person every day or if it was different people. Maybe it was somebody with a sadistic mind, or perhaps blowing the horn to wake up thousands of people was a type of punishment meant to make them feel insecure and worried that the people in their camp were going to kill them. Because this was something that Caelwen was considering. Not blowing the horn, but killing whoever was doing it. They probably had orders to do it, but she didn't care at the moment.

All she knew was that it was still dark enough outside that there wasn't much in the way of light coming through the crack in the tent, and the light that was coming in was mostly from the flickering fires outside. But here she was, warm, in a relatively comfortable bed, listening to some asshole blow a horn. She tried to will her eyes to stay closed, but she knew she couldn't. Next to her, Mariokos shifted. He didn't seem to mind the horn, and she suspected that was because he'd accepted his place in damnation. Or maybe he was ignorant of how the world was meant to be. It was hard to tell, and in Caelwen's current state of frustration, anything was possible. She closed her eyes.

The horn blared again.

She opened her eyes and groaned. "I'm going to kill them," she said softly.

She heard Mariokos chuckle, and he gave her a small squeeze.

"I'm not joking," she said.

He smiled over at her. "You can't kill them. They change every day."

She glared. "So, I have to kill everybody in the Legion, is what you're telling me?"

He grinned and laughed. "I suppose that's what I'm telling you."

In her still partially sleep-addled mind, she considered if she could do it. Could she kill five thousand soldiers and all the support staff? When she thought about it, she didn't think she'd have to kill much of the support staff. They'd all probably think she was a hero for keeping the horn quiet. Then a thought came to her, and she looked over at her husband.

"Will you have to blow the horn? Is that something that you have to do?" she asked, wondering if she would have to kill him as well.

He grinned."Am I about to be your first victim?" he asked.

She scowled at him, and he chuckled. "Sometimes I pull the duty, but I usually hand it off to an Essaerite. That said, you'll find that most of the people who do the horns are lower-ranking or trying to make it in the Legion. It's not a duty that most of us who are higher up pull."

"So you'll be one of the last to die," she said.

He laughed, and she felt herself shake with it as he held her close. "I suppose that's what I'm saying," he said.

He looked at her and said, "I'm guessing you'd manage it."

This made her smile. As she was waking up, she felt a little bit less murderous, but the sensation was still there. She sat up in bed and stretched her arms above her head and cracked her neck.

"So what's the plan today? Are we going to sit around more, or do you have duty?" she asked.

He sat up next to her. He put his arm around her and kissed her shoulder. "Today we march," he said.

She looked at him and was surprised to feel trepidation inside of her.

"We march?" she said.

He nodded. "We march."

She nodded and thought for a moment. "And what does marching entail for me?"

"Marching for you entails being with the support caravan. Unfortunately, you can't be with me when I march because I have to be with my unit, and the Legion's very firm about this."

"So I'll be on my own, is what you're telling me?" she said, "or tending to the people from my settlement?"

He smiled. "I'm telling you that you're going to be with Fioralba all day, but you can spend time with your settlement if you like. It doesn't really matter. That said, there's not a lot of downtime when we march. We'll make twenty miles today, unless the Legion is in a hurry, in which case we'll do twenty-five."

Her eyes widened. "We're going to do twenty miles today and then build a camp just like this one?"

"Yes. We're all going to do twenty miles today, but the Legion is going to build a camp just like this one. That's not something you have to help with, and isn't something that's expected of you."

She frowned for a moment. "I don't mind helping. I'm your wife, and I'm part of this. I feel like I should help."

He smiled good-naturedly. "Okay. I'm sure at some point in time you can help, but today, just watch." And then before she could argue, he added, "Fioralba doesn't help set up the camp either. It's not that she can't or that she isn't capable, and she helps the Legion all the time. It's just that every Legion does this every day, and they're very meticulous about it. It's not so much that we don't want the help. It's that generally speaking, we just don't need it. And it would take us longer to train somebody than it would to just do the work ourselves," he said, but then added, "but you're also an Essaerist, so that could be different. I'm sure once you've seen the camp built a few times, we'll find a way of being able to work you into it."

He stood, and she watched him create a tunic and belt. She joined him, creating her own clothes, feeling the soft fabric against her skin. He continued to explain, "It's pretty boring work, actually. About half the Legion will either watch or forage while the rest of us build the camp, but it won't take us very long. Then before you know it, it'll be dinner time and we'll be going to sleep."

She joined him as they made breakfast and ate, her mind rolling over what he had said and what she had learned about the Legions from Wulfgren.

It sounded like her days were going to consist of walking for twenty or twenty-five miles and then building a camp. She amended that assumption: Her days would start by tearing down a camp, then walking twenty or twenty-five miles, building another camp, making dinner, going to sleep, and then doing it again the next day. That was unless, of course, the Legion had to battle somebody. In which case, she would stay in the camp, presumably, while the Legion did whatever it did.

Overall, she was fine with this when she thought about it. It wasn't that much different than what she did at home, minus the marching and building the camp. She supposed when she thought about it, it was completely different than what she did at home, but emotionally it felt the same. There would be a routine to the day and a cadence that she could run her life to, just like she had at home. And she had no doubt that on the road there would be plenty to see and do, but even if there wasn't, part of her was fine with the idea of moving, sleeping, and then moving again. And even though she knew there would be plenty of dangers on the road, she felt more secure being with a Lysandrian Legion than she did being the sole guardian for her people.

As she finished her meal, the Legion was finishing up roll call, and Mariokos turned to her. "I have to go hook up with my unit."

Behind her, the tent and everything inside of it vanished. She looked over at the blank patch of ground and then back to him. "At least breaking camp is easy," she said.

He grinned. "It really is for us." He thought for a moment. "But tonight, we'll create our tent and bed together, okay?"

She nodded, but she felt nervous about it. He read her expression and smiled. "Don't worry about it. We'll do it together. I know you haven't done this before, but trust me, it's easier than you think."

She gave a shrug, trying to play it off, though a part of her disliked that he was able to evoke unease that easily. "I'm not worried about it," she said, and he walked off. Around her, she could see others taking down tents and putting out fires.

She walked over to a small wooden box that she had created, which held what was left of her life's possessions. She picked it up and walked over to the tent that Xavieno and Fioralba shared, except there wasn't a tent anymore, and Xavieno wasn't there. She found Fioralba placing her own belongings in a cart.

She walked up to the other woman. "Good morning," she said.

Fioralba turned, and Caelwen registered shock in the woman's expression for just a moment as she remembered who Caelwen was, and that she wasn't, in fact, a Gwenthari there to slit her throat. Fioralba smiled.

"Sorry, you startled me. Good morning," she said. She looked down at Caelwen's box. "What is that?" she asked.

Caelwen shrugged. "It's all my possessions," she said honestly.

"Oh, I see," Fioralba said, trying not to sound awkward. "Well, do you have a cart for them?"

Caelwen shrugged. "No? Should I? I figured I could put it with my settlement if I needed to."

Fioralba shook her head and gave a motherly look. "No, no, you can put your box with us." She walked over and took the box from Caelwen and set it in the cart.

Caelwen was surprised she didn't resist, but instead just went with it. "Thank you," Caelwen said. "I suppose I'll have to create or buy a cart at some point."

Fioralba smiled. "Yeah, you will eventually, but don't worry about it for now. At some point in time, we'll be able to get you one when the Legion isn't on the move."

The cart was small, and Caelwen was thankful for the space on it. She saw Fioralba wave her hand noncommittally, and a small Essaerite appeared. It had thick legs, with what looked like a hook that could attach to the cart.

Caelwen cocked an eyebrow. "Handy," she said.

Fioralba smiled. "Extremely handy."

She finished packing what was left on the ground in the cart, and she turned back to Caelwen. "So, would you like to join me today?"

Caelwen smiled genuinely. "I was told that was the plan." She looked around. Everyone was done taking down their tents now, and she could see men along the walls. They were digging them up, pulling down the poles.

The smell of burning wood grew, and Caelwen looked around, seeing fires around different parts of the camp. Fioralba answered her unasked question.

"Anything that the Legion doesn't take with it, it burns," she said.

Caelwen nodded. "Nothing for the enemy to get, I see."

Fioralba smiled tightly. "No, there isn't."

In the distance, Caelwen made out the form of a large Essaerite. It was ripping down a watchtower. She looked over to Fioralba. "One of yours?"

Fioralba smiled. "Nope. That's your husband's."

Caelwen looked at it again. It was strange-looking, all function over form, but it looked powerful. It pulled down the tower with ease and used giant, blade-like arms on its front that almost looked like teeth to hack it into smaller pieces. She saw smaller Essaerites pulling the pieces away to throw them into bonfires.

"I haven't seen one that big before," Caelwen said.

Fioralba nodded. "It's his Essaerithon."

Caelwen looked at her. "Essaerithon?"

Fioralba nodded. "Yes. Most Essaerists have them in Lysandrian society. It's our crowning achievement, if you will. It's our most powerful Essaerite and usually has most of our Essaeris put into it," she explained. "In the case of my husband, he doesn't have one but can make multiple versions of his. They're smaller and not as powerful as, say, Mariokos's over there. Though Xavieno's are geared towards combat, whereas Mariokos's is not."

"I see," Caelwen said. "I suppose I have one of those then too."

Fioralba raised an eyebrow, curious.

"I can create an Essaerite that I can step inside. It's made of vines and branches, and it has a skull for a helmet with antlers coming out of it," Caelwen said.

Fioralba looked impressed. "It sounds like an Essaerithon," she said. "Have you been able to create it for long?"

Caelwen was about to answer when she heard the sound of horns. They were a different cadence than what she had heard before.

"The Legion is starting to move," Fioralba said.

Around them, Caelwen saw men forming up into small formations that turned into larger ones. They began to move, and Caelwen looked over at Fioralba. "We won't go for a little while," she said. "The rest of the Legion has to get moving.

"So you were telling me how long you've been able to create this Essaerithon," Fioralba said.

"Yes," Caelwen said. "I've only been able to create it for maybe a year or so. Does that sound about right for an Essaerithon?"

Fioralba shrugged. "It sounds about right. It's usually when we start getting to our most powerful and our most advanced state that we're able to do it."

Caelwen was curious. "Do you have an Essaerithon?"

Fioralba smiled. "I do. Mine's similar to Mariokos's, but not as mobile. I tend to have mine focused on making fabrics or millstones or things of that nature. They're much more common for female Lysandrian Essaerists to make."

At this, Caelwen felt a mixture of embarrassment and pride. She tried to place the emotions. The pride was easy enough to spot; she was proud of the fact that she could do something that other female Essaerists could not, or at least not ones that were in Lysandrian. But the embarrassment came in that she was an outsider to the society, and it looked like that wasn't going to change.

"It wasn't what I really wanted to create," Caelwen said after a moment.

"And what did you want to create?" Fioralba asked. "And you can always create another one."

Caelwen frowned and thought. "I don't think I had anything I wanted to make I suppose. I just knew that I needed to create that to be able to defend my settlement."

Around them, she saw some of the other support staff begin to move into place, and Fioralba gestured for her to follow. Caelwen did. In front of them, Fioralba's cart began to move, lining up with the rest of the support wagons. Ahead of them was a small cloud of dust as the Legion moved forward.

Caelwen started plodding along next to Fioralba, surprised at how quickly they were moving. "Is this how fast the Legion always moves?" Caelwen asked.

Fioralba grimaced. "Yes, it'll be like this all day. We don't even stop for lunch."

"Wow," Caelwen said, unsure of what to think of it. The Legion was something completely different to her, and she didn't know if she would ever fully understand it. The whole concept of it was completely alien compared to anything she'd been raised with. She had heard of Gwenthari armies before, but they didn't work the way the Lysandrian ones did. And she suspected that was why the Lysandrian ones were as effective as they were.

They were silent for a while, just making sure they were part of the caravan and not being run over. As they left the area they were in, they started to be surrounded by forests, and Caelwen felt herself relax.

All around her, she could hear the commotion of people talking and shouting orders at each other, along with the sound of wheels rolling on rough ground and the sound of animals. But somehow, the noise all collected into a single sound, a din that was able to blot out thought and almost relax her in a way.

She felt Treftune crawl up her back and perch on her shoulder. Fioralba looked at it wide-eyed.

"What is that?" she asked.

Caelwen smiled and scratched under the Valfglidea's ear. "It's a Valfglidea," she said. "They're common in this area."

Fioralba didn't look convinced. "We haven't seen any."

Caelwen chuckled. "I'm sure you haven't, and you won't. Just because they're common doesn't mean they're easy to find."

Treftune moved down Caelwen's body, trying to get into a pouch she had on her belt, looking for food. Caelwen untied the pouch, allowing the little Valfglidea to go in and grab a tidbit. He went back up to her shoulder and gnawed on a nut.

"They're Essaerists, see," Caelwen said. "They can create other versions of themselves. They can change their teeth and claws and fur. They're very clever, and they live for a very long time. Treftune here was my mother's before he was mine. And he probably will outlive me," she said honestly.

Fioralba looked amazed. "I didn't know that. I haven't heard of many creatures like that before," she said. "I mean, we have a few of them in Lysandrian, but not very many."

Caelwen nodded. "There's plenty up here. There are a few different types. There's the Valfglideas, but there are some other animals that are up here as well. Most of them are very intelligent and long-lived.

"But because they're intelligent and live long enough to gain that intelligence, you'll rarely see them," she said. "So even though these Valfglideas are common enough and we will probably pass a dozen of them over the next few days, you won't see any of them. Well, other than Treftune here," she said fondly.

The Valfglidea chitted a little bit and jumped off her shoulder. As he did, he spread out his legs wide and glided over to the cart. He began looking through Fioralba and Caelwen's items.

Fioralba looked like she wanted to stop him, and Caelwen stopped her. "Trust me, if you make him think that you don't want him in something, he's more likely to get into it," she said.

Fioralba sighed, but then smirked. "Well, that's a problem, but he is really cute," she said.

Treftune poked his head up and looked over at Fioralba, chitting. He ran over and jumped. Fioralba squeaked as Treftune landed on her.

"Treftune," Caelwen said, "be nice."

Fioralba looked a little concerned, but Caelwen said, "He must like you. He doesn't often go to people that he doesn't like. Well, unless he's stealing from them, but you wouldn't know that he was there if he was trying to steal from you, and he would probably use one of his Essaerites," she explained.

Fioralba was looking at the Valfglidea as it ran around her, looking for things to nibble on. As he came up to her shoulder, she smiled at him tentatively and ran her finger along his head.

"He's soft," Fioralba said and smiled.

Caelwen grinned. "Very. And they're really friendly, once you get to know them."

Treftune nuzzled along Fioralba's neck and ears, making her laugh. "Oh, that tickles," she said, as he ran his tail under her chin, making her laugh more.

Caelwen smiled. "It does, but be careful. Sometimes when he's doing that, it's because he's found a mark and he's trying to distract you from what he's trying to steal."

Fioralba glared playfully at the little creature. "I have no doubt. Here," she said. She reached down into a pouch and pulled out a little chunk of bread. Treftune took it and nibbled on it.

Caelwen shook her head kindly and snickered. "He already has you trained, doesn't he?"

Fioralba smiled. "Maybe."

Treftune distracted Fioralba for a while, and Caelwen checked in on a handful of hawks that she had in the area. Even though she wasn't part of the Legion, she still felt the need to watch and protect. After a moment, she looked over to see Fioralba looking at her curiously.

Caelwen blushed. "I was checking on some Essaerites I had in the area. I'm sorry. I didn't mean to be rude. It's a habit," she said.

Fioralba didn't look bothered. "You have some Essaerites in the area?"

Caelwen nodded. "A handful of hawks. Just looking for anything," she said. And then, realizing she might have made a mistake, said, "Should I not be doing that?"

Fioralba shook her head. "No, you're fine to do that. In fact, I dare say the Legion would appreciate it. You can never have too many scouts. Or at least that's what Xavieno tells me."

"No, you really can't," Caelwen said. "Though with the trees around here, the hawks may not be of huge assistance," she said. But then she amended, "But I suppose I'm used to looking for small raiding parties. And anything that would pose a threat to the Legion, I would be able to see even through the trees."

Fioralba said. "We will get attacked, or I've heard of other Legions being attacked while on the march, but usually it's with smaller groups or with fast attack groups. It hasn't been something we've really had to deal with, though."

Caelwen nodded. "You will," she said darkly.

Fioralba didn't look convinced, and Caelwen didn't push the subject. She liked Fioralba. She could tell that they were going to be friends—the woman was kind and easy to talk to. But Caelwen could also tell that she wasn't as experienced in many of the ways of the world as Caelwen was, and it seemed that Fioralba had an attitude of "things happen to others." She could just tell from the brief conversations that they had. This was a person who didn't expect for things to go wrong or to go sideways. That was no delusion that Caelwen held. She worked under the assumption that at some point in time, something would go wrong or would go sideways; the column would be attacked, or there would be some other catastrophe that would happen.

So she kept her hawks in the area, and she had her pumas close enough by. Mariokos had told her that so long as they were kept far away from the Legion, they wouldn't have anything to worry about until an arrangement could be made. In a way, this was fine with her. The pumas were able to roam around looking for threats far away from the column. And with both Xavieno and Mariokos being aware of them and knowing what they looked like, they wouldn't raise a false alarm. Caelwen very much doubted any of the Lysandrian scouts would notice the cats, as few people did.

Next to her, Fioralba looked to be thinking about something. "Is there something on your mind?" Caelwen asked.

Fioralba looked thoughtful. "I don't want to pry," she said.

Caelwen smiled. "That sounds like something someone says right before they pry," she said good-naturedly.

Fioralba smiled sheepishly. "I suppose so."

"Go ahead and pry," Caelwen said.

"Thanks," Fioralba said, and then she asked, "You said that you created your Essaerithon to protect your settlement, and you have pumas that you also use to protect your settlement, right?"

Caelwen nodded. "Yes, I do. Why?"

"Did they protect your settlement from men or from animals?" Fioralba inquired.

Ah, this makes sense, Caelwen thought. Fioralba wanted to know if Caelwen was a warrior. She knew enough about the Lysandrians to know that they thought the Gwenthari were barbarians, and she could only wonder what Fioralba thought of her people, and doubly so for what she would think of an Essaerist.

Caelwen answered, "Both, honestly. Most of the time they were just used for animals. For example, there's a type of animal that can create Essaerites, that's called a Wolxaran," she explained. "They're extremely intelligent, and they can produce up to five versions of themselves. So I would use the pumas to protect the settlement against those, though attacks from them were very rare."

Fioralba looked curious. "Why is that?"

Caelwen gestured indifferently. "Well, they tend to keep themselves away from people, and with their Essaerites, they're able to hunt small game and have the Essaerites bring it back to them. But on occasion, we will see juveniles come after livestock. Usually, you can scare them away. I don't think I've ever killed an actual Wolxaran in my life, I don't think I've ever killed an actual Wolxaran in my life, which is a good thing because it would risk angering the gods," she said.

"And then there's other animals as well. We had your normal predators that would attack livestock, and so the cats kept them away, but they were also for people attacking us too," she said.

Fioralba looked thoughtful. "Is it true that with the Gwenthari, women fight alongside the men?"

This made Caelwen smile. "Yes, it is."

"I see," Fioralba said. "Lysandrian women don't do that," she said, almost like she was bothered by the idea of a woman having to fight.

Caelwen thought for a moment. "You don't like the idea of women fighting, do you?"

Fioralba shook her head. "No, I don't," she said honestly. "I'm sorry, I'm not trying to criticize your culture."

Caelwen waved off the comment. "You're not. It's fine. I dare say we're going to have a lot of differences between our cultures," she said with a smile. "But let me ask you this. If you were to be attacked, even by more Lysandrians, would they not harm or kill or rape the women?"

Fioralba's eyes widened a little bit at the last statement, and she spluttered, "Well, yes, I suppose so."

Caelwen nodded. "So even though Lysandrian women don't fight, they can be killed by people who do?"

Fioralba looked thoughtful. "Well, yeah. What's your point?"

"So Gwenthari women fight as well. It means that we can defend ourselves, and it means that we can help others in battle," Caelwen said. "Yes, we're mothers, and we're homemakers, and we're all those things. But we also can fight. My mother was a warrior. My grandmother was one. It's a part of our people and our heritage, and while I may not like how violent some of my culture is, I can understand it, and I can respect it. I would have died many times had I not had that ability."

Fioralba seemed to be taking this in. "So you've been in battles before?" she finally asked.

Caelwen inclined her head. "Many times, yes. I've defended my settlement from being raided, and I've taken part in raiding parties," she said, her tone honest. "It's the way of my people. And like I said, I don't necessarily agree with it, but it's what it is."

Fioralba was looking ahead, her expression thoughtful. "You can ask what you want to ask," Caelwen said, sensing her hesitation.

Fioralba blushed slightly. "Sorry. Again, I don't want to pry, but... I guess I do want to pry," she admitted.

Caelwen laughed, then answered the unasked question. "Yes, I've killed," she said simply.

It looked like Fioralba was expecting this answer, but she still reeled a little bit from it. Caelwen continued, "I know you know killers. I know for a fact that Mariokos has killed; I watched him do it. And I dare say your husband has as well."

Fioralba gave a small nod. "I know they have. But I haven't seen it, and I don't like the thought of it," she said, glancing over at Caelwen apologetically. "Sorry."

Caelwen smiled warmly. "There's nothing to be sorry for."

After a moment of silence, Fioralba ventured another question. "How many people have you killed, if you don't mind me asking?"

Caelwen looked up, thinking. "Over my whole life? I'd say maybe thirty or forty," she replied, her honesty unflinching.

Fioralba's eyes widened. "Really? Thirty or forty? I don't think Mariokos or Xavieno have killed that many," she said, surprise in her voice.

"Unfortunately, I have," Caelwen said. "Most of them have been people attacking my settlement. And sad to say, a lot of it has been over the last year or so," she added, a touch of sorrow in her tone. "I'm not proud that I've killed, but I'm not ashamed of it either."

"And you shouldn't be," Fioralba said firmly.

She had been worried that she would be judged by Fioralba, but it didn't seem that was going to be the case.

"Thank you for your understanding," Caelwen said. "So, I take it you've never been in a fight or in a battle at all?"

Fioralba shook her head and laughed dryly.

"Honestly, I don't think I would know what to do with myself," Fioralba said. "I don't react well to violence. I don't even like it when they're training. When the Legion was getting ready to move, Xavieno and Mariokos created Essaerites that the Legion would train on, and I helped a little bit. I'd create shields or spears or whatever they needed for training. I hated it," she said. "Even though I knew it was just Essaerites that were being attacked and doing the attacking and that nobody was actually getting hurt, it still bothered me."

"Then this must be hard for you," Caelwen said, "being on the march like this."

Fioralba looked around and shrugged.

"I try not to think about it, honestly, but also being in the support wagon, we're far back from any action that happens, or at least we have been so far," she said.

Caelwen was curious. "How many interactions has the Legion gotten into since coming in this area?"

"A handful, but they've all been small, or it's been like what you and Mariokos experienced," she said. "We haven't seen a dedicated Gwenthari army yet, and part of me wonders if we will. From what we've been told, all the Gwenthari are barbarians, and are only in this for money and supplies, and that they won't band together," Fioralba said, and then instantly regretted her words. Her face flushed, and Caelwen laughed.

"It's fine," she said. "And at some point, we will face a Gwenthari army. In a lot of ways, you're right; our people are scattered and are just a collection of cities and settlements. We aren't as cohesive as we once were," Caelwen explained, "but when threatened, they will come together."

CHAPTER 35

S pring sunlight shone down on Xavieno, warming his back and shoulders as he marched. The air was warm as well, but not sweltering or stifling. It was nice—just the perfect temperature for marching, in his opinion. All around them, spring was taking hold, though he usually only saw it from the birds that he had flying above Legion as it snaked its way across the land.

He was in the center of his formation, as was the norm, so he could check on his Essaerites while they marched. When he wasn't checking on them, he was looking at the back of the head of the man in front of him. It didn't make for a very scenic view, but he knew his lot was better than some, because he at least had his Essaerites to check in on.

It was still warm when they made it to their campsite. Above them, the sky was a crystal-clear expanse of blue, while the mountains stood tall, their jagged peaks piercing the horizon. All of them were covered in dense forest. He could see the beauty in it, but in many ways, it made him long for home. He much preferred the rolling hills, vineyards, and fields of Dionisiana over this mountainous territory.

As they arrived at their campsite, his squad was informed that they were going to help set up camp and would not be taking part in guard duty or foraging. He reached inside himself and created several legionnaire Essaerites to assist them. He knew Mariokos preferred creating simpler Essaerites for this task, but Xavieno preferred these. He had never quite become as adept as his friend at some of the more simplistic construction-type Essaerites.

"We're on wall duty," Geraldox shouted to Xavieno and his squad.

Next to him, Isaios and Pandros grunted. They set their packs and armor down, and Xavieno created a shovel. He joined his squad, heading over to where the engineers said the wall was to be built. He could already see Mariokos's

Essaerithon getting to work. It was chewing through the ground, creating a deep trench that would move around the camp as it dug. Xavieno's nose filled with the scent of dirt and ground being turned up. The smell always relaxed him, and he joined his squad as they began to dig a counter trench where they would place some of the poles to create the wall.

He let his mind wander as he dug with his squad and Essaerites. He could hear Pandros and Isaios talking about something, but he didn't pay much attention to it. Instead, he plodded along, letting his mind drift. He would never admit it to Mariokos, but he always found this type of work peaceful. He enjoyed it—there was something about the sun on your back, the smell of the dirt as you turned it up, and the feel of it on your hands. He enjoyed the way it made his muscles stretch and work. Though he was sure that if he had to spend day after day doing this, he would feel otherwise.

Still, he lost himself in the work, and they built the wall in no time at all. As they were completing it, Geraldox sent them on other tasks around the base to get it set up for the night.

There was a rhythm to setting up camp, and it didn't matter what duty you pulled. It was a part of the day, and it was a part of his routine that he'd become accustomed to, and in a way, fed on. It created a cadence to his day and evening, and as the camp was built, his mind settled, as did his emotions.

This campaign had been so different from what he thought it would be. They'd encountered a few Gwenthari groups, but they'd all been small. Xavieno had assumed that they would have been in great battles at this point, but they hadn't been. They'd been in small skirmishes at best and dealt with annoyances. But it hadn't been what he thought, nor had been killing. Before coming on this campaign, he had been in plenty of fights, and he had hurt people, but he'd never killed before, nor had any of his Essaerites. Now he had, as had his Essaerites, and he wasn't sure what he thought about it.

He didn't have a hard time sleeping at night, which surprised him. At first, he'd assumed that once he'd taken a life for the first time, it would bother him, but it really hadn't. It had been gruesome, and it had been brutal, but it had all happened so fast, and so much was going on around him when it had happened, and while he felt emotions from it, they weren't as difficult to bear as he thought they would be. He knew Mariokos had had a harder time with it, but neither of them had been as disturbed as they thought they should have been. It was probably a good thing, Xavieno thought.

As they wrapped up the completion of the camp, Xavieno walked over to where he and Fioralba's tent would be. As he approached her, he saw Caelwen with her. Xavieno was curious about Mariokos's new wife. There was something mysterious and alien about her—not in an off-putting sort of way, but just in the way that she was unique and different. She looked at him, her eyes calculating. She had an exotic beauty to her as well, with her blue eyes, pale skin, and brilliant red hair. He was sure that it was a beauty that Mariokos could appreciate.

Xavieno walked up to his wife and gave her a hug. Her arms wrapped around his neck, and she smiled up at him.

"How was your day, my love?" he asked.

She smiled. "It was good." She leaned up and kissed him. Her lips were soft, warm, and inviting. His arms wrapped around her waist, pulling her tighter.

"Good, I'm happy to hear that." He looked over at Caelwen. "How was your first day on the march?"

"It was fine," she said.

Xavieno felt something on his back, and he jumped a little and turned, seeing a bushy tail. "What the fuck?" he said, starting to turn around.

Fioralba stopped him. "That's just Treftune."

"Treftune?" he asked, feeling something moving on him.

Caelwen sighed. "I'm sorry. He's my Valfglidea."

Xavieno looked down, seeing a little creature trying to get into a pouch on his belt. He tried pushing it away. "Ouch. It bit me!" He gasped.

He felt anger flare for a moment. But Fioralba said, "Don't fight it. Trust me, it's easier not to fight it."

"Treftune, that's enough," Caelwen said, coming over to him.

"What's it want?" Xavieno asked.

"Food," Fioralba said. "That seems to mostly be what he steals."

"He steals?" Xavieno asked.

The Valfglidea jumped from him, landing on Caelwen's shoulder. She chided it, but it didn't seem like her heart was in it.

"You have an animal that steals food?" Xavieno asked.

Caelwen sighed. "Yes, I'm sorry. He also steals other things, though. If he sees anything shiny or something that he likes, he's bound to take it."

"But look at how cute he is," Fioralba said, walking up to Caelwen. She scratched underneath the chin of the little creature, and as she did, his fur turned a pale blue.

"Yeah, real cute," Xavieno commented. He sucked his finger where the animal bit him. "Very cute."

Fioralba glared at him. "Be nice. I like him."

Xavieno chuckled. "Of course you like him. He bit me. What's not to like?"

Fioralba grinned. "There you go. See? You're starting to understand why I like him already."

He couldn't help but smirk. "You're the only one I like being bitten by."

She snorted. "I know that's not true for a fact."

Xavieno looked over Caelwen's shoulder, seeing Mariokos approach. He came up to them and smiled.

He greeted Caelwen. "How was your day?" he asked.

"Fine," she said. "How was yours? I saw that Essaerite of yours working on the camp."

Mariokos smirked. "It's useful for sure."

Treftune leapt onto Mariokos's shoulder, and he stroked it a few times before handing it a little piece of bread from his pocket.

"Has it bitten you?" Xavieno asked.

Mariokos looked over at him. "Has what bitten me? Treftune?"

Xavieno nodded.

Mariokos shook his head. "No. He hasn't. I just give him what he wants, and he's fine. He's pretty cuddly and cute, though, don't you think?"

Xavieno sighed. "Traitors, all of you."

Mariokos looked over at Caelwen. "I spoke to Command a little bit about you today."

Her eyebrows went up. "About what?"

"About you potentially helping the Legion, if you want," he said. "They wanted to see some of your Essaerites this evening before dinner and have Xavieno, Fioralba, and I take a look at them."

Next to Xavieno, Fioralba perked up. "They want my help?" she asked.

Mariokos nodded. "You're an Essaerist, and a talented one at that."

"I am talented, it's true," she said.

Xavieno snorted. "I miss marching already."

Fioralba hit his shoulder, and Xavieno noticed that Caelwen looked concerned. "You'll be alright," Xavieno said.

Mariokos echoed it. "You're very talented. You have nothing to be worried about, and even if you were a horrible Essaerist, you're still an Essaerist."

"Okay, yeah. I can show them my Essaerites," she said with a sigh.

Mariokos reached out and gave her a reassuring squeeze on the shoulder. "You have nothing to be worried about." He looked at the others. "Shall we do this?"

They made their way out of camp and were joined by Damianello, Alessandros, Theoliano, Erastos, and Geraldox, along with Caelwen's brother Wulfgren. Mariokos led them to a patch outside of the main wall where he had a few of his Legionnaire Essaerites standing around. With them were two large cats that looked similar to pumas.

Xavieno whistled. "Those are impressive," he said as he walked up to the Essaerites.

They all came and stood around the Essaerites, and Damianello looked at them quizzically. Next to Damianello, Xavieno noted that Alessandros seemed apprehensive of them. He resisted the urge to smirk. *Coward,* Xavieno thought.

Damianello looked at Caelwen. "Thank you for being willing to show us these."

She nodded. "Of course. What would you like to see?"

"Tell me about them," Damianello said, and then he looked at Mariokos, Fioralba, and Xavieno. "I want you to look at them as well."

Xavieno approached one of the pumas and looked over at Caelwen. "Am I fine to touch it?"

"Of course. If you'd like, I can make it stand on two legs so you can get a better view of it," she said.

"That'd be great," Xavieno said.

The big cat stood on its two hind legs. It was tall when it stood like this, and he could see just how large and intimidating it was. Next to him, Fioralba looked at it curiously.

"How heavy is it?" Mariokos asked.

"It's three-hundred pounds. Usually, I keep them around one-fifty or two-hundred pounds, and I've created some all the way up to six-hundred, but I found three-hundred tends to be the sweet spot," she said.

"Why is that?" Theoliano asked. "Wouldn't it be better to have them be larger? I've heard about some big cats in some foreign lands that can get up to close to six-hundred pounds."

"No, three-hundred sounds about right," Xavieno said, looking at the Essaerite appreciatively. "It's important to note that it probably doesn't have any organs like a normal animal would," he said and looked over at Caelwen. "All muscle? Teeth and bone?"

"Yes," Caelwen said.

The Essaerite opened its mouth, and Xavieno couldn't help but smile. "The entire mouth is metal," he mused.

"That'd be effective. Armor's not going to do shit to it," Mariokos said next to him.

"That it won't," Damianello was closer to it now, looking at it. He ran his fingers over the fur. "It's soft. For some reason, I didn't expect it to feel like fur."

"Most of it's like regular flesh and bone, just like a normal animal," Caelwen supplied, and Damianello nodded.

"Ours aren't like that, are they?" he asked.

Mariokos shrugged. "Some of them are, yes, but, for example, Xavieno's more advanced Essaerites aren't. Their skin feels more like stone."

Xavieno went on to explain. "Yes, they're a lot more advanced than this one probably is, but they're also my highest level of Essaerite. I've been working on them for years, but this seems like a very efficient use of power." He ran his finger along the teeth, feeling how sharp they were. "They look almost like daggers. I would expect to have seen more slicing ability in them. And the mouth looks," Xavieno said, trailing off.

"The mouth is deeper than a regular cat's," Caelwen said, "and as for the teeth, they tend to do more gripping than anything else. But that jaw is powerful. It can easily snap through bone."

Damianello nodded, and Theoliano asked, "Have they needed to do that a lot? And why would you need something that powerful?"

"I use them a lot to protect the settlement from larger predators," she said.

Theoliano seemed to understand. "Right. Big, heavy, muscular animals. Large bones. Makes sense now. It also makes sense why the mouth is so much deeper."

Xavieno looked at the paws. "These also look different, too."

"Yes, they're able to grip more. And then there's the claws," she said.

Xavieno saw long claws come out of the paws, but they looked slightly different than what he was expecting. He smiled. "They're much sharper than the teeth. They for slashing?"

"Yes, but," she said. And then a lower part of the claw went back in, leaving a secondary claw out that looked almost like a hook.

Next to him, Mariokos smirked. "Very interesting," he said, with pride.

He looked over at Caelwen. "And what do these do?"

"They'll grip onto something. They won't shred through tissue the same way that sharper claws will, but with the paws being able to grip more, and the strength of the animal, they're able to grip on and rip things apart," she said.

"I could see why that would be effective," Fioralba said next to them.

He knew that Fioralba hated violence, but he also knew that she was intrigued by the Essaerites of others, and he could see her getting into inspecting Caelwen's. He could also see how impressed she was by her. Xavieno had to agree. Even if Caelwen had come from the Empire, this level of skill was impressive.

Xavieno looked over at Caelwen. "You created all this without any training? Fuck, I'm sure glad you're on our side."

Damianello glanced over at Caelwen in surprise. "You haven't been trained?"

Caelwen blushed. "No. I haven't." And then after a moment, "You seem pleased," she said, sounding confused. "Sorry, I didn't mean to question you."

Damianello waved a hand. "You're not part of the Legion. You're welcome to question me, however much you please. And I am pleased. Because if you're willing to help us, and you were able to create this without any training, I can only imagine what will happen after you spend some time working with our Essaerists," he said, looking at the puma. "This thing is a specimen, to say the least. I can only imagine what it does on the battlefield."

"They're effective," Wulfgren said, and Damianello looked over at him.

"Have you seen these in combat before?" he asked.

Wulfgren nodded. "Several times." He looked over to his sister and then shook his head. "They're terrifying. Sometimes, I have a hard time believing they came from my little sister."

This made Damianello smirk. "I can only imagine. Do you have anything else that you can create?" he asked Caelwen.

She nodded. "Yes, I have a larger Essaerite that I wear like a suit."

Mariokos started speaking. "That's what you had on when we first met, wasn't it? And then when we were attacked?"

"Yes, it wasn't the full version of it; that takes a lot more Essaeris to create, but it was a type of version of it." she said.

Damianello looked at her. "May we see it?"

"Of course," she said.

She took a few steps away from them, and Xavieno watched as she closed her eyes and breathed deeply. After a few moments, he started to see vines winding around, covering her body. He saw her raise her foot, and they grew down below her foot. And then the next foot came up. Soon she was taller than Xavieno and Mariokos. More of the vines wound around, creating thick arms, and then a helmet that looked like the skull of a deer or an elk, with antlers coming out of it. Xavieno couldn't help but grin. The thing was terrifying. Something, he suspected, Alessandros felt, as the man seemed to almost shrink a little bit, seeing the Essaerithon.

Damianello seemed pleased; he even caught a grunt of approval. Xavieno walked up to it along with Mariokos and Fioralba. They ran their hands along it, and Mariokos commented, "Large blades along the forearm. I could see those being deadly," he said, looking up at the skull and smiling.

The voice that came out was Caelwen's, but deeper and more ethereal. "Yes, I can also change the eyes' colors and make things glow on it."

Xavieno nodded in appreciation. "There's something to be said for the effect of an Essaerite," he said. "I'm sure this one is intimidating. Do you use any other sounds? That voice is unsettling."

"Yes, it's a kind of roar," she said.

"Let's hear it," Damianello said.

The Essaerithon let out a loud roar that was a mix of animals with low notes and a high keening sound at the same time. Everyone flinched at the sound, and Xavieno felt every hair on his body stand up. Nearby legionnaires looked at them, a few backing away or grabbing their weapons.

After a moment, Damianello started to laugh; he clapped his hands. "Terrifying! That sound will haunt my dreams."

Xavieno agreed. He walked around Caelwen. "What are those on the back?"

Some vines came out that were thicker than some of the other ones, with weird ends on them, almost like fingers. "They can grip onto things," she said, and a spike came out of the end. "They have spikes on them, or," she said, holding up the other one. It puffed up near the end, and a spike shot out of it that was metal and buried itself in a tree a distance away.

He heard Fioralba gasp a little bit, but Xavieno just grinned wider.

"These, with the pumas, will be extremely effective," Theoliano said.

"How many of the pumas can you create and have this?" he asked.

"Three of the size that I have now, with this," Caelwen admitted. "Maybe four, if I kept the pumas around for a while."

Theoliano nodded and looked over at Damianello. Damianello looked at the Essaerite curiously as he walked around. "Yes, these would be useful. Not in the standard formations, mind you, but in the skirmish lines, perhaps, or if the lines are broken," he said.

"That's what I was thinking," Theoliano said. "I'm sure they'd be effective in the skirmish line, but I would hate risking an Essaerist like that."

"How strong are you in this?" Damianello asked her.

"Very strong," she said. "I can easily knock over a horse." They heard a snort from Wulfgren. They all turned and looked at him.

"I think you can do more than knock over a horse," Wulfgren said. "She can knock over carts with that; she can probably pick them up and throw them."

"Well, I've never had to do that before," Caelwen said.

Wulfgren shrugged. "Doesn't mean that you couldn't."

Damianello nodded in approval and looked over at Xavieno, Mariokos, and Fioralba. "Do you think you can help her improve these?" he asked, "or are they at their pinnacle?"

Fioralba smiled. "Nothing's ever at its pinnacle," she said.

"That's what I like to hear," Damianello said. "Thank you, Caelwen. I sincerely appreciate your time and effort. I would like to ask that you work with Fioralba while on the road, to hone your abilities. I wish I could say that you could spend the days working with Xavieno and Mariokos and Fioralba, but unfortunately, Xavieno and Mariokos need to be in the main formations."

He looked over at Fioralba. "That is, if this is okay with you."

Fioralba nodded. "Yes, sir, it's my pleasure."

————

AFTER DINNER THAT EVENING, XAVIENO SAT ON HIS COT, LOOKING OVER AT FIORALBA. SHE had been talkative during dinner, but she seemed off to him as the night wore on. He looked over at her.

"What's wrong, my love?" he asked. "Did your day not go as well as you said?"

She looked over at him and then back at whatever she was doing. She shook her head. "No, it was fine. It's just," she started, and then came and sat next to him. She looked over at him.

"Caelwen is different," she said.

He raised an eyebrow. "Bad different?"

She shook her head quickly. "No, not at all. In so many ways, I'm almost jealous of her. She has a confidence that I don't have, though I also see her insecurities as well. But..." Fioralba said, trailing off.

"But what?" he asked.

"But she's killed," Fioralba said.

Xavieno gave a shrug. "So have I and Mariokos. That doesn't bother you? Unless there's something that you're not telling me."

Again, she shook her head. "No, it doesn't bother me that you've killed, and I guess it doesn't bother me that Caelwen has killed either, but she's killed more than you and Mariokos, and I understand she had to to protect her people, but it's just," she said, trailing off.

"It's just that she's a woman," Xavieno said.

Fioralba nodded. "Yeah. I mean, how many Lysandrian Essaerists that are women do you know that have killed anybody?"

Xavieno thought and shook his head. "None. I haven't met any at all."

"Exactly," Fioralba said, "but for Caelwen it was expected that she would. It just—I don't know, it's something to think about."

And it was something to think about. In some ways, Caelwen was far more experienced than both Xavieno and Mariokos. They'd now both seen combat, though it had been minor. Xavieno had used his Essaerites to fight and kill, but Caelwen had done that so many more times. In many ways, she was more advanced than they were. But in other ways, she was wholly unadvanced and simplistic.

It was an interesting situation to be in, but he also thought there was an advantage to it as well. With her different background, it would give her the ability to help and push Xavieno and Mariokos in ways that they wouldn't be pushed by a Lysandrian Essaerist. And in return, Caelwen would have the opportunity to grow and experience the benefits of formalized training and regiment that would make her Essaeris more effective.

He had been able to tell when he looked at her Essaerithon that it was lacking in some fundamental ways. She wasn't using her power in the most efficient way possible, and he suspected that with some work, she would be able to produce many more Essaerites that would be far more powerful than what they currently were. But it would take some time—time that she had a lot of.

Xavieno reminded himself of that, and he knew that Fioralba was just the person to teach her. While she may not have liked fighting, Xavieno wasn't sure there were many people he knew who had a more solid understanding of Essaeris and how to use it, as well as how to create and control Essaerites. Fioralba would be perfect for Caelwen, and he suspected that Caelwen would be good for Fioralba as well.

CHAPTER 36

The Legion had been on the move for days, and Fioralba was looking forward to them finding a place to camp for at least a few nights. Over that time, they had been moving through the mountains—many of them tall with sheer cliff sides. But others were more rolling in nature, although all of them were rocky. It made for a windy path that the Legion had to travel through, and the rough terrain meant that it took them longer to set camp every night as they had to clear any forest rocks and debris before they could settle down for the evening.

The whole time, the rear supply lines had been harassed by Gwenthari raiding parties, and scouts had spotted others in the distance. On occasion, the Legion would pause and send out a squad or a platoon to deal with a raiding party or scare it away. But these weren't problems that Fioralba generally had to deal with. The reality of it was that the trip for her was mostly boring, though she was getting to know Caelwen and was starting to count her as a friend. Caelwen was fascinating to Fioralba, and she suspected that the fascination went both ways. Caelwen was so different and had such a different view of the world than Fioralba did. It was fascinating to her.

There was plenty that they didn't agree on, but for some reason, because Caelwen was so different from Fioralba, this didn't seem to bother either of them. They couldn't comprehend where the other person came from at all. Though, she had learned that the Gwenthari had the same dedication to family that Lysandrian society did. And by and large, people lived the same kind of life. They farmed, they worked, and they did what they needed to provide for their loved ones and families.

They had learned that they were heading towards the Ulfgarath city of Hroldenfell. Fioralba obviously knew nothing about the city, but she wondered if Caelwen did.

"Do you think we're far from Hroldenfell now?" she asked.

Caelwen looked over at her. "I would think we would arrive there today or tomorrow. The roads here are widening, and it appears that they are well-traveled. I think we're very close."

Fioralba frowned. "This seems like an odd sort of place to build a city."

Caelwen smiled. "It is, I suppose. But it didn't used to be. You see, Hroldenfell is built on top of one of these mountains. It'll be more of a fortress than what you would think of a city to be."

"Have you been to Hroldenfell before?" she asked after a moment.

Caelwen chuckled and shook her head. "No, I haven't been."

"Why do you find that amusing?" Fioralba asked.

"I'm Wulfharboria. There's not a lot of Wulfharborias who go to Hroldenfell. We aren't exactly welcome there," she said with a shrug.

Fioralba cocked an eyebrow. "I guess I don't understand that. The Ulfgarath are Gwenthari, aren't they? And the Wulfharborias are also Gwenthari, correct?" she confirmed.

Caelwen thought for a moment. "Yes, we're all Gwenthari, but it doesn't mean that we're all the same people," she explained. "We all used to be our own nations." And then, reading the look of confusion on Fioralba's face, she said, "How much do you know about us?"

Fioralba felt a little self-conscious, and she felt herself blush. "Not much. I'm sorry. I've always been told that they're all barbarians," she paused and blushed deeper. "Again, I'm sorry," she added.

This didn't seem to bother Caelwen. "Honestly, many of our people are, I suppose, compared to what Lysandrians would consider society to be."

Caelwen sighed, thinking aloud, "Well, maybe it's just easier to explain this to you. If you don't know much about Gwenthari history, I can see where a lot of this would be confusing for you. There are basically five Gwenthari peoples," she explained.

"You have the Ulfgarath; this is the territory we're in now. Then you have Valfarans, Rothmornians, Eirfrosti, and Wulfharboria," Caelwen continued. "I'm Wulfharboria."

Fioralba took in the information. "I believe I've heard of the Rothmornians before."

"You probably have," Caelwen said. "They didn't lose as much as the others did over time. They're still their own country, and I know they're more friendly with Lysandrians than any other Gwenthari peoples. For example, my brother Wulfgren fought in one of their wars recently with Lysandrian legions."

Fioralba nodded. "Yes, yes, I know about that. It's odd. I never thought of them as being Gwenthari before, but I suppose they are, aren't they?"

Caelwen inclined her head. "Yes, they are. They're just much closer to you than they are to what you would consider a Gwenthari to be."

Fioralba was fascinated, hearing about this. "Please, tell me more."

Caelwen smiled, seeming to enjoy the opportunity to share her culture with someone else. "Well, we're all Gwenthari, but again, we're all different, and you can tell when you look at us. For example, you had to have noticed that everyone from my settlement has blue eyes, red hair, and pale skin."

Fioralba nodded. "That was pretty obvious," she said with a smirk.

Caelwen chuckled. "Exactly. We're Wulfharboria. That's how we look. Now, if you look at the Ulfgarath, for example, they have blonde hair and blue eyes, generally speaking, sometimes green, but almost always blue. The Valfarans are very similar to the Ulfgarath. You'll see a lot of blonde hair and blue eyes. Their skin will be a little bit lighter than the Ulfgarath sometimes, and occasionally their hair is so blonde it almost looks white."

Fioralba perked up at that. "That's interesting."

Caelwen went on. "Now, the Rothmornians, you probably didn't know they were Gwenthari because they look so similar to you. They don't have the same tan or olive skin that you do, or the dark hair. Their hair tends to be more sandy, but they do have green eyes, and sometimes brown eyes."

Fioralba nodded, logging the information away. "And the Eirfrosti?" she asked.

"The Eirfrosti are like us in some ways. They have blue eyes, generally speaking, and where my skin tends to be more pale, an Eirfrosti person's skin will be almost as white as freshly fallen snow," Caelwen said, "and their hair is a deep coal black."

They were starting to come around a corner now, and Fioralba could make out something in the distance. Atop one of the taller hills in the area, she could see a city coming into view, though it wasn't a city like she was used to seeing in Lysandrian. It appeared that the hill had been flattened on the top. She could see a stone wall running all along the top of it. The sides of the hill, or she supposed it was a mountain, were clear of trees, save for some along the bottom, giving the defenders on the wall a view for miles.

She felt her eyes widen just a bit. "It's larger than I thought, but so different than what I thought it would be too."

"Yes, like I said, it's more of a fortress than a city," Caelwen noted.

Fioralba looked at her. "Are these common around here?"

Caelwen shrugged. "They used to be. You'll find abandoned fortresses like this all over, but people don't live in them much anymore. There's still a few that are populated, like Hroldenfell, but most of the cities that are around now are in better areas."

This confused Fioralba. "Better areas?"

"Yes." Caelwen gestured around. "Farming in this land is a nightmare. All the soil is full of clay and rocks, and you don't get good yields out of it. That's why so many of these cities were abandoned."

"Then why did you have them to begin with?" Fioralba asked.

"We changed," Caelwen said.

"Changed?" Fioralba echoed.

Caelwen explained, "There was a time when the Gwenthari were not a warrior people," Caelwen said, and Fioralba could tell that she was thinking hard about how to explain things. She could see a sense of nostalgia, or concern on her face. Maybe not concern so much as introspection.

Caelwen went on, "We were craftsmen, and we were farmers and merchants and traders. Our goods were better than anybody else's in the world, including that of Lysandrian's," she said, looking over at Fioralba. Then she continued, "But then that changed. The people started changing. They started moving over towards raiding and gaining wealth and power that way, along with resources." Caelwen said "it was extremely effective.

"You see, back then each of the peoples were more like nations, and as time changed and the people changed, they put more and more of an emphasis on war and less of an emphasis on everything else that we did, and much of that was born here," she said, gesturing around. "The Ulfgarath were the ones who raided the Lysandrian capital, as I'm sure you're well aware, but then they pushed out into the rest of the Gwenthari territory. As the rest of us changed, these types of fortresses became normal. They had to be. And even though these were all nations, they were loose. And so there was a lot of infighting amongst us," she admitted.

"And then inside of these cities, with the lack of food, disease was able to spread. People got sick, starved, and eventually, they started abandoning these hilltop fortresses, going back to settlements like we used to have before," Caelwen said.

Fioralba nodded. "That's very interesting. You seem sad about it."

Caelwen shrugged. "In a way, I am. Our people used to be strong and advanced and amazing in so many ways, but now so many of us are just killers, and we believe that's what matters, being a warrior," she said, almost like a scoff. She shook her head. "And it all started here, not in Hroldenfell, mind you, but with Ulfgarath."

She laughed coolly.

"What's so funny?" Fioralba asked.

Caelwen pointed at Hroldenfell. "This used to be a small fortress for them. They were the strongest among us, and now they're the weakest," she said. She looked over at Fioralba, "which is apparent by us being here."

Fioralba cocked an eyebrow. "What does that mean?" she asked, curious.

"If the Ulfgarath were strong, do you think the legions would be here now? Because the answer is no, they would not be. Maybe they would be bothering the Valfarans, or maybe even the Rothmornians, though I doubt that because the Rothmornians are close to Lysandrian. You have a lot of ties with them," she said.

Fioralba was curious. "Why didn't you say the Wulfharborias or the Eirfrosti?"

"Well, to go after the Wulfharborias, you would have to first go through the Ulfgarath lands to do that, even though a lot of Wulfharborias are moving into what used to be Ulfgarath," Caelwen said. "But we were also never as cohesive as the other Gwenthari nations. We've always been more transient than the others. And while we're a people, it's more cultural than it is a defined political structure, and we also range very far north. We cover a huge territory, though again, that's starting to change.

"For example, my settlement's only been in the Ulfgarath area for the last several generations. We moved down a while ago. Others of my kind have. Plus, there's a lot of Wulfharborias that will work as mercenaries with the Lysandrian legions, so I don't think it's exactly in Lysandrian's best interest to try to attack a people with its own people," she said with a smirk.

Fioralba laughed. "I suppose that's true. And the Eirfrosti?"

"The Eirfrosti are on an island far to the north," Caelwen said. "And while Valfarans, Wulfharboria, and Ulfgarath may have fractured back into the tribes that we once were, the Eirfrosti have not. They are still tribes, but they are controlled by one individual and by bodies of individuals. They are still very strong, and they are seafaring people. I do not think it would be wise for anyone to attack them," Caelwen said honestly. "But we're here because the Ulfgarath are weak. They've lost the most in the time since we were once strong. And so, here we are."

Fioralba found all of this interesting, and she noted it in her mind. "So, basically, they don't like you here because you're Wulfharboria, and because some of your people have moved into their areas?"

"Mostly, yes," Caelwen said, "but the Ulfgarath have always seen themselves above the other nations, and while they occasionally get along with Valfarans, they don't do well with the others. They also blame us for much of their downfall. They say it was Wulfharborias who brought in diseases that killed off their cities, and they blame us now for our raiding activity, and as we push into their territory. Though, in that case, they are right to be frustrated with us, I suppose.

"Also, it's easy to tell us apart. I would stick out pretty easily if I walked into a group of Ulfgarath people, wouldn't I?" she said with a smile.

Fioralba grinned. "That you would."

"I'm not sure if that's a compliment or not," Caelwen said.

Fioralba linked her arms with Caelwen and said, "It's a compliment. You are a rarity, for sure, in the Legion. It's not just that you're a Gwenthari."

Caelwen raised an eyebrow. "Because I'm an Essaerist?"

Fioralba chuckled. "There's that, but also, you are beautiful no matter where you are from. There is beauty to you that everyone sees. I see it in the eyes of every Legionnaire who looks at you, even those who hate the Gwenthari. They're all mesmerized by you in a way."

Caelwen rolled her eyes. "I do not believe that."

"You don't have to believe me, it's true. And you seem to have a good head on your shoulders. Mariokos is very lucky to have you," she said.

Caelwen's cheeks reddened. "Thank you. I don't think he's as lucky as you think, though," she said, her voice dark.

"And why is that?" Fioralba asked.

And before Caelwen could say anything, she said, "Because you can't have children."

Caelwen's eyes widened for just a moment, and then she looked down. "You know about that?"

"Yes, I know about that," Fioralba said. "But that doesn't mean that Mariokos isn't lucky."

Then she thought for a moment. In a way, she'd stepped in it. She sighed. "Xavieno and I have lost pregnancies before. Well, we lost one, I should say." Fioralba admitted.

Caelwen looked over at her. "You did? I'm so sorry to hear that."

"Thank you," Fioralba said. "But that's being an Essaerist, isn't it?"

Caelwen cocked an eyebrow. "What do you mean, 'that's being an Essaerist'?"

Fioralba shrugged. "Essaerist females struggle to bring children to term, and the men struggle to get a woman pregnant in the first place. Usually, we lose them within the first couple of months. It's our power. It goes kind of crazy, if you will, and some think that it hurts the baby, but I'm not sure. Most of us don't have families because of it. Did you not know that?"

Caelwen looked surprised, "I didn't know that." She thought for a moment. "When my uncle was making the deal with the legion, Damianello said he didn't care if I could breed or not. I just thought it was him being dismissive at the time."

"He wasn't," Fioralba said, "and it won't be something that bothers Mariokos. He accepted it a long time ago." She chuckled, "Xavieno and I are the weird ones for hoping for a family someday."

———

MARIOKOS LOOKED AROUND AS THE LEGION CAME TO A STOP. HROLDENFELL WAS LOCATED atop a mountain that appeared to have a flat top. It was in about the worst position imaginable if you were a Lysandrian legion. All around were other mountains that were similar to Hroldenfell, but they tended to have more jagged cliffs and steeper terrain. He suspected that the Gwenthari had built in this place for a reason. It was very easy to defend, though he suspected that getting supplies in and out could be difficult.

He also noted that there wasn't any suitable land in the area for agriculture, meaning that Hroldenfell was completely supported by trade. That wasn't something that he thought was a great idea, but as it had turned out, he hadn't been alive or around when the city planners of Hroldenfell had made their little settlement here.

The other three legions that had gone into the frontier with them were already on site. Mariokos's legion took up a position to the east of the city. The other legions were at the north, south, or west ends, effectively surrounding

Hroldenfell. This was the idea, after all. As the other legions had arrived sooner, they already had camps established and were working on building fortifications in the area.

This would be one of the things he knew the Gwenthari would find confusing. Up to this point, they hadn't faced a modern Lysandrian army. They were about to.

Mariokos worked with his Essaerithon to create the camp. It was just as much of a chore as he thought it would be. They had to clear trees from the site, along with several large rocks. His Essaerithon struggled to dig a trench around the camp, as the soil wasn't really soil so much as clay and rock.

It took them far more effort than it normally would have, and he was sure that the other legions that didn't have Essaerists would be extremely jealous of Mariokos's, as even though it took a while, his Essaerithon was able to do it. But as he watched it dig through the clay and rock, he realized there were going to be other challenges to Hroldenfell.

The other town that they had encountered had been easy for it to just dig through the dirt and timber wall. Here that wouldn't be the case; they'd be dealing with a stone wall, but also that stone wall would be largely on clay or rock, meaning that tunneling into it wouldn't take him just a few minutes to do, if that was the decision and the path Command decided to go down.

As his camp was being finished, he found Caelwen. She had already cleared out an area for their tent, and he came up to her. She was looking at Hroldenfell.

"Does this bother you?" he asked.

She shook her head. "No, not really." And she looked over at him, curious. "Why aren't you attacking it, though?"

He smiled. "We will, just not yet. Shall we create our tent?"

"Sure," she said.

He reached out, and she took his hand, and he felt their power mixing with each other's. It was an odd sort of sensation. With everyone else he had been with, this mixing of Essaeris had felt not intimate but friendly and familiar. With Caelwen, it was different. There was an intimacy to it somehow, as if their powers touching spoke to a deeper bond that was building between them, even though they had only been together for a few weeks.

He reached out, and their power channeled through them, creating a tent and cot along with some pots and pans to make their dinner with.

He let go of the Essaeris but held her soft hand, the act of it feeling natural to him. She wound her fingers in his and smiled softly.

"What?" he asked.

She shrugged. "This has just been easier than I thought it would be."

He smiled. "I'm glad to hear it, and yes, it has been. I suppose I thought it was going to be more work than it has been."

She smiled softly. "I can't even begin to agree with you enough on that."

She looked back at the city. "So, why aren't we attacking it again?"

He grinned. "Well, you've probably noticed all the legions that are around in different spots."

"Yes," she said.

"Well, we're going to be clearing timber and clearing the area, and we're going to be building a counter-fortification around it," he said.

"A counter what?" she asked.

He chuckled. "Counter-fortifications. Every camp will still have the same fortifications that it does now, though those will build with time, as the longer we're in an area, the more we fortify a camp. But around this whole mountain, we will build watchtowers, trenches, and walls to keep the people of Hroldenfell inside."

She raised an eyebrow. "Really? I've always just heard of armies trying to bang down the gates or climb over the walls, or maybe try to hold out for a while, though not for very long."

He gave her hand a squeeze. "You're talking about Gwenthari armies. Now you're with a Lysandrian one."

She raised an eyebrow. "And that's different how?"

"It's different in that we have defined supply lines," Mariokos said. "We will siege Hroldenfell, but we'll also attack it. The difference is that once we're dug in, we can be here for months or years if that's what it takes."

She looked a little surprised. "I see. And what do you mean about defined supply lines?"

"There will be legionnaires working on fortifying the roads in the area and making sure that caravans can make it here with supplies. You had to have noticed when we were marching back to the camp the first time, the roads that we marched back to the camp on."

"Yes, they were pretty decent roads, I guess. I didn't think much about it at the time," she said.

Mariokos agreed. "Most people don't. They were more than decent. We leveled them. We built them up. We put in drainage. In short, we made sure that they were easy to travel on. That's one of the reasons why the legions do so well. We're builders and warriors, and we make sure that the legions always have food and supplies. The empire will be supplying us the entire time, though we will also get many of our supplies from the local area," Mariokos said. "But in the case of Hroldenfell, since they don't seem to care about farming around here, we're going to be dependent upon those supply lines from the empire."

She looked thoughtful. "What are you thinking?" he asked.

"I don't think you're going to need all that," she said. "I have a way that you can beat Hroldenfell within a few days."

He chuckled. "I had no idea you were such a military tactician. Do tell me. What is your plan?"

She looked at him and shrugged. "It's simple. Those cunts that blow the horns every morning? Just have them do it closer to Hroldenfell, trust me. The people will surrender in no time."

He snorted a laugh. "I really am worried one of these days you're going to kill one of them," he said playfully.

She looked over at him and smiled. "There's no sense in worrying about the inevitable."

He laughed.

———

THE NEXT DAY, MARIOKOS FELT SWEAT ROLLING DOWN HIS BACK AND NECK AS HE WORKED. It was a warm day, and they had been busy clearing forest the entire day. He had been helping his Essaerites—his large Essaerithon would knock over or rip out a tree, and then he had other smaller ones that would cut off branches, while the larger one would then move it into place. All the legions had been doing this, and now it was Mariokos's legion's turn to join in.

Presently, they were working on building a watchtower that was going to be along the edge of the perimeter that the legion had set around Hroldenfell. There were always men standing watch, making sure that no one got in or out of the city. None of those had been tested yet. They also built watch fires all around, and there were some legionnaires that were venturing up towards the mountain to cut some of the woods that were there in order to use them for supplies and to rid the area of its cover.

There had been a handful of archers that had tried to fire down at the legionnaires from the city, but the legion had kept too far away; therefore, nothing of any real excitement had happened yet. But he knew that would change, and it would change soon. It wouldn't take the legion long before they were testing the city's defenses. And while what he had told Caelwen the night before was true—they were willing to be here for months or years if needed— that's not what it would take. He knew it wouldn't take very long before the legions would be testing the defenses, and not long after that, those defenses would fall.

———

CAELWEN FOUND HER BROTHER, ALONG WITH SOME OF HIS MEN, NEAR THE END OF THE camp where her settlement was being kept. He looked up at her as she walked over and smiled. He came over and embraced her.

"It's been too long," he said.

She laughed. "It's only been a few days. You missed me already?"

"Oh, I'm used to having you in the house... You know, after yours was burned down by your jealous lover," he teased.

She scowled. "It wasn't burned down by a jealous lover," she retorted. "It was burned down by a former lover that I maybe tried to kill," she clarified.

He chuckled. "Oh, sorry. I keep on forgetting. But anyway, after your house got burned down, you know, by that guy who you slept with, who was mad at you, I kind of got used to having you around. It was nice having someone to cook for me," he joked.

She rolled her eyes. "Well, I'm glad to hear that you miss me."

She saw that he was buckling on some of his armor and loading up his horse, along with some of the other men. "What are you up to? Do they have you patrolling the area?"

He shook his head. "No, we're going to go scavenge. There are other farms and settlements in this area. We're going to go and see if they will pay tribute to the Lysandrian army," he said, trying to sound dignified and pompous.

She chuckled. "Seriously? That's what you're going to go do?"

"Yeah, that's exactly what we're going to go do. And they'll pay," he assured.

"What makes you so sure?" she probed.

He sighed. "Because Hroldenfell is completely surrounded, and there's four legions in the area. Plus, there's us," he said, gesturing at his men.

"They have choices. They can help the legions, and they can help in a capacity that doesn't harm them, or we can take what they have, and they can help us that way," he stated matter-of-factly.

"I suppose raiding makes sense," she conceded.

"It's only kind of raiding," he corrected, "but this is pretty common for every army to do."

"I'm sure it is," she agreed.

"Did you do a lot of this work when you were mercenaries?" she asked.

He loaded some more stuff on his saddle. "Yeah, we did."

"And how'd it go?" she asked.

"If it's a farm or a small settlement, they'll give us what they have. If it's a larger settlement, they might resist, but in the end, they'll cave. Because either they can deal with us and give us what they have to spare, and we'll be reasonable about it because we don't want to deal with them, or they can have us raid them, or worse, they can have us show back up with a couple of platoons of Lysandrian soldiers. In that case, they might get away with keeping their lives and not being turned into slaves, but that's not a guarantee at that point in time," he explained.

She had to agree that was pretty sound logic, and logic that she knew most people would follow. Her brother wouldn't have to push hard.

"So you show up and say, 'give me your food?'" she teased.

"Pretty much something like that, but it also means that there's potential jobs for people, too," he added.

"Look, I'm not saying that war is pretty," Wulfgren said, "but I am saying that the Lysandrians are different than the Gwenthari when it comes to it."

"How so?" she asked.

He thought for a moment, trying to figure out how to explain. "It's much more transactional than it is with us. For example, these settlements that we're going to go and talk to, they will have options, and if they agree to help the Legion, in some cases it can work rather well for them."

A mocking smile crossed her face. "I can see that. They don't have to worry about all the food that they're going to eat."

He laughed. "I'm being serious. Yes, it's a pain for them to give over food, but that will change with time. Once the Lysandrians are in control of this area, yes the people will pay tribute, but it's not horrible, and they'll also get security from the Lysandrians. But what I'm talking about is in other goods. Carpenters can sell more than they have to the legions, but there also are smiths, and carpenters, and all of that, that are in these settlements. Lysandrians will pay," he said.

She was surprised by this. "Seriously? They'll pay them? They just won't make them work or turn them into slaves?"

He shook his head. "No, not generally. If they work with them, no. Now, if the legion has to take over a settlement or a town, they might, but generally speaking, that's not how they work. They will do some horrible, violent, shitty things," Wulfgren said. "Don't get me wrong. In many ways, they're just like us when it comes to the end of a battle. When Hroldenfell falls, half these Lysandrians will gladly rape the women of Hroldenfell and kill them along with their children and enslave them and everything else, just like we do when we raid someplace. It's the victor's right, after all, but Lysandrians don't always work that way. If somebody works with them, they would rather have compliance, willing compliance, I should say, than somebody they have to force."

"So, you're telling me that this may not be all bad for the people you're about to visit," she said.

"It may not be, but it might be as well," he said. Then he looked at Hroldenfell darkly. "But it's not going to be good for them," he said.

"Why is that?" she asked.

He looked at the city. "Just a feeling I have," he said. "Maybe," he started and then shook his head. "I don't know, just call it a gut feeling. When you've been around the legions long enough, you start to know what's going to happen with them to a certain extent," he said, "and I just don't think things are going to go well for Hroldenfell," he said darkly, "but if they had been attacked by a Gwenthari army," he shrugged, "well, I suppose it wouldn't have gone well for them either in that case."

"No, it wouldn't," Caelwen said, looking back at the city, knowing exactly what would happen if the city of Hroldenfell fell to a Gwenthari army. It would not go well for them at all.

CHAPTER 37

Since the incident a few weeks ago with the other Essaerist, Valfric and his team had seen nothing but bad luck. Not only had they lost almost every person who had been in the raiding party with them, but they had also lost all the things they had stolen, save for what they'd had on their person when the attack happened, which wasn't much. This meant they had spent their time recovering, hunting, and otherwise bartering, trying to get food and supplies.

But they were determined. They were not going to go out this way. They would win, and they would come home to their settlement proud.

Settlements. That was another problem that had been coming into play. As the Lysandrian legions had approached ever closer to Hroldenfell, many settlements had either turned tail and run north, dispersed into the woods, or, more often than not, moved to Hroldenfell to help fortify the city and to be safe. That was one of the frustrating parts. Not so much that the people wanted to be safe or wanted to fortify the city—he thought that was the right thing to do—but that there was nobody around for them to barter with. It made him angry to no end.

Then they had come across what could be called some luck. They'd found a small settlement, if you could even call it that, where most of the people had left, save for a handful of the elderly who didn't care to travel to Hroldenfell, and one foolish farmer and his wife.

Presently, said farmer's wife, was under Valfric, tied to the bed with some Essaeris ropes. She'd been just what Valfric and the others had needed to relieve some stress and frustration. He pushed deep inside her and heard her whimper just slightly. His seed flooded inside her, he panted and stopped moving.

"Thank you, that's exactly what I needed," he said, smiling down at her.

Her eyes looked up at his blankly, and he ran his fingers along her cheek. "You did very good. I bet you didn't see this coming today, did you? This morning you started out as just a normal wife for some dumb farmer. And look at you now," he said with a grin.

She looked away from him.

He heard someone at the door and turned to look, seeing Aelric standing there. The man looked concerned and frustrated. Valfric could see the anger just under the surface, tensing his muscles.

Valfric looked back down at the woman. "I don't think you're going to enjoy the rest of your afternoon," he said and laughed.

He pulled out of her and put on some pants, walking over to his friend. "Ready for your turn, friend?"

"In a minute," Aelric said, his voice gruff.

Valfric frowned and joined him outside. Laying on the ground, tied up and covered in blood, was the farmer. Valfric glanced over at him and smirked.

The man looked up at him, balefully. "If you hadn't been a coward, and had just joined those of your settlement to go defend Hroldenfell, this wouldn't be happening now, would it?" Valfric said.

He turned to Aelric. "What is it?"

"Do you remember that guy we sent to run word to our settlement a few days back?" he asked.

Valfric nodded. "Yes. What about him?"

"Well, he's back," Aelric said.

"Already?" Valfric said.

Aelric nodded. "Yes. Apparently, he ran into Durnara and the others not far from Hroldenfell. They said they were going there to help fortify the city."

Valfric instantly felt concerned. "Fuck, and we've been out here messing around."

Aelric nodded. "Yes. That's exactly what we've been doing. But I assume that's going to change, right, boss?"

Valfric nodded. "Yeah, it is."

He looked at Aelric, seeing the hardness in his eyes and the man's jaw twitch just a little bit. Valfric thought he needed Aelric's head clear.

He looked back at the house. "Go clear your mind," he said. "Enjoy yourself. The rest of us will pack up and get ready to leave."

Aelric started trudging off toward the house, and Valfric heard the farmer call out and beg him to leave his wife alone.

Valfric turned to him. "That's not going to happen."

He reached out to some of the Essaerites that he had in the area. They were all in the forms of rats on the shoulders of Ilara and Thraindel. They scratched around the two of them, letting them know that it was time to come back to Valfric.

Ilara was the first to arrive. Her horse came trotting up, and she got off it.

"What is it?" she asked.

"The settlements in Hroldenfell," he said. "We need to go. Did you find any supplies for the road?"

She nodded. "I did. They left some things behind, but no animals. Just what we can carry," she said.

Before she could say anything else, they heard a blood-curdling scream from inside the house. Valfric turned and looked at it, then looked back to Ilara, who smiled.

"Aelric, I take it?" she said.

There was another scream and loud keening begging.

Valfric nodded. "I told him to take out some frustrations."

The screaming got worse, and they heard Aelric yelling inside. Ilara laughed and looked over at the farmer.

"I don't think she's enjoying herself. In fact, I don't think she's going to be much good for you after this," she said with a snicker.

Now Thraindel was riding up to them. He glanced over at the house, hearing the screaming and yelling, and barked a laugh.

"Well, at least he'll be better to be around now," he said.

Valfric filled Thraindel in on what was going on and what they needed to do. He nodded, and Valfric took the few moments it took to put what little items they had found onto his saddle. They waited patiently, and after the screams and yells stopped, Aelric came out of the house. Valfric breathed a sigh of relief. The tension and anger in Aelric's face seemed to be absent. Instead, he was calm and collected. He even gave them a small smile.

He walked up to Valfric and clapped him on the shoulder. "Thank you. I didn't know how badly I needed that."

"Is she alive?" Ilara asked.

Aelric shrugged. "For now, maybe. She won't make it long, though." He looked back at the farmer. "Should we take care of that one?"

Valfric released the Essaeris cords that were inside the house, holding the woman to the bed, and shook his head.

"No. Let him live with knowing what happens to cowards," he said, and got on his horse.

The journey to Hroldenfell wasn't a long one, only taking them about a day to make it there. Once they did, though, they slowed down. They were riding up, cresting over one of the low mountains in the area, when they saw Hroldenfell come into view, and with it, the legions.

"Fuck," Thraindel said softly, next to them on his own horse.

"Fuck is right," Ilara said. Her tone was etched with stress and concern, and it was right to be.

Valfric tried not to gape as he looked at the scene below him. Around the mountain's base, he could make out the legions, and with them, he could see what seemed to be towers and walls that the legions were building.

"Are they building walls around the city? Did they already take it?" Aelric asked.

Valfric shook his head. "I don't think so. I think we'd see smoke or something, and there's no chance that Hroldenfell would fall that fast," he said.

"It's walls to keep them in," Ilara said, making the connection first. "They aren't trying to defend against people coming into Hroldenfell. They're keeping them inside the city," she said.

Thraindel chuckled. "Joke's on them. Those legionnaires are going to die."

Valfric shook himself and then decided he agreed.

"Yes, they will. They're not going to last against Hroldenfell," he said.

"Agreed," Aelric said. "Obviously, they are planning for a siege, but they won't last long, and Hroldenfell will have provisions inside," Aelric said with confidence in his voice. And they would. All the settlements that had been coming through had taken everything they had with them. When they had gone to the city, there would be plenty of food, livestock, warriors, blacksmiths, and craftsmen to keep the city armed and working.

Now, the Lysandrians were stupid if they thought they were going to win this. But still, it wasn't exactly as if Valfric and his friends could just walk up to the city gates and walk in.

He thought, *We're going to need to find a place to lay low until we can either sneak into the city, or we'll have to find a way of helping them.*

"Assuming that the folks from our settlement are even there," Thraindel said.

"True," Valfric conceded. "If we can find someplace that the legions aren't going to bother us, I can send some hawks over and see what I can find."

Everyone nodded, and they went back down the mountain. They kept well clear of any paths in the area and found a deep thicket near a cliff face where they could make camp. Valfric didn't think the smoke from a fire would carry very far, but they would still need to be careful about it. Just because the legions were focused on the city didn't mean that they wouldn't have scouts in the area, and while Valfric was confident in their ability to take care of any scouts, he didn't care to be ambushed. They had learned their lesson about underestimating small units of Lysandrian soldiers.

The sun was beginning to set as their camp was built and finished. Valfric closed his eyes and felt his Essaeris. He created a couple of hawks that flew off into the area, going high above them.

"I'll see if I can find anybody we know there," Valfric said, "and get an idea of what the city's situation looks like," he added.

His mind moved into one of the hawks. It flew high in the air, moving toward the city. As it moved closer, Valfric could see just how much the Lysandrians had built, and he didn't voice it, but he felt a little amazed. *They couldn't have only been here for a few days,* he thought, yet already he could see so much. There were four forts, or at least they appeared to be forts, that were on the outside of the city. Two of them looked to have been pretty complete and advanced, with a third that was far along and a fourth that mostly consisted of just walls and trenches. He could see men scurrying around, adding to the fortress.

They looked like the base that they had seen the legion at a while back. The hawk moved in closer, making out some of the banners, and he realized it was indeed the same legion. Then it hit him. This camp looked exactly the same way that the other one they had seen looked, though the one they had seen before seemed to have been more advanced. At the time, Valfric had assumed the Lysandrians were building a fort in the area or some other kind of permanent structure, but they had burned it and destroyed it when they had left.

Now he felt a small pit in his stomach as he began to realize that they hadn't been seeing a permanent base, but just a temporary one, just a camp.

And if the progress he was seeing on the other camps was any indication for the future, those camps would just get stronger and stronger as time went on.

The hawk banked, moving toward the city. As it got closer to the city walls, he could see it. They were full of people. Some of them were in makeshift tent camps along the wall's edge, and others filled up the rest of the streets.

The hawk was assaulted by the scent of smoke and livestock as it flew over, though it didn't appear that the city had been attacked or even harassed at all. He could make out the forms of men and women along the walls, keeping watch.

The hawk dipped down and looked around. After what felt like an eternity, it was over a section of tents, and he caught the first glimpse of someone he knew.

"I see Durnara," Valfric said to the others. He pulled himself back into his body. "Durnara's down there, and you know that means the rest of the settlement is as well."

The others took this news to be good. They all smiled and nodded.

"Well, then I guess we know we're in a good spot," Thraindel said. "I take it you're not seeing any easy ways into the city?"

"No, not yet," Valfric said. He was about to speak when he felt something from his hawk. His mind moved into it. It was tumbling in the air and registering damage on one of its wings.

"What the fuck," Valfric said softly.

And then he saw another hawk, though this one was not one of his. It closed in and grabbed onto Valfric's hawk's wings. The hawk twisted in the air, trying to attack the other one, and Valfric's Essaerite registered another one on its other wing. The two birds pulled, ripping Valfric's hawk into pieces.

"What the fuck is this?" he said. "Dammit, they have Essaerists checking the air!"

And then a moment later, his other hawk registered an attack. He didn't bother connecting with it and just released it instead.

He huffed and looked over at the others. "Put out the fire," he said.

They did so quickly and looked at him, concerned.

"They attacked your hawks?" Ilara asked. "No one's ever done that before," she said, her voice filled with concern.

Valfric gritted his teeth and shook his head. "No, no one has ever done that before. I'm amazed they're even thinking to look for it," he said, and then huffed. "I suppose we shouldn't be surprised; we know that there's Essaerists with the legions."

Aelric spoke, his voice grim, "That could make this more interesting."

Valfric nodded. "Yes, that's one way of putting it." He sat down and thought, "I don't think we're going to be able to get into Hroldenfell."

Aelric said that he agreed, and Ilara asked, "Then what are we going to do?"

After a moment of thought, he shrugged and said, "We deal with the Lysandrian supply lines. If we can keep a decent distance away from the city, we shouldn't have to worry about the Essaerists. I'm sure they're going to be focused on the city, and I suppose we knew this was going to happen. There was an Essaerist in that group that we attacked, so this is what it's going to be. They're not going to be able to take Hroldenfell, so we hit their supply lines. We make it so the Lysandrians have to leave."

The others nodded their agreement, and Valfric sighed. And here he thought their luck was changing. After all, the morning had gone so well.

CHAPTER 38

Mariokos stood at a drafting table, looking out of the tent at the city before them. The tent was situated on top of a platform outside the city's counter fortifications. In front of them was a wall, and on the other side of that wall was a trench. The tent opened up, allowing the engineers to supervise the work from a distance.

The head of the Legion's engineers was an older gentleman named Aresio. He had been in the Legion for years. Mariokos respected him, and Aresio seemed to respect Mariokos as well. Presently, they were looking at the Legion's progress.

They had made several probing attacks on the city, but nothing more than to harass or gain information. The real work was still ongoing. Leading up to the city walls—or almost to the city walls—the Legion had been building a ramp that was covered in timber and stone as it got closer to the city. It provided the legionnaires protection as they continued to build.

As they had gotten closer to the city, archers had begun firing upon the ramp but hadn't been able to do much damage. It appeared that Hroldenfell did not have any dedicated siege weapons like catapults inside that they could use to hurl something heavier at the ramps, which had made everyone's lives easier. Well, except for the residents of Hroldenfell—for them, that was just poor planning.

Mariokos looked down at the table, seeing plans that had been drawn up. "Alright, so how soon do you think you'll be ready for me to send up my Essaerithon?"

Aresio, inspected the plans for a moment. "Soon, I think. That ramp we're building doesn't have a very tall roof on it, but your Essaerithon should be able to make it through."

"And once it gets up to the top, you want me to start tunneling?" Mariokos asked.

Aresio nodded. "Yes."

The man moved a piece of paper and pulled out another one that showed schematics for just how Mariokos was to tunnel. The idea was relatively straight-forward. Mariokos's Essaerithon would begin digging mostly ahead of itself, moving toward the city. The goal was for it to get underneath the main wall and then dig tunnels along that wall.

As that happened, workers and Essaerites would be fortifying the tunnel, giving it supports with timbers so the tunnel would not collapse. At least, it wouldn't collapse yet. Once they had a wide enough section of tunnels built, engineering teams would set the internal supports on fire, and as they burned, the tunnel would cave in, bringing down a section of the wall. A section that was more than large enough for the Legion to go through.

Simultaneously, work crews would continue working on the exterior, building the ramp closer and closer to the wall. This would give legionnaires a straight shot into the city. Once an initial force had captured the surrounding areas, others would begin the march up the hill to take the rest of the city.

The rub was going to be the makeup of the mountain and if the Gwenthari had any Essaerists in the city that would be able to counter them. From what they had experienced so far, they did know that Essaerists were in the area as they had attacked some scouting hawks early on, but they hadn't seen a lot since then. There were likely some Essaerists in Hroldenfell. The question would be whether they would be listening to the ground or know what the legionnaires were planning to do. If they did, it could get interesting for Mariokos, or at least for his Essaerites. If they were met with a counter tunnel and Gwenthari troops pushing them out, it might give the Legion a way into the city, but more than likely, it would just allow the Gwenthari the opportunity to clog up the tunnels and otherwise make it so that they couldn't use that route for entry.

He would have to hope that that wouldn't be the case. It would also mean that he would have to be smart and slow about what he did. This was something he decided to voice to Theoliano, who was also with them while they did this.

"I'm going to have to make sure I'm going slow and not making too much racket down there," Mariokos said.

Theoliano looked at him. "People will be able to hear you down there?"

Mariokos gave a noncommittal shrug. "Depends on what kind of Essaerist are in town. If they have rats or moles in little tunnels underneath the city, which is something that I would do, then they're certainly going to hear us digging, especially because that ramp they're already seeing right now is going to make it pretty obvious where we're going," he explained.

Theoliano thought about it for a moment and sighed. "I'll tell command, but it's not going to change the plan."

"No, it shouldn't change the plan at all, but I'm just warning you, we're not going to be able to fly through this." Mariokos looked up at the mountain. "Plus, I don't think that terrain will be easy to dig through."

Theoliano barked a laugh. "Of that, I have no doubt. The land in this area has been a bitch to try to work in."

"Yes," one of the engineers said, "I suspect that's why they abandon places like this. There's no farming here."

Mariokos shook his head. "My wife said something along those lines. She said that these cities used to be popular, but they required raiding, and they pushed resources too far, so people left. They moved to more fertile lands."

"I'm sure they did," Theoliano said. He looked to Mariokos. "When are you going to get started?"

Mariokos kept looking up at the mountain. "I'll get started today. I want to walk up that ramp and see what we're looking at to make sure that my Essaerithon can make it in, and then I'll create it, and we'll start tunneling."

Theoliano gave a curt nod. "Report back to me when you have more."

"I will," Mariokos said.

A short time later, he found himself at the entrance to the ramp that was heading up the side of the mountain. He walked with some of the engineers, being cast in darkness. There were torches lit along the walls, but otherwise, there was little in the way of light. As Mariokos walked, he looked around, making sure there was enough clearance for his Essaerithon. He could tell they were getting closer to the city as he could hear the occasional bang or hit against the roof or side of the tunnel.

"We're close to the city now, I take it," he asked one of the engineers.

"Yes," the man said, "we're very close. Right up here, you can see the area we're going to need you to start working in."

They walked up a ways further, and Mariokos saw an opening ahead of him, a spot where they were still building walls and a roof.

This was where most of the danger lay. At the opening were legionnaires holding their shields up, providing cover for other legionnaires who were engaged in construction. Mariokos got closer to the entrance and poked his head out, looking up. Above him, he could see men and women on the walls, throwing rocks and shooting arrows down at them. He came back into the tunnel and looked over at the engineer.

"This is where you want me to start digging?" he asked.

The engineer nodded. "A little ways back, actually," he said. "How far in do you need to be before we can go back to working on this ramp?"

Mariokos surveyed the area. "Once I get partway in, there's going to be a lot of dirt coming out of here. I would recommend halting the progress of the ramp until we have everything tunneled out underneath here. Then we can put some wood over it for the legionnaires to walk on."

The engineer nodded. "Thought you might say something like that. Very well. Give me an hour to get this area sealed up, and then it's all yours."

Mariokos went back down the ramp and behind the main counter fortification wall. He closed his eyes and reached inside himself, controlling his breathing, feeling his power well up. He had been holding it in reserve all day, knowing that this task was about to start. Part of him looked forward to being able to taunt and tease Xavieno about how it would be Mariokos who would truly be responsible for bringing down Hroldenfell. After all, it would be his Essaerithon—and Essaerites—that would do the bulk of the work bringing down the wall, not one of Xavieno's. Not that Mariokos actually saw it as a competition, but he knew that Xavieno did, and he was looking forward to getting under his skin.

The energy built inside him, and it came rippling out. In front of him, his Essaerithon formed. Its exterior was black and leathery-looking. He created a few other smaller Essaerites and changed the underneath of the Essaerithon to be able to push out more dirt as it dug and moved. As he finished his inspection of it, the engineers returned, saying that Mariokos was good to do his thing.

He sent it up the ramp. It passed by men who looked at it with slight amazement, and he noted that many of the men working on this section were not part of his legion but part of one of the other legions that didn't have Essaerists with them. As it got to its designated spot, Mariokos turned to Aresio.

"You're going to need to have men in there to pull out dirt as this thing digs," he said.

"We're already on it," Aresio said.

Mariokos could see lines of legionnaires holding shovels and buckets, waiting for the task. Mariokos's mind moved into that of his Essaerithon, and with a thought, it drove its shovel teeth into the ground. They didn't go in as deep as one would have hoped. They struck a large rock with a clang. The Essaerithon began moving around, digging around, exposing more and more of the rock. Its teeth came down again with another clang. A chunk of rock fell off. It dug around some more, and Mariokos sent some other smaller Essaerites into the space to clear out some debris around it. He sighed, and Aresio looked at him.

"Already found a big rock, that's all," Mariokos said.

Aresio grunted, not surprised.

His Essaerithon couldn't move past the enclosed space it was in unless it wanted to destroy what the legionnaires had already built and also deal with all of the Gwenthari firing on it and probably destroying it. While they had stayed inside the city, Mariokos had no doubt that the second they saw an Essaerithon digging around their wall, they would send out men. And while it was tough, it wasn't *that* tough.

So instead, he had to use his smaller Essaerites to dig around the rock while using the larger one to help out. It took him roughly an hour to clear out the first stone. The Essaerithon gripped onto the giant rock and pulled it down the ramp. It was too large to move past the Essaerithon, and Mariokos found it unlikely that it would be faster to have the legionnaires try to move it out of the way.

The Essaerithon came out of the tunnel with the giant rock and rolled it over to the side. It moved back up the ramp and started digging around the space that the rock had just cleared. There were more giant rocks that it brought down, but he hadn't found any other *big* ones yet. Still, his Essaerithon chewed through the ground carefully and slowly, the clay making it hard and the rock slowing it down.

Again, it found another giant rock. Mariokos huffed. It began trying to dig around, seeing where the rock ended. After a bit, he groaned. He pulled himself back into his body and looked over at Aresio.

"This one's bigger. We're going to have to go through it," he said.

The engineer looked concerned. "How long?"

Mariokos thought for a moment. "Depends on how big it is. Some of those Essaerites up there that I have that are smaller are good masons, or can be, I should say. I'll have them start digging through it, breaking up what they can. The larger one will help them. But this is not going to be quick."

And quick it wasn't. Mariokos worked for a few more hours before they finally made it through the rock and began digging again. He felt happy until a few minutes later when they found another one.

———

CAELWEN SAT ON THE GROUND WITH HER LEGS TUCKED BENEATH HER. HER EYES WERE closed, and she focused solely on her breathing—the cool air entering through her nose and escaping gently from her mouth. She inhaled, counting to herself, then exhaled for the same rhythmic count. With each cycle of breath, she could sense her Essaeris stirring within.

Exhaling deeply, a steel cube materialized on the ground before her. As Caelwen's eyes fluttered open, they fell upon the cube.

Beside her, Fioralba sat closely observing the scene. Curled up in Fioralba's lap, Treftune slumbered soundly, oblivious to the world around him. A smirk tugged at the corner of Caelwen's lips. "Traitor," she mused silently.

Fioralba, picking up the newly crafted cube, studied it intently. "Better," she remarked, a hint of approval in her voice. "Much better. But work on the internal structure of the metal," she advised. "You're getting close."

Caelwen received a cube of metal from Fioralba. With her powers, Caelwen sensed the subtle nuances distinguishing Fioralba's metal from her own. Fioralba then handed Caelwen a cube of authentic metal. Holding a cube in each hand, Caelwen closed her eyes once more, reaching out with her abilities.

Touching the real metal, she found she could perceive its very makeup, its intricate construction. Before this moment, she would have sworn her creation was indistinguishable from the genuine thing. Now, however, discerning her work from the authentic cube revealed minute differences. Yet, comparing Fioralba's metal to the real one, they seemed identical, except for the latent Essaeris Caelwen could detect in Fioralba's cube—it had details she had initially deemed trivial, but now it irked her ceaselessly.

All her past creations, once perceived as flawless, were now subject to her scrutinizing doubt.

Still, she was grateful for Fioralba and her time. Mariokos and Xavieno had also worked with her, and she'd found all of their lessons to be helpful. She had assumed they would start working with her on some advanced techniques that she had never heard of before, but they hadn't. They had focused entirely on basic principles and concepts. She had flown through much of the training at the beginning as they were just looking for holes in her abilities, but with each thing she learned that was basic and fundamental to them, she found some little gap that she was missing, or she found some workaround that she'd come up with that was actually hindering her in some way.

She was getting better, and she could feel it, and that part made her happy. But she could also see just how outclassed she was by Lysandrian Essaerists, though she suspected that wouldn't last long.

Caelwen closed her eyes and made another block of metal. This one was closer.

"Do you feel the differences now?" Fioralba asked.

Caelwen nodded, looking over at her. "I can feel them," she said.

"What do you feel?" Fioralba asked.

Caelwen thought. "Mine aren't complete," she said in realization. "It's like they're partially created, but not completely created."

Fioralba smiled. "Exactly. That's a big part of it. When we finish creating something, it doesn't take as much Essaeris to keep around, right?"

Caelwen nodded. "Yes. And some of that Essaeris we use to create goes back in us."

"In this way, the better you are at creating these foundational items, the more efficient you will be, which means you can create more complicated items or create a lot more of them," Fioralba said.

Caelwen understood this principle, or she thought she understood it, but she was beginning to realize that she didn't quite understand it the way Fioralba meant it. But she was starting to. The reason why they put so much effort into creating basic raw materials was so that they had much more reserves to do something else.

The sun was starting to set, and Caelwen heard people approaching. She looked and smiled, seeing Mariokos coming over to them. She stood and walked over to him, and Treftune joined her. Treftune ran up the side of his tunic and onto his shoulder, and to Mariokos's credit, he just petted the little creature and walked up to Caelwen. She put her hands on his chest and looked up into his face.

"You look tired," she said.

He smiled, and she felt his hands on her hips.

"I am extremely tired," he said, "and frustrated."

He leaned down and kissed her. His lips were salty and warm, and she kissed him back, feeling herself press against him. As she broke the kiss, she looked back up at him.

"What has you frustrated?" she asked.

He made a sour face. "Just digging through this fucking mountain. How's your training going?" he asked, his voice softer.

She led him over to where Fioralba was sitting, and Mariokos greeted her.

"We're working on cubes," Caelwen said.

She picked up her cube and handed it to Mariokos. She could feel him examining it with his Essaeris, but it wasn't something that she disliked. After a moment, he nodded in approval.

"You're learning, and you're learning quickly. Are you trying to make us all look bad?" he asked playfully.

She smirked. "I mean, it's not like it's that hard... well, other than Fioralba," she commented.

Fioralba stood up and laughed. "The woman speaks truth, Mariokos. What can I say?"

Mariokos rolled his eyes. "Wonderful. I still don't know if I like the idea of you two spending the day together plotting against Xavieno and I."

Fioralba grinned. "It doesn't take up too much time. After all, it is pretty easy to outsmart the dim-witted."

Caelwen smiled, and soon Xavieno joined them. They worked on cooking dinner together, and Mariokos and Xavieno spent a little time working with Caelwen until the sun was down and they were all sitting around the fire.

Caelwen was tired in a way that she wasn't used to. It was more mental than anything else, but she could also feel the strains on her Essaeris. Her reserves were depleted, but it felt nice in a way because they weren't depleted from exhaustion of necessity. They were depleted from work.

As they sat around talking, Caelwen asked how progress was going.

"It's fine," Mariokos said. "It's just a lot of rocks and clay that we're digging through. How about you, Xavieno?"

"Mostly patrols. We haven't seen any more Essaerites that we've had to take out of the air," he said. "But that doesn't mean that there's none around. I'd be surprised if there's not a handful of Essaerists in that city."

Caelwen nodded. "I agree, it's very unlikely that there isn't, but I don't think there's as many as you might think."

"Why is that?" Xavieno asked.

"Hroldenfell is a fort, and it's a city, but it's not a major one," she said after a moment. "In those, you'll find more Essaerists. But out here, they're very dependent upon trade. The city really only does well at the beginning of the year when people are going out of their minds with boredom and need some place to trade, and towards the end of the year when they're coming to sell crops and other things."

"So it's not a big hub year-round, is what you're saying," Xavieno said.

She shook her head. "No. But some of the other cities will be. And thank you all again for helping train me. I really appreciate it, and I hope to be able to help you out soon," she said.

She felt Mariokos give her a squeeze.

"Of course. We're happy to do it," he said.

Xavieno nodded, and Fioralba smiled.

"I'm sure you will help us at some point, and you are more than welcome," Xavieno said.

Caelwen thought for a moment, looking over at Fioralba. "I could help you now, I suppose. You've been teaching me. I could teach you."

Fioralba cocked an eyebrow. "Of course, I would love to learn some of the Gwenthari techniques for Essaeris."

Caelwen shook her head. "No, not those. I'm happy to teach you those as well, but they're just things I figured out on my own. But I mean how to fight," she said.

There was silence for a moment. And then Fioralba started chuckling.

"You want to teach me how to fight?" she asked incredulously.

Caelwen shrugged. "Why not? I mean, after all, at some point in time, if you run into problems, it might be handy knowing how to do it. Not to the same level as Mariokos or Xavieno, obviously, or even myself, if you didn't want, but that way you would know something."

Fioralba didn't look convinced. "I'm fine. But thank you. I do appreciate the offer."

Caelwen was considering pushing the subject when she felt Mariokos touch her back softly. She glanced over at him, and his eyes gave an almost imperceptible back-and-forth movement. She chose not to push the subject any further, but still wanted to.

Later, when she was back in her tent with Mariokos, she asked, "Why did you stop me from telling Fioralba to fight or learn how to do it? I'm sorry. Did I overstep?"

Mariokos shook his head. "No, you didn't overstep," he said. "In fact, I agree with you, and I think Xavieno does, too. I could see it in his face."

"So then why'd you stop me?" she asked.

"Because Fioralba's stubborn as any mule out there," he said. "If she digs in her heels, she's not going to do anything or listen to anyone. Xavieno will convince her, I think."

"Why won't she want to do it?" Caelwen asked, sitting down on the cot.

Mariokos sat next to her. He placed his hand on her leg. It was a warm, nice feeling.

"Well, Fioralba doesn't like violence. That you already know. But also, Lysandrian women don't, strictly speaking, learn combat. Even Essaerists. And it's a little bit of a social thing. She won't be looked down upon for it, but she's not likely to do it. Fioralba does care about appearances a bit."

"I'm sure she would care a lot more about dying and not being able to defend herself from it," Caelwen said.

Mariokos smiled. "I agree with you. And I think it's dumb that we don't at least give the people out here in the support staff a little bit of help. And

Essaerists especially," he leaned over and kissed her cheek. "It was a good idea. And I think you're the perfect person to teach her."

She smirked. "Why is that? Is it because I'm a small, frail female?"

He laughed. "There's nothing frail about you," he said good-naturedly. "But you are pretty small. You're very short."

She hit his arm. "You like that I'm short."

He grinned. "I do. But I also think that you'll be good for a couple of reasons. One, you're another woman, so she's going to feel more comfortable with you. And two, you are much more similar in size and stature to Fioralba than Xavieno and I. And from what I've seen and experienced of Gwenthari fighting, it's not the same kind of fighting that the Legion does. We do a lot of one-on-one combat, but we spend a lot of time in formations and learning how to fight that way. Your people aren't that. They're brawlers." He said honestly. "I don't mean to sound offensive with that."

She considered what he'd said and shook her head. "You're not being offensive about that at all. We are. We put a lot of focus on the abilities of the individual warrior, not so much about the group."

"Which is why you would be perfect for her," he said.

She smiled. "I'm glad you think so."

———

FIORALBA FELT XAVIENO ROLL OFF OF HER. SHE ROLLED ON HER SIDE AND SIGHED, LAYING her head on Xavieno's chest. His fingers were running through her hair in the most relaxing and delightful way possible. Cool air kissed her skin, cooling it. She kissed his chest and looked up at him.

"That was nice," she said.

He smiled and looked down at her, kissing her. "I could say the same thing to you. I married very well," he said in a teasing tone.

She smiled. "I'm glad you think so."

"Speaking of marrying well, it looks like Caelwen and Mariokos are doing very well," she said.

He smiled again. "They really are. They seem so much more natural together after just a few weeks than he and Biankara did after months."

Fioralba laughed. "That they do. Gods, I'm relieved about it though, aren't you?"

"You have no idea," he said.

"And you and she seem to be getting along pretty well as well," he said.

She shifted in his arms. "We are. She's different, to be sure. She's much more pragmatic and blunt than most Lysandrians are, but I like her. With Caelwen, you know exactly where you stand with her. She's very talented as an Essaerist. I could see her and I becoming good friends," she said with a smile. "And she's funny."

Xavieno raised an eyebrow. "Yeah? What's funny about her?"

Fioralba giggled. "Fighting? Tonight? Come on," she said. "It's sweet that she thinks I should learn how to fight, but also a little scary too. I can only imagine what it was like for her growing up as a Gwenthari. In so many ways, they are barbarians, though I have a hard time seeing Caelwen that way."

"Somehow, I don't think Caelwen would fault you for thinking of her as a barbarian," he said. "She seems to not mind what people's opinions of her are." And then he paused and said, "but her idea isn't that bad."

She looked at her husband, surprised, and then she laughed. "You almost had me for a minute."

He got serious. He sat up a little bit in the bed. "I am being serious."

She frowned. "You really want me to learn how to fight? Xavieno, you can't—" She started, but he held up a hand.

"Look, I don't think you should be on the front lines of any legion," he said. And then paused. "But she's not wrong. Look, before we came up here, I would have said otherwise. But we've seen enough action to know that it doesn't matter if you're a man or a woman or if you're young or old. You can die just the same. And you're my wife. I love you. And I worry about you."

"You don't have to worry about anything," Fioralba countered. "I'm in the support caravan, and I'm in the center of the camp all the time. If something were to happen to me, it would mean the legion lost."

He sighed. "I know. But still. The thought of you not being able to defend yourself," he said, "I know you could create an Essaerite, but if that Essaerite doesn't know what it's doing..."

She could see the concern on his face, and it made her heart soften a bit. She sighed. "Would it really make you feel better if I learned a thing or two?"

He looked at her, his expression soft, and he nodded, "yes."

She sighed again. She reached out and caressed his cheek. "How can I say no to a face like that?" she said. "Fine. I will learn a few things, but this is not what I'm going to spend the bulk of my time doing."

He smiled. "I'd hope not, but thank you, my love."

She smiled back. "You're welcome."

CHAPTER 39

V alfric was finding the siege of Hroldenfell to be a mixture of successes and failures, though if he was being honest with himself, there were far more failures than successes. At first, his optimism had been high. He'd assumed that they would be able to hinder or stop Lysandrian supply lines, and that at some point, the Lysandrians would leave, but it didn't appear that was going to happen at all. In fact, the opposite was happening.

Valfric and his team had watched as the Lysandrians built more and more around the city of Hroldenfell. They'd constructed a wall around it, with ramps leading up to the city's walls. He had seen a few skirmishes along those walls but nothing major yet. Still, the ramps were ominous. They were covered and armored, giving the soldiers more access to the wall. They hadn't attempted to breach it yet, but Valfric knew it was only a matter of time until they would. And then the question remained: what would happen then?

So, they had gone into the surrounding area, looking for warriors to help support the city. If they could just crack the Lysandrian supply lines, Valfric knew that they would be able to win. But finding fighters had proven difficult. Most in the area had moved into the city for either protection or to help defend it, leaving the countryside alarmingly empty. There were some settlements and small farming communities out there, but the people there were generally either too old to fight or far too young to do so. He'd also discovered that many of them had given supplies to the Lysandrians.

And while he wanted to fight this and rail against it, he knew the people hadn't had choices. That still hadn't stopped him from taking out some frustrations on some people. But it left them not only short on supplies themselves but short on warriors.

They also discovered, after a handful of times they'd harassed locals for supporting the Lysandrians or for not supporting Valfric and his people the way he wanted them to, that they came under Lysandrian pressure. It appeared that the people were all too happy to tell their new conquerors that they were threatened. This, too, angered Valfric. Had these people really fallen that far? He wondered how they had forgotten what they once were, what they were supposed to be.

But he reminded himself that the people of Hroldenfell were different. They had moved there to defend their home, to show the Lysandrians what was coming for them. Those who were helping the Lysandrians or who were still in their farms or villages—those people were cowards, and there was no way to save them. When this whole conflict was said and done, Valfric vowed to himself that he would put those people in their places—that they would become slaves or dead or would just be punished. He wasn't sure how, but he would make sure it happened.

First, he needed to take care of Hroldenfell and to ensure that the city not only didn't fall but won. If they did, he was sure the Lysandrians would turn tail and run back to their empire in the south. And within a few years, his people—Valfric's people—would be raiding those lands.

Perhaps in a generation or so, when they had recovered their numbers, one of Valfric's descendants would go and sack the Lysandrian capital again, proving once and for all that the Gwenthari were more powerful than the Lysandrians. Of course, he had to make that happen first.

He was happy to find that he wasn't the only one in the area who had been harassing Lysandrian supply lines, though he suspected that much of the harassment from other groups was just for personal gain. He had seen raiding parties that were Ulfgarath, but he'd also seen plenty that were Valfarans and Wulfharboria. And while he hated the Wulfharborias, he couldn't argue with them raiding Lysandrian supply lines, though he'd also seen several of those Wulfharboria groups move towards the legions to work as mercenaries for them.

So Valfric's team had been raiding daily. They didn't keep much of what they took. They only kept food and any supplies they might need. For the most part, Valfric and his people burned whatever supplies they were able to capture, which was difficult to do. In the early days when he had been raiding Lysandrian territories, there'd been little in the way of guards for caravans. Now merchant trains had not only grown but had more guards with them. That made his life difficult. It meant having to be cunning about what they were doing and having to pick off wagons and caravans that were either small or had fallen behind a larger group.

On occasion, they would hit something at night. For him, it was easier because he had his Essaerites he could use, and the team was relying on those Essaerites more and more. His wolves could get closer and could kill animals or people in the middle of the night. It wasn't the great victory that he was hoping for, but he knew it was wearing them down. And with each attack that the legions found out about, the more soldiers they had to send out to defend the territory. That was soldiers they were losing for building whatever it was they were constructing on those ramps and for being able to attack the city.

This made the whole enterprise worth it, in Valfric's opinion. The group he was with was around fifteen strong, so nothing that could take on a large caravan, but they could make quick work of a smaller one. The missions had become fairly routine and templated. They would attack, hit hard, take anything they might need, and kill everybody in the caravan. There was no time to savor and enjoy the moment. They weren't able to take the time to enjoy killing, or making people suffer, or to take slaves, or any gold or silver. No, this was all about making it harder for the Lysandrians.

Also, what they had started doing was if anyone came to defend the caravan, Valfric and his team would leave. They wouldn't engage any cavalry that were coming to assist, or any ground troops either. On occasion, they would see Wulfharboria mercenaries who were working with the legions. Most of the time, they'd be on horseback. And then Valfric and his people would flee. Oftentimes, the party would split up, going in different directions, and then rendezvous back at a designated point to decide what their next move was going to be.

If someone did not make it back to camp fast enough, the camp moved. They had learned that this had to be something they needed to do the hard way, as several people had been captured and tortured during this whole affair. It had led to a few close encounters with their camp almost being ambushed by Lysandrian troops. So now they had this system in place. Back at their camp, everything was ready to go. They couldn't be too careful.

And while he hated it, part of him thrilled at it. They had failed more over the last little while than he had in his entire life, and in a way, it had made him feel so much more alive than he had throughout most of his life. It was exhilarating. He went from being the best to occasionally being the hunted.

Today, as so many days had started, Valfric was hiding in a clump of trees as he watched a caravan moving down the road.

It was a large merchant caravan that had many guards, and Valfric had zero intention of attacking it. At best, they could piss off the guards, and at worst, they would all die. Not the guards, that is, but Valfric and his people. So they waited patiently to see if there were any stragglers that would fall behind. If he was lucky, there would be. As the caravan moved, he saw dust kicked up from the animals and people. He counted the wagons, trying to figure out what might be in them.

Next to him lay Ilara, Thraindel, and Aelric.

"What do you think they're bringing in?" Ilara asked conversationally.

Valfric shrugged. "Probably food," he said. "They haven't gotten in many engagements in Hroldenfell, so I don't see them needing a lot of weapons or shields, but I could be wrong."

He looked over at her. She had a look of boredom. He suspected he shared the same look. This was the boring part of the day, wasn't it? And there was a chance that they wouldn't be able to do anything at all. If the caravan held tight and moved past without any stragglers, and another one didn't come by for the day, they'd be left empty-handed. It wouldn't be the first time, and he suspected it wouldn't be the last.

So he waited and watched. After a while, the caravan passed. As they grew distant, he looked down the road to see if there was anything coming along. He'd stopped using hawks a while ago, as, after the experience over Hroldenfell, he'd realized that any overt use of Essaeris that was out in the open had a chance of being a liability rather than a help.

Thraindel had told him that he was being paranoid, but Aelric and Ilara both agreed with Valfric. There was no reason to risk it. Instead, his scouts had moved over to something more simplistic and easy. There was a rat down the road that was perched on a branch looking ahead. It was unlikely that anyone would be able to spot it. The rat was the same color as the bark, and it hadn't moved in some time.

He supposed he could have had a bird sitting in the branch that would have given him the ability to move things around more, but he thought the rat was still a better call. Things in the air were easy to spot, but their patience appeared to have paid off.

Coming up the road was one last cart. Valfric's mind moved into that of the rat, and he looked at the cart. It seemed to be laden with heavy jugs and pots. It likely was full of olive oil. The Lysandrians imported a lot of it from back down in the south as rations for their soldiers.

There were a handful of men on the cart, and they looked to be worn and irritated. Valfric could make out one of the wheels. It looked to be damaged, not from a fight necessarily, but probably from hitting a rut in the road. He smiled.

"I think we have our mark," he said.

"What are they?" Aelric asked.

"It's just one cart. Looks like only four or five men are on it, and if I had to guess, the cart got damaged while they were moving. It's kind of wobbling along," he said.

Thraindel grinned. "That would make for a very frustrating day, fixing a cart while you're part of a large caravan. I think it would be wrong of us not to make it so they didn't have to worry about that damaged cart anymore, don't you think?"

Valfric smiled. "That's the polite thing to do, after all."

He sent word down through their group, letting them know that once the cart was in view, they were going to hit it. This would be one of their standard smash-and-grab jobs. Valfric enjoyed the oil that the Legion imported, but he had more than enough of it. And while it wasn't likely that the loss of some jugs of olive oil would stop the Legion hard in its tracks, it would make life more irritating for the Legionnaires. And sometimes that's the best you could hope for in a day.

So he waited. He had four large wolves that he had created for the task, and he had enough Essaeris and reserves to be able to heal them or to create any other small ones that he needed. This had also been a change. In the past, he had always spent as much power as possible at any given time, and he never thought about the prospect of having to repair his Essaerites once a fight began. But he learned better after their encounter with the other Gwenthari Essaerist, and most certainly after their encounter with the Wulfharboria and Lysandrian Essaerists.

That would not be an experience that he would forget any time soon. And he hoped to have the opportunity to repay those Essaerists at some point in his life, especially the Wulfharboria. He hated the Lysandrian one too, but that man was just doing his job. He was part of the Legion and was doing what he was supposed to do. Valfric didn't like the Lysandrians, but he could respect somebody who was doing what their duty was supposed to be. But for that Wulfharboria Essaerist, she was going to pay. She had turned her back on her own people and was helping the enemy, and in Valfric's opinion, there was no coming back from that.

He wondered if he would see her again. He suspected at some point he would or would have the opportunity to find her. No doubt she and her people were now mercenaries for the Lysandrians, which would mean that she would be in some battle. If the Lysandrians left after they lost at Hroldenfell, he suspected that she would try to go back to her homelands. And he would find her. He would find all of them that helped the Lysandrians. Every mercenary that was Gwenthari would pay for their treachery.

The cart was fully in view now, being pulled by two horses. Valfric gave the word, and he stood and mounted his horse. He charged out of the woods along with everyone else. His wolves darted ahead of him, running up to the horses. Valfric and his people covered the short open space between the woods and the road quickly. As they neared, they saw surprise and shock on the men's faces. And then they smiled. Why would they smile, he wondered.

The large pile of jugs and urns full of oil vanished. In their place, they had been covering a type of horror. Valfric felt himself pull the reins on his horse, stopping it. But it was too late. Too many were closer.

Out of the cart stood four Essaerites. They looked like men, but they weren't men. They were taller, and their skin was white like marble. Their eyes were terrifying pitch black. Their legs looked more like wolves', and they had four arms. Before people truly understood what was going on, they leaped off the cart.

"Retreat, run!" Valfric yelled as loud as he could, but it was too late.

Some of the men were already at the cart, and Valfric watched in horror as the Essaerites came down, each holding two blades. His mind seemed to stop for a moment; he could only watch. He wasn't able to move or think or feel or breathe as time slowed. He saw one of the Essaerites' blades lash out, removing a horse's leg. The animal tumbled, and the Essaerites stabbed the man on top of it. A shield appeared in one of the Essaerites' arms, stopping somebody from hitting it with an axe. The next man died.

People were realizing their mistakes, and they were pulling back, prepared to leave. Time came back to Valfric, and he sent his Essaerites to attack the others to distract them, but it appeared they were too late. Men were already falling and dying, and then one of his rats registered something even worse coming from the north. Out of the forest, two massive cats came running toward the caravan, and he felt dread fill his gut. The Wulfharboria Essaerist. She was here, or her Essaerites were.

"Retreat! Retreat!" Valfric was shouting.

So was Aelric. People were starting to back away, and Valfric turned his horse and spurred it on. Next to him, Ilara and Aelric moved, along with Thraindel. An arrow whizzed by them, and Valfric looked back, seeing that one of the white Essaerites was now back on the cart. It had created a bow and was shooting at them. A man dropped. The Essaerite was turning its attention to one of the other groups that was fleeing the area, and Valfric saw others die. His Essaerites were now turning to try and slow down the other Essaerites, trying to give the people some chance at living.

Hating himself for it, he knew he couldn't allow the Essaerites to be engaged for too long. He might need the power. They were almost to the woods now and entering it, and Valfric knew what he needed to do. Again, he felt that hatred. The giant cats were there now, and Valfric had two of his Essaerites attack them, and he had two of the other Essaerites he'd created follow one of the other groups into the forest.

Valfric and his people were crashing through the underbrush. It was whipping against his face and hands, and he looked over to see Ilara, Aelric, and Thraindel. All their faces were pale and shocked.

"How many made it out?" Ilara shouted at him.

Valfric shook his head. "I don't think a lot. I know at least one man from one of the other groups made it into the forest, but there are a few others that are currently being chased."

"Do you have your Essaerites following us?" Aelric asked.

Valfric felt his face flush with shame and rage. He shook his head, and Aelric looked amazed.

"Were they already taken out?" he asked.

Valfric shook his head again. "They'll think that whoever has the Essaerites is the group with the Essaerist."

Aelric got quiet. As realization sank in of what Valfric had done, he'd sacrificed those people. They were almost back to the camp, and as they entered their small camp, Valfric and his were the first to arrive. He got off his horse, as did the others. Thraindel looked at him.

"What do you mean you have your Essaerites following the other groups? What if they come after us?" he said.

"That's why he did it," Aelric said, looking at Valfric. His expression was hard. "You know what you did to them, don't you?"

Valfric felt more shame boil up inside of himself. His expression became rigid and hard, just like Aelric's.

"Yes, I do. I did what I had to do to keep us alive!" he spat.

Ilara and Thraindel looked confused, and Aelric explained.

"They'll think that whoever has the Essaerites is the group with the Essaerist," he said. "Valfric assured those men are going to die."

Ilara looked at him, her expression puzzled. "Valfric, is this true?"

Thraindel also looked surprised.

Valfric looked at all of his friends and then nodded. "Yes, it's true."

Thraindel looked shocked, but not angry. Ilara almost looked disappointed, but Aelric was still giving him that hard look.

"There were two Essaerists there, Aelric. You know how this turns out!" Valfric roared.

Aelric's face turned red, and he spat at the ground. "It doesn't mean that I have to like it!"

Valfric felt his rage boiling up. "And do you think I do? Do you think I like what I did to them?"

Aelric seemed to deflate a little. "I know you didn't. And I want to beat the shit out of you for it. But another part of me wants to hug you because I know what you did for us."

"What did he do?" Thraindel asked.

"He saved our lives," Aelric said. "Two Essaerists? There's no way we would have survived that. That ambush was planned for us."

Valfric nodded. "There's no way it wasn't. Not with two Essaerists."

Ilara swore. "Fuck, so now what? What if some of them live?"

"We go," Valfric said, "but before we do, we change out our saddles and everything we have. They were shooting arrows at us. The other guy who made it away looked like he may have been clipped by one."

"And why would that matter?" Thraindel asked.

"Because they were Essaeris arrows," Valfric said.

"So?" Aelric asked.

"So if they embedded in anything, that Essaerist is going to know exactly where it is. Essaerists can find anything they've made with Essaeris, no matter where it is or how small it is."

He saw Ilara's eyes widen. "And if we have anything on us from that, they'll know exactly how to find where our camp is."

Valfric nodded. "Yes. So we take a couple of the horses that are here, with their gear, and we send the others in a different direction."

"Then what?" Thraindel asked.

"We ride away from here. And after a few days, we can come up with a different plan, but for now, we have to assume those Essaerists were hunting me, and they're not going to give up."

Aelric nodded. "That they won't."

They worked quickly. They gathered what items they could around the camp and put them on a few horses that they had sitting in reserve. Part of Valfric hated the idea of leaving whoever was left to come back to camp to find that they could be going into a trap, but he didn't see any other way around it. So they did what they had to do.

And after only a few minutes, they were back on new horses and heading out of the area. They moved quickly, moving away from Hroldenfell. Valfric turned back and looked at them.

"We'll head away from Hroldenfell for a day or so, and then circle back around to the north," he said.

"Maybe come in on the west side," Aelric said. "If those cats were with them, that's that legion that we saw, and they're on the east side of Hroldenfell."

This seemed like as good a reasoning as any to Valfric, so he nodded his assent.

"To the northwest. If we go back, we come in from the northwest," he said.

They kept riding deeper into the woods away from Hroldenfell. As they rode, Valfric felt ice forming in his gut. He had never had other Essaerists coming after him before.

In the back of his mind, his Essaerites registered that they had company. He moved into their minds, seeing two of the white marbled Essaerites closing in behind them. His Essaerites kept close to the group, and as the group stopped, he had them turn and attack the Essaerites.

As one wolf jumped at one of the Essaerites, it raised a shield, stopping the wolf and sending it sprawling. The other wolf was going for the other Essaerite, but it was caught by a spear from the one the other wolf had been going after. It hooked into the wolf and lifted it into the air, and then a blade came and cut the wolf in half.

The other Essaerite was up on its feet now, but only for a moment before it was kicked to the ground again. It registered bones being broken in its shoulders and legs, and then it looked up to see the Essaerite standing above it, its white marbled skin showing and almost seeming to glow in the light, and then the sword came down and took out the wolf.

Valfric was forced back into his body, and he felt a cold sweat cover him.

How? How could they be that powerful, he wondered, and how were they going to defend against it?

CHAPTER 40

M uch had changed in the month since Mariokos and his legion had come to Hroldenfell. All of the counter-fortifications had long since been completed, and each of the legion's camps was well defined and supplied. Roads in and out of the area had been fortified, widened, and improved, and the city of Hroldenfell was surrounded. A week or so ago, the legion had begun actually attacking the city, moving closer to the side of the mountain until they could use siege weapons to fire on it. This was predominantly in the form of ballistae and catapults. They hadn't done large amounts of damage to the city, but that hadn't really been the point of the attacks. Mariokos knew the purpose of the attacks had been to wear the defenders down, to instill fear and fatigue in the people, and to deplete resources, all in preparation for the real attack, which would be commencing shortly.

It was early in the morning, long before the horns that would wake up the legions and irritate his wife. Mariokos had Essaerites moving up into the tunnels underneath the walls of Hroldenfell. He moved into the mind of one of them and looked around. Above him, he could actually see the foundations for the walls. They were stone and solid, all of them being held up by thick timbers that made a latticework throughout the tunnel.

The work had been just as slow, if not slower, than Mariokos had assumed it would be. The mountain didn't particularly care to be tunneled into, and Mariokos had to remove a lot of rock, dirt, and clay, but the job was done now. A large section of the wall was being held up by the timbers, and from what he could tell, no one in the town was the wiser. They hadn't seen any counter-tunnels dug, with Essaerites or soldiers coming in to defend the wall. It had all been silent. Still, Mariokos had worked very quietly and diligently, making sure that they hadn't been spotted.

On the outside, other ramps had been built up, going directly against other sections of the wall, allowing the Legionnaires to soon make it to the top of the wall without Mariokos's help at all. This was occurring all around the city, and the residents would fire and throw things down on the Legionnaires as they moved and worked, but Mariokos didn't think that the Legion had suffered much in the way of losses yet. He knew that would change once they made it into the city.

The Gwenthari were not to be trifled with, and once it came to close-quarters urban fighting, he had no doubt that many men would lose their lives or be injured. For him, once the main push started, he would be held back, in reserves at best, but most of his energy had been spent on breaking the city. All of his Essaeris had been put into the Essaerites that were around finishing their work, so he probably wouldn't be engaged during the actual fight. He was fine with that. He didn't particularly find battle to be horrifying or negative per se, but it wasn't something that he enjoyed either, and he certainly wouldn't enjoy what would happen to Hroldenfell.

The Emperor had decided that Hroldenfell was going to be a message, and the message was clear. The legions were here to take what they wanted, and they would do whatever was necessary and whatever the Emperor wanted. In this case, it would mean that Hroldenfell would be razed. There would be no deal made that would give them the ability to pay tribute or to somehow work out something with the legion. They wouldn't be able to simply give their fealty to the Empire. No, the people of Hroldenfell would perish or be enslaved. Those were the options they had, and Mariokos felt bad for them.

While he knew the Gwenthari had brought this on themselves with their constant raiding and attacks to the south, he still felt for the people there. Many of them had nothing to do with those raids, and yet they would be paying the price. As he finished the last of his inspections, other Essaerites began coming in, carrying with them tinder of all sorts, some in the form of small wood shavings. Others were dry grass and other flammable materials. They began stacking them and building them around all the supports for the walls.

As they did, they made sure there was plenty of ventilation, and there were holes that had been dug right up almost to the surface near the walls of the city. When the time came for them to burn the structures, Mariokos would have Essaerites inside finish those tunnels to the outside, providing holes that were roughly the size of a man, where air could move in and out, allowing it to stoke the flames. Other Essaerites would stay inside as long as they could, making sure the fire burned correctly and quickly, ensuring that the wall would come down.

As his work wrapped up, he opened his eyes and turned to a messenger who was standing next to him. "It's ready," he said. The legionnaire nodded and left the tent that Mariokos was in to deliver the message that the wall was ready to come down. Mariokos sat and waited patiently for the order to come. It was no surprise to him when men entered the room to give him the order.

However, what did surprise him were some of the men that joined them.

Damianello, Alessandros, and Theoliano were present, but the two that surprised him were Tangelo, who was the senator for their province, and Feliciano, the emperor himself. Mariokos stood and then bowed his head, quickly feeling a jolt of fear at his disrespect. "Dominaro," Mariokos said, feeling his heart race; he chided himself. He should have been standing, waiting at attention for whoever arrived.

"Rise," a deep voice said. Mariokos did so and looked, realizing that for the first time in his life he had heard the voice of the emperor of Lysandrian. The man was older-looking and regal. His armor was beautiful, well-crafted, and expensive. Aides were around him, and he looked at Mariokos, not giving any sign of irritation or pride. His expression was emotionless.

Tangelo was the one to speak. "The wall is ready to come down?"

Mariokos nodded. "Yes, senator. I am ready to start the fires that will bring down the wall of Hroldenfell."

"How long will it take?" the emperor asked.

Mariokos thought quickly, trying to remember back to what the engineers had estimated when they'd come up with the design for him. "It shouldn't take long, Dominaro, maybe an hour or two at the most."

The emperor nodded. "Very well. Begin," he commanded.

Mariokos nodded in return. He turned and went to a brazier, lighting some torches. Essaerites came up to him. They were small and spindly. Each reached out, taking a torch, and then they made their way up the covered ramp that would lead them to the tunnels underneath Hroldenfell. As Mariokos finished lighting the last of the torches and handing it off, he stood and focused deeply, moving into the mind of some of the Essaerites.

The first were inside the tunnels now. They moved carefully to their designated spots and stood waiting. Mariokos's mind slid into other Essaerites that were positioned inside the small holes that would soon emerge from the ground. With a flick of his thoughts, those Essaerites drove metal bars into the dirt and manipulated the debris. Soil cleared away, and soon they were breaking open.

As this happened, Mariokos issued a command, and the Essaerites started the tinder alight. Returning to his own body, he faced the emperor, senator, and general. "It has begun," he reported.

The emperor nodded with approval. "Good. Thank you for your service," he acknowledged, then turned to leave the tent, accompanied by the senator, Damianello, and Alessandros. Theoliano lingered behind, offering Mariokos a proud smile before leaving as well.

As soon as they were gone, Mariokos allowed himself to breathe. He hadn't realized he had been holding his breath the entire time.

He had just interacted with the Emperor. "I hope this works," he murmured to himself.

Checking on the tunnels, he noticed that some of his Essaerites had already succumbed to the flames, which were now raging uncontrollably. Stepping outside of the tent, he saw the smoke building up near the base of the walls.

Gwenthari soldiers on top tried to assess the situation, only to be met with arrows, ballista shots, and catapults from the legions below. Despite the height advantage of the Gwenthari, the legions' primary job was distraction, to keep the enemy from halting the flames, though Mariokos knew they couldn't succeed.

He had strategically planned numerous air holes; some deeper than others. The fire inside the tunnels needed air, and it wouldn't be long before the results showed. Thick black smoke spewed from the holes, and elsewhere, smoke seeped from ground fractures. Inside, every one of his Essaerites was now a victim of the blaze, and those at the tunnel entrances felt the extreme heat. Looking in, they could see nothing but inferno.

Mariokos's estimates had been precise. Within two hours, the tunnels started to collapse. He watched the wall shift as the underground structure failed. Ground broke around it, spewing more smoke and flames. Then a vast portion of the wall came crashing down.

Mariokos watched as the once formidable barricade crumbled forward in defeat, its chunks tumbling down the slopes toward the retreating legions.

As the wall came down, he heard horns blare. The time for the attack had come.

———

ONE OF VALFRIC'S ESSAERITES WAS THE FIRST TO SPOT IT. HE HAD MOVED BACK TO USING hawks, though he kept them very far away from Hroldenfell and high in the air, giving him a general view of what was going on in the city. He hadn't dared send any others above the city since the first day. Their raiding activities had resumed after a short period, but it had proven not to be extremely fruitful. It had been a frustrating endeavor, and he could see the hit to morale among his people. They had picked up a handful of others in the area who had once been part of raiding parties that had either been scattered or destroyed, along with a few people from the north who had come to see what was going on in Hroldenfell and to lend assistance.

The hawk saw pillars of smoke along Hroldenfell's wall, and he risked edging closer to the city. He went over to his people.

"Something's going on," he said, worried.

Aelric looked up at him, concerned. "What?"

"There's smoke along the wall," he said.

Aelric stood, as did Thraindel and Ilara.

"There's a peak we should be able to see the city from," Valfric said.

Valfric nodded and got on his horse. They rode up the side of the sheer mountain they were on and made it to the top. At the top, they could see for miles around them, including the city of Hroldenfell. Smoke was rising high in the sky now, making a smudge above the city.

"Fuck, what is that?" Thraindel said next to him.

Valfric moved into his hawk, which could go much closer and see much better than any of them could.

"It looks like the wall is coming down." He couldn't hide the horror in his voice. "Fuck, how did they?" And then he saw another section come down. It appeared to almost be falling into the ground as it fell.

"They dug tunnels underneath," Valfric said almost to himself.

"They did what?" Thraindel asked.

"Tunnels. There's tunnels underneath the wall. They must have been having them held up by something; it's burning. Fuck. A huge section of wall just came down," he said.

The hawk was moving in closer. Valfric didn't care if it was at risk. He had to know what was going on. As it got closer, he felt his heart pump faster with dread. Columns of soldiers were moving up ramps along the side of the mountain. As they got closer to the walls, he saw them engage with the citizens of Hroldenfell. But the legions didn't slow. They had been watching for days now, as the legions had made attacks on the walls and the city. Each time they had attacked, they had backed away. He had thought that it was because they were afraid of the people of Hroldenfell, but that had been wrong. They had just been probing attacks. He could see that now. He could see it because the legions moved forward, unstoppable and unfazed by everything that the people threw at them. They came to the break in the wall, and Valfric watched as warriors from inside the city came spilling out in full armor.

"The fight is happening," Valfric said.

The people clashed with the legionnaires, who created a line. Like an unstoppable wall, they crashed into the Gwenthari defenders of Hroldenfell.

The legions stopped moving forward with the onslaught. They pressed against the people of Hroldenfell. And Valfric watched on, unable to do anything. Even if he had Essaerites that could fight, they could never reach the city in time, and even if they tried to, they'd be stopped at one of the camps.

He saw those white Essaerites that he'd seen before at the forefront of the fight. There were six of them. They wound through the Gwenthari in the area, stabbing and killing, and throwing them about. It was awe-inspiring in so many ways, but horrifying at the same time. There was another one too; it was large with blades on the front cutting through people.

The legion was also killing, and Valfric could see now the only reason why the front had stopped wasn't because the legion was being pushed back, but because they had a seemingly never-ending line of Gwenthari men and women coming up to kill.

The legion slowly started to move forward, and Valfric watched, his blood running cold as the legion made it to the break in the wall, and then they were inside. Once they were inside, the slow-moving formation seemed to stop. People were scattering, and the legionnaires began moving quickly.

Valfric's voice was heavy and thick. "They've breached the wall."

He pulled back into himself and looked over at his friends. They looked concerned, but still somehow optimistic. Thraindel smiled.

"I bet they're paying for that," Thraindel said.

Valfric shook his head. "No, they're not. They're losing."

"The legion's losing?" Aelric confirmed.

Valfric looked at him. "The people of Hroldenfell."

He moved back into the eyes of the hawk, seeing what was going on. The legionaries were spilling into the city now, and as they did, they were killing as they went. He saw buildings start to burn. The legionaries would set torches on them, starting their roofs on fire, or the interiors. He saw men, women, and children jump out of windows or run out of doors on fire.

Realization dawned on him. "Ulfgara," Valfric said, "they're going to raze the city."

The legions were moving through. As they came to people, even unarmed ones who held up their hands, the legionaries fell on them, beating them, killing them, stabbing them, throwing them into the burning buildings still alive.

He moved back out of the eyes of the hawk, seeing that the greasy smear of smoke coming from the city was growing as more of it was lit on fire. He shook his head.

All they could do was watch. They couldn't do anything to stop it.

He moved back into the hawk's eyes, seeing as the carnage spread. He could see it now. He could see what was going to happen to these people. There wasn't going to be a surrender that they could give. There wasn't going to be any amount that could be paid.

Hroldenfell was lost, and so was every person inside of it. He felt his heart ache. Their settlement was in there. He saw the legionaries moving to the part of the city where their settlement was.

Their people came running out, clad in armor, Durnara at their head. "Durnara's fighting now," Valfric said.

Thraindel said nothing. Valfric felt a bloom of pride inside his chest as he saw his settlement clash with the legionaries. They fought valiantly. He saw some of them killing some of the legionaries, and he was happy to see the city would not go down without a fight.

And then, he saw them begin to lose. He saw the people from his settlement begin to fall back, the good fighters having already perished.

And then he saw the most heartbreaking thing that he'd ever seen in his life. He saw Durnara on the ground, crawling away from a legionnaire. The hawk moved in closer, and he could see that she was covered in blood. She was crawling away, not towards the fight, but crawling away from it. She rolled on her back, her hands up, and he could tell she was begging. Begging for her life.

He wasn't sure what he felt. He couldn't decide. Was she a coward for begging? Was she not?

And then, he watched as a spear came down into her gut. She curled up, and he saw the legionnaires laughing as she slowly bled out.

He felt hot tears rolling down his cheeks, and he pulled back into his body. He collapsed in on himself. In a moment, Ilara was there.

"What is it, Valfric? What did you see?" she said.

He looked up at his friends, seeing fear in their eyes.

"Durnara's dead," he said. "All of them are dead."

Ilara sat down in front of him, and he could see defeat on her face. Aelric and Thraindel had blank expressions.

"Already?" Thraindel said. "They already died? But the Lysandrians just— the Lysandrians just got in," he said, his voice halting and staggering.

"I know," Valfric said.

"Well maybe—" Thraindel started and then stopped.

Maybe nothing.

They all knew what was going on. They all knew what happened. Durnara was dead. Their settlement was gone. Hroldenfell was falling. Not everyone inside of it was dead or captured yet. That would take the Lysandrians hours to do. But it was inevitable.

Valfric could see that now. From the moment the legions had arrived at Hroldenfell, it had been inevitable. And all of their counterattacks, all of their raiding had done nothing. It had never done anything. Hroldenfell was too small. It couldn't hold back the legions.

He could see that now. And he could see that the legions had known it from the word go. It's why they had taken their time. It's why they hadn't attacked in earnest.

And it was why they had done everything they had. Valfric had watched as they had built up the roads in the area and everything else. They hadn't been doing it to help their attack against Hroldenfell as he had once thought they were doing. They had been doing it because they wanted better roads and supply lines for the legion as it pushed north after it was done with Hroldenfell. So that way the legions could move forward and finish killing everything else that Valfric held dear. Every Ulfgarath city would fall. Every settlement would be taken or enslaved or would become part of the Empire and pay tribute to it.

Rage and despair turned in his gut. *Why,* he thought to himself, *why was this happening? Why are the Lysandrians here?* And a voice in his head said, *You know why they're here.* The voice was right. He knew why they were here. They were here because of him. Because of Valfric's raiding, looting, raping, and killing of Lysandrian citizens in their settlements. But that's what needed to be done, wasn't it? That was what they had to do. That's what their people were. He'd only been trying to remind his people.

"This is our fault," he said softly.

Aelric looked at him. "How is it our fault? We tried."

Valfric looked at him. "We're the ones who angered the Lysandrians."

Aelric barked a humorless laugh. "There were many of us who raided those lands, and this has been coming for a long time. This won't be the last city attacked, but it will be the last one to fall," he said, looking at Valfric seriously.

"Hroldenfell was small, but we both know there are bigger, more powerful cities. And Hroldenfell was also on its own," Aelric said. He pointed to the smoke column in the distance. "And you cannot tell me that after this, that after this atrocity that is occurring down there to our people, that all of the settlements in all of Ulfgarath won't join together and push back the Lysandrians from here and put them back where they belong!"

Valfric could hear the fury in Aelrics voice and could hear the confidence in it. It resonated with him. It was true. What was he thinking? This wasn't Valfric's doing. And even if it was, then so be it. Maybe this is what his people needed to remember their past.

He nodded and stood. "You're right, Hroldenfell is just one city, and the Lysandrians lost people today too." He nodded. "There will be people that will make it out of the city. There will be survivors that will run from the area," Valfric said.

"Your point?" Thraindel asked.

"We'll find them. We'll help them. They'll tell their story to others. And when they do, others will join," he said.

"So what's the plan then?" Ilara asked.

"The plan is to find survivors when they come out of the city. We're not going to be able to go in and rescue anybody, but we can find those who make it. Some will make it at night. There's no way the Lysandrians can stop them all. And when they do, we'll help them," he said. "We'll find larger cities to go to. We'll help fortify them. We know how the Lysandrians fight now. We can and will counter it," he said, feeling his confidence build.

They would stop this. They could stop this. The Lysandrians were just men, no different than any other men. They could and they would die. He felt revenge boiling inside his chest, and he grinned.

"We'll show them what happens when they fuck with the Gwenthari," he said. "We'll avenge Hroldenfell. I promise you that."

ABOUT THE AUTHOR

Nicholas Taylor is a fantasy and science fiction author. He was born in 1981 in Denver, Colorado, where he lives with his wife and family. Nicholas was an imaginative child who enjoyed writing stories and daydreaming about new worlds and places from a young age.

In his twenties, Nicholas rekindled a love for reading and consuming fantasy and science fiction. The culmination was his decision to write a novel in the winter of 2007. That first novel was Legon Awakening, which ran as a weekly podcast and was later released in print, digital, and audio editions that thousands have enjoyed.

Nicholas enjoys writing fiction that pulls readers into immersive worlds with likable and relatable characters. He strives to draw the reader into the scene with the characters, allowing them to explore magical realms or distant planets.

For more about Nicholas Taylor
Visit:
www.NicholasTaylor.co